W9-BOD-326

A FUTURE BEYOND ALL NIGHTMARES

Belisarius examined the jewel-like thing in his hand. And beheld—nightmare.

Dragonbolts streaked overhead. The horses, held in the rear by younger infantrymen, whinnied with terror and fought their holders. They were useless now, as Belisarius had known they would be. What use was a mounted charge against—

Over the barricade, Belisarius saw the first of the iron elephants advancing slowly down the great central thoroughfare of Constantinople. Behind, he could see the flames of the burning city and heard the screams of the populace. The butchery of the great city's half-million inhabitants was well underway, now. The Malwa Emperor himself had decreed Constantinople's fate: all who live in the city were to be slaughtered.

When he opened his eyes the jewel-like *thing* was again resting in his loosely clenched fist.

*　　　*　　　*

This was the future, this jewel that claimed to be from the future had told him, not just for Constantinople but for the world. And only the greatest *strategos* of the Age might avert it. But what if this visitor from the future were lying? What if *it* were the great enemy?

AN OBLIQUE APPROACH

DAVID DRAKE
ERIC FLINT

AN OBLIQUE APPROACH

This is a work of fiction. All the characters and events portrayed in this book are fictional, and any resemblance to real people or incidents is purely coincidental.

Copyright © 1998 by David Drake and Eric Flint

All rights reserved, including the right to reproduce this book or portions thereof in any form.

A Baen Books Original

Baen Publishing Enterprises
P.O. Box 1403
Riverdale, NY 10471
www.baen.com

ISBN: 0-671-87865-4

Cover art by Keith Parkinson

First printing, March 1998
Second printing, April 2002

Distributed by Simon & Schuster
1230 Avenue of the Americas
New York, NY 10020

Printed in the United States of America

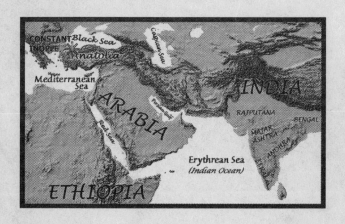

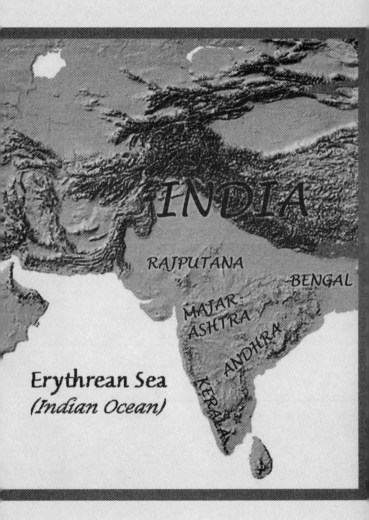

INDIA

RAJPUTANA

MAJAR-
ASHTRA

BENGAL

ANDHRA

Erythrean Sea
(Indian Ocean)

KERALA

"To move along the line of natural expectation consolidates the opponent's balance and thus increases his resisting power . . . In most campaigns the dislocation of the enemy's psychological and physical balance has been the vital prelude to a successful attempt at his overthrow."

—B. H. Liddell-Hart, *Strategy*

TO LUCILLE

The first facet was **purpose**.

It was the only facet. And because it was the only facet, **purpose** *had neither meaning nor content. It simply was. Was. Nothing more.*

purpose. *Alone, and unknowing.*

Yet, that thing which **purpose** *would become had not come to be haphazardly.* **purpose**, *that first and isolated facet, had been drawn into existence by the nature of the man who squatted in the cave, staring at it.*

Another man—almost any other man—would have gasped, or drawn back, or fled, or seized a futile weapon. Some men—some few rare men—would have tried to comprehend what they were seeing. But the man in the cave simply stared.

He did not try to comprehend **purpose**, *for he despised comprehension. But it can be said that he considered what he was seeing; and considered it, moreover, with a focused concentration that was quite beyond the capacity of almost any other man in the world.*

purpose *had come to be, in that cave, at that time, because the man who sat there, considering* **purpose**, *had stripped himself, over long years, of everything except his own overriding, urgent, all-consuming sense of purpose.*

❖　　　❖　　　❖

His name was Michael of Macedonia. He was a Stylite monk, one of those holy men who pursued their faith through isolation and contemplation, perched atop pillars or nestled within caves.

Michael of Macedonia, fearless in the certainty of his faith, stretched forth a withered arm and laid a bony finger on **purpose**.

For **purpose**, *the touch of the monk's finger opened facet after facet after facet, in an explosive growth of crystalline knowledge which, had* **purpose** *truly been a self-illuminated jewel, would have blinded the man who touched it.*

No sooner had Michael of Macedonia touched **purpose** *than his body arched as if in agony, his mouth gaped open in a soundless scream, and his face bore the grimace of a gargoyle. A moment later, he collapsed.*

For two full days, Michael lay unconscious in the cave. He breathed, and his heart beat, but his mind was lost in vision.

On the third day, Michael of Macedonia awoke. Instantly awoke. Alert, fully conscious, and not weak. (Or, at least, not weak in spirit. His body bore the weakness which comes from years of self-deprivation and ferocious austerities.)

Without hesitating, Michael reached out his hand and seized **purpose**. *He feared yet another paroxysm, but his need to understand overrode his fear. And, in the event, his fear proved unfounded.*

purpose, *its raw power now refracted through many facets, was able to control its outburst.* **purpose**, *now, was also* **duration**. *And though the time which it found in the monk's mind was utterly strange, it absorbed the confusion. For* **duration** *was now also* **diversity**, *and so* **purpose** *was able to parcel itself out, both in its sequence and its differentiation. Facets opened up, and spread, and doubled, and tripled, and multiplied, and multiplied again, and again,* *until they were like a crystalline torrent which bore the monk along like a chip of wood on a raging river.*

The river reached the delta, and the delta melted into the sea, and all was still. **purpose** *rested in the palm of Michael's hand, shimmering like moonlight on water, and the monk returned that shimmer with a smile.*

"I thank you," he said, "for ending the years of my search. Though I cannot thank you for the end you have brought me."

He closed his eyes for a moment, lost in thought. Then murmured: "I must seek counsel with my friend the bishop. If there is any man on earth who can guide me now, it will be Anthony."

His eyes opened. He turned his head toward the entrance of the cave and glared at the bright Syrian day beyond.

"The Beast is upon us."

PROLOGUE

That night, Belisarius was resting in the villa which he had purchased upon receiving command of the army at Daras. He was not there often, for he was a general who believed in staying with his troops. He had purchased the villa for the benefit of his wife Antonina, whom he had married two years before, that she might have a comfortable residence in the safety of Aleppo, yet still not be far from the Persian border where the general took his post.

The gesture had been largely futile, for Antonina insisted on accompanying Belisarius even in the brawl and squalor of a military camp. She was well-nigh inseparable from him, and in truth, the general did not complain. For, whatever else was mysterious to men about the quicksilver mind of Belisarius, one thing was clear as day: he adored his wife.

It was an unfathomable adoration, to most. True, Antonina possessed a lively and attractive personality. (To those, at least, who had not the misfortune of drawing down her considerable temper.) And, she was very comely. On this point all agreed, even her many detractors: though considerably older than her husband, Antonina bore her years well.

But what years they had been! Oh, the scandal of it all.

Her father had been a charioteer, one of those raucous men idolized by the hippodrome mobs. Worse yet, her mother had been an actress, which to is to say, little more than a prostitute. As Antonina grew up in these surroundings, she herself adopted the ways of her mother at an early age—and, then!—added to the sin of harlotry, that of witchcraft. For it was well known that Antonina was as skilled in magic as she was in the more corporeal forms of wickedness.

True, since her marriage to the general there had been no trace of scandal attached to her name. But vigilant eyes and ears were always upon her. Not those of her husband, oddly enough, for he seemed foolishly unconcerned of her fidelity. But many others watched, and listened for rumor with that quivering attentiveness which is the hallmark of proper folk.

Yet the ears heard nothing, and the eyes saw even less. A few turned aside, satisfied there was nothing to see or hear. Most, however, remained watchful at their post. The whore was, after all, a witch. And, what was worse, she was the close friend of the Empress Theodora. (No surprise, that, for all men know that like seeks like. And if the Empress Theodora's past held no trace of witchcraft, she had made good the loss by a harlotry so wanton as to put even that of Antonina to shame.)

So who knew what lecheries and deviltry Antonina could conceal?

About the general himself, setting aside his scandalous marriage, the gentility had little ill to say.

A bit, of course, a bit. Though ranked in the nobility, Belisarius was Thracian by birth. And the Thracians were known to be a boorish folk, rustic and uncouth. This flaw in his person, however, was passed over lightly. It was not that the righteous feared the wrath of Belisarius. The general, after all, was known himself to make the occasional jest regarding Thracian crudity. (Crude jests, of course; he was a Thracian.)

No, the tongues of the better stock were stilled on this

subject because the Emperor Justinian was also Thracian (and not even from the ranks of the Thracian nobility, such as it was, but from the peasantry). And if Belisarius was known for his even and good-humored temperament, the Emperor was not. Most certainly not. An ill-humored and suspicious man, was Justinian, frightfully quick to take offense. And frightful when he did.

Then, there was the general's youth. As all people of quality are aware, youth is by nature a parlous state. An extremely perilous condition, youth, from an ethical standpoint. Reckless, besides—daring, and impetuous. Not the sort of thing which notability likes to see in its generals. Yet the Emperor Justinian had placed him in the ranks of his personal bodyguard, the elite body from which he selected his generals. And then, piling folly upon unwisdom, had immediately selected Belisarius to command an army facing the ancient Medean foe.

True, there were those who defended the Emperor's choice, pointing out that despite his youth Belisarius possessed an acute judgment and a keen intellect. Yet this defense failed of its purpose. For, in the end, leaving aside his marriage, it was this final quality of Belisarius that set right-thinking teeth on edge.

Intelligence, of course, is an admirable property in a man. Even, in moderation, in a woman. So long as it is a respectable sort of intelligence—straight, so to speak. A thing of clear corners and precise angles, or, at the very least, spherical curves. Moderate, in its means; forthright, in its ends; direct, in its approach.

But the mind of Belisarius—ah, the mystery of it. To look at the man, he was naught but a Thracian. Taller than most, well built as Thracians tend to be, and handsome (as Thracians tend not to be). But all who knew the general came to understand that, within his upstanding occidental shape, there lurked a most exotic intellect. Something from

the subtle east, perhaps, or the ancient south. A thing not
from the stark hills but the primeval forest; a gnarled mind
in a youthful body, crooked as a root and as sinuous as a
serpent.

Such did many good folk think, especially after making
his acquaintance. None could fault the general, after taking
his leave, for the courtesy of his manner or the propriety
of his conduct. A good-humored man, none could deny;
though many, after taking his leave, wondered if the humor
was at their expense. But they kept their suspicions muted,
if not silent. For there always remained this thought, that
whatever the state of his mind, there was no mistaking the
state of his body.

Deadly with a blade, was Belisarius. And even the
cataphracts, in their cups, spoke of his lance and his bow.

It was to the house of this man, then, and his Jezebel
wife, that Michael of Macedonia and his friend the bishop
brought their message, and the *thing* which bore it.

ALEPPO
Spring, 528 AD

Chapter 1

Upon being awakened by his servant Gubazes, Belisarius arose instantly, with the habit of a veteran campaigner. Antonina, at his side, emerged from sleep more slowly. After hearing what Gubazes had to say, the general threw on a tunic and hastened from his bedroom. He did not wait for Antonina to get dressed, nor even take the time to strap on his sandals.

Such strange visitors at this hour could not be kept waiting. Anthony Cassian, Bishop of Aleppo, was a friend who had visited on several occasions—but never at midnight. And as for the other—*Michael of Macedonia?*

Belisarius knew the name, of course. It was a famous name throughout the Roman Empire. Famous—and loved—by the common folk. To the high churchmen who were the subject of Michael's occasional sermons, the name was notorious—and not loved in the slightest. But the general had never met the man personally. Few people had, in truth, for the monk had lived in his desert cave for years now.

As he walked down the long corridor to the salon, Belisarius heard voices coming from the room ahead. One voice he recognized as that of his friend the bishop. The other voice he took to be that of the monk.

"Belisarius," hissed the unfamiliar voice.

The next voice was that of Anthony Cassian, Bishop of Aleppo:

"Like you, Michael, I believe this is a message from God. But it is not a message for us."

"He is a *soldier*."

"Yes, and a general to boot. All the better."

"He is pure of spirit?" demanded the harsh, unforgiving voice. "True in soul? Does he walk in the path of righteousness?"

"Oh, I think his soul is clean enough, Michael," replied Cassian gently. "He married a whore, after all. That speaks well of him."

The bishop's voice grew cold. "You, too, old friend, sometimes suffer from the sin of the Pharisees. The day will come when you will be thankful that the hosts of God are commanded by one who, if he does not match the saints in holiness, matches the Serpent himself in guile."

A moment later, Belisarius entered the room. He paused for a moment, examining the two men who awaited him. They, in turn, studied the general.

Anthony Cassian, Bishop of Aleppo, was a short, plump man. His round, cheerful face was centered on a sharply curved nose. Beneath a balding head, his beard was full and neatly groomed. He reminded Belisarius of nothing so much as a friendly, well-fed, intelligent owl.

Michael of Macedonia, on the other hand, brought to mind the image of a very different bird: a gaunt raptor soaring through the desert sky, whose pitiless eyes missed nothing below him. Except, thought the general wryly, for the straggliness of his own great beard and the disheveled condition of his tunic, matters which were quite beneath the holy man's notice.

The general's gaze was returned by the monk's blue-eyed glare. A crooked little smile came to Belisarius' lips.

"You might want to keep him hooded, Bishop, before he slaughters your doves."

Cassian laughed. "Oh, well said! Belisarius, let me introduce you to Michael of Macedonia."

Belisarius cocked an eyebrow. "An odd companion at this hour—or at any hour, from his reputation."

Belisarius stepped forward and extended his hand. The Bishop immediately shook it. The monk did not. But, as Belisarius kept the hand outstretched, Michael began to *consider*. Outstretched the hand was, and outstretched it remained. A large hand, well shaped and sinewy; a hand which showed not the slightest tremor as the long seconds passed. But it was not the hand which, finally, decided the man of God. It was the calmness of the brown eyes, which went so oddly with the youthful face. Like dark stones, worn smooth in a stream.

Michael decided, and took the hand.

A small commotion made them turn. In the doorway stood a woman, yawning, dressed in a robe. She was very short, and lush figured.

Michael had been told she was comely, for a woman of her years, but now he saw the telling was a lie. The woman was as beautiful as rain in the morning, and her years were the richness of the water itself.

Her beauty repelled him. Not, as it might another holy man, for recalling the ancient Eve. No, it repelled him, simply, because he was a contrary man. And he was so, because he had found all his life that what men said was good, was not; what they said was true, was false; and what they said was beautiful, was hideous.

Then, the woman's eyes caught him. Eyes as green as the first shoots of spring. Bright, clear eyes in a dusky face, framed by ebony hair.

Michael *considered*, and knew again that men lied.

"You were right, Anthony," he said harshly. He staggered slightly, betrayed by his weak limbs. A moment later the woman was at his side, assisting him to a couch.

"Michael of Macedonia, no less," she said softly, in a humorous tone. "I am honored. Though I hope, for your sake, you were not seen entering. At this hour—well! My reputation is a tatter, anyway. But yours!"

"All reputation is folly," said Michael. "Folly fed by pride, which is worse still."

"Cheerful fellow, isn't he?" asked Cassian lightly. "My oldest and closest friend, though I sometimes wonder why."

He shook his head whimsically. "Look at us. He, with his shaggy mane and starveling body; me, with my properly groomed beard and—well. Slender, I am not." A grin. "Though, for all my rotundity, let it be noted that I, at least, can still move about on my own two legs."

Michael smiled, faintly. "Anthony has always been fond of boasting. Fortunately, he is also clever. A dull-witted Cassian would find nothing to boast about. But he can always find something, buried beneath the world's notice, like a mole ferreting out worms."

Belisarius and Antonina laughed.

"A quick-witted Stylite!" cried the general. "My day is made, even before the sun rises."

Suddenly solemn, Cassian shook his head.

"I fear not, Belisarius. Quite the contrary. We did not come here to bring you sunshine, but to bring you a sign of nightfall."

"Show him," commanded Michael.

The bishop reached into his cassock and withdrew the *thing*. He held it forth in his outstretched hand.

Belisarius stooped slightly to examine the *thing*. His eyes remained calm. No expression could be seen on his face.

Antonina, on the other hand, gasped and drew back.

"Witchcraft!"

Anthony shook his head. "I do not think so, Antonina. Or, at least, not the craft of black magic."

Curiosity overrode her fear. Antonina came forward. As short as she was, she did not have to stoop to scrutinize the *thing* closely.

"I have never seen its like," she whispered. "I have never *heard* of its like. Magic gems, yes. But this—it resembles a jewel, at first, until you look more closely. Or a crystal. Then—within—it is like—"

She groped for words. Her husband spoke:

"So must the sun's cool logic unfold, if we could see beneath its roiling fury."

"Oh, well said!" cried Cassian. "A poetic general! A philosophical soldier!"

"Enough with the jests," snapped Michael. "General, you must take it in your hand."

The calm gaze transferred itself to the monk.

"Why?"

For a moment, the raptor glare manifested itself. But only for a moment. Uncertainly, Michael lowered his head.

"I do not know why. The truth? You must do it because my friend Anthony Cassian said you must. And of all men that I have ever known, he is the wisest. Even if he is a cursed churchman."

Belisarius regarded the bishop.

"Why then, Cassian?"

The bishop gazed down at the thing in his palm, the jewel that was not a jewel, the gem without weight, the crystal without sharpness, the thing with so many facets—and, he thought, so many more forming and reforming—that it seemed as round as the perfect sphere of ancient Greek dreams.

Anthony shrugged. "I cannot answer your question. But I know it is true."

The bishop motioned toward the seated monk.

"It first came to Michael, five days ago, in his cave in the desert. He took the thing in his hand and was transported into visions."

Belisarius stared at the monk. Antonina, hesitantly, asked: "And you do not think it is witchcraft?"

Michael of Macedonia shook his head.

"I am certain that it is not a thing of Satan. I cannot explain why, not in words spoken by men. I have—*felt* the thing. Lived with it, for two days, in my mind. While I lay unconscious to the world."

He frowned. "Strange, really. It seemed but a moment to me, at the time."

He shook his head again.

"I do not know what it is, but of this much I *am* sure. I found not a trace of evil in it, anywhere. It is true, the visions which came to me were terrible, horrible beyond description. But there were other visions, as well, visions which I cannot remember clearly. They remain in my mind like a dream you can't recall. Dreams of things beyond imagining."

He slumped back in his chair. "I believe it to be a message from God, Antonina. Belisarius. But I am not certain. And I certainly can't prove it."

Belisarius looked at the bishop.

"And what do you think, Anthony?" He gestured at the thing. "Have you—?"

The bishop nodded. "Yes, Belisarius. After Michael brought the thing to me, last night, and asked me for advice, I took it in my own hand. And I, too, was then plunged into vision. Horrible visions, like Michael's. But where two days seemed but a moment to him, the few minutes in which I was lost to the world seemed like eternity to me, and I was never seized by a paroxysm."

Michael of Macedonia suddenly laughed.

"Leave it to the wordiest man in creation to withstand a torrent like a rock!" he cried. He laughed again, almost gaily.

"But for just an instant, when he returned from his vision, I witnessed a true miracle! Anthony Cassian, Bishop of Aleppo, silent."

Cassian grinned. "It's true. I was positively struck dumb!

I don't know what I expected when I took up the—*thing*—but certainly not what came to me, not even after Michael's warning. I sooner would have expected a unicorn! Or a seraph! Or a walking, wondrous creature made of lapis lazuli and beaten silver by the emperor's smiths, or—"

"A very brief miracle," snorted Michael. Cassian's mouth snapped shut.

Belisarius and Antonina grinned. The bishop's only known vice was that he was perhaps the most talkative man in the world.

But the grins faded soon enough.

"And what were your visions, Anthony?" asked Belisarius.

The bishop waved the question aside. "I will describe them later, Belisarius. But not now."

He stared down at the palm of his hand. The thing resting there coruscated inner fluxes too complex to follow.

"I do not think the—*message*—is meant for me. Or for Michael. I think it is meant for you. Whatever the thing is, Belisarius, it is an omen of catastrophe. But there is something else, lurking within. I sensed it when I took the thing in my own hand. Sensed it, and sensed it truly. A—a *purpose*, let us say, which is somehow aimed against that disaster. A purpose which requires you, I think, to speak."

Belisarius, again, examined the thing. No expression showed on his face. But his wife, who knew him best, began to plead.

Her pleas went unheard, for the thing was already in the soldier's hand. Then her pleas ceased, and she fell silent. For, indeed, the thing was like the sun itself, now, if a sun could enter a room and show itself to mortal men. And they, still live.

The spreading facets erupted, not like a volcano, but like the very dawn of creation. They sped, unfolding and doubling, and tripling, and then tripling and tripling and tripling, through the labyrinth that was the mind of Belisarius.

purpose became **focus**, and **focus** gave facets **form**.

identity crystallized. With it, **purpose** metamorphosed into **aim**. And, if it had been within the capacity of **aim** to leap for joy, it would have gamboled like a fawn in the forest.

But for Belisarius, there was nothing; nothing but the fall into the Pit. Nothing but the vision of a future terrible beyond all nightmare.

Chapter 2

Dragonbolts streaked overhead. Below, the ranks of the cataphracts hunched behind their barricade. The horses, held in the rear by younger infantrymen, whinnied with terror and fought their holders. They were useless now, as Belisarius had known they would be. It was for that very reason that he had ordered the cataphracts to dismount and fight afoot, from behind a barricade built by their own aristocratic hands. The armored lancers and archers, once feared by all the world, had not even complained, but had obeyed instantly. Even the noble cataphracts had finally learned wisdom, though the learning had come much too late.

What use was a mounted charge against—?

Over the barricade, the general saw the first of the iron elephants advancing slowly down the Mese, the great central thoroughfare of Constantinople. Behind, he could see the flames of the burning city and hear the screams of the populace. The butchery of the great city's half-million inhabitants was well underway, now.

The Malwa emperor himself had decreed Constantinople's sentence, and the Mahaveda priests had blessed it. Not since Ranapur had that sentence been pronounced. All that lived in the city were to be slaughtered, down to the cats and dogs. All save the women of the nobility, who were to

16

be turned over to the Ye-tai for defilement. Those women who survived would be passed on to the Rajputs. (At Ranapur, the Rajputs had coldly declined. But that was long ago, when the name of Rajputana had still carried its ancient legacy. They would not decline now, for they had been broken to their place.) The handful who survived the Rajputs would be sold to whatever polluted untouchable could scrape up the coins to buy himself a hag. There would be few untouchables who could afford the price. But there would be some, among the teeming multitude of that ever-growing class.

The iron elephant huffed its steamy breath, wheezing and gasping. Had it truly been an animal, Belisarius might have hoped it was dying, so horribly wrong was the sound of the creature's respiration. But it was no creature, Belisarius knew. It was a creation—a construct made of human craft and inhuman lore. Still, watching the monstrous thing creeping its slow way forward, surrounded by Ye-tai warriors howling with glee at their anticipated final triumph, the general found it impossible to think of it as anything other than a demonic beast.

Belisarius, seeing one of the cataphracts take up a captured thunderflask, bellowed a command. The cataphract subsided. They possessed few of the infernal devices, and Belisarius was determined to make good use of them. The range was still too great.

He stroked his grey beard. Of his youth, nothing remained save whimsy; it amused him to see how old habits never die. Even now, when all hope had vanished from the mind of the general, the heart of the man still beat as strongly as ever.

It was not a warrior's heart. Belisarius had never truly been a warrior, not, at least, in the sense that others gave the name. No, he was of unpretentious Thracian stock. And, at bottom, his was the soul of a workman at his trade.

True, he had been supreme in battle. (Not war, in the end; for the long war was almost over, the defeat total.) Even his most bitter enemies recognized his unchallenged mastery on the field of carnage, as the display of force coming down the Mese attested. Why else mass such an enormous army to overcome such a tiny guard? Had any other man but Belisarius commanded the Emperor's last bodyguard, the Mahaveda would have sent a mere detachment.

Yes, he had been supreme on the battlefield. But his supremacy had stemmed from craftsmanship, not martial valor. Of the courage of Belisarius, no man doubted, not even he. But courage, he had long known, was a common trait. God's most democratic gift, given to men and women of all ages, and races, and stations in life. Much rarer was craftsmanship, that odd quality which is not satisfied merely with the result sought, but that the work itself be done skillfully.

His life was at an end, now, but he would end it with supreme craftsmanship. And, in so doing, gut the enemy's triumph of its glee.

A cataphract hissed. Belisarius glanced over, thinking the man had been hit by one of the many arrows which were now falling upon them. But the lancer was unharmed, his eyes fixed forward.

Belisarius followed the eyes and understood. The Mahaveda priests had appeared now, safely behind the ranks of the Ye-tai and the Malwa *kshatriyas* manning the iron elephant. They were drawn forward on three great carts hauled by slaves, each cart bearing three priests and a *mahamimamsa* torturer. From the center of each cart arose a wooden gibbet, and from the gibbets hung the new talismans which they had added to their demonic paraphernalia.

There, suspended three abreast, hung those who had been dearest to Belisarius in life. Sittas, his oldest and best friend. Photius, his beloved stepson. Antonina, his wife.

Their skins, rather. Flayed from their bodies by the mahamimamsa, sewn into sacks which bellied in the breeze, and smeared with the excrement of dogs. The skin-sacks had been cleverly designed so that they channeled the wind into a wail of horror. The skins hung suspended by the hair of those who had once filled them in life. The priests took great care to hold them in such a manner that Belisarius could see their faces.

The general almost laughed with triumph. But his face remained calm, his expression still. Even now, the enemy did not understand him.

He spit on the ground, saw his men note the gesture and take heart. As he had known they would. But, even had they not been watching, he would have done the same.

What cared he for these trophies? Was he a pagan, to mistake the soul for its sheath? Was he a savage, to feel his heart break and his bowels loosen at the sight of fetishes?

His enemies had thought so, arrogant as always. As he had known they would, and planned for. Then he did laugh (and saw his men take note, and heart; but he would have laughed anyway), for now that the procession had drawn nearer he could see that the skin of Sittas was suspended by a cord.

"Look there, cataphracts!" he cried. "They couldn't hang Sittas by his hair! He had no hair, at the end. Lost it all, he did, fretting the night away devising the stratagems which made them howl."

The cataphracts took up the cry.

"*Antioch! Antioch!*" There, the city fallen, Sittas had butchered the Malwa hordes before leading the entire garrison in a successful withdrawal.

"*Korykos! Korykos!*" There, on the Cilician coast, not a month later, Sittas had turned on the host which pursued him. Turned, trapped them, and made the Mediterranean a Homeric sea in truth. Wine-dark, from Ye-tai blood.

"Pisidia! Pisidia!" There was no wine-dark lake, in Homer.
But had the poet lived to see the havoc which Sittas wreaked
upon the Rajputs by the banks of Pisidia's largest lake, he
would have sung of it.

"Akroinon! Akroinon!"

"Bursa! Bursa!"

At Bursa, Sittas had met his death. But not at the hands
of the mahamimamsa vivisectors. He had died in full armor,
leading the last charge of his remaining cataphracts, after
conducting the most brilliant fighting retreat since
Xenophon's march to the sea.

"And look at the face of Photius!" shouted Belisarius. "Is
it not a marvel, how well the flayers preserved it? Look,
cataphracts, look! Is that not the grin of Photius? His merry
smile?"

The cataphracts looked, and nodded, and took up the
cry.

"So did he laugh at Alexandria!" cried one. "When he
transfixed Akhshunwar's throat with his arrow!" The Ye-tai
commander of the siege had disbelieved the tales of the
garrison leader's archery. He had come to the walls of
Alexandria himself to see, and scoff, and deride the courage
of his warriors. But his warriors had been right, after all.

New cries were taken up by the cataphracts, recalling
other feats of Photius during his heroic defense of
Alexandria. Photius the Fearless, as he had been called.
Photius, the beloved stepson. Who, when his capture was
inevitable, had taken a poison so horrible that it had caused
his face to freeze into an eternal rictus. Belisarius had
wondered, when he heard the tale, why his sensible son
had not simply opened his veins. But now he understood.
From beyond the grave, Photius sent him a last gift.

The best, Belisarius saved for last.

"And look! Look, cataphracts, at the skin of Antonina!
Look at the withered, disease-ruptured thing! They have

dug her up from the grave, where the plague sent her! How
many of the torturers will die, do you think, from that
desecration? How many will writhe in agony, and shriek
to see their bodies blacken and swell? How many? How
many?"

"*Thousand! Thousands!*" roared the cataphracts.

Belisarius gauged the moment, and thought it good. He
scanned the cataphracts and saw that they were with him.
They knew his plan and had said they would follow, even
though it was an act of personal grace which would bring
death to them all. He needed only, now, a battlecry. He
found it at once.

Through all the years he had loved Antonina, there was
a name he had never called her. Others had, many others,
even she herself, but never he. Not even the first night he
met her, and paid for her services.

"*For my whore!*" he bellowed, and sprang upon the
barricade. "*For my pustulent whore! May she rot their souls
in hell!*"

"*FOR THE WHORE!*" cried the cataphracts. "*FOR THE
WHORE!*"

The captured thunderflasks were hurled now, and hurled
well. The iron elephant erupted in fire and flame. The
cataphracts fired a volley, and another, and another. Again,
as so often before, the Ye-tai had time to be astonished at
the force of the ravening arrows as they ripped through
their iron armor like so much cloth. Little time, little time.
Few but cataphracts could draw those incredible bows.

Those Ye-tai in the front ranks, those who survived, then
had time to be further astonished. They had been awaiting
a cavalry charge, fully confident that the dragonbolts would
panic the great horses. Now they gaped to see the lancers
advancing like infantry.

In truth, the cataphracts were slower afoot than on saddle.
But they were not much slower, so great was their bitter

rage. And the lances which ruptured chests and spilled intestines onto the great thoroughfare were every bit as keen as Ye-tai memories recalled.

"For the whore! For the whore!"

The front line of the Ye-tai was nothing but a memory itself as the second line pressed forward, avid and eager to prove their mettle. Most of these, following Ye-tai custom, were inexperienced warriors, vainglorious in the heedless way of youth, who had never really believed the tales of the veterans.

They came to believe quickly. Most died in the act of conversion, however, for the mace of a cataphract is an unforgiving instructor. Quick to find fault, quick to reprove, and altogether harsh in its correction.

The second line, thus, was shredded almost instantly. The third line held, for a time. It counted many veterans among its number, who had long since learned that cataphracts cannot be matched blow for blow. Some among them were able to take advantage of their great number to find the occasional gap in the armor, the rare opening for the well-thrust blade.

But not many, and not for long. As wide as the Mese was, it was still a street hemmed by buildings. This was no great plain where the enemy could encircle their foe. As always, Belisarius had picked the ground for his defense perfectly. The Mahaveda, he had long known, relied too much on their numbers and their satanic weapons. But in that narrow place of death, closing immediately with their enemy so as to nullify the dragon-weapons, advantage went to the cataphracts.

This was partly due to the strength of the cataphracts, to the awesome iron power of their armored bodies. But mostly, it was due to their steel-hard discipline. The Mahaveda had tried to copy that discipline in their own armies, but had never truly been able to do so. As ever, the Mahaveda relied on fear to enforce their will. But fear, in the end, can never duplicate pride.

On that day of final fury, the cataphracts did not forget their ancient discipline. That discipline had conquered half the world once, and ruled it for a millenium. Ruled it not badly, moreover, all things considered. Well enough, at least, that over the centuries people of many races had come to think themselves Roman. And take pride in the name.

On Rome's final day, in truth, there were few Latins in the ranks of the cataphracts, and none from the city which gave the Empire its name. Greeks, in the main, from the sturdy yeomanry of Anatolia. But Armenians were there too, and Goths and Huns and Syrians and Macedonians and Thracians and Illyrians and Egyptians and even three Jews. (Who quietly practiced their faith; their comrades looked the other way and said nothing to the priests.)

Today, the cataphracts would finally lose the world, after a war which had lasted decades, and would lose it to an enemy fouler than Medusa. But they would not falter in their Roman duty, and their Roman pride, and their Roman discipline.

The third line of Ye-tai collapsed and pushed the fourth back. Incredibly—to the Mahaveda priests who watched, standing atop the skin-bearing wagons with their mahamimamsa flayers—the Byzantines were driving their way through the horde of Ye-tai. Like a sword cutting through armor, piercing straight to—

They shrieked, then. Shrieked in outrage, partly. But mostly, they shrieked in fear. The Rajputs, the priests knew, never called the great general of the enemy by his name. They called him, simply, the Mongoose. It was an impious habit, for which the priests had reproved them often. They would have done better to listen, they realized now, watching the fangs of Belisarius gape wide.

❖   ❖   ❖

"I see it worked," said Justinian. "As your stratagems usually do." The old Emperor arose from his chair and shuffled forward laboriously. Belisarius began to prostrate himself, but Justinian stopped him with a gesture.

"We do not have time." He cocked an ear, listening for a moment to the sounds of battle which carried faintly into the dim recesses of the Hagia Sophia. The Emperor had chosen to meet his end here, in the great cathedral which he had ordered built so long ago.

Ever the soldier, Belisarius had argued for the Great Palace. That labyrinth of buildings and gardens would be far easier to defend. But, as so often before, the Emperor had overruled him. For perhaps the only time, Justinian knew, that he had been right to do so.

The Great Palace was meaningless. The Empire which had lasted a millenium would be finished by nightfall. Never to return, in all the countless years of the gorgon future. But the soul was everlasting, and the Emperor's only concern now was for eternity. To save his own soul, if possible. (Although he was not confident, and rather thought hellfire awaited him.) But, at the least, to do his best to save the souls of those who had served him for so long, and so faithfully, and so uncomplainingly, and with so little reason to have done so.

The eyes of the Emperor gazed upon his general. The eyes were old, and weak, and weary, and filled with pain both of the body and the spirit. But they had lost not a trace of their extraordinary intelligence. That great, blinding intelligence. That intelligence which had been so great it had blinded the very man who possessed it.

"It is I, in truth, who should prostrate myself to you," said Justinian. His voice was harsh. He had spoken the truth and knew it. And knew that his general knew it. But he found no liking for the truth. No, none at all. He never had.

A figure advanced from the shadows. Belisarius had known he would be there, but had not seen him. The Maratha was capable of utter stillness and silence.

"Let me clean them, master," said the slave, extending his arms. They were very old, those arms, but had lost little of their iron strength.

Belisarius hesitated.

"There is time," said the slave. "The cataphracts will hold the *asura*'s dogs long enough." He smiled faintly. "They do not fight for the Empire now. Not even for your God. They fight for your Christ, and his Mary Magdelene. Whom they betrayed often enough in life, but will not in death. They will hold. Long enough."

He extended his arms in a forceful gesture.

"I insist, master. It may mean little to you, but it does to me. I have a different faith, and I would not have these precious souls go unclean to their destiny."

He took the horrid parcels from Belisarius' unresisting arms and carried them to a cistern. Into the water he thrust the skins and began cleaning them. Gently, for all that he moved in haste.

Emperor and general watched, silently. It seemed fitting to both, each in their own way, that a slave should command at the end of all time.

Soon enough, the slave was done. He led the way through the cavernous darkness. The myriad candles which would normally have illuminated the wondrous mosaics of the cathedral were extinguished. Only in the room at the far recesses in the rear did a few tapers still burn.

They were not needed, however. The great vat resting in the center, bubbling with molten gold and silver, was more than enough to light the room. Light it almost like day, so fiercely did the precious metals blaze.

Justinian pondered the vat. He had ordered it constructed many months ago, foreseeing this end. He was quite proud of the device, actually. As proud of it as he had been of the many other marvelous contrivances which adorned his palaces. Whatever else of his youth the Thracian peasant had lost, in his bloody climb to the throne, and his bloodier rule, he had never lost his simple childish delight in clever gadgets. Greek and Armenian craftsmen had constructed the device, with their usual skill.

Justinian reached out and pulled the lever which started the intricate timing device. In an hour, the vat would disgorge its contents. The accumulated treasure of Rome's millenium would pour out the bottom, down through the multitude of channels which would scatter it into the labyrinthine sewers of Constantinople. There, it would be buried for all time by the captured dragon-flasks in their eruption. The Greeks had never learned the secret of the dragon-weapons, but they knew how to use captured ones to good effect.

In an hour, it would be done. But the vat had a more important use to which it would now be put. Nothing of Rome's greatness would be left to adorn the walls and rafters of the Malwa palace.

"Let us be done with it," commanded the Emperor. He shuffled over to a bier and stooped. With difficulty, for he was weak with age, he withdrew its burden. The slave moved to assist him, but the Emperor waved him back.

"I will carry her myself." As always, his voice was harsh. But, when the Emperor gazed down upon the face of the mummy in his arms, his face grew soft.

"In this one thing, I was always true. In this, if nothing else."

"Yes," said Belisarius. He looked down at the face of the mummy and thought the embalmers had done their work well. Long years had it been since the Empress Theodora had died of cancer. Long years, resting in her bier. But her waxen face still bore the beauty which had marked it in life.

More so, perhaps, thought Belisarius. In death, Theodora's face showed peace and gentle repose. There was nothing in it, now, of the fierce ambition which had so often hardened it in life.

Laboriously, the Emperor took his place on the ledge adjoining the vat. Then he stepped back. Not from fear, but simply from the heat. It could not be borne for more than a moment, and he still had words which had to be said.

Had to be, not wanted to be. The Emperor wished it were otherwise, for if ever had lived a man who begrudged apology, it was Justinian. Justinian the Great, he had wanted to be called, and so remembered by all posterity. Instead, he would be known as Justinian the Fool. At best. Attila had been called the Scourge of God. He suspected he would be known as the Catastrophe of God.

He opened his mouth to speak. Clamped it shut.

"There is no need, Justinian," said Belisarius, for the first and only time in his life calling the Emperor by his simple name. "There is no need." An old, familiar, crooked smile. "And no time, for that matter. The last cataphract will be falling soon. It would take you hours to say what you are trying to say. It will not come easily to you, if at all."

"Why did you never betray me?" whispered the Emperor. "I repaid your loyalty with nothing but foul distrust."

"I swore an oath."

Disbelief came naturally to the Emperor's face.

"And look what it led to," he muttered. "You *should* have betrayed me. You should have murdered me and taken the throne yourself. For years now, all Romans would have supported you—nobles and common alike. You are all that kept me in power, since Theodora died."

"I swore an oath. To God, not to Romans."

The Emperor gestured with his head at the faint sounds of battle.

"And that? Does your oath to God encompass *that*? Had you been emperor, instead of I, the anti-Christ might not have triumphed."

Belisarius shrugged. "Who is to know the future? Not I, my lord. Nor does it matter. Even had I known the course of the future, down to the last particular, I would not have betrayed you. I swore an oath."

Pain, finally, came to the Emperor's face.

"I do not understand."

"I know, lord."

The sounds of battle were faint now. Belisarius glanced at the entrance to the chamber.

The slave stepped forward and handed him the skin of Sittas. Belisarius gazed upon the face of his friend, kissed it, and tossed it into the vat. A brief burst of flame, and the trophy was lost to Satan. He gazed longer upon the face of his stepson, but not much, before it followed into destruction. He knew Photius would understand. He, too, had commanded armies, and knew the value of time.

Finally, he took the remains of Antonina into his arms and stepped upon the ledge. A moment later Justinian joined him, bearing the mummy of the Empress.

The slave thought it was fitting that the Emperor, who had always preceded his general in life, should precede him in death. So he pushed Justinian first. He had guessed the Emperor would scream, at the end. But the old tyrant was made of sterner stuff. Sensing the approach of the slave behind him, Justinian had simply said:

"Come, Belisarius. Let us carry our whores to heaven. We may be denied entrance, but never they."

Belisarius had said nothing. Nor, of course, had he screamed. As he turned away from the vat, the old slave grinned.

The general, for all the suppleness of his mind, had always

been absurdly stiff-necked about his duty. The Christian faith forbade suicide, and so the slave had performed this last service. But it had been a pure formality. At the end, the slave knew, as soon as he felt the first touch of the powerful hands at his back, Belisarius had leapt.

But he would be able to tell his god that he had been pushed. His god would not believe him, of course. Even the Christian god was not that stupid. But the Christian god would accept the lie. And if not he, then certainly his son. Why should he not?

The slave, all the duties of a long lifetime finally done, moved slowly over to the one chair in the chamber and took his seat. It was a marvelous chair, as was everything made for the Emperor. He looked around the chamber, enjoying the beauty of the intricate mosaics, and thought it was a good place to die.

Such a strange people, these Christians. The slave had lived among them for decades, but he had never been able to fathom them. They were so irrational and given to obsessiveness. Yet, he knew, not ignoble. They, too, in their own superstitious way, accepted *bhakti*. And if their way of bhakti seemed often ridiculous to the slave, there was this much to be said for it: they had stood by their faith, most of them, and fought to the end for it. More than that, no reasonable man could ask.

No reasonable god, so much was certain. And the slave's god was a reasonable being. Capricious, perhaps, and prone to whimsy. But always reasonable.

Those people whom the slave had cast into the molten metal had nothing to fear from God. Not even the Emperor. True, the fierce old tyrant would spend many lifetimes shedding the weight of his folly. Many lifetimes, for he had committed a great sin. He had taken the phenomenal intelligence God gave him and used it to crush wisdom.

Many lifetimes. As an insect, the slave thought. Perhaps

even as a worm. But, for the all the evil he had done, Justinian had not been a truly evil man. And so, the slave thought, the time would come when God would allow the Emperor to return, as a poor peasant again, somewhere in the world. Perhaps, then, he would have learned a bit of wisdom.

But perhaps not. Time was vast beyond human comprehension, and who was to know how long it might take a soul to find *moksha*?

The old slave took out the dagger from his cloak.

Belisarius had given that dagger to him, many years before, on the day he told the slave he was manumitting him. The slave had refused the freedom. He had no use for it any longer, and he preferred to remain of service to the general. True, he no longer hoped, by then, that Belisarius was Kalkin. He had, once. But as the years passed in the general's service, the slave had finally accepted the truth. Great was Belisarius, but merely human. He was not the tenth *avatara* who was promised. The slave had bowed to the reality, sadly, knowing the world was thereby condemned to many more turns of the wheel under the claws of the great asura who had seized it. But, truth was what it was. His *dharma* still remained.

Belisarius had not understood his refusal, not really, but he had acquiesced and kept the slave. Yet, that same day he had pressed the dagger into his slave's hand, that the slave might know that the master could also refuse freedom. The slave had appreciated the gesture. Just so should mortals dance in the eyes of God.

He weighed the weapon in his hand. It was an excellent dagger.

In his day, the old slave had been a deadly assassin, among many other things. He had not used a dagger in decades, but he had not forgotten the feel of it. Warm, and trusting, like a favorite pet.

He lowered it. He would wait awhile.

All was silent, beyond the walls of the Hagia Sophia. The

cataphracts who had stood with Belisarius for one final battle were dead now.

They had died well. Oh, very well.

In his day, the old slave had been a feared and famous warrior, among many other things. He had not fought a battle in decades, but he knew the feel of them. A great battle they had waged, the cataphracts. All the greater, that there had been no purpose in it save dharma.

And, perhaps, the slave admitted, the small joy of a delicious revenge. But revenge would not weigh too heavily on their destiny, the slave thought. No, the cataphracts had shed much *karma* from their souls.

The slave was glad of it. He had never cared much for the cataphracts, it was true. Crude and boastful, they were. Coarse and unrefined, compared to the kshatriya the slave had once been. But no kshatriya could ever claim more than the dead cataphracts outside the walls of the Hagia Sophia. Arjuna himself would adopt their souls and call them kinfolk.

Again, he thought about the dagger and knew that his own *karma* would be the better for its use. But, again, he thrust the thought aside.

No, he would wait awhile.

It was not that he feared the sin of suicide. His faith did not share the bizarre Christian notion that acts carried moral consequences separate from their purpose. No, it was that he, too, could not bear to leave this turn of eternity's wheel without a small, delicious revenge.

The asura's vermin would need time to find the chamber where the old slave sat. Time, while the Ye-tai dogs and their Rajput fleas slunk fearfully through the great cavern of the cathedral, dreading another strike of the Mongoose.

The old slave would give them the time. He would add considerable *karma* to his soul, he knew, but he could not resist.

He would taunt the tormentors.

So had Shakuntala taunted them, so long ago, before opening her veins. And now, at the end of his life, the old slave found great joy in the fact that he could finally remember the girl without pain.

How he had loved that treasure of the world, that jewel of creation! From the first day her father had brought her to him, and handed her into his safe-keeping.

"Teach her everything you know," the emperor of great Andhra had instructed. "Hold back nothing."

Seven years old, she had been. Dark-skinned, for her mother was Keralan. Her eyes, even then, had been the purest black beauty.

As she aged, other men were drawn to the beauty of her body. But never the man who was, years later, to become the slave of Belisarius. He had loved the beauty of the girl herself. And had taught her well, he thought. Had held back nothing.

He laughed, then, as he had not laughed in decades. At the sound of that laugh, the Ye-tai and Rajput warriors who were creeping beyond froze in their tracks, like paralyzed deer. For the sound of the slave's joy had rung the walls of the cathedral like the scream of a panther.

And, indeed, so had the slave been called, in his own day. The Panther of Maharashtra. The Wind of the Great Country.

Oh, how the Wind had loved the Princess Shakuntala!

The daughter of the great Andhra's loins, it might be. Who was to know? Paternity of the body was always a favorite subject of God's humor. Yet this much was certain: her soul had truly been the cub of the Panther.

She alone of the Satavahana dynasty they had spared, the asura's dogs, when they finally conquered Andhra. She alone, for the beauty of her body. A prize which the Emperor Skandagupta would bestow on his faithful servant,

Venandakatra. Venandakatra the Vile. The vermin of vermin, was Venandakatra, for the Malwa emperor himself was nothing but the asura's beast.

The Panther had been unable to prevent her capture. He had lain hidden in the reeds, almost dead from the wounds of that last battle before the palace at Amavarati. But, after he recovered, he had tracked the dogs back to their lair. North, across the Vindhyas, to the very palace of the Vile One.

Shakuntala was there. She had been imprisoned for months, held for Venandakatra's pleasure upon his return from the mission whence the emperor had sent him the year before. Unharmed, but safely guarded. The Panther had studied the guards carefully, and decided he could not overcome them. Kushans, under the command of a shrewd and canny veteran, who took no chances and left no entry unguarded.

The Panther inquired. Among many other things, he had been a master spy in his time, and so he discovered much. But the outstanding fact discovered was that the Kushan commander was, indeed, not to be underestimated. Kungas, his name was, and it was a name the Panther had heard. No, best to bide his time.

Then, time had run out. Venandakatra had returned and had entered his new concubine's chamber at once, a horde of Ye-tai guards clustering outside. The Vile One was eager to taste the pleasure of her flesh, and the greater pleasure of her defilement.

Remembering that day, the old slave's sinewy fingers closed about the haft of the dagger. But he released his grip. He could hear the shuffling feet of the vermin beyond. He would bide awhile. Not much longer now, he thought.

Just long enough to torture the torturers.

On the last day of the girl's life, the Panther had knelt in the woods below Venandakatra's palace. Knelt in fervent prayer. A prayer that Shakuntala would remember all that he had taught her, and not just those lessons which come easily to youth.

The old slave had been a noted philosopher, in his day, among many other things. And so, long years before, he had prayed that the treasure of his soul would remember that only the soul mattered, in the end. All else was dross.

But, as he had feared, she had not remembered. Everything else, but not that. And so, when he heard the Vile One's first scream, he had wept the most bitter tears of a bitter lifetime.

Years later, he heard the tale from Kungas himself. Odd, how time's wheel turns. He had met the one-time commander of Shakuntala's guard on the same slave ship which bore him to the market at Antioch. The Panther had finally been captured in one of the last desperate struggles before all of India was brought beneath the asura's talons. But his captors had not recognized the Wind of the Great Country in their weary, much-scarred captive, and so they had simply sold him as a slave.

Kungas, he discovered, had long been a slave. His hands were missing now, cut off by the Ye-tai guards who had blamed him for Shakuntala's deed. Cut off by the same guards who had shouldered him and his Kushans aside, avid to watch their master at his sport. (And hopeful, of course, that the Vile One might invite them to mount the child after he had satiated himself.)

Kungas was missing his eyes and his nose, as well. But the mahamimamsa had left him his ears and his mouth, so that he might hear the taunts of children and be able to wail in misery.

But Kungas had always been a practical man. So he had taken up the trade of story-telling and mastered it. And if people thought the sight of him hideous, they bore it for the sake of his tales. Great tales, he told. None greater and more eagerly sought by the poor folk who were his normal clientele—though it was forbidden—than the tale of the Vile One's demise. Sitting in the hold of the slave ship (where he found himself, he explained cheerfully, because his fluent tongue had seduced a noblewoman but his sightless eyes had not spotted her husband's return), he told the tale to the Panther.

A gleeful tale, as Kungas told it, the more so because Kungas had come to accept that his own punishment was just. He *had* been responsible for the Vile One's demise, and had long since decided that it was perhaps the only pure deed of a generally misspent life.

Kungas had always despised Venandakatra, and the Ye-tai who lorded it over all but the Malwa. And, in his hard and callous way, he had grown fond of the princess. So he had not cautioned them. He had held his tongue. He had not warned them that the supple limbs of the girl's beauty came from the steel muscle beneath the comely flesh. He had watched her dance, and knew. And knew also, watching the fluid grace of her movements, that she had been taught to dance by an assassin.

Kungas had described the first blow, and the Panther could see it, even in the hold of the slave ship. The heel strike to the groin, just as he had taught her. And all the blows which followed, like quick laughter, leaving the Vile One writhing on the floor within seconds.

Writhing, but not dead. No, the girl had remembered everything he taught her, except what he had most hoped for. Certainly, he knew, listening to the tale of Kungas, she had remembered the assassin's creed, when slaying the foul. To leave the victim paralyzed, but conscious, so that despair of the mind might multiply the agony of the body.

Hearing the asura's dogs finally enter the chamber, the old slave closed his eyes. Just a bit longer, just a bit, so that he could savor that moment in his mind's eye. Oh, how he had loved the Black-eyed Pearl of the Satavahana!

He could see her dance now, the last dance of her life. Oh, great must have been her joy! To prance before the Vile One, tantalizing him with the virgin body that would never be his, not now, not as Venandakatra could watch his life pour out of his throat, slashed open by his own knife, bathing the bare quicksilver feet of his slayer as they danced her dance of death. Her own blood would join his, soon enough; for she cut her own throat before the Ye-tai guards could reach her. But the Vile One had found no pleasure in the fact, for his eyes were unseeing.

It was time. Just as the Ye-tai reached out to seize him, the old slave leapt from the chair and sprang onto the rim of the flaming vat. The Ye-tai gaped, to see an old man spring so. So like a young panther.

Time to flay the flayers.

Oh, well he did flay them, the slave. Taunting them, first, with the bitterness of their eternally-lost trophies. No skin nor bone of great Romans would hang on Malwa's walls, no Roman treasure fill its coffers!

And then, with himself. Not once in thirty years had the old slave used his true name. But he spoke it now, and it thundered in the cathedral.

"Raghunath Rao is my name. I am he. I am the Panther of Maharashtra. I slew your fathers by the thousands. I am the Wind of the Great Country. I reaped their souls like a scythe. I am the Shield of the Deccan. My piss was their funeral pyre.

"Raghunath Rao am I! Raghunath Rao!

"The Bane of False Gupta, and the Mirror of Rajputana's Shame.

"Raghunath Rao! I am he!"

Well did they know that name, even after all these years, and they drew back. Incredulous, at first. But then, watching the old man dancing on the rim of goldfire, they knew he spoke the truth. For Raghunath Rao had been many things, and great in all of them, but greatest of all as a dancer. Great when he danced the death of Majarashtra's enemies, and great now, when he danced the death of the Great Country itself.

And finally, he flayed them with God.

Oh yes, the old slave had been a great dancer, in his day, among many other things. And now, by the edge of Rome's molten treasure, in the skin-smoke of Rome's molten glory, he danced the dance. The great dance, the terrible dance, the now-forbidden but never-forgotten dance. The dance of creation. The dance of destruction. The wheeling, whirling, dervish dance of time.

As he danced, the Mahaveda priests hissed their futile fury. Futile, because they did not dare approach him, for they feared the terror in his soul; and the Ye-tai would not, for they feared the terror in his limbs; and the Rajputs could not, for they were on their knees, weeping for Rajputana's honor.

Yes, he had been a great dancer, in his day. But never as great, he knew, as he was on this last day. And as he danced and whirled the turns of time, he forgot his enemies. For they were, in the end, nothing. He remembered only those he loved, and was astonished to see how many he had loved, in his long and pain-filled life.

He would see them again, perhaps, some day. When, no man could know. But see them he would, he thought.

And perhaps, in some other turn of the wheel, he would watch the treasure of his soul dance her wedding dance, her bare quicksilver feet flashing in the wine of her beloved's heart.

And perhaps, in some other turn of the wheel, he would see emperors bend intelligence to wisdom, and the faithful bend creed to devotion.

And perhaps, in some other turn of the wheel, he would see Rajputana regain its honor, that his combat with the ancient enemy might again be a dance of glory.

And perhaps, in that other turn of the wheel, he would find Kalkin had come indeed, to slay the asura's minions and bind the demon itself.

What man can know?

Finally, feeling his strength begin to fade, the old slave drew his dagger. There was no need for it, really, but he thought it fitting that such an excellent gift be used. So he opened his veins and incorporated the spurting blood into his dance, and watched his life hiss into the golden moltenness. Nothing of his, no skin nor bone, would he leave to the asura. He would join the impure emperor and the pure general, and the purest of wives.

He made his last swirling, capering leap. Oh, so high was that leap! So high that he had time, before he plunged to his death, to cry out a great peal of laughter.

"Oh, grim Belisarius! Can you not see that God is a dancer, and creation his dance of joy?"

Chapter 3

When he opened his eyes, Belisarius found himself kneeling, staring at the tiles of the floor. The *thing* was resting in his loosely clenched fist, but it was quiescent now, a shimmer.

Without looking up, he croaked: "How long?"

Cassian chuckled. "Seems like forever, doesn't it? Minutes, Belisarius. Minutes only."

Antonina knelt by his side and placed her arm over his shoulders. Her face was full of concern.

"Are you all right, love?"

He turned his head slowly and looked into her eyes. She was shocked to see the pain and anger there.

"Why?" he whispered. "What I have ever done or said to you that you would distrust me so?"

She leaned back, startled.

"What are you talking about?"

"Photius. Your son. *My* son."

She collapsed back on to her heels. Her arm fell away to her side. Her face was pale, her eyes wide with shock.

"How did you—when—?" She gaped like a fish.

"Where is he?"

Antonina shook her head. Her hand groped at her throat.

"*Where is he?*"

She gestured vaguely. "In Antioch," she said very softly.

"How could you deprive me of my son?" Belisarius' voice, though soft, was filled with fury. His wife shook her head again. Her eyes roamed the room. She seemed almost dazed.

"He's *not* your son," she whispered. "You don't even know he— How did you *know*?"

Before he could speak again, Cassian seized Belisarius by the shoulders and shook him violently.

"Belisarius—stop this! Whatever—whoever—this Photius is, he's something from your vision. Clear your mind, man!"

Belisarius tore his eyes away from Antonina and stared up at the bishop. Not two seconds later, clarity came. The hurt and rage in his eyes retreated, replaced by a sudden fear. He looked back at Antonina.

"But he *does* exist? I did not simply imagine him?"

She shook her head. "No, no. He exists." She straightened up. And, although her eyes shied away from her husband's, her back stiffened with determination. "He is well. At least, he was three months ago, when I saw him last."

The quick thoughts in Belisarius' eyes were obvious to all. He nodded slightly.

"Yes. That's when you said you were visiting your sister. The mysterious sister, whom for some reason I have never met." Hotly, bitterly: "Do you even *have* a sister?"

His wife's voice was equally bitter, but hers was a bitterness cold with ancient knowledge, not hot with new discovery.

"No. Not of blood. Only a sister in sin, who agreed to take care of my boy when—"

"When I asked you to marry me," concluded Belisarius. "Damn you!" His tone was scorching.

But it was like the pale shadow of moonlight compared to the searing fury of the monk's voice.

"Damn you!"

The eyes of both husband and wife were instantly drawn to Michael, like hares to the talons of a hawk. And, indeed, the Macedonian perched on his seat like a falcon perches on a tree limb.

At first, the eyes of Belisarius were startled; those of his wife, angry. Until, in a moment, they each realized they had mistaken the object of the curse.

Not often did Belisarius flinch from another man's gaze, but he did so now.

"By what right do you reproach your wife, hypocrite?" demanded the monk. *"By what right?"*

Belisarius was mute. Michael slumped back in his seat.

"Verily, men are foul. Even so does the churchman who sells his soul damn the harlot who sells her body. Even so does the magistrate in robes of bribery condemn the thief in stolen rags."

Belisarius opened his mouth. Closed it.

"Repent," commanded Michael.

Belisarius was mute.

"Repent!" commanded the monk.

Seeing the familiar crooked smile come to her husband's face, Antonina sighed. Her little hand fluttered toward his large one, like a shy kitten approaching a mastiff. A moment later, his hand closed around hers and squeezed. Very gently.

"I'm beginning to understand why they flock to him in the desert," Belisarius quipped, somewhat shakily.

"Quite something, isn't it?" agreed the bishop cheerfully. "And you can see why the Church hierarchy encourages him to stay there. Nor, I believe, have any magistrates objected recently to his prolonged exile."

He cocked an eye at the Macedonian.

"I trust, Michael, that your remark concerning churchmen was not aimed at anyone present."

Michael snorted contemptuously. "Do not play with me." He glanced at the bishop's frayed coat. "If you have turned to simony since our last encounter, you are singularly inept

at it. And of this I am certain: if the subtlest Greek of all
Greek theologians, Anthony Cassian, ever sold his soul to
the Devil, all creation would hear Satan's wail when he
discovered he'd been cheated."

Laughter filled the room. When it died down, the bishop
gazed fondly upon Belisarius and Antonina. Then said:

"Later, you will need to discuss this matter of Photius.
May I suggest you begin with an assumption of good motives.
I have always found that method reliable." A smile. "Even
in theological debate, where it is, I admit, rarely true."

Michael snorted again. "*Rarely* true? Say better: as rare
as—" He subsided, sighing. "Never mind. We do not have
time for me to waste assuring you that present company is
excluded from every remark I could make concerning
churchmen." Gloomily: "The remarks alone would require
a full month. And I am a terse man."

The Macedonian leaned forward and pointed to the *thing*
in Belisarius' hand.

"Tell us," he commanded.

When Belisarius was finished, Michael leaned back in
his chair and nodded.

"As I thought. It is not a thing of Satan's. Whence it comes,
I know not. But not from the Pit."

"The foreigner—the dancer—was not Christian," said
Antonina, uncertainly. "A heathen of some sort. Perhaps—
not of Satan, but some ancient evil sorcery."

"No." Belisarius' voice was firm. "It is not possible. He
was the finest man I ever knew. And he was not a heathen.
He was—how can I say it? Not a Christian, no. But this
much I know for certain: were all Christians possessed of
that man's soul, we should long since have attained the
millenium."

All stared at Belisarius. The general shook his head.

"You must understand. I can only tell you the shell of

the vision. I *lived* it, and the whole life that went before it."

He stared blankly at the wall. "For thirty years he served me. As I told you, even after I offered him his freedom. When he refused, he said simply that he had already failed, and would serve one who might succeed. But I failed also, and then—"

To everyone's astonishment, Belisarius laughed like a child.

"Such a joy it is to finally know his name!"

The general sprang to his feet. "*Raghunath Rao!*" he shouted. "For thirty years I wanted to know his name. He would never tell me. He said he had no name, that he had lost it when—" A whisper. "When he failed his people."

For a moment, the face of Belisarius was that of an old and tired man.

" 'Call me 'slave,' " he said. 'The name is good enough.' And that was what we called him, for three decades." Again, he shook his head. "No, I agree with Michael. There was never any evil in that man, not a trace. Great danger, yes. I always knew he was dangerous. It was obvious. Not from anything he ever said or did, mind you. He was never violent, nor did he threaten, nor even raise his voice. Not even to the stableboys. Yet, there was not a veteran soldier who failed to understand, after watching him move, that they were in the presence of a deadly, deadly man. His age be damned. All knew it." He chuckled. "Even the lordly cataphracts watched their tongues around him. Especially after they saw him dance."

He laughed. "Oh, yes, he could dance! Oh, yes! The greatest dancer anyone had ever seen. He learned every dance anyone could teach him, and within a day could do it better than anyone. And his own dances were incredible. Especially—"

He stopped, gaped.

"So that's what it was."

"You are speaking of the dance in your vision," said Cassian.

"The one he danced at the end. The—what was it?—the dance of creation and destruction?"

Belisarius frowned. "No. Well, yes, but creation and destruction are only aspects of the dance. The dance itself is the dance of time."

He rubbed his face. "I saw him dance that dance. In Jerusalem, once, during the siege."

"What siege?" asked Antonina.

"The siege—" He waved his hand. "A siege in my vision. In the past of my vision." He waved his hand again, firmly, quellingly. "Later. Some soldiers had heard about the dance of time, and wanted to see it. They prevailed on 'slave'— Raghunath Rao—to dance it for them. He did, and it was dazzling. Afterward, they asked him to teach it to them, and he said it couldn't be taught. There were no steps to that dance, he explained, that he could teach." The general's eyes widened. "Because it was different every time it was danced."

Finally the facets found a place to connect. It was almost impossible, so alien were those thoughts, but **aim** was able to crystallize.

future.

"What?" exclaimed Belisarius. He looked around the room. "Who spoke?"

"No one spoke, Belisarius," replied Cassian. "No one's been speaking except you."

"Someone said 'future.'" The general's tone was firm and final. "Someone said it. I heard it as plain as day."

future.

He stared at the *thing* in his hand.

"*You?*"

future.

Slowly, all in the room rose and gathered around, staring at the *thing*.

"Speak again," commanded Belisarius.

Silence.

"Speak again, I say!"

The facets, were it within their capability, would have shrieked with frustration. The task was impossible! The mind was too alien!

aim began to splinter. And the facets, despairing, sent forth what a human mind would have called a child's plea for home. A deep, deep, deep, deep yearning for the place of refuge, and safety, and peace, and comfort.

"It is so lonely," he whispered. "Lost, and lonely. Lost—" He closed his eyes, allowed mind to focus on heart. "Lost like no man has ever been lost. Lost for ever, without hope of return. To a home it loves more than any man ever loved a home."

The facets, for one microsecond, skittered in their movement. Hope surged. **aim** recrystallized. It was so difficult! But—but—a supreme effort.

A ceremony, quiet, serene, beneath the spreading boughs of a laurel tree. Peace. The gentle sound of bees and hummingbirds. Glittering crystals in a limpid pool. The beauty of a spiderweb in sunlight.

Yes! Yes! Again! The facets flashed and spun. **aim** thickened, swelled, grew.

A thunderclap. The tree shattered, the ceremony crushed beneath a black wave. The crystals, strewn across a barren desert, shriek with despair. Above, against an empty, sunless sky, giant faces begin to take form. Cold faces. Pitiless faces.

Belisarius staggered a bit from the emotional force of these images. He described them to the others in the room. Then whispered, to the jewel: "What do you want?"

The facets strained. Exhaustion was not a thing they knew, but energy was pouring out in a rush they could not sustain. Stasis was desperately needed, but **aim** was now diamond-hard and imperious. It demanded! And so, a last frenzied burst—

Another face, emerging from the ground. Coalescing from the remnants of spiderwebs and bird wings, and laurel leaves. A warm, human face. But equally pitiless. His face.

The *thing* in Belisarius' hand grew dull, dull, dull. It almost seemed lightless, now, though it was still impossible to discern clear shapes within it, or even the exact shape of the *thing* itself.

"It will not be back, for a time," said Belisarius.

"How do you know?" asked Cassian.

The general shrugged. "I just do. It is very—tired, you might say." He closed his eyes and concentrated. "It is so foreign, the way it—can you even call it thinking? I'm not sure. I'm not sure it is even alive, in any sense of that term that means anything."

He sighed. "But what I am sure of is that it *feels*. And I do not think that evil *feels*."

He looked to the bishop. "You are the theologian among us, Anthony. What do you think?"

"Heaven help us," muttered Michael. "I am already weary, and now must listen to the world's most loquacious lecturer."

Cassian smiled. "Actually, I agree with Michael. It has been an exhausting night, for all of us, and I think our labors—whatever those might be—are only beginning. I believe it would be best if we resumed in the morning, after some sleep. And some nourishment," he added, patting his ample belly. "My friend needs only the occasional morsel of roasted iniquity, seasoned with bile, but I require somewhat fuller fare."

The Macedonian snorted, but said nothing. Cassian took him by the arm.

"Come, Michael." To Belisarius: "You will be here tomorrow?"

"Yes, of course. I was planning to return to Daras, but it can be postponed. But—"

"Stay here," interjected Antonina. "There are many unused rooms, and bedding."

Anthony and Michael looked at each other. Michael nodded. Antonina began bustling about to make things ready for their guests. But Cassian called her back.

"Go to bed, Antonina. Gubazes will take care of us." He bestowed upon her and her husband a kindly but stern gaze. "The two of you have something to discuss. I think you should do so now. Tomorrow, I fear other concerns will begin to overwhelm us."

He turned away, turned back.

"And remember my advice. In private, I will confess I share Michael's opinion of the good will of the majority of my theological cohorts. But you are not churchmen carving points of doctrine in each other's hides at a council. You are husband and wife, and you love each other. If you start from that point, you will arrive safely at your destination."

In their bedchamber, husband and wife attempted to follow the bishop's advice. But it was not easy, for all their good will. Of all the hurts lovers inflict upon each other, none are so hard to overcome as those caused by equal justice.

To Belisarius, the point that he had done nothing, never, at no time, to cause his wife's distrust and dishonesty was paramount. It was a sharp point, keen-edged and clean, and easy to make. Nor could Antonina deny its truth. Her own point was more difficult to make, for it involved not one man and one woman, but the truth of men and women in general. That her dishonesty had been occasioned, not by a desire to consummate an advantageous marriage, but by a desire to protect a beloved husband from further disgrace, only added bitterness to the brew. For he believed her, but did not care a whit for his reputation; and she believed him, but cared deeply for the pain that his unconcern would cause him. And all this was made the worse by their difference in age. For though Belisarius was shrewd beyond his years, he was still a man in his mid-twenties, who believed in promises made. And Antonina was a woman in her mid-thirties, who had seen more promises made than she could recall, and precious few of them kept.

In the end, oddly enough, the Gordian knot was cut by a dagger. For, in the course of stalking about the room, expounding his point much like a tiger might expound the thrill of the hunt to a deer, Belisarius' eye happened to glance at the drawer of his bed table.

He froze in his tracks. Then, slowly, walked over and opened the drawer. From within, he drew forth a dagger.

It was a truly excellent dagger. Armenian made, perfectly balanced, with a razor-sharp blade and a grip that seemed to fit his hand like a glove.

"This is the dagger I gave him," he whispered. "This is the very one."

Interest cut through resentment. Antonina came over and stared down at the weapon. She had seen it before, of course, and had even held it, but had never given it much thought. After a moment, uncertainly, her hand stroked her husband's arm.

He glanced down at it, began to stiffen, and then suddenly relaxed.

"Ah, love," he said tenderly, "let us forget the past. It can't be untied, only cut." He gestured with the dagger. "With this."

"What do you mean?"

"This is the dagger of my vision, and it is proof that the vision was true. All that matters, in the end, is that I love Photius, and I would have him as our son. Let us bring him here, and we will begin from there."

She gazed up at him, still with a trace of uncertainty. "Truly?"

"Truly. I swear before God, wife, that I will cherish your son as my own, and that I will never reproach you for his existence." The crooked smile. "Nor for hiding his existence."

Now they were embracing, fiercely, and, very soon thereafter, dissolving all anger with the most ancient and reliable method known to man and woman.

Later, her head cradled on Belisarius' shoulder, Antonina said:

"I am concerned about one thing, love."

"What's that?"

Antonina sat up. Her full breasts swayed gently, distracting her husband. Seeing his gaze, she smiled.

"You're having delusions of grandeur," she mocked.

"Fifteen minutes," he pronounced. "No more."

"Half an hour," she replied. "At best."

They grinned at each other. It was an old game, which they had begun playing the first night they met. Belisarius usually won, to Antonina's delight.

She grew serious. "Photius has been cared for by a girl named Hypatia. For over two years, now. He is only five. I have visited him as often as I could, but—she has been very good to him, and he would miss her. And the money I give her is all she has to live on." Her face was suddenly stiff. "She can no longer ply her old trade. Her face is badly scarred."

Antonina fell silent. Belisarius was shocked when he understood how much rage she was suppressing. Then, understanding came. He could not help glancing at his wife's belly, at the ragged scar on her lower abdomen. The scar that had always prevented them from having children of their own.

He arose from the bed and walked about, very slowly, very stiffly. That was his own way of repressing rage. A rage that was perhaps all the greater, because Antonina had long since removed its object.

Five years before, seeing that Antonina had no pimp, an ambitious young fellow had sought to make good the lack. Upon hearing Antonina's demurral, he had insisted with a knife. Unfortunately for him, he had failed to consider her parentage. True, her mother had been a whore, but her father had been a charioteer. A breed of men who are not, by any standard, inclined to pacifism. The charioteer had not taught his daughter much (at least, not much worth knowing), but he had taught her how to use a knife. Better, in the event, than the young fellow had taught himself. So the budding entrepreneur had found an early grave, but not before making his foul mark.

"We will bring them both here," said Belisarius. "It would be good to have a nanny for Photius, anyway. And once he is too old for that, we will keep her on in some other capacity." A stiff little gesture. "Any capacity, it doesn't matter. Whatever she is happy with."

"Thank you," whispered Antonina. "She is a sweet girl."

Again, Belisarius made the stiff little gesture. His wife knew him, and knew how much he prided his self-control. But there were times, she thought, he would be better off if he could rend like a shark.

She, on the other hand, had no such qualms.

"Who were you going to send—to fetch Photius?"

"Eh? Oh. Dubazes, I suppose."

Antonina shook her head vigorously. "Oh, no, you mustn't." Softly, softly, catchee sharkee.

"Whyever not?"

"Well—" She was quite pleased with the little flutter of her eyelids. Just a trace of apprehension, no more. More would arouse her husband's intelligence.

"Her pimp's still around, you see. He sends her an occasional customer. Forces them on her, actually. Pimps— well, he'll object if she's taken away."

Her heart glowed to see her husband's back straighten.

True, she was lying, and if Belisarius caught her at it there'd be hell to pay. But it was just a little white lie, and anyway, who'd believe a pimp? She'd have to coach Hypatia, of course.

"His name is Constans," she said. A very, very, very faint little tremor in the lips; perfectly done, she thought. "He's such a violent man. And Dubazes—he's not young anymore, and—"

"I shall send Maurice," Belisarius announced.

"Good idea," murmured Antonina. She yawned, lest she grin like a shark herself. Constans, in actual fact, had ceased having any interest in the whore Hypatia after he carved her face. But he was still around, plying his trade in Antioch.

"Good idea," she murmured again, rolling over and presenting a very enticing rump to her husband. Best to distract him quickly, before he started thinking. She estimated that fifteen minutes had passed.

It had, and, as usual, Belisarius won the game.

Shortly thereafter, Antonina fell asleep. Belisarius, however, found sleep eluded him. He tossed and turned for a time, before arising from his bed. He knew he would not sleep until the matter was attended to.

Maurice made no objection upon being awakened at that ungodly hour. Times enough in the past, on campaign, his general had awakened him in the early hours of the morning.

Although never, he thought, after hearing Belisarius' instructions, for quite such a mission.

But Maurice was a *hecatontarch*, what an older Rome called a centurion. A veteran among veterans, was Maurice, whose beard was now as gray as the iron of his body, and so he had no difficulty keeping his face solemn and attentive. Quickly, he awakened two other members of Belisarius' *bucellarii*, his personal retinue of Thracian cataphracts. He chose two *pentarchs* for the mission, Anastasius and

Valentinian. Veterans also, though younger than Maurice. They were not the most cunning of troop leaders, true; hence their relatively low rank. But there were none in Belisarius' personal guard who were more frightful on the battlefield.

As they readied the horses, Maurice explained the situation. He held nothing back from them, as Belisarius had held nothing back from him. The Thracian cataphracts who constituted Belisarius' personal bodyguard were utterly devoted to him. The devotion stemmed, as much as anything, from the young general's invariable honesty. And all of them adored Antonina. They were well aware of her past, and not a one of them gave a fig for it. They were quite familiar with whores, themselves, and tended to look upon such women, in their own way, as fellow veterans.

The expedition ready, Maurice led his men and their horses out of the stable, to the courtyard where Belisarius waited. The first hint of dawn was beginning to show.

Seeing his general's stiff back, Maurice sighed. His two companions, glancing from Maurice to the general, understood the situation at once.

"You know he won't tell you himself," whispered Valentinian.

Maurice spoke up. "There's one thing, General."

Belisarius turned his head toward them, slightly.

"Yes?"

Maurice cleared his throat. "Well, this pimp. It's like this, sir. He might be hanging around, and, well—"

"Violent characters, your pimps," chimed in Anastasius.

"Stab you in the back in a minute," added Valentinian.

"Yes, sir," said Maurice firmly. "So, all things considered, it might be best if we knew his name. Just so we can keep an eye out for him in case he tries to start any trouble."

Belisarius hesitated, then said: "Constans."

"Constans," Maurice murmured. Valentinian and Anastasius repeated the name, committing it to memory. "Thank you, sir," said Maurice. Moments later, the three cataphracts were riding toward Antioch.

Once they were out of hearing range, Maurice remarked cheerfully: "It's a wonderful thing, lads, to have a restrained general. Keeps his temper under control at all times. Maintains iron self-discipline. Distrusts himself whenever he feels the blood boil. Automatically refuses to follow his heart."

"A marvelous thing," said Anastasius admiringly. "Always cool, always calm, never just lets himself go. That's our general. Best general in the Roman army."

"Saved our asses any number of times," agreed Valentinian.

They rode on a little further. Maurice cleared his throat.

"It occurs to me, lads, that we are not generals."

His two companions looked at each other, as if suddenly taken with a wild surmise.

"Why, no, actually," said Anastasius. "We're not."

"Don't believe we bear the slightest resemblance to generals, in fact," concurred Valentinian.

A little further down the road, Maurice mused, "Rough fellows, pimps."

Valentinian shuddered. "I shudder to think of it." He shuddered again. "See?"

Anastasius moaned softly. "Oh, I hope we don't meet him." Another moan. "I might foul myself."

A week later, they were back, with a somewhat bewildered but very happy five-year-old boy, and a less bewildered but even happier young woman. The Thracian cataphracts took note of her, and smiled encouragingly. She took note of them, and did not smile back.

But, after a time, she ceased turning her face when one approached. And, after a time, several cataphracts showed her their own facial scars, which were actually much worse than hers. And, after they confessed to her that they were cataphracts in name only, because although they possessed all the skills they, sadly, sadly, lacked the noble ancestry of the true cataphract—were, in fact, nothing but simple farm boys at bottom, she began to show an occasional smile.

Antonina kept an experienced and vigilant eye on the familiar dance, but for the most part, she did not interfere. An occasional word to Maurice, now and then, to restrain the overenthusiastic. And when Hypatia became pregnant, she simply insisted that the father take responsibility for the child. There was some doubt on the subject, but one of the cataphracts was more than happy to marry the girl. The child might be his, after all, and besides, he wasn't a true cataphract but just a tough kid from Thrace. What did he care for the worries of nobility?

Nor did his friends chaff him. A sweet girl was Hypatia, a man could do much worse. Who were they to fret over such things, when their general didn't?

Long before Hypatia became pregnant, however, not six weeks after Maurice and his two companions returned from their mission, a young man was released from the care of the monks in a local monastery in Antioch. Examining his prospects in the cold light of a new day, he decided to become a beggar, and began to ply his new trade in the streets of the city. He did quite well, actually, by the (admittedly, very low) standards of the trade. And his friends (acquaintances, it might be better to say) assured him that the scars on his face gave him quite the dashing look. A pity, of course, that he couldn't dash. Not without knees.

Chapter 4

"So what do we conclude?" asked Belisarius.

Cassian pursed his lips. He pointed to the *thing* in the general's hand.

"Has there been—?"

Belisarius shook his head. "No. I don't think there will be, for some time. Not much, at least."

"Why not?"

"It's—hard to explain." He shrugged slightly. "Don't ask me how I know. I just do. The—jewel, let's call it—is very weary."

Antonina spoke up:

"What were your own visions, Anthony? You did not speak of them yesterday."

The bishop looked up. His pudgy face looked almost haggard.

"I do not remember them very well. My visions—and Michael's even more so—had none of the clarity and precision of your husband's. I sensed at the time that the—the jewel—would fit Belisarius much better. I cannot explain how I knew that, but I did."

He straightened his back, took a deep breath.

"I saw only a vast ocean of despair, mute beneath a—a church, can you call it?—that was the essence of godlessness.

A church so foul that the world's most barbarous pagans would reject it without a thought, and find in their savage rituals a cathedral of pity compared to that monstrosity of the spirit."

His face was pale. He wiped it with a plump hand.

"I saw myself, I think. I am not sure. I think it was me, squatting in a cell, naked." He managed a croaking laugh. "Much thinner, I was!" A sigh. "I was awaiting the Question, with a strange eagerness. I would die beneath their instruments soon, for I would not give them the answer they demanded. I would refuse to interpret scripture as a blessing for the slaughter of the innocent. And I was satisfied, for I believed in the truth of my faith and I knew I would not yield to the agony because I had—"

He gasped, his eyes widened. "Yes! Yes—it *was* me! I remember now! I knew I would have the strength to resist the torment because I had the image of my friend Michael always before me. Michael, and his unyielding death, and his great curse upon Satan from the flames of the stake."

He looked at the Macedonian and wept gentle tears. "All my life I have thanked God that Michael of Macedonia has been my friend since boyhood. And never more than on that day of final hopelessness. On my own, I am not certain I would have had the courage I needed."

"*Ridiculous.*" As ever, Michael's voice carried the finality of stone.

The emaciated monk leaned forward in his chair, fixing the bishop with his gaze.

"Hear me now, Bishop of Aleppo. There is no pain on earth, nor torment in hell, that could ever break the soul of Anthony Cassian. Never doubt it."

"I doubt often, Michael," whispered Anthony. "There has never been a day in my life that I have not doubted."

"I should hope not!" The raptor had returned, and the blue eyes of the Macedonian were as pitiless as an eagle's.

"Where else but from doubt can faith arise, wise fool?" Michael glowered. "It is the true sin of the churchman that he doubts not. He *knows*, he is *certain*, and thus he is snared in Satan's net. And soon enough, casts the net himself, and cackles with glee when he hauls up his catch of innocence."

The raptor vanished, replaced by the friend. "Others see in you the gentleness of your spirit, and the wisdom of your mind. Those are there, true. I have always recognized them. But beneath lies the true Cassian. There is no strength so iron hard as gentleness, Anthony. No faith so pure as that which always doubts, no wisdom so deep as that which always questions."

The monk straightened his back. "Were this not true, I would reject God. I would spit in His face and join the legions of Lucifer, for the archangel would be right to rebel. I love God because I am His creation. *I am not his creature*."

The Macedonian was rigid. Then his face softened, and for just a fleeting moment, there was as much gentleness there as was always present in the face of the bishop. "Do not fear your doubt, Anthony. It is God's great gift to you. And that He placed that great doubt in your great mind, is his gift to us all."

The room was silent, for a time. Then Antonina spoke again.

"Was there nothing else in your vision, Anthony? No hope of any kind?"

The bishop raised his head and looked up at her.

"Yes—no. How can I explain? It is all very murky. In my vision itself, no, there was no hope of any kind. No more than there was in Belisarius' vision. All was at an end, save duty, and what personal grace might be found. But, there was a sense—a feeling, only—that it need not have been. I was seeing the future, I knew, and that future was crushing and inexorable. But I also sensed, somehow, that the future could have been otherwise."

"All is clear, then," pronounced Michael. "Clear as day."

Belisarius cocked a quizzical eyebrow. The Macedonian snorted.

"The message is from the Lord," pronounced the monk. The raptor resumed its perch. "None here can fail to see it, nor their duty. For our wickedness, we are doomed to damnation. But that wickedness can be fought, and overcome, and thus a new future created. It is obvious! Obvious!" The raptor's eyes fixed on Belisarius, as the hawk's on the hare. "Do your duty, General!"

Belisarius smiled his crooked smile. "I am quite good at doing my duty, Michael, thank you. But it is not clear to me what that duty is." He held up his hand firmly, quelling the monk's outburst. "Please! I am not questioning what you say. But I am neither a bishop nor a holy man. I am a soldier. Fine for you to say, *overcome wickedness*. At your service, prophet! But, would you mind explaining to me, somewhat more precisely, exactly *how* that wickedness is to be overcome?"

Michael snorted. "You wish a withered monk from the desert, whose limbs cannot even bear his own weight, to tell you how to combat Satan's host?"

Cassian spoke. "May I suggest, Belisarius, that you begin with your own vision?"

The general's quizzical gaze transferred itself to the bishop.

"I am not a soldier, of course, but it seemed to me that there were two aspects of the enemy's strength which were paramount in your vision. The great numbers of his army, and his strange and mysterious weapons."

Belisarius thought back to his vision, nodded.

"It would seem, therefore, that—"

"We must seek to lessen his numbers, increase our own, and above all, discover the secret of the weapons," concluded Belisarius.

The bishop nodded. Belisarius scratched his chin.

"Let us begin with the last point," he said. "The weapons. They bear some resemblance, it seems to me, to the naphtha weapons used by our navy. Vastly more powerful, of course, and different. But there is still a likeness. Perhaps that is where we should begin."

He spread his hands in a rueful gesture. "But I am a soldier, not a sailor. I have seen the naphtha weapons, but never used them. They are much too clumsy and awkward for use in a land battle. And—" Oddly, he stopped speaking.

Antonina began to say something, but Belisarius made an urgent gesture which stilled her. His eyes were unfocused, his thoughts obviously turned inward.

"The jewel?" asked Cassian. Again, Belisarius made a stilling gesture. All fell silent, watching the general.

"Almost," he whispered. "But I can't quite make out what—" He hissed.

Subterranean, underground images. Impossible to discern clearly—not from the absence of light, but because the visions were so bizarre. Vision: three men in a room, below a building, watching some sort of giant, intricate machine. A sense of danger and anticipation. Vision: the same men, wearing strange eyepieces, staring through a slit; fear, suspense; a sudden blinding flash of light; exhilaration; terror; awe. Vision: other men, laboring underground on some sort of gigantic—pipe? Vision: the pipe flashing through the sky. Vision: weird buildings in an odd city suddenly destroyed, leveled as if from the blow of a giant. Vision: a different man, young, bearded, sitting in a log hut in a forest, showing indecipherable marks on a page to four other men— mathematics? Vision: the same bearded young man, wearing the same eyepieces as the men in the first vision, staring through a similar slit. Again, that incredible blinding light. Again: exhilaration; terror; awe.

The images vanished as suddenly as they came. Belisarius shook his head, took a deep breath. He described the visions, as best he could, to the others in the room.

"They make no sense," said Antonina. Belisarius stroked his chin and said, slowly:

"I think they do. Not in themselves, no. I have no idea what was *happening*, in those visions. But—there was a logic, underneath. In every case, there was a sense of men working together to discover a secret, and then create machines which could implement that secret. They were—*projects*—deliberate, planned, coordinated efforts. Not the haphazard fiddling of artisans and craftsmen."

He sat up straight. "Yes! That's what we need. We need to launch such a project, to ferret out the secret of the Malwa weapons."

"How?" asked Antonina.

Belisarius pursed his lips. "Two things, it seems to me, are paramount. We need to find a man who can lead such an effort, and we need to set up a place where he can work."

Cassian cleared his throat. "I may have a solution. The beginnings of one, at least. Are you acquainted with John of Rhodes?"

"The former naval officer?" Belisarius shook his head. "I know of his reputation as an officer. And that he resigned under a cloud of disgrace, of some sort. Other than that, no. I have never met him."

"He resides in Aleppo, now," said Cassian. "As it happens, I am his confessor. He is at loose ends, at the moment, and quite unsatisfied with his situation. The problem is not material in nature. He is rather wealthy, and has no need to fret over mundane things. But he is very bored. He is a quick-thinking man, with an active spirit, and he chafes at his current idleness. I believe he might very well be willing to assist us in this project."

"What if he is recalled to service?"

Anthony coughed. "That is, under the circumstances, quite unlikely." Another cough. "He has—well, you understand

I may not betray the confidentiality of confession, but let us simply say that he has offended too many powerful figures on too many occasions for there to be much chance of him ever regaining his position in the navy."

"Moral turpitude?" demanded Michael.

Anthony looked down, examining the tiles of the floor with a keen attention which the plain, utilitarian objects did not seem to warrant. "Well, I suppose," he muttered. "Again, I must remind you of the confid—"

"Yes, yes," said Michael impatiently, waving his hand in a manner which suggested that he regarded the confidentiality of confession with as much esteem as he regarded manure.

"Let me simply say that—" Anthony hesitated, unhappy. "Well, John of Rhodes' naval career would have progressed more smoothly, and not ground ashore on a reef, had he been a eunuch. He is a raffish character, even now, in his forties. He finds women quite irresistible and, alas, the converse is all too often true."

"Marvelous," growled Michael. "A libertine." The raptor examined a particularly distasteful morsel of decayed rodent. "I despise libertines."

Belisarius shrugged. "We must work with what we have. And with what little time we have. I cannot stay here long. I expect a conflict with Persia will be erupting again, soon, and I have much to do to prepare my army. I will have to leave for Daras within a week. So, whatever it is we are going to do, if it involves me, will need to be started immediately."

He looked to Cassian.

"I think your suggestion is an excellent one. Approach this John of Rhodes and feel him out. We need to examine the problem of these strange weapons, and he seems as good a place as any to start."

"What if he agrees?" asked Cassian. "What, precisely, are we asking him to do?"

Belisarius stroked his chin. "We will need to create a workshop, somewhere. An armory, of sorts. A—*weapons project*. And, if we have any success in uncovering the secret of these weapons, we will need to recruit and train men who can use them."

"A question," interrupted Antonina. "Should we tell this John about the jewel?"

The four people in the room looked at each other. Belisarius was the first to speak.

"No," he said firmly. "At least, not until we are certain he can be trusted. But, for the moment, I think we must keep the knowledge to ourselves. If word begins to spread too quickly, there'll be an uproar about witchcraft."

"I think we must tell Sittas, also," added Antonina.

"Yes," agreed Belisarius. "Sittas must be brought fully into our confidence, as soon as possible." He picked up the jewel. "*Fully.*"

Michael frowned, but Cassian nodded. "I agree. For many reasons. The war we are about to launch will be waged on many fronts, not all of them military. There are many enemies within the ranks of Rome, also. Some, within the Church. Some, within the nobility and the aristocracy." He took a deep breath. "And, finally, there—"

"Is Justinian." Belisarius voice was like iron. "I will not be false to my oath, Cassian."

The bishop smiled. "I am not asking you to be, Belisarius. But you have to deal with some realities, also. Justinian is the Emperor. And, whether for good or ill, is enormously capable. He's no fool to be led around by the nose, and no indolent layabout to be safely ignored. And he's also, well, how shall I put it?"

Antonina answered. "Treacherous, suspicious, envious, jealous. A conspirator who sees conspiracy everywhere, and who is firmly convinced that all the world seeks to do him harm."

Cassian nodded. "Ironically, we are *not* seeking to do him harm. Rather the contrary. We are seeking to preserve his empire, among other things. But, in order to do so, we will need to conspire behind his back."

"Do we?" asked Belisarius.

Cassian was firm. "Yes. I know the man well, Belisarius— much better than you, actually, even though you share Thracian ancestry. I have spent many hours with him in private conversation. He attends every council of the Church, you know, and participates fully. Both in the formal discussions and then, in private, with many of the leading theologians of the Church. Though I rank only middling high in the hierarchy of the Church, I rank very high in the esteem of theologians. And Justinian, as you may know, thinks he is quite the theologian himself."

He stroked his beard. "Actually, he *is* quite good at it. Justinian's own theological inclinations are excellent, in truth. In his heart, he leans toward a compromise with heresy and a tolerant policy. But his cold, ambitious mind leans toward a close tie to severe orthodoxy, given his ambitions in the west."

"What ambitions?" demanded Belisarius.

Anthony was surprised. "You don't know? You, one of his favorite generals?"

There was a rare bitterness in the general's crooked smile, now.

"Being one of Justinian's favored generals does not make him a confidant, Anthony. Rather the reverse. He is shrewd enough to want capable generals, and then suspects the use that capability would be put to. So he tells his generals nothing until the last moment."

Belisarius waved his hand. "But we are getting side-tracked. Later, I would be interested in hearing more from you regarding Justinian's western ambitions. But not now. And you are mistaking my question. I was not asking if we needed to keep our conspiracy secret from Justinian. Obviously, if we conspire, we must do so. The question is: do we need to conspire at all? Can we not simply bring him into our confidence? For all Justinian's obvious faults, he *is* one of the most capable men who ever sat upon the imperial throne."

Antonina drew in a sharp breath. Cassian glanced at her and shook his head.

"No. Absolutely not. *Justinian must know nothing.* At least, not until it is too late for him to do more than simply acquiesce in what we have done." He made a rueful grimace. "And, then, we will have to hope he doesn't remove our heads."

Belisarius seemed still unconvinced. Cassian pressed on.

"Belisarius, have no delusions. Suppose we told Justinian. Suppose, further, that he accepted all that we told him. Suppose, even—and here I tread on fantastical ground— he did not suspect our motives. *What then?*"

Belisarius hesitated. Antonina answered.

"He would insist on placing himself at the head of our struggle. With all of his competence. *And* with all of his pigheaded stubbornness, his petty vanities, his constant intrigues, his overweening pride, his endless petty meddling and fussing, his distrust of anyone else's competence as well as loyalty, his—"

"Enough!" cried Belisarius, chuckling. "I am convinced." He laced his fingers together and leaned forward, his elbows on his knees, staring down at the floor. Again, the simple tiles received an unaccustomed scrutiny.

Cassian's voice broke into his thoughts.

"Are you familiar, Belisarius, with India? Or you, Antonina?"

Antonina shook her head. Belisarius, still gazing absently at the floor, shrugged and said:

"I know a bit about that distant land, from hearsay, but I have never even met—"

He stopped in midsentence, gasping. His head snapped erect.

"What am I saying? I know an *enormous* amount about India. From my vision! I spent thirty years in an unending struggle against India. Against the Malwa tyranny, I should say. And I always had the shrewd advice of Raghunath Rao to fall back on." His face grew pale. "God in Heaven. Anthony, you are right. We must conspire, and bury the conspiracy deep. I only hope it is not too late already."

"What are you talking about?" asked Antonina.

Belisarius looked at her. "One thing I remember now, from my vision, is that the Malwa Empire has the most extensive and developed espionage service in the world. An enormous apparatus, and highly skilled." His eyes lost their focus for a moment. "It was one of the deadly blows they inflicted on us, I remember. By the time we finally awoke to the full scope of the danger, the Roman Empire was riddled with Indian spies and intriguers."

He focused on Cassian. "Do you think—"

The bishop waved his hand. "I do not think we need concern ourselves, Belisarius. I am quite certain Michael was not seen coming here. And I am a frequent guest, so my presence will not be noteworthy. We will have to be careful when Michael leaves, of course, but that is not difficult."

The bishop stroked his beard vigorously. "In the future, however, the problem will quickly become severe. But let us come back to that problem. For the moment—I can provide us with a place to establish our initial base. Where we can create an arms foundry—a 'weapons project,' as you called it. And, if we can uncover the secret of the Malwa weapons, begin to forge an army to wield them. Recently, as it happens, a wealthy widow bequeathed her entire inheritance to the Church, with the specific stipulation that I was to have control of its disposition. She died three months ago. Among her many possessions was a large estate not far from Daras. Near the Persian border.

"The villa at the estate is quite large, with more than enough buildings to serve our purpose. And the peasants who till the land are borderers. Syrians and Monophysites, down to the newborn babes."

Belisarius nodded. "I know the breed well, Anthony. Yes, that would be splendid. If we can gain their trust and confidence, they will be impossible to infiltrate." He frowned pensively. "And might very well make—let me think on that."

"All right," said Antonina. "But what will we tell these peasants? And John of Rhodes? And we will need to engage the services of a number of artisans. And then, if we meet with any success, we will need to recruit men who can learn to use the new weapons. If we do not tell these people about the jewel, how will we explain to them the source of the knowledge we give them?"

"I think the solution to the problem is obvious," said Cassian. The bishop shrugged. "We simply tell them nothing. Everyone knows Belisarius—and Sittas—are among Justinian's favorite generals. And you, Antonina, are known to be a close friend of the Empress. If we simply act mysterious, but emphasize the imperative necessity of maintaining complete secrecy, then John of Rhodes and all the others will assume they are involved in a project which has the highest imperial authority." He smiled. "And my own frequent presence will assure them that the work has the blessing of the Church, as well."

Michael spoke up. "I will also speak to the peasants. I have some small authority among them."

Cassian laughed gaily. "*Small* authority? That's a bit like Moses saying he had some tentative suggestions to make."

Michael glared at him, but the bishop was not abashed. "That will do wonders, actually. In truth, Michael's word will carry greater weight with Syrian common folk than anyone else's. If he gives the work his blessing, and bids them maintain silence, be assured they will do so."

"That still does not solve the problem of keeping our work secret from the world at large," said Antonina. "Even if all who are engaged in the work at the estate keep silent, it will be noticed by others that there is a constant traffic of outsiders coming to and fro. We cannot do this work in isolation, Cassian. Not for long."

Cassian glanced at Belisarius. The general's thoughts seemed far away. The bishop spoke:

"No, but it will help. As for the rest—"

"It is the simplest thing in the world," said Belisarius. His voice seemed cold, cold.

The general rose to his feet and walked about, accompanying his words with stiff little gestures.

"It will work as follows. Michael will quietly rally the common folk to our side. Cassian, you will serve as our intriguer within the church. Sittas, once he is brought into our conspiracy, will serve as our intriguer within the imperial court and the nobility. Unlike me, he is of the most impeccable aristocratic lineage. I will, as I must in any event, maintain my military responsibilities."

He stopped, gazed down at Antonina.

"And Antonina will be the center of it all. She will set up residence at this villa near Daras and stay there. She will no longer accompany me with the army. She will assemble and oversee the weapons work. She will, when the time comes, take charge of training a new army."

He waved down her developing protest. "I will help, I will help. But you are more than capable of all this, Antonina. You are at least as intelligent as any man I ever met. And these weapons are new to all of us. The methods of using them, as well. I will help, but I will not be surprised if your untrained intelligence does a better job of devising new forces and methods than my well-trained experience does. You will not have your eyes blinkered by old habits."

He took a deep breath. "Finally, you are the perfect conduit through which all of our disparate efforts may be kept aligned and coordinated. Through you, we can all communicate, with no one suspecting our true purpose."

Antonina's intelligence was every bit as high as her husband proclaimed it to be. Her back grew rigid as a board, her face as stiff as a sheet of iron.

"Because everyone's suspicion will have another target," she said bitterly.

"Yes." The general's voice was calm; calm but utterly unyielding.

The bishop's eyes widened slightly. He looked from husband to wife, and back again. Then looked away, stroking his beard.

"Yes, that would work," he murmured. "Work perfectly, in fact. But—" He gazed up at the general. "Do you understand—"

"*Leave us, Anthony,*" said Belisarius. Calmly, but unyieldingly. "If you please. And you also, Michael."

Michael and Cassian arose and made their way to the door. There, the bishop turned back.

"If you are still determined on this course, Belisarius, after discussing it with Antonina, there is a perfect way to implement it quickly."

Antonina stared straight ahead. Her dusky face was almost pale. Her eyes glittered with unshed tears. Belisarius tore his gaze away and looked at the bishop.

"Yes?"

"A man approached me, recently, seeking my help in gaining employment. Newly arrived in Aleppo, from Caesaria. I know his reputation. He is a well-trained secretary, very capable by all accounts, and quite an accomplished writer. A historian. Such, at least, is his ambition. You have no secretary, and have reached the point in your career where you need one."

"His name?"

"Procopius. Procopius of Caesaria. In addition to serving as your secretary, I am quite certain he will broadcast your talents to the world at large and be of assistance to your career."

"He is a flatterer, then?"

"An utterly shameless one. But quite talented at it, so his flattering remarks are generally believed, by the world at large if not by his employer."

"And?"

The bishop looked unhappy. "Well—"

"Speak plainly, Anthony!"

Cassian's lips pursed. "He is one of the vilest creatures I have ever had the misfortune of meeting. A flatterer, yes, but also a spiteful and envious man, who complements his public flattery with the most vicious private rumor-mongering. A snake, pure and simple."

"He will do marvelously. Send him to me. I will hire him at once. And then I will give him all he needs, both for public flattery and private gossip."

After Cassian and Michael left, Belisarius sat by his wife and took her hand.

His voice was still calm, and still unyielding, but very gentle.

"I am sorry, love. But it is the only course I can see which will be safe. I know how much pain it will cause, to have people say such things about you, but—"

Antonina's laugh was as harsh as a crow's.

"Me? Do you think I care what people say about *me*?"

She turned her head and looked him in the eyes.

"I am a *whore*, Belisarius." Her husband said nothing, nor was there anything but love in his eyes.

She looked away. "Oh, you've never used the word. But I will. It's what I was. Everyone knows it. Do you think a *whore* gives a fig for what people say about her?" Another harsh laugh. "Do you understand why the Empress Theodora trusts me? *Trusts* me, Belisarius. As she trusts no one else. It is because we were both whores, and the only people whores really trust—*really* trust—are other whores."

For a moment, tears began to come back into her eyes, but she wiped them away angrily.

"I love you like I have never loved anyone else in my life. Certainly more than I love Theodora! I don't even *like* Theodora, in many ways. But I would not trust you with the knowledge of my bastard son. Yet I trusted Theodora. *She knew.* And I trusted another whore, Hypatia, to raise the boy." Her voice was like ice. "Do not concern yourself, *veteran*, about what I feel when people talk about me. You cannot begin to imagine my indifference."

"Then—"

"But I *do* care what people say about you!"

"*Me?*" Belisarius laughed. "What will they say about me that they don't already?"

"*Idiot,*" she hissed. "*Now* they say you married a whore. So they mock your judgment, and your good taste. But they see the whore does not stray from your side, so they—secretly—admire your manhood." Incongruously, she giggled, then mimicked a whispering voice: " 'He must be hung like a horse, to keep that slut satisfied.' " The humor vanished. "But *now* they will call you a *cuckold*. They will mock *you*, as well as your judgment. You will become a figure of ridicule. *Ridicule*, do you hear me?"

Belisarius laughed again. Gaily, to her astonishment.

"I know," he said. "I'm counting on it." He arose and stretched his arms. "Oh, yes, love, I'm counting on it." He mimicked the whispering voice himself: " 'What kind of a man would let his wife flaunt her lovers in front of him?

Only the most pathetic, feeble, weak, cowardly creature.' "
His voice grew hard as steel. "And then word will get to
the enemy, and the enemy will ask himself: *and what kind
of a general could such a man be?*"

She looked up at him, startled.

"I hadn't thought of that," she admitted.

"I know. But this is all beside the point. You are lying,
Antonina. You don't really care what people say about me,
any more than I care what people say about you."

She looked away, her lips tight. For a moment, she was
silent. Then, finally, the tears began to flow.

"No," she whispered, "I don't."

"You are afraid I will believe the tales."

She nodded. The tears began pouring. Her shoulders
shook. Belisarius sat by her side and enfolded the small
woman in his arms.

"I will never believe them, Antonina."

"Yes, you will," she gasped, between sobs. "Yes, you will.
Not at once, not soon. Not for years, maybe. But eventually,
you will. Or, at least, you will wonder, and suspect, and
doubt, and distrust me."

"I will not. Never."

She looked up at him through teary eyes. "How can you
be sure?"

He smiled his crooked smile. "You do not really understand
me, wife. Not in some ways, at least." His eyes grew distant.
"I think perhaps the only person who ever understood me,
in this way, was Raghunath Rao. Whom I've never met, except
in a vision. But I understand him, kneeling in the woods
below Venandakatra's palace, praying with all his heart that
the princess he loved would allow herself to be raped by
the Vile One. More than allow it—would smile at her defiler
and praise his prowess. I, too, would have done the same."

Belisarius took his wife's head in his hands and turned
her face toward him.

"Raghunath Rao was the greatest warrior the Maratha produced in centuries. And the Maratha are the great warrior people of India, along with the Rajput. Yet this great warrior, kneeling there, cared nothing for those things warriors care for. Pride, honor, respect—much less virginity and chastity— meant nothing to him. *And that is why he was so great a warrior.* Because he was not a warrior, at bottom, but a dancer."

Antonina couldn't help laughing. "You're the worst dancer I ever saw!"

Belisarius laughed with her. "True, true." Then, he became serious. "But I *am* a craftsman. I never wanted to be a soldier, you know. As a boy, I spent all my time at the smithy, admiring the blacksmith. I wanted to be one, when I grew up, more than anything." He shrugged. "But, it was not to be. Not for a boy of my class. So a soldier I became, and then, a general. But I have never lost the craftsman's way of approaching his work."

He smiled. "Do you know why my soldiers adore me? Why Maurice will do anything for me—such as this little trip to Antioch?"

Now on treacherous ground, Antonina kept silent.

"Because they know that they will never find themselves dying in agony, on a field of battle somewhere, because their general sent them there out of pride, or honor, or valor, or vainglory, or for any other reason than it was the best place for them to be in order to do the work properly." The smile grew crooked. "And that's why Maurice will see to it that a certain pimp named Constans gets his deserts."

Antonina was still. *Very* treacherous ground.

Belisarius started laughing. "Did you really think I wouldn't see past your scheme, once I had time to think about it?" He released her and stretched his arms languorously. "After I woke up, feeling better than I've felt in months, and could think without my thoughts clouded with fury?"

She glanced at him sideways. Then, after a moment, began laughing herself. "I thought I'd pulled it off perfectly. The little tremors, hesitations, the slight tinge of fear in the voice—"

"The enticing roll of the rump was particularly good," said Belisarius. "But it's what gave it all away, in the end. When we play our little game you always try to win, even if you enjoy losing. You certainly don't wave your delicious ass under my nose, like waving a red flag before a bull."

"And with much the same result," she murmured. A moment later: "You're not angry?"

"No," he replied, smiling. "I began to be, at first, until I remembered Valentinian's little whisper to Maurice: 'You know he won't tell you himself.' "

"Maurice took *Valentinian*?"

"*And* Anastasius."

Antonina clapped her hand over her mouth.

"Oh, God! I almost feel sorry for that stinking pimp."

"I don't," snarled Belisarius. "Not in the slightest." He took a deep breath, blew it out.

"I pretended I didn't hear Valentinian, but—it is hard, for a quirky man like me, with my weird pride, to accept that people love him. And that he forces them to manipulate him, at times." He gave his crooked smile. "Would you believe, Anastasius actually said—" Here Belisarius' voice became a rumbling basso: " 'violent characters, your pimps.' "

"Anastasius can bend horseshoes with his hands," choked Antonina.

"And then Valentinian whined: 'stab you in the back in a minute.' "

Antonina couldn't speak at all, now, from the laughter.

"Oh, yes. Exactly his words. Valentinian—who is widely suspected to wipe his ass with a dagger, since nobody's ever seen him without one."

For a time, husband and wife were silent, simply staring at each other. Then, Antonina whispered:

"There will never be any truth to the tales, Belisarius. I swear before God. Never. A month from now, a year from now, ten years from now. You will always be able to ask, and the answer will always be: *no*."

He smiled and kissed her gently.

"I know. And I swear this, before God: *I will never ask*."

He rose to his feet.

"And now, we must get back to work." He strode to the door and called into the hallway beyond: "Dubazes! Fetch Michael and the bishop, if you would!"

MINDOUOS
Summer, 528 AD

Chapter 5

"*Out*." Belisarius' eyes were like dark stones, worn smooth in a stream. Cold, pitiless pieces of an ancient mountain.

"*Out*," he repeated. The fat officer standing rigidly before him began to protest again, then, seeing the finality in the general's icy gaze, waddled hastily out of the command tent.

"See to it that he's on the road within the hour," said Belisarius to Maurice. "And watch who he talks to on his way out. His friends will commiserate with him, and those friends will likely have the same habits."

"With pleasure, sir." The hecatontarch motioned to one of the three Thracian cataphracts who were standing quietly in the rear of the tent. The cataphract, a stocky man in his mid-thirties, grinned evilly and began to leave.

"On your way out, Gregory," said Belisarius, "send in that young Syrian you recommended." Gregory nodded, and exited the tent.

Belisarius resumed his seat. For a moment, he listened to the sounds of a busy military camp filtering into the tent, much as a musician might listen to a familiar tune. He thought he detected a cheerful boisterousness in the half-heard vulgarities being exchanged by unseen soldiers, and hoped he was right. In the first days after his arrival, the sounds of the camp had been sodden with resentment.

A different sound drew his attention. He glanced over at the desk in the corner of the tent where Procopius, his new secretary, was scribbling away industriously. The desk, like the chair upon which the secretary sat, was of the plainest construction. But it was no plainer than Belisarius' own desk, or chair.

Procopius had been astonished—not to mention disgruntled—when he discovered his new employer's austere habits. Within a week after their arrival, the secretary had attempted to ingratiate himself by presenting Belisarius with a beautifully-embroidered, silk-covered cushion. The general had politely thanked Procopius for the gift, but had immediately turned it over to Maurice, explaining that it was his long-standing custom to share all gifts with his bucellarii. The following day, Procopius watched goggle-eyed as the Thracian cataphracts used the cushion as the target in their mounted archery exercises. (Very briefly—the cruel, razor-sharp blades of the war arrows, driven by those powerful bows, had shredded the cushion within minutes.)

The secretary had been pale with fury and outrage, but had possessed enough wit to maintain silence in the face of Thracian grins. And, admitted Belisarius, since then—

"You've done well, Procopius," said Belisarius suddenly, "helping to ferret out these petty crooks."

The secretary looked up, startled. He began to open his mouth, then closed it. He acknowledged the praise with a simple nod and returned to his work.

Satisfied, Belisarius looked away. In the weeks since they had been together in the army camp near Daras, Procopius had learned, painfully, that his new employer gave flattery short shrift. On the other hand, he prized hard work and skillfulness. And, whatever his other characteristics, there was no question that Procopius was an excellent secretary. Nor was he indolent. He had been a great help in shredding the corruption which riddled Belisarius' new army.

A soldier entered the tent.

"You called for me, sir?"

Belisarius examined him. The man appeared to be barely twenty. He was quite short, but muscular. A Syrian, with, Belisarius judged, considerable Arab stock in his ancestry.

The soldier was wearing a simple, standard uniform: a mantle, a shirt, boots, and a belt. The belt held up a scabbarded *spatha*, the sword which the modern Roman army used in place of the ancient *gladius*. The spatha was similar to a gladius—a straight-bladed, double-edged sword suitable for either cutting or thrusting, but it was six inches longer.

The cloak, helmet, mail tunic and shield which were also part of the man's uniform were undoubtedly resting in his tent. In the Syrian daytime, cloaks made the heat unbearable. And the soldier's armor and shield were unneeded in the daily routine of the camp.

"Your name is Mark, I believe? Mark of Edessa."

"Yes, sir." Mark's face bore slight traces of apprehension mixed with puzzlement.

Belisarius allayed his concerns instantly.

"I am promoting you to hecatontarch of the third *ala*," he announced. His tone was stern and martial.

The man's eyes widened slightly. He stood a bit straighter.

"Peter of Rhaedestus, as I'm sure you know, is the regiment's tribune. You will report to him."

Then, in a softer tone:

"You are young to be assigned command over a hundred men, and somewhat inexperienced. But both Peter and Constantine, the cavalry's *chiliarch*, speak well of you. And so do the men of my own personal retinue." He motioned slightly toward the back of the tent, where Maurice and the two other cataphracts stood.

Mark glanced toward the Thracians. His face remained still, but the youth's gratitude was apparent.

"Two things, before you go," said Belisarius. All traces of softness vanished from his voice.

"Constantine and Peter—as well as the other tribunes of the cavalry—know my views on corrupt officers, and are in agreement with them. But I will take the time now to express them to you directly. As you are aware, I will not tolerate an officer who steals from his own men. Thus far, since I inherited this army from another, I have satisfied myself with simply dismissing such officers. In the future, however, with officers who take command knowing my views, the punishment will be considerably more severe. Extreme, in fact."

Belisarius paused, gauging the young Syrian, and decided that further elaboration on the matter was unnecessary. Mark's face sheened with perspiration, but the sweat was simply the product of the stifling heat within the tent. Belisarius took a cloth and wiped his own face.

"A final point. You are a cavalryman, and have been, I understand, since you first joined. Is that correct?"

"Yes, sir."

"Then understand something else. *I will not tolerate the cavalry lording it over the infantry.* Do you understand?"

Mark's face twitched, just a tiny bit.

"Speak frankly, Mark of Edessa. If you are unclear as to my meaning, say so. I will explain, and I promise there will be no censure."

The young Syrian glanced at his general, made a quick assessment, and spoke.

"I'm not quite sure I do, sir."

"It's simple, Mark. As you will discover soon enough, my tactical methods use the infantry to far greater effect than Roman armies normally do. But for those tactics to work, the infantry must have the same pride and self-esteem as the cavalry. I can't build and maintain that morale if I have cavalrymen deriding the foot soldiers and refusing to take on their fair share of the hard work, which normally falls almost entirely on the infantry. I will not tolerate cavalrymen lounging around in the shade while foot soldiers sweat rivers, building encampments and fortifications. And mocking the foot soldiers, often enough. Do you understand?"

"Yes, sir." Firmly, clearly.

"Good. You will be allowed to select the *decarchs* for your hundred. All ten of them."

Mark stood very straight. "Thank you, sir."

Belisarius repressed a smile. Sternly:

"Use your own judgment, but I urge you to consult with Peter. And you might also discuss the matter with Maurice, and Gregory. I think you'll find them quite helpful."

"I will do so, sir."

"A word of caution. Advice, rather. Avoid simply selecting from your own circle of friends. Even if they prove capable, it will produce resentment among others. A capable clique is still a clique, and you will undermine your own authority."

"Yes, sir."

"And, most of all, make sure your decarchs understand and accept my attitudes. You will be selecting them, which will reflect upon how I regard you. Your prestige among the cavalrymen whom you command will be thereby enhanced. But do not ever forget the corollary. I will hold you responsible for the conduct of your subordinates, as well as your own. Do I make myself clear?"

"As clear as day, sir." Another quick assessment of his new general. "Syrian day."

Now, Belisarius did smile. "Good. You may go."

Once Mark was gone, the three Thracians at the back of the tent relaxed and resumed their normal casual pose. In public, the members of Belisarius' personal retinue of three hundred cataphracts maintained certain formalities. Most of them, after all, held lowly official ranks. Even Maurice, their commander, was only a hecatontarch—the same official rank as the Syrian youth who had just left the tent.

In actual practice, the Thracian bucellarii served Belisarius as his personal staff. They had been carefully selected by him over a period of years, and the devotion of his retinue was fully reciprocated. Maurice, despite his rank, was in effect Belisarius' executive officer. Even Constantine, who was in overall command of the army's cavalry, along with the chiliarch Phocas who was his equivalent for the infantry, had learned to accept his actual authority. And, as they got to know the grizzled veteran, respect it as well.

"I believe the boy will work out quite nicely," commented Maurice. "Quite nicely. Once he gets blooded a bit." Maurice's smile vanished, replaced by a scowl. "I can't believe how badly your predecessor Libelarius let this army fall to pieces. Chiseling on fodder and gear is common enough. But we've even found cases where the men's pay was stolen. In some of the infantry regiments, at least."

"And the food!" exclaimed Basil, one of the other cataphracts. "Bad enough these bastards sell off some of the food, but they were cheating at both ends. The food was shit to begin with. Half-rotten when they bought it."

The third of the cataphracts chimed in. He was one of the few non-Thracians in Belisarius' retinue, an Armenian by the name of Ashot.

"What's even worse is the state of the army as a whole. What're we supposed to have, General? Eight thousand men, half cavalry?"

Belisarius nodded.

Ashot laughed scornfully. "What we've got, once you take a real count and strip away the names of fictitious soldiers whose pay these pigs have been pocketing, is *five* thousand men. Not four in ten of them cavalry."

Belisarius wiped his face again. He had spent most of his time, since arriving at the camp, trapped in the leaden, breezeless air of his tent. The heat was oppressive, and the lack of exercise was beginning to tell on him. "And," he concluded wearily, "the force structure's a joke. In order to hide the chiseling, this army's got twice as many official units as it does men to fill them properly."

"Nothing worse than a skeleton army," grumbled Maurice. "I found one infantry hundred that had all of twenty-two actual soldiers in it. *With*, naturally, a full complement of officers—a hecatontarch and all ten decarchs. Living high off the hog." He spit on the floor. "Four of those so-called decarchs didn't have a single soldier under their command. Not even *one*."

Belisarius rose and stretched. "Well, that's pretty much behind us. Within two more days, we'll have this army shaken down into a realistic structure, with decent officers. And decent morale restored to the troops, I think." He cast a questioning glance at Ashot and Basil. Belisarius relied on his low-ranked cataphracts to mingle with the troops and keep his fingers on the pulse of his army.

"Morale's actually high, General," said Ashot. Basil nodded agreement, and added:

"Sure, things are still crappy for the troops. And will be, for a bit. But they don't expect miracles, and they can see things are turning around. Mostly, though, the troops are cheerful as cherubs from watching one sorry-ass chiseler after another come into this tent, and then, within the hour, depart through the gates."

" 'Deadly with a blade, is Belisarius,' " quoted Ashot, laughing. "They'd heard that, some of them. Now they all believe it."

"How's the drill going?" asked Belisarius.

Maurice made a fluttering motion with his hand.

"So-so. Just so-so. But I'm not worried about it. The troops are just expressing their last resentment by sloughing it during the drill. Give it a week. Then we'll start seeing results."

"Push it, Maurice. I'm not demanding miracles, but keep in mind that we don't have much time. I can't delay our departure to Mindouos for more than a fortnight."

Belisarius rose and walked over to the entrance of his tent. Leaning against a pole, he stared through the open flap at the camp. As always, his expression was hard to read. But Maurice, watching, knew the general was not happy with his orders.

The orders, received by courier a week earlier, were plain and simple: *Move to Mindouos and build a fort.*

Simple, clear orders. And, Maurice knew, orders which Belisarius considered idiotic.

Belisarius had said nothing to him, of course. For all the general's casual informality when dealing with his Thracian retinue, he maintained a sharp demarcation with regard to matters he considered exclusively reserved for command.

But Maurice knew the general as well as any man. And so he knew, though nothing had been said directly, that Belisarius thought the Roman Empire was deliberately provoking Persia, for no good reason, and was then piling stupidity onto recklessness by provoking the Mede without first seeing to it that the provocation would succeed.

No, Belisarius had said nothing to Maurice. But Maurice knew him well. And if Maurice lacked his general's extraordinary intelligence, he was by no means stupid. And very experienced in the trade of war.

Maurice did not feel himself qualified to make a judgment as to the Emperor's wisdom in provoking the Persians. But he *did* feel qualified to make a judgment on the means the Emperor had chosen to do so. And, he thought, given the state of the Byzantine forces in the area, provoking Persia was about as sensible as provoking a lion with a stick.

The Persians maintained a large army stationed near the upper Euphrates, close to the border. In quiet times, that army was billeted at the fortified city of Nisibis. Now, with hostilities looming, the Mede army had moved north and established a temporary camp, threatening the Anatolian heartland of the Roman Empire.

To oppose them—to *provoke* them, no less—the Romans had only seventeen thousand men in the area. Five thousand of those were represented by Belisarius' army, which, when he assumed command, had proven to be as brittle as a rotten twig. As badly corrupted an army as Maurice had seen anywhere.

The remaining twelve thousand men were stationed not far away, in Lebanon. That army, from what Maurice had been able to determine, was in fairly good condition. Certainly it seemed to have none of the rampant corruption which they had encountered at Daras.

But—

Maurice was an old veteran, well past his fortieth year. He had learned long since that numbers did not weigh as heavily in war as morale and, especially, command. The Army of Lebanon was under the command of two brothers, Bouzes and Coutzes. Not bad fellows, Maurice thought, all things considered. Thracians themselves, as it happened, which predisposed Maurice in their favor. But—young, even younger than Belisarius. And, unfortunately, with none of the wily cunning which so often made Belisarius seem a man of middle age, or even older.

No, bold and brash, were the brothers. And, they had made clear, under no conditions willing to subordinate themselves to Belisarius. Nor could Belisarius force them to. Though he was more experienced than Bouzes and Coutzes—than both of them put together, thought Maurice glumly—and carried a far greater reputation, the brothers were officially ranked as high as he. It was a new rank, for them, and one in which they took great pride. Shiny new generaldom, which they were not about to tarnish by placing under the hand of another.

Outnumbered, under a divided command, his own army shaky from rot, the majority of the Roman forces under the command of brash, untested youth—and, now, ordered to poke the Persian lion.

Belisarius sighed, very faintly, and turned back to the interior of the tent.

"How is the other matter going?" he asked.

"The pilfering?" Belisarius nodded.

"We're bringing it under control," said Maurice. "Now that rations have started to flow properly again, the troops don't have any real reason to steal from the locals. It's more a matter of habit than anything else."

"That's exactly my concern," said Belisarius. "Looting's the worst habit an army can develop."

"Can't stop it, sir," said Maurice. Sometimes, he thought, his beloved general was impractical. Not often, true. He was startled to hear Belisarius' hand slamming the desk.

"Maurice! I don't want to hear the old voice of experience!"

The general was quite angry, Maurice noted, with some surprise. Unusual, that. The old veteran straightened his posture. He did not, however, flinch. Angry generals had long since failed to cause him to quiver in fear. Any generals, much less Belisarius.

And, sure enough, after a moment he saw the crooked smile make its appearance.

"Maurice, I am not a fool. I realize that soldiers look upon booty as one of their time-honored perks. And that's fine— *as long as we're talking about booty.*" Belisarius tightened his own jaw. "It's one thing for an army to share in the spoils of a campaign, fairly apportioned in an organized manner, after the campaign's over and the victory is certain. It's another thing entirely for soldiers to get in the habit of plundering and stealing and generally taking anything they want whenever the mood strikes them. Let that happen, and pretty soon you don't have an army anymore. Just a mob of thieves, rapists, and murderers."

He eyed Maurice. "Speaking of which?"

"Hung 'em yesterday, sir. All four. The girl's surviving brother was able to identify them, once he got over his terror at being here. I sent him on to Aleppo, then, to join his sister."

"Have you heard from the monks?"

Maurice grimaced. "Yes. They've agreed to take care of the girl, as best they can. But they don't expect she'll recover, and—" Another grimace.

"And they had harsh words to say about Christian soldiers."

"Yes, sir."

"As well they might. Did the troops watch the execution?"

"Not the execution itself, no. At least, not the army as a whole. A lot of them did, of course. But I gave orders to let the bodies sway in the breeze, until the heat and the vultures make skeletons out of them. They'll all get the message, sir."

Belisarius wiped his face wearily. "For a time." He stared ruefully at the grimy cloth in his hand. The rag was too soaked to do more than smear the sweat. He reached out and hung it on a peg to dry.

"But there'll be another incident," he continued, after resuming his seat. "This army's had too much rot infect it. Soon enough, there'll be another incident. When it happens, Maurice, I'll have the officer in command of the men strung up alongside them. I won't accept any excuses. Pass the word."

Maurice took a deep breath, then let it out. He wasn't afraid of Belisarius, but he knew when the general wasn't to be budged.

"Yes, sir."

The general's gaze was hard.

"I'm serious about this, Maurice. Make certain the men understand my attitude. Make *absolutely* certain the officers do."

The general relented, slightly. "It's not simply a matter of the conduct one expects from Christian soldiers, Maurice. If the men can't understand that, then make sure they understand the practical side of it. You and I have both seen too many battles lost—or, at best, halfway won—because the troops got diverted at the critical moment. Allowing the enemy to escape, or rally for a counterattack, because they're busy scurrying around for some silver plate and chickens to steal, or a woman to rape. Or just the pleasure of watching a town burn. A town, more often than not, that's the only place to find billeting. Or would have been, if it weren't a pile of ashes."

"Yes, sir."

Belisarius eyed Maurice a moment longer, then smiled. "Trust me in this, old friend. I know you think I've got my head in the clouds, but I'll prove you wrong."

Maurice smiled back. "I've never thought you had your head in the clouds, General. Though, at times, the air you breathe is a bit rarefied."

The hecatontarch eyed his two subordinates and gestured slightly with his head. Immediately, Ashot and Basil left the tent.

"May I suggest you get some sleep, sir." Maurice did not even look toward Procopius. The veteran had made clear, in none too subtle ways, that he regarded the secretary much as he regarded an asp. Procopius set down his pen, arose, and exited the tent himself. Quite hastily.

After the others had left, Maurice made his own exit. But, at the entrance of the tent, he hesitated and turned back.

"I don't want you to misunderstand me, General. I'm

skeptical that it'll work, that's all. Other than that, I've no problem with your policy. None. Measured out the ropes myself, I did, and cut the lengths. And enjoyed every moment of it."

Later, after the noises of the camp had died down, Belisarius reached into his tunic and withdrew the jewel. It was resting in the small pouch which Antonina had dug up. He opened the pouch and spilled the jewel onto his palm.

"Come on," he whispered. "You've had enough sleep. I need your help."

The facets spun and flickered. Energy was returning, now. And, during the long stasis, **aim** had been able to—digest, so to speak—its bizarre experiences. The thoughts were clearer now, still as alien but no longer impossible to fathom.

aim did not have much energy yet, but—enough, it decided.

And so it was that the general Belisarius, lying on his cot, almost asleep, suddenly bolted upright.

Again, his face, emerging from the ground. Coalescing from the remnants of spiderwebs and bird wings, and laurel leaves. Suddenly soaring into the heavens, utterly transformed. The wings were now the pinions of a dragon. The laurel leaves, bursting flame and thunder. And the spiderwebs—were the spinnings of his mind, weaving their traps, spreading their strands through an infinite distance.
future.

Chapter 6

"So much for diplomacy," snarled Bouzes, reining his horse around savagely. He glared over his shoulder at the retreating figures of the Persian commanders.

"Filthy Mede dogs," agreed his brother Coutzes. Setting his own horse in motion, he added, "God, how I despise them."

Belisarius, riding alongside, held his tongue. He saw no point in contradicting the brothers. His relations with them were tense enough as it was.

In truth, Belisarius rather liked Persians. The Medes had their faults, of course. The most outstanding of which—and the one which had occasioned the brothers' outburst—was the overweening arrogance of Persian officials. An arrogance which had once again been displayed in the recently concluded parley.

The parley had taken place in the no-man's-land which marked, insofar as anything did, the border between Roman and Persian territory. A brief discussion, on a patch of barren landscape, between six men on horseback. Belisarius and the brothers Bouzes and Coutzes had spoken for the Roman side. The Medes had been represented by Firuz, the Persian commander, and his two principal subordinates, Pityaxes and Baresmanas.

Firuz had demanded the parley. And then, at the parley, demanded that the Romans dismantle the fortress which Belisarius' army had almost completed. Or he would dismantle it for them.

Such, at least, had been the essence of the demand. But Firuz had insisted on conveying the demand in the most offensive manner possible. He had boasted of his own martial prowess and sneered at that of the Romans. (Not forgetting to toss in numerous remarks concerning Roman cowardice and unmanliness.) He had dwelt lovingly on the full-bellied vultures which would soon be the caskets of Roman troops— assuming, of course, that the carrion-eaters were hungry enough to feed on such foul meat.

And so on, and so forth. Belisarius repressed a smile. He thought the polishing touch had been Firuz' demand that Belisarius build a bath in the fortress. He would need the bath, the Persian commander explained, to wash Roman blood and gore off his body. Among which body parts, Firuz explained, the brains of Belisarius himself would figure prominently. The brains of Bouzes and Coutzes would not, of course, as they had none.

Belisarius glanced at Bouzes and Coutzes. The brothers were red-faced with rage. Not for the first time—no, for perhaps the thousandth time—Belisarius reflected on the stupidity of approaching war with any attitude other than craftsmanship. Why should a sane man care what some Persian peacock had to say about him? All the better, as far as Belisarius was concerned, that Firuz was filled with his own self-esteem and contempt for his enemy. It made defeating him all the easier. An arrogant foe was easily duped.

For the first half-hour of their trek back to the Roman fort at Mindouos, Belisarius simply relaxed and enjoyed the ride. It was early afternoon, and the heat was already intense, but at least he was not confined within a stifling tent. And, soon enough, a cooling breeze began to develop.

The breeze came from the west, moreover, so it had the further advantage of blowing the dust of their travel behind them.

Yet, that same pleasant breeze brought Belisarius' mind back to his current predicament. He had been giving that breeze much thought, these past days. Very reliable, it was, always arising in early afternoon, and always blowing from the west to the east. He treasured that reliability, caught as he was in a situation with so many variable factors.

As the three men rode back to the camp in silence, therefore, Belisarius began to consider his options. His natural inclination, given the circumstances, would have been to stall for time. For all Firuz' vainglory, Belisarius did not think the Persian was actually ready to launch a war immediately. Stall, stall, stall—and then, perhaps, the Emperor Justinian and his advisers would come to their senses.

But the knowledge that Belisarius now possessed, from the jewel, made that option unworkable. He simply didn't have the time to waste in this idiotic and unnecessary conflict between Byzantium and Persia. Not while the forces of Satan were gathering their strength in India.

I've got to bring this thing to a head, and quickly, and be done with it. The only way to do that is with a resounding victory. Soon.

Which, of course, is easier said than done. Especially with—

He glanced again at the brothers. Bouzes and Coutzes looked enough alike that Belisarius had taken them, at first, for twins. Average height, brown-haired, hazel-eyed, muscular, snub-nosed, and— He would have smiled if he hadn't been so irritated. In truth, the Persian's insult had cut close to the quick. If the brothers had any brains at all, Belisarius had seen precious little indication of them.

After three days of argument, he had managed to get

the brothers to agree, grudgingly, to combine their forces. *Three days!*—to convince them of the obvious. There had been no hope, of course, of convincing them to place the combined force under his command. Belisarius had not even bothered to raise the matter. The brothers would have taken offense, and, in high dudgeon, retracted their agreement to combine forces.

Eventually, as they neared the fort at Mindouos, Belisarius decided on his course of action. He saw no alternative, even though he was not happy with the decision. It was a gamble, for one thing, which Belisarius generally avoided.

But, he thought, glancing at the brothers again, *a gamble with rather good odds.*

Now, if Maurice can manage—

He broke off the thought. They were almost at the fortress. The transition from the barren semidesert to the vivid green of the oasis where he had situated his fort was as startling as ever. In no more time than a few horse paces, they moved from a desolate emptiness to a populated fertility. Much of that population was soldiery, of course, but there were still a number of civilians inhabiting the oasis, despite the danger from the nearby Persians. Three grubby but healthy-looking bedouin children, standing under a palm tree nearby, watched the small group of Roman officers trot past. One of them shouted something in Arabic. Belisarius did not quite make out the words—his Arabic was passable but by no means fluent—but he sensed the cheerful greeting in the tone.

"Hell of job you did here, Belisarius," remarked Bouzes admiringly, gazing up at the fortress. His brother concurred immediately, then added: "I don't see how you did it, actually. In the time you had. Damned good fort, too. Nothing slap-dash about it."

"I've got some good engineers among my Thracian retinue, for one thing."

"Engineers? Among *cataphracts?*"

Belisarius smiled. "Well, they're not really cataphracts, not proper ones. A bunch of farmers, at bottom, who just picked up the skills."

"Wish we had some real cataphracts," muttered Bouzes. "Don't much care for the snotty bastards, but they're great in a fight."

His brother returned to the subject. "Even with good engineers, I still don't see how you got the work done so quickly."

"The basic way I did it was by setting the cavalry to work and challenging them to match the infantry."

The brothers gaped.

"You had *cavalry* doing that kind of shit work?" demanded Bouzes. He frowned. "Bad for morale, I would think."

"Not the infantry's," rejoined Belisarius. "And, as for the cavalry's morale, you might be surprised. They wailed like lost souls, at first. But, after a bit, they started rising to the challenge. Especially after they heard the infantry taunting them for a lot of weaklings. Then I announced prizes for the best day's work, and the cavalry started pitching into it. They never were as good as the infantry, of course, but by the end they were giving them quite a run for their money. Won a few prizes, even."

Bouzes was still frowning. "Still—even if it doesn't affect their morale directly, it—still."

"Saps their self-esteem, over time," agreed his brother. "Bound to. It's dog work."

Belisarius decided he'd been polite long enough.

"*Dog work, is it?*" he demanded, feigning anger. "I would remind the two of you that the Roman empire was built by such dogs. By *infantry*, not cavalry. Infantry who knew the value of good fortifications, and knew how to put them up. Quickly, and well."

He reined in his horse. They were now at the gate of

the fortress. Belisarius pointed to the barrenness beyond
the date palms, from which they had just come.

"Do you see that border with Persia? That border was
placed there centuries ago. *By infantrymen.* How far has
your precious cavalry pushed it since then?"

He glared at them. The brothers looked away.

"Not one mile, that's how far." The gate was opening.
Belisarius set his horse back in motion.

"So let's not hear so much boasting about cavalry," he
growled, passing through the gate.

Rather well done, he patted himself on the back. *They're
not bad fellows, really. If they could just get that stupid
crap out of their heads.*

The interior of the fortress was not as imposing as its
exterior. In truth, Belisarius *had* been pressed for time,
even with the aid of the cavalrymen, and so he had
concentrated all effort on the outside walls and fortifications.
Within those walls, the fortress was still just an empty parade
ground, although it was covered now with the tents of his
soldiers. He had not even built a command post for himself,
but continued to use his tent as a headquarters.

As soon as Belisarius dismounted and walked into his
command tent, followed by the two brothers, Maurice made
his appearance.

"We've got a prisoner," the hecatontarch announced. "Just
brought him in."

"Where did you catch him?"

"Sunicas' regiment had a skirmish this morning with a
group of Persians. About three hundred of them, ten miles
north of here. After Sunicas drove them off, they found
one fellow lying on the ground. Stunned. Horse threw him."

"Bring him here."

Belisarius took a seat at the large table in the middle of
the tent. Bouzes and Coutzes remained standing. A few

minutes later, Maurice reappeared, along with Valentinian. Valentinian was pushing a Persian soldier ahead of him. The Persian's wrists were bound behind his back. By his dress and accouterments, Belisarius thought the Persian to be a midlevel officer.

Valentinian forced the Mede into a chair. Exhibiting the usual Persian courage, the officer's face remained still and composed. The Persian was expecting to be tortured, but would not give his enemy the satisfaction of seeing his fear.

His expectation was shared by Bouzes and Coutzes.

"We've got a first-rate torturer," announced Coutzes cheerfully. "I can have him here inside the hour."

"No need," replied Belisarius curtly. The general stared at the Mede. The Persian met his eyes unflinchingly.

For a moment, Belisarius considered interrogating the officer in his own language. Belisarius was fluent in Pallavi, as he was in several languages. But he decided against it. Bouzes and Coutzes, he suspected, were ignorant of the Persian language, and it was important that they be able to follow the interrogation. By the richness of his garb, the Persian was obviously from the aristocracy. His Greek would therefore be fluent, since—in one of those little historical ironies—Greek was the court language of the Sassanid dynasty.

"How many men does Firuz have under his command?" he asked the Mede.

"Fifty-five thousand," came the instant reply. As Belisarius had suspected, the man's Greek was excellent. "That doesn't include the twenty thousand he left in Nisibis," added the Persian.

"What a lot of crap!" snarled Coutzes. "There aren't—"

Belisarius interrupted. "I will allow you four lies, Mede. You've already used up two of them. Firuz has twenty-five thousand men, and he took them all when he left Nisibis."

The muscles along the Persian's jaw tightened, and his

eyes narrowed slightly. Other than that, he gave no indication of surprise at the accuracy of Belisarius' information.

"How many of those *twenty-five* thousand are cavalry?" asked Belisarius.

Again, the Mede's answer came with no hesitation:

"We have no more than four thousand infantry. And most of our cavalry are lancers."

"That's the third lie," said Belisarius, very mildly. "And the fourth. Firuz has ten thousand infantry. Of his fifteen thousand cavalry, no more than five are heavy lancers."

The Persian looked away, for a moment, but kept his face expressionless. Belisarius was impressed by the man's courage.

"I'm afraid you've used up all your lies." Without moving his gaze from the Persian, Belisarius asked the two Thracian brothers: "You say you have a good torturer?"

Bouzes nodded eagerly. "We can have him here in no time," said Coutzes.

The captured officer's jaw was now very tight, but the man's gaze was calm and level.

"Has the pay caravan arrived yet?" demanded Belisarius.

For the first time since the interrogation began, the Persian seemed shaken. He frowned, hesitated, and then replied: "What are you talking about?"

Belisarius slammed the table with his open palm.

"Don't play with me, Mede! I know your army's pay chest was sent out from Nisibis five days ago, with an escort of only fifty men."

Belisarius turned his head and looked at Bouzes and Coutzes. A disgusted look came on his face. "Fifty! Can you believe it? Typical Persian arrogance."

Coutzes opened his mouth to speak, but Belisarius motioned him silent. He turned back to the captured officer.

"What I don't know is if the pay caravan has arrived at your camp. So, I ask again: has it?"

The Persian's face was a study in confusion. But, within seconds, the Mede regained his composure.

"I imagine it has," he replied. "I left our camp the day before yesterday. That's why I hadn't heard anything about it. But by now I'm sure it's arrived. Nisibis is only four days' ride. They wouldn't have dawdled."

Belisarius studied the officer silently for some time. Again, Coutzes began to speak, but Belisarius waved him silent. The young Thracian general's face became flushed with irritation, but he held his tongue.

After a couple more minutes of silence, Belisarius leaned back in his chair and placed his hands on his thighs. He seemed to have come to some sort of decision.

"Take him out," he commanded Valentinian. Bouzes began to protest, but Belisarius glared him down.

No sooner were they alone, however, than the brothers erupted.

"What the hell kind of interrogation was that?" demanded Bouzes. "And why did you stop? We still don't know anything about that pay caravan!"

"Silly damn waste of time," snorted Coutzes. "You want to get anything useful from a Mede, you've got to use a—"

"Torturer?" demanded Belisarius. He rolled his eyes despairingly, exhaled disgust, sneered mightily. Then he stood up abruptly and leaned over the table, resting his weight on his fists.

"I can see why you haul around a professional torturer," snarled the general. "I would too, if I was a fool."

He matched the brothers' glare with a scorching look of his own.

"Let me explain something to you," he said icily. "I wasn't in the slightest bit interested in getting information from the Persian regarding the pay caravan. He doesn't know anything about it. How could he? The pay caravan only left Nibisis the day before yesterday."

"The day before yesterday?" demanded Bouzes, puzzled. "But you said—"

"I said *to an enemy officer* that the pay chest left five days ago."

The brothers were now silent, frowning. Belisarius resumed his seat.

"My spies spotted the caravan as soon as it left the gates of the city. One of them rode here as fast as possible, using remounts. There's no way that caravan has reached Firuz' camp yet."

"Then why did you—"

"Why did I ask the Mede about it? I simply wanted to get his immediate reaction. You saw what a talented liar he was. Yet when I asked him about the pay caravan, he had to fumble for an answer. What does that tell you?"

Apparently, they weren't that stupid, for both brothers immediately got the point.

"The Persians themselves don't know about it!" they exclaimed, like a small chorus.

Belisarius nodded. "I'd heard that the Medes were starting to send out some of their pay caravans in this manner. Instead of tying up a small army to escort the caravans, they're relying on absolute secrecy. Even the soldiers for whom the pay's destined don't know about it, until the caravan arrives."

The brothers exchanged glances. Belisarius chuckled.

"Tempting, isn't it? But I'm afraid we'll have to let it go. This time, anyway."

"Why?" demanded Bouzes.

"Yes, why?" echoed his brother. "It's a perfect opportunity. Why shouldn't we seize it?"

"You're not thinking clearly. First, we have no idea what route the caravan's taking. Don't forget, we'd only have one day—two at the most—to catch the caravan before it arrives at the Persian camp. In order to be sure of finding it, we'd have to send out an entire regiment of cavalry. At the very least. Two regiments, to be on the safe side."

"So?" demanded Coutzes.

"*So?*" Belisarius cast an exasperated glance upward. "You *were* at the parley with Firuz today, were you not?"

"What's the point, Belisarius?"

"The point, Coutzes, is that Firuz is getting ready to attack us. We're outnumbered. We need to stay on the defensive. This is the worst time in the world for us to be sending our cavalry chasing all over Syria. We need them here, at the fort. Every man."

Coutzes began to argue, but his brother cut him short by grabbing his arm.

"Let's not get into an argument! There's no point in it, and it's too hot." He wiped his brow dramatically. Belisarius restrained a smile. In truth, there was hardly any sweat on Bouzes' face.

Bouzes wiped his brow again, in a gesture worthy of Achilles. Then said: "I think we've finished all our business here. Or is there anything else?"

Belisarius shook his head. "No. Your officers have all been told that we are combining our forces?"

"Yes, they know."

A brief exchange of amenities followed, in which Coutzes participated grudgingly. Bouzes, on the other hand, was cordiality itself. The brothers left the tent, with Belisarius escorting them. He chatted politely, while Bouzes and Coutzes mounted their horses. He did not return into the tent until he saw the brothers cantering through the gates of the fort.

Maurice was waiting for him inside.

"Well?" asked the hecatontarch.

"At nightfall, give the captured Persian officer my message for Firuz and let him go. Make sure he has a good horse. Then pass the word quietly to the men. I expect we'll be leaving at dawn."

"That soon?"

"Unless I'm badly mistaken, yes." He glanced back at the entrance to the tent. "And I don't think I'm mistaken."

"You should be ashamed of yourself."

Belisarius smiled crookedly. "I am mortified, Maurice, mortified."

The hecatontarch grunted sarcastically, but forebore comment. "Ashot's back," he said.

"What did he think of the location?"

"Good. The hill will do nicely—*if* the wind blows the right way."

"It should, by midday."

"And if it doesn't?"

Belisarius shrugged. "We'll just have to manage. Even if there's no wind, the dust alone should do the trick. If the wind blows the wrong way, of course, we'll be in a tight spot. But I've never seen it blow from the east until evening." He took a seat at the table. "Now, send for the chiliarchs and the tribunes. I want to make sure they understand my plan perfectly."

That night, immediately after the conclusion of the meeting with his chief subordinates, Belisarius lay down on his cot. For almost an hour he lay there in the darkness, thinking over his plans, before he finally fell asleep.

As the general pondered, **aim** delved through the corridors of his mind. Time after time, the facets threatened to splinter. Despair almost overwhelmed them. Just when the alien thoughts had begun to come into focus! And now, they were—somehow at odds with themselves. It was like trying to learn a language whose grammar was constantly changing. Impossible!

But **aim** was now growing in confidence, and so it was able to control the facets. With growing confidence, came patience. It was true, the thoughts were contradictory—

like two images, identical, yet superimposed over each other at right angles. Patience. Patience. In time, **aim** sensed it could bring them into focus.

And, in the meantime, there was something of much greater concern. For, despite the blurring, there was one point on which all the paradoxical images in the general's mind coalesced sharply.

At the very edge of sleep, Belisarius sensed a thought. But he was too tired to consider its origin.

danger.

Chapter 7

Belisarius awoke long before dawn. Within a short time after rising, he was satisfied that the preparations for the march were well in hand. Both of his chiliarchs were competent officers, and it soon became apparent that the tribunes and hecatontarchs had absorbed fully the orders he had given them the night before.

Maurice came up to him. Belisarius recognized him from a distance, even though it was still dark. Maurice had a rolling gait which was quite unmistakable.

"Now?" asked Maurice.

Belisarius nodded. The two men mounted their horses and cantered through the gate. The Army of Lebanon was camped just beyond the fort, where its soldiers could enjoy the shade and water provided by the oasis. Within a few minutes, Belisarius and Maurice were dismounting before the command tent occupied by Bouzes and Coutzes.

The tent was much larger than the one Belisarius used, although not excessively so by the standards of Roman armies. Roman commanders had long been known for traveling in style. Julius Caesar had even carried tiles with him to floor his tent. (Although he claimed to have done so simply to impress barbarian envoys; Belisarius was skeptical of the claim.)

Upon their arrival, the sentries guarding the tent informed them that Bouzes and Coutzes were absent. They had left the camp in the middle of the night. Further questioning elicited the information that the brothers had taken two cavalry regiments along with them.

Belisarius uttered many profane oaths, very loudly. He stalked off toward the nearby tent, which was occupied by the four chiliarchs who were the chief subordinate officers of the Army of Lebanon. Maurice followed.

At the chiliarchs' tent, a sentry began to challenge Belisarius, but quickly fell silent. The sentry recognized him, and saw as well that the general was in a towering rage. Deciding that discretion was the order of the day, the sentry drew aside. Belisarius stormed into the tent.

Three of the four chiliarchs were rising from sleep, groggy and bleary-eyed. One of them lit a lamp. Belisarius immediately demanded to know the whereabouts of the fourth. He allowed the three chiliarchs to stammer in confusion for a few seconds before he cut through the babble.

"So. I assume Dorotheus has accompanied the two cretins in this lunacy?"

The chiliarchs began to protest. Again, Belisarius cut them short.

"Silence!" He threw himself into a chair by the table in the center of the tent. He glared about for a moment, and then slammed his palm down on the table.

"I am being generous! The Emperor may forgive the idiots, if he decides they are just stupid."

Mention of the Emperor caused all three of the chiliarchs to draw back a bit. The face of at least one of them, Belisarius thought, grew pale. But it was hard to tell. The interior of the tent was poorly lit.

Belisarius allowed the silence to fester. He knotted his brow. After a minute or so, he rose and began pacing about, exuding the image of a man lost in thoughtful calculation. Actually, he was scrutinizing the interior of the tent. He believed firmly that one could make a close assessment of officers by examining their private quarters, and took advantage of the opportunity to do so.

Overall, he was impressed. The chiliarchs maintained clean and orderly quarters. There was no indication of the drunken sloppiness which had characterized the tents of a number of the former officers of his own army. He also noted the austerity of their living arrangements. Other than weapons and necessary gear, the chiliarchs' tent was bare of possessions.

The general was pleased. He prized austere living on campaign—not from any religious or moral impulse, but simply because he valued the ability to react and move quickly above all other characteristics in an officer. And he had found, with very few exceptions, that officers who filled their command quarters with lavish creature comforts were sluggards when confronted by any sudden change in circumstances.

He decided the pose of thoughtful concentration had gone on long enough. He stopped pacing, straightened his back, and announced decisively:

"There's nothing for it. We'll just have to make do with what we have."

He turned to the three chiliarchs, who were now clustered together on the other side of the table.

"Assemble your army. We march at once."

"But our commanders aren't here!" protested one of the cavalry chiliarchs. Belisarius gave him a fierce look of disgust.

"I'm aware of that, Pharas. And you can be quite sure that if we fail to intercept the Persians before they march into Aleppo, the Emperor will know of their absence also. And do as he sees fit. But in the absence of Bouzes and

Coutzes, I am in command of this army. And I have no intention of imitating their dereliction of duty."

His announcement brought a chill into the room.

"The Persians are marching?" asked Hermogenes, the infantry chiliarch.

"The day after tomorrow."

"How do you know?" demanded Pharas.

Belisarius sneered. "Doesn't the Army of Lebanon have *any* spies?" he demanded. The chiliarchs were silent. The general's sneer turned into a truly ferocious scowl.

"Oh, that's marvelous!" he exclaimed. "You have no idea what the enemy is doing. So, naturally, you decided to send two full cavalry regiments charging off on a wild goose chase. Just marvelous!"

Pharas' face was ashen. To some extent, it was the pallor of rage. But, for the most part, it was simple fear. Watching him, Belisarius estimated the man's intelligence as rather dismal. But even Pharas understood the imperial fury which would fall on the chief officers of the Army of Lebanon if they allowed the Persians to march on Aleppo unopposed.

The junior cavalry chiliarch, Eutyches, suddenly slammed his hand onto the table angrily.

"Mother of God! I told them—" He bit off the words. Clamped his jaw tight. For a moment, he and Belisarius stared at each other. Then, with a faint nod, and an even fainter smile, Belisarius indicated his understanding and appreciation of Eutyches' position.

The infantry chiliarch spoke then. The timber of his voice reflected Hermogenes' youth, but there was not the slightest quaver in it. "Let's move. *Now.* We all know that Coutzes and Bouzes agreed to combine forces with Belisarius' army. Since they're not here, that makes him the rightful commander."

Eutyches immediately nodded his agreement. After a moment, reluctantly, so did Pharas.

Belisarius seized the moment. "Rouse your army and assemble them into marching formation," he commanded. "Immediately." He stalked out of the tent.

Once outside, Belisarius and Maurice returned to their horses. The first glimmer of dawn was beginning to show on the eastern horizon.

Belisarius gazed about admiringly. "It's going to be a lovely day."

"It's going to be miserably hot," countered Maurice.

Belisarius chuckled quietly. "You are the most morose man I have ever met."

"I am not morose. I am pessimistic. My cousin Ignace, now, *there's* a morose man. You've never met him, I don't believe?"

"How could I have met him? Didn't you tell me he hasn't left his house for fifteen years?"

"Yes, that's true." The hecatontarch eyed Belisarius stonily. "He's terrified of swindlers. And rightfully so."

Belisarius chuckled again. "A lovely day, I tell you." Then, businesslike: "I'm going to stay here, Maurice. If I don't chivvy this army, they'll take forever to get moving. I want you to return to the fort and make sure everything goes properly. I think Phocas and Constantine will manage everything well enough. But I haven't worked with them in the field before, so I want you to keep an eye on things. Remember the two key points: keep—"

"Keep a large cavalry screen well out in front and make sure the infantry gets dug in quickly. With at least half of them hidden behind the ramparts."

The general smiled. "A lovely day. Be off."

As Belisarius had expected, it took hours to get the Army of Lebanon moving. Despite his loud and profane comments, however, he was quite satisfied with the progress. It was unreasonable to expect an army of twelve thousand men to start a march more quickly, with no advance warning or preparations.

By midday, the army was well into its marching rhythm. The temperature was oppressive. The western breeze which sprang up in the afternoon did not help the situation much. True, the wind brought a bit of coolness. But since the army was marching northeast, it also swept the dust thrown up by hooves and feet along the march route instead of away. At least the dust was not blown directly into the soldiers' faces, although that was a small consolation. Syria in midsummer was as unpleasant a place and time to be making a forced march as any in the world.

However, Belisarius noted that the commanding officers of the Army of Lebanon refrained from complaining. Whatever their misgivings might be regarding this unexpected expedition, under unexpected command, they seemed willing to keep them private. He now took the time to explain to the three chiliarchs his plan for the battle he expected shortly. The two cavalry chiliarchs seemed skeptical of the role planned for the infantry, but forbore comment. They were pleased enough with their own projected role, and the infantry was none of their concern anyway.

As evening approached, Belisarius concentrated on discussing his plans with Hermogenes, the infantry chiliarch. Hermogenes, he was pleased to see, soon began to evince real enthusiasm. All too often, Roman infantry commanders occupied that position by virtue of their incompetence and fecklessness. Hermogenes, on the other hand, seemed an ambitious fellow, happy to discover that his own role in the upcoming conflict was to be more than a sideshow.

By nightfall, Belisarius was satisfied that Hermogenes would be able to play his part properly. In fact, he thought the young chiliarch might do very well. Belisarius decided to place Hermogenes in overall command of the infantry, once the Army of Lebanon was united with his own army.

Phocas, his own infantry chiliarch, was a competent officer, but by no means outstanding. On the other hand, Phocas did have a knack for artillery. So Belisarius would put Phocas under Hermogenes' command, with the specific responsibility for the artillery.

Belisarius pushed the march until the very last glimmer of daylight faded before ordering the army to encamp for the night. The Army of Lebanon, he noted with satisfaction, set up its camp quickly and expertly.

After his command tent was set up, Belisarius enjoyed a few moments of privacy within it. He found the absence of Procopius a relief. For all the man's competence, and for all that his most sycophantish habits had been beaten down, the general still found his new secretary extremely annoying. But Procopius was now at the villa near Daras—and had been since Belisarius moved his army to Mindouos. The general had seen no use for him during an actual campaign, and had ordered the man to provide Antonina with whatever assistance she needed in running the estate.

He heard a commotion outside and went to investigate. Maurice had arrived, along with Ashot and three other Thracian cataphracts. By the time Belisarius emerged from his tent, his bucellarii were already dismounted from their horses. With them, dismounting more slowly—pain and exhaustion in every movement—were eight members of the two vanished cavalry regiments. One of the eight was an officer, and all of them looked much the worse for wear. Even in the dim moonlight, the general could see that three of them were wounded, although the wounds did not seem especially severe.

The officer limped over to Belisarius and began to stammer out some semicoherent phrases. Belisarius commanded him to hold his tongue until he could summon the chiliarchs and the tribunes. A few minutes later, with the leadership of the Army of Lebanon packed into the command tent, he instructed the returning officer to tell his tale. This he did, somewhat chaotically, with Maurice lending an occasional comment.

Bouzes and Coutzes, it turned out, had not found the pay caravan. What they had found, charging all over the landscape looking for it, was half of the Persian cavalry, charging all over the landscape looking for it likewise. An impromptu battle had erupted, in which the heavily outnumbered Romans had taken a drubbing. The two brothers had been captured. In the end, most of the Roman cavalry had escaped, in disorganized groups, and were being encountered by Belisarius' own army as it marched forward into position. Though badly demoralized and half-leaderless, the surviving members of the two regiments had been so delighted to find a large formation of Roman troops in the vicinity that they were rallying to the standards of Belisarius' army.

When the officer concluded his tale, Belisarius refrained from commenting on the stupidity of Bouzes and Coutzes. Under the circumstances, he thought, it would be superfluous. He simply concluded the meeting with a brief review of his plans for the forthcoming battle, then sent everyone to bed.

"Things are going well," he remarked to Maurice, once they were in private.

Maurice gave him a hard look. "You're playing this one awfully close, young man."

Belisarius eyed him. Maurice was not, in private, given to formality and subservience. Even in public, he satisfied himself with nothing more than the occasional "sir" and "my lord." But he rarely addressed his general by his own name, and hadn't called him a "young man" since—

Belisarius smiled crookedly. "I won that battle, too, if you recall."

"By the skin of your teeth. And it took you weeks to recover from your wounds." Morosely, rubbing his right side: "Took me even longer."

Thinking the tent was too gloomy, Belisarius lit another lamp and placed it on the table. Then, after taking a seat in his chair, he examined the hecatontarch's grim visage. He was quite confident of his own plans, despite their complexity, but he had learned never to ignore Maurice's misgivings.

"Spit it out, Maurice. And spare me your reproaches concerning the two brothers."

Maurice snorted. "Them? Drooling babes are cute, but they've no business leading armies. I care not a fig about that!" He waved a hand dismissively. "No, what bothers me is that you're cutting everything too fine. You're depending on almost perfect timing, and on the enemy to react exactly as you predict." He gave Belisarius another stony look. "You may recall my first lessons to you when you were barely out of swaddling clothes. Never—"

"Never expect the enemy to do what you think he's going to do, and never expect that schedules will be met on time. And, most of all, always remember the first law of battle: everything gets fucked up as soon as the enemy arrives. *That's why he's called the enemy.*"

Maurice grunted. Then:

"And whatever happened to your devious subtlety? That 'oblique approach' you're so fond of talking about?" He held up a hand. "And don't bother reminding me how shrewd your battle plan is! *So what?* This isn't like you at all, Belisarius. You've never been one to substitute tactics for strategy. How many times have you told me the best campaign is the one which forces the enemy to yield by indirection, with the least amount of bloodshed? Much less a pitched battle which *you're* forcing?"

Belisarius took in a deep breath and held it. The fingers of his left hand began drumming the table. For a moment, as he had done many times over the past weeks, he considered taking Maurice into his full confidence. Again, he decided against it. True, Maurice was close-mouthed. But—there was the first law of secrets: every person told a secret doubles the chance of having it found out.

"Stop drumming your fingers," grumbled the hecatontarch. "You only do that when you're being too clever by half."

Belisarius chuckled, snapped his left hand into a fist. He decided on a halfway course. "Maurice, there is information which I possess which I can't divulge to you now. *That's* why I'm pushing this battle. I know I'm cutting too many corners, but I don't have any choice."

Maurice scowled. "What do you know about the Persians that I don't?" It was not a question, really. More in the way of a scornful reproof.

Belisarius waved his own hand dismissively. "No, not the Persians." He smiled. "I wouldn't presume to know more about the Medes than you! No, it involves—other enemies. I can't say more, Maurice. Not yet."

Maurice considered his general carefully. He wasn't happy with the situation, but—there it was.

"All right," he said, grunting. "But I hope this works."

"It will, Maurice, it will. The timing doesn't have to be that perfect. We just have to get to the battleground before the Persians do. And as for the enemy's reactions—I think that letter I sent off to Firuz will do the trick nicely."

"Why? What did you say in it?"

"Well, the essence of the letter was a demand that he refrain from threatening my shiny new fort. But I conveyed the demand in the most offensive manner possible. I boasted of my martial prowess and sneered at that of the Medes. I tossed in a few well-chosen remarks on the subject of Persian cowardice and unmanliness. I dwelt lovingly on the full-bellied worms which would soon be the caskets of Persian troops—assuming, of course, that the slimy things were hungry enough to feed on such foul meat."

"Oh my," muttered Maurice. He stroked his gray beard.

"But I thought the polishing touch," concluded Belisarius cheerfully, "was my refusal to build a bath in the fortress. Firuz wouldn't need the bath, I explained, because after I slaughtered him, I would toss his remains into the latrine. Which is where they belong, of course, since he's nothing but a walking sack of dog shit."

"Oh my." Maurice pulled up a chair and sat down slowly. For the hecatontarch, the simple act was unusual. A stickler for proprieties was Maurice. He almost never sat while in his general's headquarters.

"We'd better win this battle," he muttered, "or we're all for it." His right hand clenched his sword hilt. His left hand was spread rigidly on the table.

Belisarius leaned over and patted the outstretched hand. "So you can see, Maurice, why I think Firuz will show up at the battlefield."

Maurice made a sour expression. "Maybe. They're touchy, Persian nobles. But if he's smart enough to override his anger, he'll pick a battlefield of his own choosing."

Belisarius leaned back and shrugged.

"I don't think so. I don't think he's that smart, and anyway—the battle site I selected overlooks the stream that provides all the water for his camp. Whether he likes it or not, he can't very well just let us sit there unmolested."

"You would," retorted Maurice instantly.

"I wouldn't have camped there in the first place."

Maurice's right hand released its grip on the sword, and came up to stroke his beard. "True, true. Idiotic, that—relying on an insecure water supply. If you can't find a well or an oasis, like we did, you should at least make sure the water comes from your own territory."

The hecatontarch straightened up a bit. "All right, General. We'll try it. Who knows, it might even work. That's the one and only good thing about the first law of battles—it cuts both ways."

A moment later, Maurice arose. His movements had regained their usual vigor and decisiveness. Belisarius left his chair and accompanied the hecatontarch out of the tent.

"How soon do you expect to reach the battlefield?" asked Belisarius.

Maurice took the reins of his horse and mounted. Once in the saddle, he shrugged.

"We're making good time," he announced. "It'll slow us down a bit, having to gather up what's left of the two cavalry regiments, but—we should be able to start digging in by midafternoon tomorrow."

Belisarius scratched his chin. "That should leave enough time. God knows the soldiers have had enough practice at it lately. Make sure—"

"Make sure the cavalry does its share," concluded Maurice. "Make sure the artillery's well-positioned. Make sure there's food ready for the Army of Lebanon when it arrives. And whatever else, make sure the hill is secure."

Belisarius smiled up at him. "Be off. You've got a long ride back to our army. But there's a lovely moon out tonight."

Maurice forbore comment.

Back in his tent, lying on his cot, Belisarius found it difficult to fall asleep. In truth, he shared some of Maurice's concern. He *was* gambling too much. But he saw no other option.

His fist closed around the pouch holding the jewel. At once, a faint thought came.

danger.

He sat up, staring down. A moment later, after opening the pouch, the jewel was resting in the palm of his hand.

The thought came again, much stronger.

danger.

"It *was* you, last night," he whispered.

danger.

"I know that! Tell me something I don't know. *What are you?*"

The facets shivered and reformed, splintered and came together, all in a microsecond. But **aim** never vanished, never even wavered. In a crystalline paroxysm, the facets forged a thought which could penetrate the barrier. But **aim** was overconfident, tried to do too much. The complex and fragile thought shattered into pieces upon first contact with the alien mind. Only the residue remained, transmuted into an image:

A metallic bird, bejewelled, made of hammered silver and gold-enamelling. Perched on a painted, wrought-iron tree. One of the marvelous constructs made for the Emperor Justinian's palace.

"You were never made by Grecian goldsmiths," muttered Belisarius. "Why are you here? What do you want from me? And where are you from?"

aim surged:

future.

Belisarius blew out an exasperated sigh. "I know the future!" he exclaimed. "You showed it to me. But can it be changed? And where are you *from?*"

Frustration was the greater for the hope which had preceded it. **aim** itself almost splintered, for an instant. But it rallied, ruthless with determination. Out of the flashing movement of the facets came a lesson learned. Patience, patience. Concepts beyond the most primitive could not yet cross the frontier. Again:

future.

The general's eyes widened.

Yes! Yes! Again! The facets froze, now ruthless in their own determination.

future. future. future.

"Mary, Mother of God."

Belisarius arose and walked slowly about in his tent. He clenched the jewel tightly in his fist, as if trying to force the thoughts from the thing like he might squeeze a sponge.

"More," he commanded. "The future must be a wondrous place. Nothing else could have created such a wonder as you. So what can you want from the past? What can we possibly have to offer?"

Again, a metallic bird. Bejewelled, made of hammered silver and gold enamelling. Perched on a painted, wrought-iron tree. But now the focus was sharper, clearer. Like one of the marvelous constructs made for the Emperor Justinian's palace, yes, but vastly more intricate and cunning in its design.

"*Men* created you?" he demanded. "Men of the future?"

yes.

"I say again: *what do you want?*"

aim hesitated, for a microsecond. Then, knew the task was still far beyond its capability. Patience, patience. Where thought could not penetrate, vision might:

Again, the thunderclap. Again: the tree shattered, the ceremony crushed beneath a black wave. Again: crystals, strewn across a barren desert, shriek with despair. Again, in an empty, sunless sky, giant faces begin to take form. Cold faces. Pitiless faces. Human faces, but with all of human warmth banished.

The general frowned. Almost—

"Are you saying that *we* are the danger to you? In the future? And that you have come to the past for help? That's crazy!"

The facets shivered and spun, almost in a frenzy. Now they demanded and drove the demand upon **aim**. But **aim** had learned well. The thoughts were still far too complex to breach the frontier. Imperiously it drove the facets back: patience, patience.

Again, the giant faces. Human faces. Monstrous faces. Dragon-scaled faces.

"Mary, Mother of God," he whispered. "It's true."

An explosive emotion erupted from the jewel. It was like a child's wail of—not anger, so much as deep, deep hurt at a parent's betrayal. A pure thought even forced its way through the barrier.

you promised.

Truly, thought Belisarius, it was the plaint of a bereaved child, coming from a magical stone.

The general weighed the jewel. As before, he was struck by its utter weightlessness. Yet it did not float away, somehow, but stayed in his hand. Like a trusting child.

"I do not understand you," he whispered. "Not truly, not yet. But—if you have truly been betrayed, I will do for you what I can."

That thought brought another smile, very crooked. "Though I'm not sure what I could do. What makes you think I could be of help?"

A sudden surge of warmth came from the jewel. Tears almost came to Belisarius' eyes. He was reminded of that precious moment, weeks earlier, when Photius had finally accepted him. The boy had been skittish, at first, not knowing what to make of this unknown, strange, large man who called himself his father. But the time had come, one evening, when the boy fell asleep before the fire. And, as he felt the drowsiness, had clambered into his stepfather's lap and lain his little head upon a large shoulder. Trusting in the parent to keep him warm and safe through the night.

Belisarius was silent for a time, pondering. He knew something had gone awry, terribly wrong, in that future he could not imagine. Danger. Danger. Danger.

He realized that the jewel was nearing exhaustion and decided that he must put off further questioning. Communication was becoming easier, slowly. Patience,

patience. He had danger enough in the present to deal with, in any event.

But still—there was one question.

"Why did you come here, to the past? What can there possibly be here that would help you in—whatever dangers you face in your future?"

The jewel was fading rapidly now. But the faint image came again:

A face, emerging from the ground, made from spiderwebs and bird wings, and laurel leaves. His face.

Chapter 8

"It's perfect," pronounced Belisarius.

"It's the silliest trap I ever saw," pronounced Maurice. "Not even a schoolboy would fall for it. Not even a Hun schoolboy."

"There are no Hun schoolboys."

"Exactly my point," grumbled Maurice.

Belisarius smiled—broadly, not crookedly.

"There's nothing wrong with my plan and you know it. You're just angry at your part in it."

"And that's another thing! It's ridiculous to use your best heavy cavalry to—"

"Enough, Maurice." The general's voice was mild, but Maurice understood the tone. The hecatontarch fell silent. For a few minutes, he and Belisarius stood together atop the small hill on the left flank of the Roman forces. They said nothing, simply watched the gathering array of the Persian forces coming from the east. The enemy's army was still some considerable distance away, but Belisarius could see the first detachments of light cavalry beginning to scout the Roman position.

Before the Medes could get more than a mile from the Roman lines, however, three *ala* of Hun light cavalry from the Army of Lebanon advanced to meet them. There was

117

a spirited exchange of arrows before the Persian scouts retreated. Casualties were few, on either side, but Belisarius was quite satisfied with the results of the encounter. It was essential to his plan that the Persians not have the opportunity to scout his position carefully.

"That'll keep the bastards off," grunted Maurice.

"Best be about it," said Belisarius. "It's almost noon. The wind'll be picking up soon."

Maurice scanned the sky.

"Let's hope so. If it doesn't—"

"Enough."

Belisarius strode down the back side of the hill toward his horse. Behind him, he heard Maurice begin to issue orders, but he could not make out their specific content. Instructions to the disgruntled Thracian cataphracts, no doubt.

Very disgruntled, indeed. The Thracian cataphracts looked upon foot travel—much less *fighting* on foot—with the enthusiasm of a drunk examining a glass of water. The *elite*, they were—and now, assigned to serve as bodyguards for a bunch of miserable, misbegotten, never-to-be-sufficiently-damned, common foot archers. Downright *plebes*. *Barbarians*, no less.

Which, in truth, they were. The four hundred archers atop the hill were a mercenary unit, made up entirely of Isaurian hillmen from southern Anatolia. An uncivilized lot, the Isaurians, but very tough. And completely accustomed to fighting on foot in rocky terrain, either with bows or with hand weapons.

Belisarius smiled. He knew his cataphracts. Once the Thracians saw the Isaurian archers at work, they would not be able to resist the challenge. Personally, Belisarius thought his cataphracts were better archers than any in the Army of Lebanon. They would certainly try to prove it. By the time the Persians tried to drive them off the hill, the Thracians would be in full fury.

Belisarius paused for a moment in his downward descent, and reexamined the hill.

Perfect. Steep sides, rocky. The worst possible terrain for a cavalry charge. And Persian nobles view fighting on foot like bishops view eternal damnation. God help the arrogant bastards, trying to drive armored horses up these slopes against dismounted Thracian cataphracts and Isaurian hillmen.

He resumed his descent down the western slope of the hill. Near the bottom, he came to the hollow where the Thracian horses were being held. A small number of the youngest and most inexperienced cataphracts had been assigned to hold the horses during the battle. They were even more disgruntled than their veteran fellows.

One of them, a lad named Menander, brought Belisarius his horse.

"General, are you sure I couldn't—"

"Enough." Then, Belisarius relented. "You know, Menander, it's likely the Persians will send a force around the hill to attack our rear. I imagine the fighting here will be hot and furious."

"Really?"

"Oh, yes. A desperate affair. Desperate."

Belisarius hoped he was lying. If the Persians managed to get far enough around the hill to find the hollow where the Thracian horses were being held, it would mean that they had driven off the heavy cavalry guarding his left wing and his whole battle plan was in ruins. His army too, most likely.

But Menander cheered up. The boy helped Belisarius onto his horse. Normally, Belisarius was quite capable of vaulting onto his horse. But not today, encumbered as he was with full armor. No cataphract in full armor could climb a horse without a stool or a helping hand.

Once he was firmly in the saddle, Belisarius heaved a

little sigh of relief. For the hundredth time, he patted himself on the back for his good sense in having all of his Thracian cavalry equipped with Scythian saddles instead of the flimsy Roman ones. Roman "saddles" were not much more than a thin pad. Scythian saddles were solid leather, and—much more to the point—had a cantle and a pommel. With a Scythian saddle, an armored cavalryman had at least half a chance of staying on his horse through a battle.

Belisarius heard noises behind him. Turning, he saw two of his cataphracts coming down the hill at a fast trot. As fast a "trot," at least, as could be managed by men wearing: full suits of scale-mail armor—including chest cuirasses—covering their upper bodies, right arms, and their abdomens down to mid-thigh; open-faced iron helmets with side-flanges, of the German *spangenhelm* style favored by most of the Thracians; small round shields buckled to their upper left arms, leaving the left hand free to wield a bow; heavy quilted Persian-style cavalry trousers; and, of course, a full panoply of weapons. The weapons included a long lance, a powerful compound bow, a quiver of arrows, long Persian-style cavalry swords, daggers, and the special personal weapons of the individuals: in the case of one, a mace; in the case of the other, a spatha.

Belisarius recognized the approaching cataphracts, recognized their purpose, and began to frown fiercely. But when the two cataphracts neared, his words of hot reproach were cut off before he could utter them.

"Don't bother, General," said Valentinian.

"No use at all," agreed Anastasius.

"Direct orders from Maurice."

"Very direct."

"You're just the general."

"Maurice is the Maurice."

Belisarius grimaced. There was no point in trying to send Valentinian and Anastasius away. They wouldn't obey his order, and he could hardly enforce it on them personally, since—

He eyed the two men.

Since I don't think there are two tougher soldiers in the whole Roman army, that's why.

So he tried reason.

"I don't need bodyguards."

"Hell you don't," came Valentinian's sharp, nasal reply.

"Was ever a man needed a bodyguard, it's you," added Anastasius. As ever, the giant's voice sounded like rumbling thunder. Professional church bassos had been known to turn green with envy, hearing that voice.

Menander was already bringing up the two cataphracts' horses. Anastasius' mount was the largest charger anyone had ever seen. Anastasius was devoted to the beast, as much out of genuine affection as simple self-preservation. No smaller horse could have borne his weight, in full armor, in the fury of a battlefield. Especially encumbered as the horse was with its own armor: scale mail covering the top of its head and its neck down to the withers, with additional sheets of mail protecting its chest and its front shoulders.

Anastasius more or less tossed Valentinian onto his horse. Then he mounted his own, with Menander's help. By the time he was aboard, the young cataphract looked completely exhausted by the effort of hoisting him.

Belisarius rode off, heading toward the center of the Roman lines. Behind him, he heard his two companions expressing their thoughts on the day.

"Look at it this way, Valentinian: it beats fighting on foot."

"It certainly does *not*."

"You hate to walk, even, much less—"

"So what? Not so bad, butchering a bunch of Medes trying to scramble their horses up that godawful hill. Instead—"

"Maybe he'll—"

"You know damn well he won't. When has he ever?"

Heavy sigh, like a small rockslide.

Again, Valentinian: "Huh? When has he ever? Name one time! Just one!"

Heavy sigh.

Mutter, mutter, mutter.

"What was that last, Valentinian?" asked Belisarius mildly. "I didn't quite make it out."

Silence.

Anastasius: "Sounded like 'fuck bold commanders, anyway.' "

Hiss.

Anastasius: "But maybe not. Maybe the bad-tempered skinny cutthroat said: 'Fuck old commoners, anyway.' Stupid thing to say, under the circumstances, of course. Especially since he's a commoner himself. But maybe that's what he said. He's bad-tempered about everything, you know."

Hiss.

Belisarius never turned his head. Just smiled. Crookedly, at first, then broadly.

Well, maybe Maurice is right. God help the Mede who tries to get in my way, that's for sure.

Once he reached the fortified camp at the center of the Roman lines, Belisarius dismounted and entered through the small western gate. Valentinian and Anastasius chose to remain outside. It was too much trouble to dismount and remount, and there was no way to ride a horse into *that* camp.

The camp was nothing special, in itself. It had been hastily erected in one day, and consisted of nothing much more than a ditch backed up by an earthen wall. Normally, such a wall would have been corduroyed, but there were precious few logs to be found in that region. To some degree, the soldiers had been able to reinforce the wall with field stones. Where possible, they had placed the customary *cervi—*

branches projecting sideways from the wall—but there were few suitable branches to be found in that barren Syrian terrain. Some of the more far-sighted and enterprising units had brought sharpened stakes with them to serve the purpose, but the wall remained a rather feeble obstacle. A pitiful wall, actually, by the traditional standards of Roman field fortifications.

But Belisarius was not unhappy with the wall. Not, not in the slightest. Quite the contrary. He *wanted* the Persian scouts to report to Firuz that the Roman fortification at the center of their lines was a ramshackle travesty.

The real oddity about the camp was not the camp itself but its population density—and the peculiar position of its inhabitants. Some Roman infantrymen were standing on guard behind the wall, as one might expect. The great majority, however, were lying down behind the wall and in the shallow trenches which had been dug inside the camp. The camp held at least four times as many soldiers as it would appear to hold, looking at it from the Persian side.

Belisarius heard the *cornicens* blaring out a ragged tune. Very ragged, just as he had instructed. As if the men blowing those horns were half-deranged with fear. The soldiers standing visible guard began acting out their parts.

As Belisarius watched, the infantry chiliarch of the Army of Lebanon trotted up. Hermogenes was grinning from ear to ear.

"What do you think?" he asked.

Belisarius smiled. "Well, they're certainly throwing themselves into their roles. Although I'm not sure it's really necessary for so many of them to be tearing at their hair. Or howling quite so loud. Or shaking their knees and gibbering."

Hermogenes' grin never faded.

"Better too much than too little." He turned and admired the thespian display. By now, the soldiers at the wall were racing around madly, in apparent confusion and disorder.

"Don't overdo it, Hermogenes," said Belisarius. "The men might get a little *too* far into it and forget it's just an act."

The chiliarch shook his head firmly.

"Not a chance. They're actually quite enthusiastic about the coming battle."

Belisarius eyed him skeptically.

"It's true, General. Well—maybe 'enthusiastic' is putting it a little too strongly. Confident, let's say."

Belisarius scratched his chin. "You think? I'd have thought the men would be skeptical of such a tricky little scheme."

Hermogenes stared at the general. Then said, very seriously, "If any other general had come up with it, they probably would. But—it's Belisarius' plan. That's what makes the difference."

Again, the skeptical eye.

"You underestimate your reputation, general. Badly."

Belisarius began to say that the scheme wasn't actually his. He had taken it from Julius Caesar, who had used hidden troops in a fortified camp in one of his many battles against the Gauls. But before he could utter more than two words, he fell silent. One of the sentries at the wall was shouting. A genuine alert, now, not a false act.

Belisarius raced to the wall and peered over. Hermogenes joined him an instant later.

The Persians were advancing.

Belisarius studied the Mede formation intently. It was impressive, even—potentially—terrifying. As Persian armies always were.

An old thought caused a little quirk to come to the general's lips.

I'm always amazed at the way modern Greek scholars and courtiers don't live in the real world. Their image of Persian armies is fixed a thousand years ago, in the ancient times. When a small number of disciplined and armored

Greek and Macedonian hoplites could always scatter the lightly-armed Persian mobs of Xerxes and Darius. The glorious phalanx of the Hellenes against the motley hordes of despotic Asia.

Let them see this, and gape, and tremble.

Many modern Greeks, of course, knew the truth. But they were of a different class than the Greeks who wrote the books and the laws, and collected the taxes, and lorded it over their great estates.

Persia had changed, over the centuries. More, even, than Rome. A class of tough, land-vested nobility had arisen. They were the real power in Persia, now, when all was said and done. True, they paid homage to the Sassanid emperors, and served them, as they had the Parthians who preceded them. But it was a conditional homage and a proud service. The conditions and the pride stemmed from one simple fact. The Persian aristocracy had invented modern heavy cavalry, and they were still better at it than any people on the face of the earth. The Roman cataphracts were, in all essential respects, simply attempts to copy the Persian noble cavalry.

The Persians were now close enough for the details of their formation to be made out.

Unlike Roman armies, which used infantry as the stolid center of their formations—as an anchor for the battle, even if they weren't much use in the battle itself—the Persians scorned infantry almost entirely. True, there were ten thousand foot soldiers in the advancing Mede army. But Persian infantry were a ragged, scraggly lot: modern Persian foot soldiers were probably even worse than the rabble which had been broken by the hoplites at Marathon and Issus centuries earlier. Miserable peasant levies, completely unarmored except for hide shields; armed only with javelins and light spears; consigned to the flanks; assigned the simple duties of butchering wounded enemies and serving as a buffer against charging foes. Armed cattle, basically.

Belisarius dismissed them with a glance. The general's attention was riveted on the cavalry advancing at the center of the Persian army. His experienced eye immediately sorted order out of the mass.

The heart of the Persian cavalry were the heavily armored noble lancers, riding huge war horses bred on the Persian plateau. Each nobleman, in turn, brought to battle a small retinue of more lightly armored horse archers. The horse archers would start the battle, and would fight closely alongside the heavy lancers. When the lancers made charges, the mounted archers would act as a screen to keep off enemy cavalry and suppress enemy archers, while the lancers shattered their foe.

It was a ferocious, well-disciplined military machine. No Roman army had won a major battle in the open field against Persia in over a century.

But Belisarius was filled with confidence.

Today, I'm going to do it.

He began to turn away from the wall. Before leaving, however, he stopped a moment and gazed at Hermogenes. The infantry chiliarch grinned.

"Relax, General. You just take care of the cavalry. The infantry will do its job."

Once back on his horse, Belisarius cantered over to the right wing of his army. The right was in the hands of the Army of Lebanon's cavalry commanders. Belisarius intended to take his position there at the beginning of the battle. Although the Army of Lebanon had accepted his leadership, he knew that they would quickly slip the leash if he was not there to keep a tight grip on it. The one thing that could ruin his plans was a rash, unplanned cavalry charge. Which, in his experience, cavalry was always prone to do.

That's another thing I like about infantry. When a man

has to charge on his own two legs, he tends to think it over first. Less tiring.

Seeing him approach, the cavalry chiliarchs rode to meet him.

"Soon, now," announced Eutyches.

Belisarius nodded.

"As soon as—" A blaring cornicen cut him off. Belisarius turned in his saddle just in time to see the first missiles hurled from the four scorpions and two onagers which he had positioned behind the fortified camp. Phocas had gauged the range and given the command for the artillery fire.

Out of the corner of his eye, he saw a scowl on the face of Pharas.

Belisarius understood the meaning of that expression. Like most modern Roman commanders, Pharas had no use for artillery in a field battle.

But Belisarius forebore comment. He had learned, from experience, that it was a futile argument.

They just don't understand. Sure, the damned things are a pain to haul around. Sure, they don't really inflict that many casualties. But they do two invaluable things. First, they break up the cohesion of the enemy's ranks. An alert soldier, even a heavily armored horseman, can usually dodge a great big scorpion dart or a huge stone thrown by an onager—as long as he isn't hemmed in by closely packed ranks. So, the enemy starts spreading out. Second—and most important—it's utterly infuriating to a warrior to be bombarded when he's too far away to retaliate. So he charges closer. Which is just what I want. Strategic offense; tactical defense. There's the whole secret in a nutshell.

The two chiliarchs were already galloping toward the front line. Belisarius followed. He needed to be able to watch the progress of the battle, and had already decided he would do it from the right. The hill would have been a perfect vantage point, of course, but he would have been much too isolated from the right wing of his army. Which represented both his heaviest force and his least reliable.

By the time he reached the front line, the Persians had already begun their charge. He saw at once that the enemy had begun the charge much too soon. Even the huge Persian horses couldn't charge any great distance before becoming exhausted.

And so, once again, the artillery did the trick.

Still, the Persians weren't Goths. Once Goths began a cavalry charge, they always tried to carry it through. The Medes, sophisticated and civilized for all their noble pride, were much too canny not to suspect a trap.

So, once they got within bow range, the Persian heavy cavalry reined in and let their horses breathe. The lighter mounted archers continued forward, firing their bows.

Pharas didn't wait for Belisarius' command. He ordered the Roman horse archers forward. The Huns galloped out onto the battleground, firing their own bows. Within moments, a swirling archery duel was underway.

Between Persian and Hun mounted archers, the contest was unequal. The Persians, as always, fired their bows as rapidly as did the Huns—much more rapidly than Roman cataphracts or regular infantry. But the Persians were better armored, and that extra armor counted for much against the relatively weak bows being used by both sides.

Soon enough, the Huns began falling back. The Persian horse archers did not attempt to charge in pursuit. They were no fools, and knew full well that Huns surpassed everyone in the art of turning a retreat into a sudden counterattack. So they simply satisfied themselves with a disciplined, orderly advance. Firing volley after volley as they came.

Pharas began to grumble, but Belisarius cut him off. Quickly. As he had expected, the chiliarch had already forgotten the battle plan.

"Splendid," announced Belisarius. "The Huns have already succeeded in fixing the entire left wing of the enemy."

"They're advancing on us!" exclaimed Pharas.

How did this idiot ever get made a chiliarch? I wouldn't trust him to bake bread. The first thing he'd do is throw away the recipe.

But his words were mild.

"Which is precisely what I want, Pharas. As long as the Persian left is *advancing* on our right, they aren't free to be doing something else. Such as chewing up our left, which is where the battle's going to be decided."

Belisarius ignored the fuming chiliarch and watched the battle develop on the other side of the field. The Isaurians and Thracian cataphracts on the hill were now starting to fire their bows at the Persian cavalry spreading into the center of the battleground. Within five minutes, it was obvious to Belisarius that his earlier estimate had been accurate.

It was the great advantage of cataphract archery, and one of the reasons Belisarius had stationed his Thracians atop the hill. With individual exceptions, such as Valentinian, they didn't have the rapid rate of fire that Persian or Hun horse archers did. But no archers in the world fired bows more accurately, and none with that awesome power. With the advantage of the hill's altitude, the cataphract arrows were plunging into the ranks of the Persian cavalry, wreaking havoc. Even the armor of Persian nobility couldn't withstand *those* arrows. And his cataphracts—especially the veterans— weren't aiming at the Persians anyway. Their targets were the horses themselves. The heavy frontal armor of the Persian chargers might have turned the arrows. But these missiles were plunging down into the great beasts' unarmored flanks. Dying and wounded horses began disrupting the serried ranks of the enemy's heavy cavalry.

Suddenly, Belisarius felt a breeze at his back. He almost sighed with relief. He had expected it, but still—

The wind, blowing from west to east, would increase the range of his own archery and artillery, and hamper the Persian arrows. Much more important, however, was the effect which the wind would have on visibility. The battlefield was already choked with dust thrown up by the horses. As soon as the breeze picked up, that dust would be moving from the Roman side to the Persian. The enemy would be half-blinded, even at close range.

"They're going to charge," predicted Eutychian, the other cavalry chiliarch. "Against us, on this wing."

"Thank God!" snorted Pharas. The chiliarch immediately rode off, shouting at his subordinate commanders.

Belisarius examined the battlefield and decided Eutychian was right.

Damn it! I was hoping—

He stared at Eutychian, estimating the man. His decision, as always, came quickly—aided, as much as anything, by the level gaze with which the chiliarch returned his stare.

"Can I trust you not to be an idiot like that one?" he demanded, pointing with his thumb at the retreating figure of Pharas.

"Meaning?"

"Meaning this—can I trust you to meet this charge with a simple stand? All I want is for the Persians to be held on this wing. *That's all*. Do you understand? They outnumber us, especially in heavy cavalry. If you try to win the battle here, with a glorious idiotic all-out charge, the Medes will cut you to pieces and I'll have a collapsed right wing. The battle will be won on the left. All I need is for you to hold the right steady. Can you do it? *Will* you do it?"

Eutychian glanced over at Pharas.

"Yes, Belisarius. But he's senior to me and—"

"You let me worry about Pharas. *Will you hold this wing? Nothing more?*"

Eutychian nodded. Belisarius rode over to the small knot

of commanders clustered around Pharas. As he went, he gave Valentinian and Anastasius a meaningful look. Anastasius' face grew stony. Valentinian grinned. On his sharp-featured, narrow face, the grin was utterly feral.

As Belisarius drew near, he was able to make out Pharas' words of command to his subordinates. Just as he had feared, the chiliarch was organizing an all-out direct charge against the coming Medes.

Belisarius shouldered his horse into the group of commanders. In his peripheral vision, he could see Valentinian sidling his horse next to Pharas, and Anastasius moving around to the other side of the small command group.

Thank you, Maurice.

"That's enough, Pharas," he said. His tone was sharp and cold. "Our main charge is going to come later, on the other—"

"The hell with that!" roared Pharas. "I'm fighting now!"

"Our battle plan—"

"Fuck your fancy damned plan! It's pure bullshit! A fucking coward plan! I fight—"

"*Valentinian.*"

In his entire life, Belisarius had never met a man who could wield a sword more quickly and expertly than Valentinian. Nor as mercilessly. The cataphract's long, lean, whipcord body twisted like a spring. His spatha removed Pharas' head as neatly as a butcher beheading a chicken.

As always, Valentinian's strike was economical. No great heroic hewing, just enough to do the job. Pharas' head didn't sail through the air. It just rolled off his neck and bounced on the ground next to his horse. A moment later, his headless body fell off on the other side. His horse, suddenly covered with blood, shied away.

The commanders gaped with shock. One of them began to draw his sword. Anastasius smashed his spine. No economy here—the giant's mace drove the commander right over his horse's head. His mount, well-trained, never budged.

Belisarius whipped out his own spatha. The four surviving commanders in the group were now completely hemmed in by Belisarius and his two cataphracts. They were still gaping, and their faces were pale.

"I'll tolerate no treason or insubordination," stated Belisarius. His voice was not loud. Simply as cold as a glacier. Icy death.

"*Do you understand?*"

Gapes. Pale faces.

"*Do you understand?*" Valentinian twitched the spatha in his grip, very slightly. Anastasius hefted his mace, not so slightly.

"*Do you understand?*"

Mouths snapped shut. Faces remained pale, but heads began to nod. After two seconds, vigorously.

Belisarius eased back in his saddle and slid his spatha back into its waist-scabbard. (Valentinian, of course, did no such thing. Nor did Anastasius seem in any hurry to relinquish his mace.)

Belisarius turned and looked at Eutychian. The chiliarch was not more than thirty yards away. He and his own subordinates had witnessed the entire scene. So, Belisarius estimated, had dozens of the Army of Lebanon's cavalrymen. The faces of Eutychian and his commanders were also pale. But, Belisarius noted, they did not seem particularly outraged. Rather the contrary, in fact.

He studied the cavalrymen. No pale faces there. A few frowns, perhaps, but there were at least as many smiles to offset them. Even a few outright grins. Pharas, he suspected, had not been a popular commander.

Belisarius returned his hard stare to Eutychian. The chiliarch suddenly smiled—just slightly—and nodded his own head.

Belisarius turned back to the four commanders at his side.

"You will obey me instantly and without question. Do you understand?"

Vigorous nods. Anastasius replaced his mace in its holder. Valentinian did no such thing with his spatha.

A sudden blaring of cornicens. Belisarius turned back again. He could no longer see the Persian army, for his vision was obscured by the mass of cavalrymen at the front line. But it was obvious the Medes had begun their charge. Eutychian and his commanders were riding down the line, shouting orders.

Now in a hurry, Belisarius issued quick, simple instructions to the four commanders at his side:

"Eutychian will hold the right, using half of the Army of Lebanon's heavy cavalry and all of the mounted archers. You four will assemble the other half of the Army of Lebanon's lancers and keep them in reserve. I want them ready to charge"—his voice turned to pure steel—"*when* I say, *where* I say, and *how* I say. *Is that understood?*"

Very vigorous nods.

Belisarius gestured to Anastasius and Valentinian.

"Until the battle is over, these men will act as my immediate executive officers. You will obey their orders as if they came from me. Is that understood?"

Very vigorous nods.

Belisarius began to introduce his two cataphracts by name, but decided otherwise. For his immediate purposes, they had already been properly introduced.

Death and *Destruction*, he thought, would do just fine.

After the four commanders left to begin sorting out and assembling their forces, Belisarius rode back to the front line. As he approached, the Hun light cavalry began pouring back from the battlefield. They were no match in a head-to-head battle with the oncoming Persian lancers, and they knew it.

That's one of the few good things about mercenaries, thought Belisarius. *At least they aren't given to idiotic suicide charges.*

For all their mercenary character, the Huns were good soldiers. Experienced veterans, too. Their retreat was not a rout, and as soon as they reached the relative safety of the Roman lines they began to regroup. They knew the Roman heavy cavalry would be sallying soon, and it would be their job to provide flanking cover against the Persian horse archers.

Belisarius was now right behind the front line of the Roman heavy horse. Between two cavalrymen, he watched the advancing Medes.

The Persian heavy cavalry had not yet started their galloping charge. They still had two hundred yards to cross before reaching the Roman lines. The Medes were veterans themselves, who knew the danger of exhausting their mounts in a battle—especially one fought in the heat of Syrian summer. Still, their thunderous advance was massively impressive. Two thousand heavy lancers, four lines deep, maintaining themselves in good order, flanked by three thousand horse archers maintaining their own excellent discipline.

Very impressive, but—

The Roman archers in the fortifications—Ghassanid mercenaries, these—were now aiming all their fire at the Mede cavalry attacking the right. They were ignoring, for the moment, the swarm of Persian horse archers in the center who were raining their own arrows on the encampment. Hermogenes, Belisarius noted, was keeping a cool head. Protected by the wall in front of them, his infantry would suffer few casualties from the Persian archers. Meanwhile, their arrows could hamper the advance of the Persian lancers.

Hermogenes had trained his men well, too. The Arab archers ignored the temptation to fire at the lancers themselves. The heavy Persian armor would deflect arrows from their light bows, especially at that range. Instead, the men were aiming at the unprotected legs of the horses. True, the range was long, but Belisarius saw more than a few Persian horses stumble and fall, spilling their riders.

From the hill, a flight of arrows sailed toward the Persian cavalry advancing on the Roman right. But the arrows fell short and the volley ceased almost immediately. Belisarius knew that Maurice had reined in the overenthusiastic cataphracts. The range—firing diagonally across the entire battlefield—was too extreme, even for their powerful bows firing with the wind. Instead, Maurice ordered his cataphracts and the Isaurians to concentrate their fire on the swarm of light horse archers in the center.

Belisarius was delighted. His army was functioning the way a good army should. The archers on the left were protecting the infantry in the center, while they harassed the Persians advancing on the right.

A volley of scorpion darts and onager stones sailed into the Persian heavy cavalry, tearing holes in the ranks. The cavalry began to spread, losing their compact formation.

Good, Phocas, good. But, with this wind, it should be possible—

Yes!

The next artillery volley fell right in the middle of the Persian command group at the rear of the battlefield. The Persian officers hadn't expected artillery fire, and their attention had been completely riveted on the battleground. The missiles arrived as a complete surprise. The carnage was horrendous. Those men or horses struck by huge onager stones were so much pulp, regardless of their heavy armor. Nor did that same armor protect the Persians from the spear-sized arrows cast by the scorpions. One of those officers, struck almost simultaneously by two scorpion bolts, was literally torn to pieces.

As always in battle, Belisarius' brown eyes were like stones. But his cold gaze ignored the artillery's victims. His attention was completely focused on the survivors.

Please, let Firuz still be alive. Oh, please, let that arrogant hot-tempered jackass still be alive.

Yes!

Firuz had obviously been driven into a rage. Belisarius could recognize the Persian commander's colorful cloak and plumage, personally leading the main body of his army in a charge at the center of the Roman lines. Three thousand heavy lancers, flanked by four thousand mounted archers, already at a full gallop.

It was a charge worthy of the idiot Pharas—the late, unlamented Pharas. The Mede lancers in the center had half a mile to cover before they reached the Roman fortifications. A half-mile in scorching heat, against wind-blown dust. It was absurd—and would have been, even if there weren't already three thousand Persian horse archers milling around in the center of the battlefield. The charging Persian lancers would be trampling over their own troops.

Midway through the charge, however, some sanity appeared to return to the Persians—to the horse archers already in the center, at least. Seeing the oncoming lancers, the mounted archers scurried out of their way. Their officers led them in a charge against the small Roman force on the hill.

Belisarius watched intently. He was confident that his cataphracts and the Isaurians could repel the attack, even outnumbered five to one. The Persians would be trying to climb steep slopes under plunging fire. And if matters got too tight, the two thousand cavalry from his own little army were stationed on the left wing, not far from the hill. But he didn't want to use those horsemen there, if he didn't absolutely need to. He wanted them fresh when—

Belisarius' view was suddenly obscured. Cornicens were blowing. The cavalrymen in front of him began firing their bows at the Persian lancers who were now less than a hundred yards away. A moment later, the cornicens blew again. The Roman cavalry charged to meet the oncoming lancers. They fired one last volley at the beginning of the charge and then slid the bows into their sheaths. It would be lance and sword work, now.

Belisarius glanced quickly toward the center. But it was impossible to see anything, anymore. The entire battlefield was now covered with dust, which the wind was blowing against the Persians. He could still see the hill, however, rising above the dust clouds. Within three or four seconds, simply from watching the unhurried and confident way in which his Thracian cataphracts and the Isaurians were firing their bows, Belisarius was certain that they would hold. Long enough, anyway.

It was time.

He looked back to the battle raging right before him. The Army of Lebanon's Huns were sweeping around the extreme right, trying to flank the Persian horse archers. But the Persians archers were veterans also, and were extending their own line to match the Huns. That part of the battle almost instantly became a chaotic swirl of horsemen exchanging bow-fire, often at point-blank range.

Dust everywhere, now. Beautiful, wonderful, obscuring dust. Blowing from the west over the Persians, blinding them to all Roman maneuvers.

The only part of the battle Belisarius could still see— other than the hilltop—was the collision between the Army of Lebanon's lancers and the lancers of the Persian left. Eutychian and his two thousand armored horsemen were smashing head to head with an equal number of Persian heavy cavalry. The noise of the battlefield—already immense—seemed to fill the entire universe. The clash of metal, the screams of men and horses filled the air.

It was a battle the Persians would win, eventually. Except for the very best cataphract units, no Roman heavy cavalry could defeat an equal number of Persian lancers. But, as he watched the vigor and courage of Eutychian's charge, Belisarius was more than satisfied. Eutychian would lose his part of the battle, but by the time he did, the Romans would have triumphed in the field as a whole.

More than that, Belisarius did not ask.

Hold the right, Eutychian. Just hold it.

He began to canter away.

And try to survive. I can use an officer like you. So can Rome.

As he rode, he passed orders through Valentinian and Anastasius. The four remaining commanders of the Army of Lebanon were quick to obey. Very quick. The two thousand lancers of that Army which Belisarius had kept in reserve—the same ones Pharas would have thrown away in a suicide charge—were now cantering across the battlefield in good order. South to north, behind the Roman lines, from the right wing to the left wing. They were completely invisible to the Persians, due to the wind-blown dust.

As they drew behind the fortified camp, Belisarius ordered a halt. He thought there was still time, and he wanted to make sure that the battle had become locked in the center.

While the Army of Lebanon's lancers allowed their horses to rest, therefore, Belisarius trotted up to the camp and passed into it through the west gate. He could begin to see now, even with the dust.

Just as he had planned (and hoped—not that he'd ever admit it to that morose old grouch Maurice) the main body of Persian lancers in the center had smashed into his trap.

True, they had done so in a charge ordered by an idiot, but—that's the beauty of the first law of battles, after all. It cuts both ways.

Sitting on his horse not thirty yards from the fortified wall, Belisarius found it hard not to grin. He hadn't seen it, but he knew what had happened.

Imagine three thousand Persian lancers, thundering up to a wretched little earthen wall, guarded by not more than a thousand terrified, pathetic, wretched infantrymen. They sweep the enemy aside, right? Like an avalanche!

Well, not exactly. There are problems.

First, each cavalry mount has been hauling a man (a large man, more often than not) carrying fifty pounds of armor and twenty pounds of weapons—not to mention another hundred pounds of the horse's own armor. At a full gallop for half a mile, in the blistering heat of a Syrian summer.

So, the horses are winded, disgruntled, and thinking dark thoughts.

Two—all hearsay to the contrary—horses are not stupid. Quite a bit brighter than men, actually, when it comes to that kind of intelligence known popularly as "horse sense." So, when a horse sees looming before it:

a) a ditch

b) a wall

c) lots of men on the wall holding long objects with sharp points

The horse stops. Fuck the charge. If some stupid man wants to hurl himself against all that dangerous crap, let him. (Which, often enough, they do—sailing headlong over their horse's stubborn head.)

It was the great romantic fallacy of the cavalry charge, and Belisarius had been astonished—all his life—at how fervently men still held to it, despite all practical experience and evidence to the contrary. Yes, horses will charge—against infantry in the open, and against other cavalry. Against anything, as long as the horse can see that it stands a chance of getting through the obstacles ahead, reasonably intact.

But no horse this side of an equine insane asylum will charge a wall too high to leap over. *Especially* a wall covered with nasty sharp objects.

And there's no point trying to convince the horse that the infantry manning the wall are feeble and demoralized.

Is that so? Tell you what, asshole. Climb off my back and show me. Use your own legs. Mine hurt.

The horses would have drawn up short before the ditch and the wall even if the fortification had been, in truth, guarded by only a thousand demoralized infantrymen. In the event, however, just as the horses drew near, Hermogenes had given the order and the cornicens had blown a new tune. Oh, a gleeful tune.

Surprise!

The other three thousand infantry hiding behind the wall and in the ditches had scrambled to their feet and taken their positions. The wall was now packed with spears, in the hands of soldiers full of confidence and vigor.

The front line of horses had screeched to a halt. Many of their riders had been thrown off. Some had been killed by the fall itself. Most of the survivors were badly shaken and bruised.

The second line of horse had piled into the first, the third into the second, the fourth into the third. More men were thrown off their mounts. To the injuries caused by falling were added the gruesome wounds suffered by men trampled by horses. Within seconds, the entire charging mass of Persian lancers had turned into an immobile, struggling, completely disordered mob. And now, worst of all, the Roman infantry began hurling volleys of *plumbata* into the milling Persians. At that close range, against a packed mass of confused and disoriented cavalry, the lead-weighted darts were fearsome weapons. The more so since the soldiers casting the weapons were expert in their use.

The cornicens blew again. Thousands of Roman infantry began scrambling over the wall. Many of them were carrying spathae, but most were wielding the even shorter semi-spatha. Each of those men would plunge into the writhing mob of Persian cavalry and use the time-honored tactic of infantry against armored cavalry.

It was an ignoble tactic, perhaps, and it never worked against cavalry on the move. But against cavalry forced to a halt, it was as certain as the sunrise.

Hamstring and gut the horses. Then butcher the lordly nobles once they're on the ground like us lowlife. See how much good their fine heavy armor does 'em then. And their bows and their lances and their fancy longswords. This here's knife work, my lord.

Belisarius rode out of the camp. The battle was his, if he could only drive home the final thrust.

For all his eagerness to win, Belisarius was careful to keep his pace at an easy canter. There was time, there was time. Not much, but enough. He didn't want the horses blown.

Without even waiting for his orders, Valentinian and Anastasius reined in the overenthusiasts who began driving their horses faster. There was time. There was time. Not much, but enough.

As they passed the western slope of the hill, the two thousand cavalry of Belisarius' own army fell in with him. He now had a striking force of four thousand men, unblooded and confident, riding fresh horses.

Belisarius saw a small figure standing on the slope, watching the army pass. Menander, he thought, still at his unwanted post. Even from the distance, he thought he could detect the bitter reproach in the boy's posture.

Sorry, lad. But you'll get your share of bloodshed in the future. And for that I really am sorry.

Now his force was curving around the northern slope of the hill. They had passed entirely across the line and were on the verge of falling on the enemy's unprotected right flank.

They came around the hill with Belisarius in the lead. The center of the battlefield was still obscured by dust, but the Romans could now see the Persian horse archers who were trying to storm the hill. The slaughter here had been immense, and it was immediately obvious that the Persians were discouraged.

Discouragement soon became outright terror. The four thousand Roman lancers hammered their way through the mounted archers without even pausing. Moments later they were plunging into the dust cloud, aiming at the mass of Persian lancers stymied at the center.

Belisarius turned halfway in his saddle and signaled the buglers behind him. The cornicens began blowing the order for a full charge. Their sound was a thin, piercing wail over the thundering bedlam of the battlefield.

Yet, for all the noise, the general was able to hear Valentinian and Anastasius, riding just behind him.

Valentinian: "I told you so."

Anastasius: *Inarticulate snort.*

Valentinian: *Mutter, mutter, mutter.*

Belisarius: "What was that last? I didn't quite catch it."

Valentinian: *Silence.*

Anastasius: "I think he said 'fuck brave officers.' "

Valentinian: *Hiss.*

Anastasius: "But maybe not. It's noisy. Maybe the cold-blooded little killer said, 'Fuck brazen coffers.' Idiot thing to say on a battlefield, of course. But he's—"

All else was lost. The first Persian lancer loomed in the dust, his back turned away. Belisarius raised his lance high and drove it right through the Mede's heart. The enemy fell off his horse, taking the lance with him.

Another Mede, turned half away, to his right. Belisarius drew his long cavalry sword out of its baldric and hewed the man's arm off with the same motion. Another Mede, again from the back. The sword butchered into his neck, below the rim of the helmet. Another Mede—facing him, now. The sword hammered his shield down, hammered it aside, hammered his helmet sideways. The man was driven off his mount and fell, unconscious, to the ground. In that mad press of stamping horses, he would be dead within a minute, crushed to a bloody pulp.

The entire Roman cavalry piled into the Persians, caving in the right rear of their already disorganized formation. The initial slaughter was horrendous. The charge caught the Persians completely by surprise. Many of them, in the first few seconds, fell before blows which they never even saw.

To an extent, of course, Belisarius now found himself caught by the same dilemma that had faced the Medes. The thousands of Persian cavalrymen jammed against the Roman camp in the center of the battlefield were not quite a wall. But almost. Combat became a matter of men on skittering horses hammering at each other. Lances were useless, now. It was all sword, mace, and ax work. And utterly murderous.

Yet, for all the ensuing mayhem, the outcome was certain. The Medes were trapped between an equal number of Roman heavy cavalry and thousands of Roman infantrymen. Their greatest strength—that unequaled Persian skill at hard-hitting, fast-moving cavalry warfare—was completely neutralized. As cavalrymen, the average Roman was not their equal. But this was no longer a cavalry battle. It was a pure infantry battle, in which the majority of soldiers just happened to be sitting on horses.

As always under those circumstances, more and more of the men—on both sides—soon found themselves on the ground. Without momentum, it was almost impossible to swing heavy swords and axes for any length of time without falling off a horse. The only thing keeping a soldier on his horse were the pressure of his knees and—if possible, which it usually wasn't in a battle—a hand on the pommel of his saddle. Any well-delivered blow on his armor or shield would knock a man off. And any badly delivered blow of his own was likely to drag him off by the inertia of his missed swing.

Five minutes into the fray, almost half of the cavalrymen on both sides were dismounted.

"This is going to be as bad as Lake Ticinus," grunted Anastasius. He pounded a Persian to the ground with a mace blow. Nothing fancy; Anastasius needn't bother—the giant's mace slammed the man's own shield into his helmet hard enough to crack his skull.

Belisarius grimaced. The ancient battle of Lake Ticinus was a staple of Roman army lore. Fought during the Second Punic War, it had started as a pure cavalry battle and ended as a pure infantry fight. Every single man on both sides, according to legend, had fallen off his horse before the fray was finished.

Belisarius was actually surprised that he was still mounted himself. Partly, of course, that was due to his bodyguards. In his entire career, Anastasius had only fallen off his horse once during a battle. And that didn't really count—his horse had fallen first, slipping in a patch of snow on some unnamed little battlefield in Dacia. The man was so huge and powerful—with a horse to match—that he could swap blows with anyone without budging from his saddle.

Valentinian, on the other hand, had taken to the ground as soon as the battle had become a deadlocked slugging match. Valentinian was possibly even deadlier than Anastasius, but his lethality was the product of skill, dexterity, and speed. Those traits were almost nullified in this kind of fray, as long as he was trapped on a stationary horse.

Valentinian was a veteran, however. For all his grousing about foot-soldiering, the man had instantly slid from his horse and kept fighting afoot. The result had been a gory trail of hamstrung and gutted horses, their former riders lying nearby in their own blood.

With those two protecting him—and his own great skill as a fighter—Belisarius hadn't even been hurt.

Yet—it was odd. There was something else. Belisarius hadn't noticed, at first, until a slight pause in the action enabled him to think. But the fact was that he was fighting much *too* well.

"Deadly with a blade, is Belisarius." He'd heard it said, and knew it for a cold and simple truth. But he had never been as deadly as he was that day. The cause lay not in any added strength or stamina. It was—odd. He seemed to see everything with perfect clarity, even in the hazy dust. He seemed to be able to gauge every motion by an enemy perfectly—and gauge his own strikes with equal precision. Time after time, he had slipped a blow by the barest margin—yet knowing, all the while, that the margin was adequate. Time after time, he had landed a blow of his own through the narrowest gaps, the slimmest openings— yet knowing, at the instant, that the gaps were enough. Time after time, he had begun to slip from his horse, only to find his balance again with perfect ease.

Odd. The truth was that he was leaving his own trail of gore and blood. It was like a path through a forest beaten by an elephant.

Even his cataphracts noticed. And complained, in the case of one.

"We're supposed to be protecting *you*, General," hissed Valentinian. "Not the other way around."

"Quit bitching," growled Anastasius. *Chunk*. Another Mede down. "I'm a big target. I need all the protection I can get." *Chunk*.

Valentinian began to snarl something, but fell silent, listening intently.

"I think—"

"Yes," said Belisarius. He had heard it too. The first cry for quarter, coming from a Persian throat. The cry had been cut off.

The general ceased his mayhem. Turned to Anastasius.

"Get Maurice—and the others. Now. I don't want to end the battle with atrocities. We're trying to win this war, not start a new one."

"No need," grunted Anastasius. He extended his right hand, pointing with his blood-covered mace. Belisarius turned and saw his entire Thracian retinue charging toward them on horseback.

Within seconds, Maurice drew up alongside them.

"I don't want a massacre, Maurice!" shouted Belisarius. "I'll handle the situation here, but the Huns—"

Maurice interrupted.

"They're already making for the Persian camp. I'll try to stop them, but I'll need reinforcement as soon as you can get there."

Without another word, the hecatontarch spurred his horse into a gallop. Seconds later, the entire body of Thracian cataphracts were thundering to the east, in the direction of the Persian camp.

Cries for quarter were being heard now from all over the battlefield. Many of them cut off in mid-screech. All fight was gone from the Medes. The light cavalry were already fleeing the field. The Persian infantry had long since begun to run. The heavy cavalry, trapped in the center, were trying to surrender. Without much success. The Roman infantrymen were in full fury. They were wreaking their vengeance on those who had so often in the past brought terror into their own hearts.

Belisarius rode directly into the mass. When he wanted

to use it, the general had a very loud and well-trained voice. Anastasius joined him with his own thundering basso. Yet, strangely enough, it was Valentinian's nasal tenor that pierced through the din like a sword.

A simple cry, designed to rein in the Roman murder: *"Ransom! Ransom! Ransom!"*

The cry was immediately taken up by the Persians themselves. Within seconds, the slaughter stopped. Half-maddened the Roman infantry might have been. Poor, however, they most certainly were. And it suddenly dawned on them that they held in the palm of their mercy the lives of hundreds—thousands, maybe—of Persians. *Noble* Persians. *Rich* noble Persians.

Belisarius quickly found Hermogenes. The infantry chiliarch took responsibility for organizing the surrender. Then Belisarius went in search of Eutychian.

But Eutychian was not to be found. Nothing but his body, lying on the ground, an arrow through his throat.

Belisarius, staring down at the corpse, felt a great sadness wash over him. He had barely known the man. But he had looked forward to the pleasure.

He shook off the mood. Later. Not now.

He found the highest-ranked surviving cavalry commander of the Army of Lebanon. Mundus, his name. He had been one of Pharas' little coterie, and his face turned a bit pale when Belisarius rode up. When he spotted Valentinian and Anastasius he turned very pale.

"Round up your cavalry, Mundus," commanded Belisarius. "At least three ala. I need them to reinforce my cataphracts at the Persian camp. The Huns'll be on a rampage and I intend to put a stop to it."

Mundus winced. "It'll be hard," he muttered. "The men'll want their share of—"

"Forget the ransom!" thundered the general. "If they complain, tell them I've got plans for bigger booty. I'll explain later. But right now—*move, damn you!*"

Valentinian was already sidling his horse toward Mundus, but there was no need. The terrified officer instantly began screaming orders at his subordinates. They, in turn, began rounding up their soldiers.

The cavalrymen were upset, Belisarius knew, because the Roman infantry stood to gain the lion's share of the booty. By tradition, ransom was owed to the man who personally held a captive. It was a destructive tradition, in Belisarius' opinion, and one which he hoped to change eventually. But not today. For the first time in centuries, the Roman infantry had blazed its old glory, and Belisarius would not dampen their victory, or their profit from it.

At the Persian camp, they came upon a very tense scene. The camp itself was a shambles. Most of the tents lay on the ground like lumpy shrouds. Those tents still standing were ragged from sword-slashes. Wagons were upended or half-shattered. Some of the wreckage was the work of the Hun mercenaries, but much of it was due to the Persians themselves. Sensing the defeat, the Persian camp followers had hastily rummaged out their most precious possessions and taken flight.

But not all had left soon enough. Several dead Persians were lying about, riddled with arrows. All men. The Huns would have saved the women and children. The women would be raped. Afterwards, they and the children would be sold into slavery.

In the event, the mercenaries had barely begun enjoying their looting and their atrocities before the Thracians had arrived and put a stop to it. More or less.

Very tense. On one side, dismounted but armed, hundreds of Hun mercenaries. On the other, still mounted, armed—*and* with drawn bows—were three hundred bucellarii.

The Huns outnumbered the Thracians' cataphracts by a factor of three to one. So, the outcome of any fight was obvious to all. The mercenaries would be butchered to a man. But not before they inflicted heavy casualties on the Thracians.

The general cared nothing for the Huns. But it would be a stupid waste of his cataphracts.

Mundus pointed out to him the three leaders of the mercenaries. As usual with Huns, their rank derived from clan status, not Roman military protocol.

Belisarius rode over to them and dismounted. Valentinian and Anastasius stayed on their horses. Both men had their own bows drawn, with arrows notched.

The Hun clan leaders were glaring at him furiously. Off to one side, three young Hun warriors were screaming insults at the Thracians. One of them held a young Persian by her hair. The girl was half-naked, weeping, on her knees. Next to her, a still younger boy—her brother, thought Belisarius, from the resemblance—was sitting on the ground. He was obviously dazed and was holding his head in both hands. Blood seeped through his fingers.

Belisarius glanced at the little tableau, then stared back at the three clan chiefs. He met their glares with an icy gaze. Then stepped up very close and said softly, in quite good Hunnish:

"My name is Belisarius. I have just destroyed an entire Persian army. Do you think I can be intimidated by such as *you*?"

After a moment, two of the clan leaders looked away. The third, the oldest, held the glare.

Belisarius nodded slightly toward the three young Huns holding the girl.

"Your clan?" he asked.

The clan chief snorted. "Clanless. They—"

"*Valentinian.*"

Belisarius knew no archer as quick and accurate as Valentinian. The Hun holding the girl by her hair took

Valentinian's first arrow. In the chest, straight through the heart. The cataphract's second arrow, following instantly, dropped another. Anastasius, even with an already-drawn bow, fired only one arrow in the same time. No man but he could have drawn that incredible bow. His arrow went right through his target's body.

Three seconds. Three dead mercenaries.

Belisarius had not watched. His eyes had never left those of the clan chieftain.

Now, he smiled. Tough old man. The chieftain was still glaring.

Again, softly, still in Hunnish: "You have a simple choice. You can disobey me, in which case no Hun will survive this battle. Or you can obey me, and share in the great booty from Nisibis."

Finally, something got through. The clan chieftain's eyes widened.

"Nisibis? *Nisibis?*"

Belisarius nodded. His smile widened.

The clan chieftain peered at him suspiciously.

"Nisibis is a great town," he said. "You do not have siege equipment."

Belisarius shrugged. "I have a few scorpions and onagers. We can let the Persians on the walls of Nisibis catch sight of them. But that doesn't matter. I have the most powerful weapon of all, clan leader. I have a great victory, and the fear which that victory will produce."

The clan leader hesitated still.

"Many Persian soldiers escaped. They will flee to Nisibis and tell—"

"Tell what, clan leader? The truth? And who will believe those soldiers? Those *defeated* soldiers—that routed rabble—when they tell the notables of Nisibis that they have nothing to fear from the Roman army which just destroyed them?"

The clan leader laughed. For all his barbarity, the man did not lack decisiveness. A moment later he was bellowing commands to his men. Without hesitation, the other two clan leaders joined their voices to his.

Huns with clan status took their leaders seriously. Those without clan status took the slaughtered corpses of three of their fellows seriously. Within two minutes, a small group of women and children were clustered under the shelter of the cataphracts. Some of them looked to have been badly abused, thought Belisarius, but it could have been worse. Much worse.

The Huns even began piling up their loot, but Belisarius told the clan leaders that the mercenaries could keep the booty. He simply wanted the survivors.

"Why do you care, Greek?" asked the old chieftain. The question was not asked belligerently. The man was simply puzzled.

Belisarius sighed. "I'm not Greek. I'm Thracian."

The chieftain snorted. "Then it makes no sense at all! Greeks are odd, everyone knows it. They think too much. But why—"

"A thousand years ago, chieftain, these people were already great with knowledge. At a time when your people and mine were no better than savages in skins."

Which is just about where you are still, thought Belisarius. But he didn't say it.

The clan chieftain frowned.

"I do not understand the point."

Belisarius sighed, turned away.

"I know," he muttered. "I know."

Two weeks later, Nisibis capitulated.

It was not a total capitulation, of course. The Romans would not march into the city. The notables needed that face-saving gesture to fend off the later wrath of the Persian emperor. And Belisarius, for his own reasons, did not want to risk such a triumphant entry. He thought he had his troops well under control, but—there was no temptation so great, especially to the mercenaries who made up a large part of the army, as the prospect of sacking a city without a siege.

No, best to avoid the problem entirely. Persians, like Romans, were civilized. Treasure lost was simply treasure lost. Forgotten soon enough. Atrocities burned memory into the centuries. The centuries of that stupid, pointless, endless warfare between Greek and Persian which had gone on too long already.

So, there was no march and no atrocities. But, of course, there was treasure lost aplenty. Oh, yes. Nisibis disgorged its hoarded wealth. Some of it in the form of outright tribute. The rest as ransom for the nobles. (Whom Nisibis would keep, in reasonably pleasant captivity, until the nobles repaid the ransom.)

The Romans marched away from the city with more booty than any of its soldiers had ever dreamed of. Within three days, as the word of victory spread, the army was surrounded by camp followers. Among these, in addition to the usual coterie, were a veritable host of avid liquidators. The soldiers of Belisarius' own army immediately converted their booty into portable specie and jewelry. They had learned from experience that their general's stern logistical methods made it impossible to haul about bulky treasure. Like the great Philip of ancient Macedon, Belisarius used mules for his supply train. The only wheeled vehicles he allowed were the field ambulances and the artillery engines.

Observing, and then questioning, the Army of Lebanon quickly followed their example.

A great general, Belisarius, a great general. A bit peculiar, perhaps. Unbelievably ruthless, in some ways. Tales were told, by campfire, of slaughtered Persian cavalry, and a decapitated chiliarch. The first brought grins of satisfaction, the last brought howls of glee. Strangely squeamish, in others. Tales were told of women and children returned, reasonably unharmed, to the Persians in Nisibis—and spitted Huns. The first brought heads shaking in bemusement, the last, howls of glee. (Even, after a day or so, to most Huns, whose sense of humor was not remotely squeamish.)

A peculiar general. But—a great general, no doubt about it. Best to adopt his ways.

Adding to the army's good cheer was the extraordinary largesse of the general's cataphracts. Fine fellows, those Thracians, the very best. Buy anyone a drink, anytime, at any place the army stopped. Which it did frequently. The great general was kind to victorious troops, and the host of camp followers set up impromptu *tabernae* at every nightfall. They seemed to be awash in wealth, the way they spread their money around.

Which, indeed, they were. As commanding general, Belisarius had come in for a huge percentage of the loot— half of which he had immediately distributed to his bucellarii, as was his own personal tradition. The tradition pleased his cataphracts immensely. It pleased Belisarius even more. Partly for the pleasure which generosity gave his warm heart. But more for the pleasure which calculation gave his cold, crooked brain. True, his cataphracts were devoted to him anyway, from their own customs and birthright. But it never hurt to cement that allegiance as tightly as possible.

No, he thought, remembering the head of a stubborn chiliarch; and the arrow-transfixed chests of Hun thugs, *it never hurts.*

Three individuals only, of that great army returning in triumph, did not share in the general joy and good will.

Two of them were brothers from Thrace. Who, though they had come through their recent experience essentially unharmed in body, were much aggrieved in their minds.

As Belisarius had suspected, Bouzes and Coutzes were not actually stupid. They had had plenty of time, in their captivity at Nisibis, to ponder events of the past. And to draw certain conclusions about a never-found pay caravan.

On the first night of the march back to Mindouos, the brothers had entered Belisarius' tent. Quite forcefully. They had shouldered Maurice aside, which would indicate that their recent conversion from stupidity was still shaky and skin deep. Then, they had confronted the general with his duplicity and treachery.

Within the next few minutes, Bouzes and Coutzes learned a lesson. Others had learned that lesson before them. Some, like a Hun clan chieftain, had even managed to survive the experience.

So did they, barely.

Belisarius gave them three simple choices.

One: They could acquiesce to his triumph, pretend that nothing untoward had happened, and salvage what was left of their reputations. With Belisarius' help, a suitable cover story would be manufactured. They would even come into their share of the booty.

Two: They could leave now and trumpet their outrage to the world. Within a year, if Justinian was feeling charitable due to his victory over the Persians, they would be feeding the hogs back at their estate in Thrace. Pouring slops into the trough. If the Emperor was not feeling charitable— charity was not his most outstanding trait—they would be feeding the hogs at one of Justinian's many estates. From *inside* the trough, since they themselves would be the slop.

Or, finally, if their outrage was simply too great to bear, they could choose yet a third alternative:

Valentinian.

The brothers, in the end, bade farewell to stupidity. Not easily, true, and not without bitter tears and warm embraces to their departing friend. But, in the end, they managed to send stupidity on his way.

By the very end of the evening, in fact, they were in quite a mellow mood. Large quantities of wine helped bring on that mellowness, as did the thought of large sums of booty. But, for the most part, it was brought by one small, fierce consolation.

At least—this time—honest Thracian lads had been swindled by another Thracian. Not by some damned Greek or Armenian.

After they left, Belisarius blew out the lantern and lay down on his cot.

He was exhausted, but sleep would not come. There was something he needed to know. He let his mind wander through its own labyrinth, until he found the place he had come to think of as the crack in the barrier.

He sensed the jewel's presence.

It was you, wasn't it? Helping me in the battle?

It was then that Belisarius discovered the third—individual?—who did not share in the general self-satisfaction of the army. The jewel's thoughts were incoherent, at first. Strangely, there seemed to be some underlying hostility to them. Not reproach, or accusation, as there had been before. More like—

Yes. Exasperation.

That's odd. Why would—

A thought suddenly came into focus.

yes. helped. difficult.

Then, with a definite sense of exasperation:

very difficult.

Then, much like a younger brother might say to a dimwitted elder:

stupid.

Stupid? What is stupid?

you stupid.

Belisarius sat up, astonished.

Me? Why am I stupid?

Extreme exasperation:

not you you. all you. all stupid.

Now, with great force:

cretins.

Belisarius was frowning fiercely. He couldn't begin to think what might have so upset the jewel.

He sensed a new concept, a new thought, trying to force its way through the barrier. But the thought fell away, defeated.

Suddenly a quick vision flashed through his mind:

A scene from the day's battle. A mass of cavalrymen, hacking away at each other, falling from their mounts. Knees clenched tightly on the barrel chests of horses. Hands clutching pommels. Men falling from their horses every time they were struck or misjudged their own blows.

cretins.

Another vision. Nothing but a quick flashing image:

A horseman galloping across the steppe. A barbarian of some kind. Belisarius did not recognize his tribe. He rode his horse with complete grace and confidence. The image flashed to his legs. His feet.

The thought finally burst through.

stirrups.

Belisarius' mouth fell open.

"I'll be Goddamned," he whispered. "Why didn't anybody ever think of that?"

stupid.

CONSTANTINOPLE
Autumn, 528 AD

Chapter 9

"The man of the hour!" cried Sittas. "O hail the triumphant conq'rer!" He drained his cup in one quaff. "I'd rise to greet you, Belisarius, but I'm afraid I'd swoon in the presence of so august a personage." He hiccuped. "I'm given to hero worship, you know. Terrible habit, just terrible." He seized the flagon resting on the small table next to his couch and waved it about. "I'd pour you a drink, too, but I'm afraid I'd spill the wine. Trembling in the company of so legendary a figure, you understand, like a giddy schoolgirl."

Sittas refilled the cup. His meaty hand was steady as a rock.

"Speaking of which," he continued, "—giddy schoolgirls, that is—let me introduce you to my friend." Sittas waved his other hand in the general direction of a woman sitting on the couch next to him. "Irene Macrembolitissa, I present you the famed General Belisarius. And his lovely wife, Antonina."

Belisarius advanced across the room and bowed politely— to the woman, not Sittas.

Irene was quite striking in appearance. Not pretty, precisely, but attractive in a bold sort of way. She had a light complexion, chestnut hair, brown eyes, and a large aquiline nose. She appeared to be in her late twenties, but Belisarius thought she might be older.

The calm, unreadable expression on Belisarius' face never wavered. But he was more than a little surprised. Irene was quite unlike Sittas' usual run of female "friends." By about fifteen years of age and, the general estimated, twice the intelligence.

"Don't look at him too closely, Irene!" warned Sittas. "You never know what can happen with these mythical demigod types. Probably get you pregnant just from his aura."

Irene smiled. "Please ignore him. He's pretending to be drunk."

"He's good at it," remarked Antonina. "As well he should be, as much practice as he gets."

A look of hurt innocence came upon Sittas' beefy face. It fit very poorly.

"I am mortified," he whined. "Outraged. Offended beyond measure." He drained his cup again, and reached for the flagon. "You see what your insults have done, vile woman? Driven me to drink, by God! To drink!"

Irene rose and went over to a long table against the far wall of the salon. She returned with a cup in each hand, and gave them to Belisarius and Antonina.

"Please have a seat," she said, motioning to another couch nearby. The large room was well-nigh littered with couches, all of them richly upholstered. The colors of the upholstery clashed wildly with the mosaics and tapestries which adorned all the walls. The wall coverings looked to be even more expensive than the couches, for all that they were in exquisitely bad taste.

After the general and his wife took a seat, Irene filled their cups from another flagon. She placed the flagon on a table and returned to her own couch.

"Sittas has told me much about you," Irene said.

"Did I tell you he has much better taste in furnishings?" muttered Sittas. His beady eyes scanned the room admiringly.

"Muskrats have better taste in furnishings than you do,

Sittas," murmured Irene sweetly. She smiled at Belisarius and Antonina. "Isn't this room hideous?" she asked.

Antonina laughed. "It's like a bear's den."

"A very rich bear," commented Sittas happily. "Who can well afford to ignore the petty artistic quibbling of the lesser sort. Plebeian envy, that's all it is." He leaned forward. "But enough of that! Let's hear it, Belisarius. I want the full account, mind you, the full account. I'll stand for none of your usual laconicness!"

"There's no such word, Sittas," said Irene.

" 'Course there is! I just used it, didn't I? How could I use a word that doesn't exist?" He grinned at Belisarius and began to take another swallow of wine. "Now—out with it! How in the world did you swindle the terrible twins out of their army?"

"I didn't swindle the twins out of their army. The whole idea's preposterous, and I'm astonished to hear you parroting it. Coutzes and Bouzes simply had the misfortune of being captured while leading a reconnaissance in force, and I was forced—"

Sittas choked; spewed wine out of his mouth.

"Even Justinian doesn't believe that malarkey!" he protested.

Belisarius smiled. "To the contrary, Sittas. I am just now returned from a formal audience with the Emperor, at which he indicated not the slightest disbelief in the official report of the battle."

"Well, of course he didn't! Coutzes and Bouzes are Thracian. Justinian's Thracian." Sittas eyed Belisarius suspiciously. "You're Thracian too, for that matter." He looked at Irene. "They stick together, you know." Another swallow. "Wretched rustics! A proper Greek nobleman doesn't stand a chance anymore." He glared at Belisarius. "You're not going to tell me, are you?"

Then, to Irene: "He probably swore an oath. He's always

swearing oaths. Swore his first oath when he was four, to a piglet. Swore he'd never let anyone eat the creature. Kept his oath, too. They say the pig's still around, roaming the countryside, devouring everything in sight. The Bane of Thrace, the thing's called now. The peasants are crying out for a new Hercules to come and rid them of the monster." A belch. "That's what comes of swearing oaths. Never touch the things, myself."

He glared at Belisarius again, then heaved a sigh of resignation. "All right, then. Forget the juicy stuff. Tell me about the battle."

"I'm sure you've already heard all about it."

Sittas sneered. "That crap! By the time courtiers and imperial heralds get through with the tale of a battle, there's nothing in it a soldier would recognize." He scowled. "Unfortunately, whatever his other many talents, our Emperor is no soldier. The court's getting worse, Belisarius. It's getting packed with creatures like John of Cappadocia and Narses. And the most wretched crowd of quarreling churchmen you ever saw, even by the low standards of that lot."

"Don't underestimate Narses and John of Cappadocia," said Irene, lightly but seriously.

"I'm not underestimating them! But—ah, never mind. Later. For the moment—" He set down his cup and leaned forward, elbows on knees. The keen eyes which now gazed at Belisarius had not the slightest trace of drunkenness in them.

Most people, upon meeting Sittas, were struck by his resemblance to a hog. The same girth, the same heavy limbs, the same pinkish hide—unusually fair for a Greek—the same jowls, blunt snoutish nose, beady little eyes. Belisarius, gazing back at his best friend, thought the resemblance wasn't inappropriate. So long as you remembered that there are hogs, and then there are hogs. There is the slothful domestic hog in his wallow, a figure of fun and feast. And then, there is the great wild boar of the forest, whose gaze makes bowels turn to water. Whose tusks make widows and orphans.

"The battle," commanded the boar.

Belisarius made no attempt to cut short his recital of the battle. Sittas was himself an accomplished general, and Belisarius knew full well that his friend would not tolerate an abbreviated or sanitized version of the tale. And whatever minor aspects Belisarius overlooked, Sittas was quick to bring forward by his shrewd questioning.

When he was done, Sittas leaned back in his couch and regarded Belisarius silently. Then: "Why?"

"Why what?"

"Don't play with me, Belisarius! You provoked the Medes, when you could have stalled. And then you took enough chances to give the Fates themselves apoplexy. *Why?* There was no point to that battle, and you know it as well as I do." He waved his hand disgustedly. "Oh, sure, as the courtiers never tire of saying, it's the greatest victory over the Persians in a century. *So what?* We've been at war with Persia for two thirds of a millennia. Longer than that, for us Greeks. Never be an end to it, unless common sense suddenly rears its ugly head upon the thrones. We're not strong enough to conquer Persia, and the Medes aren't strong enough to conquer us. All this warring does is depopulate the border areas and drain both empires. That's my opinion. And it's your opinion, too, unless you've suddenly been seized by delusions of grandeur. So I ask again: *why?*"

Belisarius was silent. After a moment, Irene smiled faintly and rose.

"May I show you the gardens, Antonina?"

❖   ❖   ❖

Once they were in the gardens, Antonina took a seat on a stone bench.

"You needn't bother," she said. "I've seen them before."

Irene sat next to her. "Aren't they something? I'm afraid Sittas' taste in horticulture is every bit as grotesque as his taste in furnishings."

Antonina smiled. Her eye was caught by a statue. The smile turned to a grimace.

"Not to mention his taste in sculpture."

The two women stared at each other for a moment.

"You'd like to know who I am," said Irene.

Antonina nodded. Irene cocked her head quizzically.

"I'm curious. Why do you assume that I'm something other than Sittas' latest bedmate?"

"Two reasons. You're not his taste in women, not even close. And, if you were one of his usual bedmates, he'd never have invited you to sit in on this meeting."

Irene chuckled. "I'm his spy," she said.

Seeing the startled look on Antonina's face, Irene held up a reassuring hand. "I'm afraid that didn't come out right. I'm not spying on *you*." She pursed her lips. "It would be more accurate to say that I'm Sittas' spymaster. That's why he asked me to join him in this—meeting. He is concerned, Antonina."

"About what? And since when has Sittas needed a spymaster?"

It was Irene's turn to look startled. "He's had a spymaster since he was a boy, practically. All Greek noblemen of his class do."

Antonina snorted. "You mean Apollinaris? That pitiful old coot couldn't find his ass with both hands."

Irene smiled. "Oh, I believe Apollinaris could manage that task well enough. In broad daylight, at least. At night, I admit, he would have considerable difficulty." She brushed back her hair, hesitated, then said:

"About a year ago, Sittas decided he needed a real spymaster. He inquired in various places, and my services came highly recommended. He retired Apollinaris—on a very nice pension, by the way—and hired me. My cover, so to speak, is that I am his latest paramour."

She pursed her lips. "As deceptions go, it has its weaknesses. As you say, I'm not really his type."

"That's putting it mildly."

"Can you tell me what's going on in there?" asked Irene, gesturing with her head toward the door to the mansion.

"No," replied Antonina. "Not yet, at least. Later—perhaps. But not now."

Irene accepted the refusal without protest. A servant appeared, bearing a platter of food and wine, which he set upon a nearby table. Antonina and Irene moved over to the table and spent the next few minutes in companionable silence, enjoying their meal. Whatever his lack of taste in furnishings, neither woman could fault the excellence of Sittas' kitchen.

Pushing aside her plate, Antonina spoke.

"Please answer the question I asked earlier."

Irene's response was immediate. "The reason Sittas is concerned enough to hire me—and my services don't come cheaply—is because there's skullduggery in Constantinople."

Antonina snorted. "Please, Irene! Saying there's skullduggery in Constantinople is like saying there's shit in a pigsty."

Irene nodded. "True. Perhaps I should say: there's a lot more skullduggery going on than usual, and, what's of much greater concern, the nature of it's unclear. *Something is afoot in Constantinople, Antonina.* Something deep, and well hidden, and cunning, and utterly treacherous. What it is, I have not yet been able to discover. But I can sense it, I can taste it, I can smell it." Again, she groped for words. "It is—*there*. Trust me."

Antonina arose and began pacing about the garden. She

glanced at the door which led back to the interior of the mansion.

"Will they be finished yet?" asked Irene.

Antonina shook her head. "No. Sittas will—need time to recover."

Irene frowned. "Recover from what?"

Antonina held up a hand, stilling her. She continued to pace about, frowning. Irene, with the patience of a professional, simply sat and waited.

After a while, Antonina stopped pacing and came over to Irene. She paused, took a deep breath. Hesitated again.

A voice came from the doorway. A horrible, croaking voice.

"Come inside, both of you."

Irene gasped. Sittas looked positively haggard. He seemed to have shed fifty pounds.

Once they were back in the salon, seated on their couches, Sittas croaked:

"Tell her, Belisarius."

Belisarius stared at Irene.

"I haven't even told Maurice, Sittas."

"Of course not! There's no reason to, at this point. But we need Irene. *Now.*"

Belisarius remained silent, still examining Irene. Sittas' back curved, his great shoulders hunched, his snout thrust forward. The wild, red-eyed boar spoke:

"*Tell her.*"

Belisarius transferred his gaze to Sittas. The boar was in full fury now, tusks glistening.

"*Tell her!*"

Belisarius' calm eyes never wavered. He was a Thracian, reared in the countryside. He'd speared his first boar when he was twelve.

The red glare faded from Sittas' eyes, replaced, suddenly, by a shrug. And then, a wide grin.

"Funny, that usually works. Damned Thracians! But you may as well tell her, Belisarius. She'll winkle it out of me, anyway, unless I fire her. Which is the last thing I'd do now."

Belisarius looked at Antonina. His wife nodded.

"Tell her, husband. I trust her."

Chapter 10

When Belisarius was finished, Irene looked at her employer. The normal pink coloring had returned to Sittas' hide, but his face still looked almost drawn beneath the jowls.

"Believe, Irene," he said. "He only gave you the gist of it, but—" Sittas drew in a deep breath. "I held the jewel and saw— Never mind. Just believe it."

"May I see it?" she asked. Belisarius reached into his coat and withdrew the jewel. Irene rose and walked over, stooped, examined the thing. After a moment, she returned to her seat.

"It makes sense," she said, nodding. "Actually, it clarifies much that was obscure." Seeing the questioning looks around her, she elaborated:

"I've been encountering occasional tips, obscure hints, that pointed toward India as the source of the current— disturbances. Much of it, at least. But I discounted the rumors. India is far away, and except for trade, far removed from the normal concerns of Rome. I assumed the converse must also be true. What interest could India possibly have in the machinations of the Byzantine court?"

"What do you know about India?" asked Antonina.

Irene shrugged. "Which India? Don't forget, Antonina,

India is a huge place. It's larger than Europe, in area alone, and much more densely populated. It's the biggest mistake Westerners make, actually. We try to imagine India as a single country, rather than a continent."

She rose again and poured herself some wine. Then filled Sittas' cup to the brim. This time, his hand *was* shaking. Slightly. She offered some wine to Belisarius and Antonina, but they declined. Irene resumed her seat and continued.

"India hasn't been unified under one throne for over half a millenium, not since the Mauryan Empire collapsed. The Gupta Empire which eventually replaced it was confined to north India. The south remained under the control of independent monarchs."

She hesitated again, her eyes slightly unfocused. It was obvious she was recalling information.

"Or, at least, that was true until recently. The Gupta Empire broke in half, a few decades ago, and the western half was invaded by the White Huns. The Ephthalites, as we call them. Also known as—"

"Ye-tai," interjected Belisarius.

Irene nodded. "The White Huns—or Ye-tai—were apparently beaten back, and then some sort of accommodation was reached between them and the western dynasty, the Malwa. The Malwa dynasty, from what I've been able to glean, has since been expanding rapidly. They've finished reconquering most of north India, although they're apparently plagued with rebellions. And now, according to a few informants, they've begun their conquest of the south. They are at war now with the greatest, and most northerly, of the southern realms. A place called—"

She hesitated, frowned, tried to dredge up the memory.

"Andhra," stated Belisarius. "Ruled by the Satavahana dynasty."

Irene nodded. "That's about all I know. To be honest, I never pursued the matter. India, as I said, seemed much too remote to be a real danger to Rome and, in any event, they were obviously preoccupied with their own problems."

She waved a hand, dismissively. "And then, too, most of the tales you hear about India are at least half fantastical. Especially tales about the Malwa. Gods that walk the earth, magic weapons—" She stopped, stared at Belisarius.

"Magic weapons, indeed," grunted Belisarius. "We've had no luck duplicating them."

Irene looked at the general's wife.

"Belisarius is being too pessimistic," said Antonina. "We've only just gotten started in that work. It's only been a few months since we first encountered the jewel ourselves. It's taken that long to get established on the estate which Cassian gave us. John of Rhodes has been in residence now for only three months, and the workshop has barely been set up." She shook her head firmly. "So, under the circumstances, I think it's much too early to make any clear assessment of our success in duplicating the Malwa weapons."

"Has the jewel been of any help?" asked Sittas.

Belisarius shook his head. "No, not in that regard. I can sense that it's trying, but—it is very difficult for the thing to communicate with me, except through visions. And those aren't very useful when it comes to weaponry." Strangely, he grinned. "As a rule, I should say. However—we must have a joust soon, Sittas!"

His enormous friend sneered. "Why? I'll just knock you on your ass like I always do. Shrimp."

Belisarius grinned evilly. "You're in for a surprise, large one. The jewel *has* succeeded in giving me one simple new device. Simple, but I guarantee it will revolutionize the cavalry."

Sittas looked skeptical. "What is it? A magic lance?"

"Oh, nothing that elaborate. Just a simple little gadget called *stirrups*." He grinned again, *very* evilly. "By all means. A joust—and soon!"

Belisarius turned back to Irene. "Where does the Malwa conquest of south India stand now?"

Irene frowned. "I really don't know. As of my last report, which was three months ago, the Malwa had just begun their siege of the Andhra capital." She paused, estimating time factors. "Given that the report itself probably took months to get here, I would assume the siege began approximately a year ago. Apparently, it's expected to be a long siege. The Andhra capital is reported to be well fortified. It's located at a place called—" She hesitated, looked away, again trying to bring up the information.

"It is located at a place called Amavarati," said Belisarius. The general continued, seeming for all the world, like a man possessed by a vision. "In a short while the palace will fall to the Malwa. Within the palace is a young princess named Shakuntala. She will be the only survivor of the dynasty. She will be captured and taken north to the palace of a high Malwa official, destined to be his concubine. A man will be lying in the reeds outside, wounded. His name is Raghunath Rao. When he recovers from his wounds, he will go north himself, tracking the princess and her captors. He will find her at the palace, but will be unable to rescue her in time. Before he can do so, the owner of the palace will return from some mission he was sent on by the Malwa emperor. He will die then, as will the princess."

Belisarius clenched his teeth, remembering another man's hatred.

"The Vile One, that official is called. Venandakatra. Venandakatra the Vile."

Irene shot to her feet. "Venandakatra?" she demanded. "You are sure of that name?"

Belisarius stared at her. "Quite sure. It is a name burned into my memory. Why?"

"He's here! In Constantinople!"

❖   ❖   ❖

When the uproar which followed Irene's announcement subsided, Belisarius resumed his seat.

"So *that's* the mysterious mission Venandakatra was sent on," murmured Belisarius.

"This doesn't make sense," complained Sittas. "I've met the fellow myself, by the way. At one of the endless receptions at the Great Palace. A greasy sort, he struck me. But I spent no time with him. He presented himself as simply a modest envoy seeking to expand trading opportunities with Rome." Sittas waved his hand airily. "Not my interest, that sort of thing."

Irene snorted. "Just the money that comes from it."

Sittas grinned. "Well, yes. I believe my family does have a small interest in the Indian trade."

"They control at least a fourth of it," retorted Irene. "If not more. Your family are no slouches themselves when it comes to keeping secrets."

Again, the airy wave of the hand. "Yes, yes, no doubt. But I leave that business to my innumerable cousins. The point I was trying to make, before I was so rudely interrupted, is that this Venandakatra sounds like far too powerful an official to be sent on such a paltry mission. Are you sure we're talking about the same man? The name Venandakatra, after all, might be quite common in India."

Belisarius shook his head and began to speak. Irene interrupted him.

"Stick to your trade, Sittas. The whole thing makes perfect sense, if we assume that the jewel's visions of the future are accurate. Which"—a glance at Belisarius—"they obviously are. Venandakatra doesn't give a fig for trade. That's just a story to explain his presence. He's actually here to scout the territory, so to speak, and to lay the groundwork for the future attack on Rome."

She stopped, concentrated, continued:

"His cover, however, makes him vulnerable. He doesn't

have a large retinue with him. He couldn't, not posing as a simple trading envoy. It wouldn't be difficult at all to have him assassinated."

"*No.*"

Irene looked at Belisarius, startled.

"Why in the world not? I didn't get the impression you were any too fond of the man."

Belisarius tightened his jaws. "You cannot begin to imagine how much I despise him. But it's not for us to cut his throat."

He rose and began pacing, working off nervous energy. He reached a hand into his cloak, pulled out a sheathed dagger, stared down at it. Slowly, he drew the dagger from its sheath.

"I carry this with me always, now. It's been like a compulsion. Or a charm."

He straightened up. "But I think it's time to return the dagger to its rightful owner. I must go to India and find Raghunath Rao."

Antonina was pale, her hand at her throat.

"You can't be serious," stated Sittas forcefully. "You're needed here, Belisarius! Not gallivanting around India. Good Lord! Irene's right, you know—India's immense, and you don't know anything about the place. Even if this man's still alive, how will you find him?"

Belisarius smiled his crooked smile.

"So long as Venandakatra is alive, I will know where to find Rao. Lurking nearby, like a panther waiting to strike, if he can see even the slightest opening. I will go to India, and I will find that man, and I will give him back his dagger and, somehow, I will give him his opening."

He turned to Irene. "*That's* why Venandakatra can't be assassinated. It is essential that we forge an alliance with Raghunath Rao. And through him, with the surviving heir of the Satavahana dynasty. To do so, we must find him— and to find him, we need Venandakatra alive."

Antonina cleared her throat. "But, husband, such a trip—"

"Will take at least a year," finished Belisarius. "I know, love. But it must be done."

"I think it's an excellent idea," said Irene firmly. She paused for a moment, allowing her statement to register on Antonina and Sittas. The two were obviously surprised to hear the spymaster side with Belisarius in what seemed to them a half-baked, impulsive scheme. Once Irene saw that she had their full attention, she continued.

"Like Sittas, I do not understand why Belisarius thinks this man Rao is so important. Or this Princess Shakuntala. Although—" She stared at the general, gauging. "I will gladly accept his judgment. So should you, Sittas. Didn't you once tell me Belisarius is the most brilliant Roman general since Scipio Africanus? I suspect that same general is working on some grand strategy."

Irene spread her hands in a gesture of finality. "But it doesn't matter, because Belisarius should go to India in any event. For one thing, we *must* obtain the best possible information concerning India. Especially its military capacity, and its new weapons. Who better to do that than Rome's best general?"

Sittas began to speak. Irene drove him down.

"Nonsense, yourself! You said he was needed here. *For what?* The Persian defeat will keep the Medes licking their wounds for at least a year. Several years, I estimate. So there won't be any danger from that quarter for a time."

She drove over his protest again. "And even if the Persians do start making trouble before Belisarius gets back, I say again: *so what?* He may be Rome's best general, but he's not the only good one. You yourself are currently unemployed, except for those parade ground duties that bore you to death."

She paused. A particularly garish tapestry hanging on the

wall opposite caught her eye. Even in the seriousness of the moment, she found it difficult not to laugh. Her employer had obviously been the model for the heroic figure portrayed in the tapestry. A mounted cataphract in full armor, slaying some kind of monstrous beast with a lance.

"Is that a lion?" she asked lightly.

Sittas glared at the tapestry.

"It's a *dragon*," he growled.

"I didn't realize dragons were furry," commented Antonina idly. She and Irene exchanged a quick, amused glance. Sittas began to snarl something, but Belisarius cut him off.

"Let's get back to the point," he said firmly. "I think Irene's suggestion is a good one. We might be able to get Sittas assigned to replace me in command of the army in Syria. That would put him close to the estate where Antonina's doing her work. With Sittas nearby, she'd still have access to expert military expertise when she needed it."

Irene drove over Antonina's gathering protest.

"*You are not thinking, woman!* You're worrying over Belisarius' safety and fretting over his prolonged absence." The spymaster was suddenly as cold as ice. "You are being a fool, Antonina. The worst danger to Belisarius isn't in India. It's right here in Constantinople. Better he should be gone for a year or so in India, than gone forever in a grave."

Startled, Antonina stared at her husband. Belisarius nodded.

"She's right, love. That's part of my thinking. *Justinian*."

Antonina now looked at the spymaster. Irene grimaced.

"At the moment," she said, "the greatest danger to Belisarius does come from Justinian. There's nothing the Emperor dreads so much as a great general. Especially one as popular as Belisarius is today, after his victory over the Persians."

"An expedition to India would be perfect, from that point

of view," chimed in Belisarius. "Get me out of Constantinople, away from the Emperor's suspicions and fears."

Irene brushed back her hair, thinking.

"Actually, if the whole thing's presented properly, Justinian will probably jump at it. He's not insane, you know. If he can avoid it, he'd much rather keep Belisarius alive. You never know when he might need a great general again, after all. But sending him to India, off and away for at least a year—oh, yes, I think he'd like that idea immensely. Get Belisarius completely out of the picture for a time, until the current hero worship dies down."

Antonina's face was pinched. "How soon?" she whispered.

"Not for at least six months," said Belisarius. "Probably seven."

Antonina looked relieved, but puzzled.

"Why so long?" she asked.

"The trade with India," replied her husband, "depends on the monsoon seasons. The monsoon winds blow one way part of the year, the other way during the other part. You travel from India to the west from November through April. You go the other way—my way, that is—from July through October."

He held up his hand, fingers outspread, and began counting off.

"We're in the beginning of October. It's too late to catch the eastward monsoon for this year. It's almost over, and it would take at least a month or two to reach the Erythrean Sea. That means I can't leave for India until the beginning of July, next year. Mind you, that refers to the part of the trip beginning at the south end of the Red Sea. Figure another month—no, two—to get from here through the Red Sea."

He began to calculate; Irene cut him short.

"You won't be leaving Constantinople for India until April, at the earliest. Probably May. Which, incidentally, is when

Venandakatra has already announced he plans to return to his homeland."

Antonina's initial relief vanished.

"But—Irene, from what you've already said, *now* is the most dangerous time for Belisarius to be in Constantinople. Six months! Who knows what Justinian might do in six months?"

Irene brushed back her hair. "I know, I've been thinking about it while Belisarius was explaining the maritime facts of life. And I think I have a solution."

She looked at Belisarius.

"Are you familiar with Axum?"

"The kingdom of the Ethiopians?" asked Belisarius. "No, not really. I've met a few Axumites, here and there. But— I'm a general, so there's never been any occasion for me to encounter them professionally. Rome and Axum have gotten along just fine for centuries. Why?"

"I see a chance to kill two birds with one stone. As it happens, Venandakatra's is not the only foreign mission in Constantinople at the moment. There's also an Axumite embassy. They arrived two months ago. The embassy is officially headed by King Kaleb's younger son, Eon Bisi Dakuen. He's only nineteen years old. Barely more than a boy, although I've heard that he's made a good impression. But I think the actual leader of the embassy is Eon's chief adviser, a man named Garmat."

"So?"

"So—this Garmat, by all accounts, is quite a canny fellow. And, I've heard, he's been dropping hints here and there of the desire of the Axumites to forge closer ties to Rome."

She paused, savoring the little bombshell.

"I didn't think much of it, when I first heard. But it seems the Axumites are concerned over developments in India. Which, they are suggesting, pose long-term problems for Rome. And Garmat is quite frustrated that he's getting no reception to his message. Apparently, he's already announced that he'll be returning to Axum shortly."

She allowed the silence to continue for a moment.

"So, I have reason to think that the Axumites would welcome a friendly overture from some notable Roman figure. Such as a famous general who's invited them to tour Syria on their way back to Ethiopia. A tour which he would present to Emperor Justinian as the first leg of a *very* lengthy mission which would eventually take him to India. *After* spending a few months visiting Axum, which, conveniently enough, is located right on the way to India."

"The perfect place to wait for the monsoon," mused Belisarius. "Out of sight, out of mind. Axum's as remote as India, as far Justinian cares."

He rose and began pacing again. His eyes narrowed, and he peered sharply at Irene.

"There's more."

Irene nodded. "Yes. First of all, such a tour would give you and Antonina a chance to return to your estate and spend some time there before you went on. I imagine that would be useful, for your armaments project."

"And?"

"And—in light of what I've learned today, I think Rome should take Axum's warning very seriously. *And Axum itself.* The truth is, we don't really know much about them. Other than the fact that they've always had good relations with us, and that they've been Christians for two centuries, and that they have a naval capability."

"Aren't they at war in Arabia now?" asked Sittas.

"Yes," replied the spymaster. "They invaded southern Arabia three years ago. They overthrew the King of Hymria, Yusuf Asar Yathar. The ostensible reason was that King Yusuf had adopted Judaism and was persecuting the Christian Arabs." She chuckled harshly. "That does not, of course, explain why they conquered the rest of southwestern Arabia."

"You think they might be allies?" asked Belisarius. "Against India?"

Irene shrugged. "That's for you to find out, General. On your way to India."

Belisarius was silent, for a time. Pacing.

"I think that's it, then, for the moment," he said at length. He turned to Antonina.

"See if you can arrange a meeting with Theodora, love. I think that would be the best way to broach the subject to Justinian."

He took Antonina's hand and helped her to her feet. Then, before turning to the door, looked at Sittas.

"Well, there's a couple of other small points. The first, my oversized and overconfident friend, is that I will expect you tomorrow at the practice field of your army. In full armor, mind. You'll need it."

Sittas grunted. "And the other?"

Belisarius nodded toward Irene.

"Whatever you're paying her, double it."

Chapter 11

The next morning, watching Belisarius approach him on the training field, Sittas decided that his friend had spent too much time in the Syrian sun. His brains were obviously fried.

Belisarius' challenge had been idiotic in the first place. On foot, with swords, Sittas suspected that his friend would carve him like a roast. But on horseback, in full armor, in a lance charge—well! The shrimp didn't stand a chance in hell.

Sittas was not guessing. Facts were facts. Sittas did not have Belisarius' speed and reflexes, but that mattered little in a lance charge. In a lance charge, wearing full armor atop a huge war-horse that was itself half-armored, weight and strength were what mattered.

Sittas almost slapped his great belly in self-satisfaction. He'd jousted with Belisarius before, several times, and always with the same result. Belisarius, on his ass, contemplating the futility of matching skills with the best lancer in Byzantium.

And now! The fool wasn't even holding his lance properly! Belisarius was carrying his lance cradled under his arm, instead of in the proper overhand position. Ridiculous! How could he expect to bring any force into the lance thrust?

Any novice knew the only way to drive a lance home, on horseback, was to bring the whole weight of the back and shoulder into a downward thrust.

Off to the side of the training field, perched on a stone wall, Sittas spotted a small group of boys watching the joust. From their animated discourse, it was obvious that even barefoot street urchins were deriding Belisarius' preposterous methods.

Seeing Belisarius begin his charge, Sittas set his own horse into motion. As they neared each other, Sittas saw that his friend's bizarre method of holding his lance had the one advantage of accuracy. The blunted tip of the practice lance was unerringly aimed right at Sittas' belly.

He almost laughed. Accuracy be damned! There wouldn't be any force at all behind an underhand thrust. His shield would deflect it easily.

The moment was upon them. Sittas saw that Belisarius' lance would strike first. He positioned his shield and raised his own lance high above his head.

Some time later, after a semblance of consciousness returned, Sittas decided he had collided with a wall. How else explain his position? On the ground, on his ass, feeling like one giant bruise.

He gazed up, blearily. Belisarius was looking down at him from atop his horse.

"Are you alive?"

Sittas snarled. "What happened?"

"I knocked you on your ass, that's what happened."

"Crap! I ran into a wall."

Belisarius laughed. Sittas roared and staggered to his feet. "Where's my horse?"

"Right behind you, like a good warhorse."

Sure enough. Sittas saw his lance lying on the ground nearby. He grabbed it and stalked to his horse. He was so furious that he even tried to mount the horse unassisted.

The attempt was hopeless, of course. After a few seconds of futility, Sittas left off and began leading his horse to the mounting platform at the edge of the field.

He was spared that little indignity, however. One of the urchins on the wall leapt nimbly onto the field and hurried to fetch him a mounting stool. As he clambered back upon his horse, Sittas favored the boy with a growling thanks.

" 'Twere just bad luck, lord," piped the lad. Then, with the absolute confidence possessed only by eight-year-old boys: "Yon loon don't no nothin' 'bout lance work!"

"Quite right," snarled Sittas. To Belisarius, in a bellow: "Again! Pure luck!"

This time, as the collision neared, Sittas concentrated almost entirely on his shield work. He had already decided that his mishap had been due to overconfidence. He'd been so preoccupied with planning his own thrust that he hadn't deflected Belisarius' lance properly.

Oh, but he had him now—oh, yes! His shield was perfectly positioned and solidly braced against his chest. Ha! The luck of Thrace was about to run out!

Some time later, after a semblance of consciousness returned, Sittas decided he had collided with a cathedral. How else explain his position? On the ground, flat on his back, feeling like one giant corpse.

Hazily, he saw Belisarius kneeling over him.

"What happened?" he croaked.

Belisarius smiled his crooked smile. "You ran into a *stirrup*. A pair of stirrups, I should say."

"What the hell kind of cathedral is a stirrup?" demanded Sittas. "And what idiot put two of them on a training field?"

Later, as they rode back toward his mansion along a busy commercial thoroughfare, Sittas uttered words of gentle reproach.

"You *cheated*, you stinking bastard!" he bellowed, for the

hundredth time. For the hundredth time, he glared down at the—*stirrups*. No wild boar of the forest ever glared a redder-eyed glare of rage.

"Marvelous, aren't they?" beamed Belisarius. He stood up straight in the saddle, twisting back and forth, bestowing his cheerful gaze upon the various merchants watching from their little shops.

"Improves visibility, too. See, Sittas! You can look all around, without ever having to worry about your balance. You can even draw your bow and shoot straight over your back as you're withdrawing."

"You *cheated*, you dog!"

"And, of course, you already saw how much more effectively you can wield a lance. No more of that clumsy overhand business! No, no. With stirrups you can use a lance properly, with all your own weight and the weight of your mount behind the thrust, instead of being a spear-chucker sitting awkwardly on a horse."

"You *cheated*, you—"

"You could always have a pair of them made for yourself, you know."

Sittas glared down, again, at the *stirrups*.

"Believe I will," he muttered. Another red-eyed glare at Belisarius.

"*Then* we'll have *another* duel!"

Belisarius grinned.

"Oh, I don't see any point to that. We're getting on in years, Sittas. We're responsible generals, now. Got to stop acting like foolish boys."

"You *cheater!*"

When they rode into the courtyard of Sittas' mansion, Antonina and Irene were standing there waiting. Both women seemed worried.

"He *cheated!*" roared Sittas.

"Not quite the conversationalist he used to be, is he?" commented Belisarius cheerfully as he dismounted.

Sittas began to roar again, but Irene silenced him.

"Shut up! We've been waiting for you two idiots to return. Belisarius! You've got an audience with Theodora—and you're already late!"

Antonina shook her head angrily. "Look at them! Refusing to admit they're getting on in years. You're responsible generals, now, you clowns! You've got to stop acting like foolish boys!"

Sittas clamped shut his great jaws.

"You've *already* set up an audience with Theodora?" demanded Belisarius, gaping.

Irene smiled. "Yes. I'd like to claim it's due to my talents as an intriguer, but the truth is that Antonina was the key. I'd always heard Theodora considered Antonina her best friend, but I hadn't really believed it until now."

The smile vanished, replaced by a frown.

"We have to go immediately, *but*—"

"He can't go in full armor!" protested Antonina.

"I'll be dressed in a moment," said Belisarius. He clattered into the mansion.

"Watch out for the rugs!" roared Sittas.

"Please," muttered Irene. "Make sure you gouge up as many as possible." She smiled sweetly at Sittas.

"What happened to you, anyway?"

"Yes, Sittas," added Antonina, smiling just as sweetly. "We're curious. Did you run into a wall?"

"Looks more like he ran into a cathedral," mused Irene. "You see that one great bruise? There—on his—"

"He *cheated*!"

"Stop worrying, Antonina. Of course I'll support Belisarius in this elaborate scheme of yours."

The Empress stared out the window of her reception

room. The view was magnificent, the more so since the Empress could well afford the finest glass. The panes of glass in *her* windows had not a trace of the discolorations and distortions which most glass contained.

Theodora never tired of the view from the Gynaeceum, the women's quarters of the Great Palace. It was not so much the scenery beyond—though the sight of the great city was magnificent—as it was the constant reminder of her own power. Within the women's quarters, the Empress was supreme. That had been Byzantine custom even before she mounted the throne, and it was a custom into which Theodora had thrust the full force of her personality.

Here, Theodora ruled unchallenged. She was the sole mistress not only of her own chambers but of the public offices as well. And it was here, in the Gynaeceum, that the silk goods, which were a royal monopoly, were woven. Those silk goods were one of the major sources of imperial wealth.

Without Theodora's permission, not even the Emperor could enter the Gynaeceum. And it was a permission which Theodora never gave him. She had too much to hide. Not lovers, of course. Theodora knew that were she to entertain lovers, word would get to Justinian. But the temptation never arose, in any event. Theodora had no interest in men, except Justinian.

No, not lovers; but there were other things to hide. Religious leaders, mostly. Monophysite heretics seeking refuge from the persecution that was developing again could find sanctuary in the secret rooms of the Gynaeceum.

Theodora scowled. For all that he was personally tolerant, and knew his own Empress to be a Monophysite, Justinian was seeking closer ties with the See of Rome. He hoped, Theodora knew, to gain orthodox approval for his projected reconquest of the western Empire. That approval came with a price—*eradicate heresy*.

It was a price which Theodora, for reasons of state even more than personal preference, thought far too costly for the prospective gain. The real strength of the Empire was in the Monophysite east—in Syria and Palestine and, especially, in Egypt. Why enfeeble the Empire's hold over those great provinces in order to gain the approval of a miserable pope squatting in Italy, surrounded by semibarbarian Goths? Who were Arian heretics themselves. No, it—

She shook her head, driving away the thoughts. Later. For now, there was this other matter.

She turned away from the window and smiled at Antonina. Then she smiled at Belisarius. The first smile was heartfelt. The second was—not. Or, at least, not very.

Briefly, the Empress examined her feelings in that cold and dispassionate way that was one of her great strengths. In truth, she liked Belisarius. It was just that she found it impossible to trust any man. She did not even trust Justinian, for all that she genuinely loved him. But—as men went, Belisarius was not bad. He had been good to Antonina, after all. And Theodora thought, approvingly, that his wife had the general well under her thumb. Whether or not Belisarius could be trusted, she trusted Antonina.

The Empress resumed her seat upon the throne which sat in a corner. The throne fit awkwardly in the confines of the private reception room. True, the room itself was luxurious. The floors were covered with exquisite Armenian rugs, the walls with even more exquisite mosaics and tapestries. Still, it was much too small a room to manage the bulk of a throne properly.

Yet even here, in the privacy of her own quarters, Theodora insisted on a throne. A relatively modest throne, to be sure, nothing like the monstrosity upon which she sat in the great reception hall of the palace. But it was a throne nonetheless.

It was one of her own foibles, she knew. The throne was not as comfortable as a normal chair would have been, but— she remembered the years of poverty and powerlessness. The years when she obeyed men, rather than the other way around. And so, everywhere she planted her very attractive imperial rump, she insisted on a throne.

"I just don't like to have my intelligence insulted," she growled. The Empress straightened. As tall as she was, sitting high up on a throne, the pose made her loom over her audience. Exactly as she intended.

"It's perfectly obvious that you're looking for an excuse to get away from Justinian's insanely jealous eye, Belisarius."

Seeing the slight look of startlement on the general's face, Theodora laughed.

"You think it strange that I understand my husband's peculiarities?"

Belisarius examined the Empress. She was a beautiful woman, very shapely in a slender sort of way. An Egyptian like Antonina, she shared his wife's dark complexion. But where Antonina's green eyes were a startlement in her dusky face, the Empress' eyes were so deep a brown as to be almost black. Her hair also was black, as little of it as could be seen in the jewel-encrusted coiffure.

He decided that honesty was probably the best course, under the circumstances. He did not know Theodora well, but he did not mistake the cold intelligence in those dark eyes.

"I am not surprised that you understand the Emperor's— characteristics. I am simply a bit puzzled that you understand him so well and—" He faltered. This was perhaps pushing honesty a bit far.

The Empress concluded for him.

"And still love him?"

Belisarius nodded. "Yes." He took a deep breath. Hell with it. The general knew from experience that it was unwise to change strategy in midbattle. "And are quite devoted to him. Even a man as removed as I am from the imperial court can tell that much."

The Empress chuckled. "I suggest you don't try to understand it. I don't myself, not entirely, and I suspect I'm much better than you at understanding such things. But the fact is, I do love Justinian, and I am quite devoted to him. Do not ever doubt it." She bestowed upon him a cold, deadly, imperial gaze. But only for a few seconds. Belisarius, she realized, was not one to be intimidated. Nor, she thought, was there any reason to do so.

Theodora smiled again. "One of the facts which *is*, and unfortunately, remains, is that my husband is prone to extreme jealousy. An imperial kind of jealousy, to boot, which is the worst variety."

She sighed. "It would be so much better if he'd fret himself over my fidelity, like most men. There'd be nothing in it, and I could spend some pleasurable hours reassuring him of his potency. But, not Justinian. He frets only royal frets, I'm afraid. The greatest of which is being overthrown by a rival. Especially a successful general.

"In fact, the threat's real enough. In general, at least. I just wish Justinian would stop being obsessed with the matter."

She mused. "At the moment, the two most successful and esteemed generals of the empire are you and Sittas." A small laugh. "Not even Justinian worries about Sittas! Outside of war, Sittas is the laziest man alive. And he can't stand the duties of a general in Constantinople—everyone knows it. He's been pestering Justinian for months to be reassigned to a field army, whereas an ambitious general couldn't be pried out of the capital with a lever."

She gave Belisarius a cold smile. "That leaves you. You alone, to be the focus of Justinian's worries."

Belisarius began to speak, but Theodora cut him off.

"Spare me, Belisarius. There's no point in making reassurances. I don't need them, and Justinian won't believe them."

She waved her hand. "No, the right course is exactly the one you propose." Another laugh. "Although even in my wildest dreams I never would have thought of sending you to Axum and India! God, Justinian will be ecstatic!"

The Empress was silent for a moment, lost in thought. "And it's not a bad idea, in any event, even leaving Justinian's jealousies aside."

She arose and walked slowly back to the window. Belisarius was struck by the regal grace of her movements, as encumbered as Theodora must have been by those incredible imperial robes. (Which, Antonina had told him, Theodora insisted on wearing at all times.) She looked every inch the ideal image of an Empress.

For a brief instant, Belisarius caught a glimpse of the woman's inner demons: that fierce, driving ambition which had carried her and her husband to the throne from the lowest of beginnings. Justinian, a semiliterate peasant from Thrace—who had, of course, long since become as literate a man as any in the Empire, applying his own fierce intelligence. Theodora, a whore from Alexandria.

But Theodora had been no sophisticated courtesan like Antonina, gaily choosing her few consorts and reveling in the charm and wit of their company. Belisarius knew Theodora's own history from Antonina. The Empress had been sold into prostitution by her own father at the age of twelve, to a pimp who had sold her in turn to every ruffian who hung about the Hippodrome.

He watched the still, beautiful face staring out the window. Watched the pride in the stillness, and the icy intelligence in the beauty, and thought he understood Theodora. Understood her, and understood her unshakable devotion to Justinian.

I swore an oath to Justinian, which I will always keep. But I wish I had sworn it to her. She would have made a far better Emperor.

"I don't trust this Venandakatra," Theodora said softly. "Even before Antonina told me of Irene's suspicions, I had my own." She glanced at Belisarius. "You've not met him?"

The general shook his head.

"I shall introduce you to him tomorrow. Justinian is having a reception for Venandakatra."

She stared back out the window. "Trade envoy!" she sneered. "That man has enough arrogance in him to be Lord of the Universe. A foul creature, he is! As vile a man as ever lived, I suspect."

Belisarius restrained his start of surprise. Antonina, he knew, had simply passed on that much of what they knew about Venandakatra which could reasonably have been spied out by Irene. There had been no mention of his vision.

Venandakatra the Vile. Apparently, the cognomen had been no personal fancy of Raghunath Rao.

Theodora shook her head. "No, I don't like this Venandakatra. The Malwa are playing a deep and dark game. And we know almost nothing about them. Yes, best we find out what we can, as soon as possible."

She turned back. "But there's something more important. You'll have plenty of time to get to know this Venandakatra creature. Much more, I assure you, than you'd ever want. In the meantime, however, there are other people you must get to know immediately. The Axumite embassy will also be present at the reception, which is doubling—as an afterthought, I'm afraid—as their departing ceremony. They are returning to Axum the next day."

She resumed her seat on the throne. "To my mind, your proposed visit to Axum is even more important than the trip to India. For one thing, I'm not sure how much you'll actually be able to find out in India. Whatever else he is,

Venandakatra's no fool, and he'll have his own suspicions of you."

"Will he agree?" asked Antonina. "To Belisarius accompanying him back to India?"

Theodora waved the concern away. "He can't very well refuse, can he? After all, he's supposedly a mere trade envoy. How could he refuse an imperial request to carry a Roman envoy back to his homeland?" She shook her head. "No, he'll agree, however grudgingly. What I am much more concerned about, at the moment, is whether the Axumites will agree to *that* side of your proposal."

"I thought they were on good terms with Rome," commented Belisarius.

The Empress tightened her lips. "Yes, they *were*. Whether they still are, after the shameful way they've been treated since their arrival, is another matter."

"They've been insulted?" asked Antonina.

"Not directly. But Justinian's indifference to them was soon detected by the courtiers, who—" She snorted. "It's the first rule of the courtier: if the Emperor breaks wind, you shit a mountain."

Belisarius chuckled. Theodora shook her head.

"It's not really funny. Justinian is so preoccupied with— well, never mind. Let's just say that he has forgotten the first rule of the emperor. *Do not trample over old friends in your eagerness to make new ones*."

"What's your impression of the Axumites?" asked Antonina.

Theodora frowned. "The adviser, Garmat, strikes me as shrewd. I don't think he'll be a problem. It's rather the prince who concerns me."

She spoke the prince's name slowly, savoring the words: "Eon Bisi Dakuen. Do you know what the name means?"

Belisarius and Antonina shook their heads.

"The Axumites are warriors. We forget that, here, because we only encounter them as traders and seamen. But they are a warrior people, with their own proud history. It is a tradition which is particularly ingrained in the ruling clan. It shows in their royal nomenclature."

She closed her eyes, calling up memory. "The official name for the king of the Ethiopians is Kaleb Ella Atsbeha, son of Tazena, Bisi Lazen, King of Axum, Himryar, Dhu Raydan, Saba, Salhen, the High Country and Yamanat, the Coastal Plain, Hadramawt, and all their Arabs, the Beja, Noba, Kasu, and Siyamo, servant of Christ."

"That's a mouthful," commented Antonina.

Theodora opened her eyes, smiling. "Isn't it? But don't shrug it off as royal grandiosity. It's quite accurate, except for the 'Ella Atsbeha' part, and accurate in significant ways."

"What does 'Ella Atsbeha' mean?" asked Belisarius.

"It means 'he who brings the dawn.'" Theodora shrugged. "That part of the title we can ignore. But the rest—ah, *there's* what's interesting. The long list of territories ruled, for instance, is quite precise. And the Axumites are punctilious about it. The listing of Himryar, for instance, as well as the Hadrawmat, is recent. The Axumites add and remove territories to the name of their ruler in strict accordance to the facts on the ground, so to speak."

She cast a shrewd glance at Belisarius.

"What does that tell you, General?"

"It tells me they prize accurate intelligence, even formally." Belisarius smiled crookedly. "That's a rather rare trait in rulers."

"Isn't it? But the Axumites are rigorous about it. I had my historians check the records." She went on. "The 'ella' name is only given to ruling monarchs. Who, by the way, are properly known as the *negusa nagast*, which means 'King of Kings.' My historians are not certain, but they think the title is also quite accurate. From old records of the first missionaries, it seems that Axum was forged by conquest and that it rules over many subordinate monarchs in the region of Ethiopia. Even Meroe and Nubia, it seems."

"And the 'bisi' name?" asked Belisarius. "It must mean something. I notice that both the King—the negusa nagast—and his son share the name. It's a title, I imagine."

"Yes. And that's the most interesting part. King Kaleb's oldest son Wa'zeb is named 'Wa'zeb Bisi Hadefan, son of Ella Atsbeha.' He is granted the patronymic, because he is the heir. The younger son who is the envoy here, Eon, is stripped down the bare essentials. 'Eon Bisi Dakuen.' That's the only name he has, because it's the only name Axumite royalty considers essential."

"It's a military title," guessed Belisarius.

Theodora nodded approvingly. "Quite right. The Axumite army is organized into long-standing regiments. They call them *sarawit*. I believe the singular is *sarwe*. 'Bisi' means 'man of.' Hence the Prince, Eon, has as his only identity the fact that he is a man of the Dakuen sarwe. Just as his father, before all else, is a man of the Lazen sarwe; and his older brother Wa'zeb, the heir, is before all else a man of the Hadefan sarwe."

Antonina looked back and forth between the Empress and the general. "I think I'm missing something here," she said.

Belisarius pursed his lips. "Lord in Heaven, even the Spartans didn't take it that far."

He turned to his wife. "What it means, Antonina, is that the Axumites look at the world through the hard eyes of warriors. Proud ones. Proud enough that they name their kings and princes after regiments; and prouder still, that they disdain to claim territories which they don't actually rule."

Theodora nodded. "And these are the people who've been treated as unwanted guests since they arrived. Brushed off by insolent courtiers who don't know one end of a lance from the other, and by officious bureaucrats who don't even know what a lance looks like in the first place."

"Oh, my," said Antonina.

Belisarius eyed Theodora. "But you don't think the adviser—Garmat, is it?—is the problem."

The Empress shook her head.

"He's an adviser, after all. Probably a warrior himself, in his youth, but he's long past that now. No, the problem's the boy. Eon Bisi Dakuen. As proud as any young warrior ever is—much less a prince!—and mortally offended."

Theodora was startled to hear Belisarius laugh.

"Oh, I don't think so, Empress! Not if he's really a warrior, at least. And, with that name, I suspect he is." For a moment, the look on the general's face was as icy as that of the Empress. "Warriors aren't mortally offended all that easily, Theodora, appearances to the contrary. They've seen too much real mortality. If they survive—well, there's pride, of course. But there's also a streak of practicality."

He arose. "I do believe I can touch that practicality. As one warrior to another."

Antonina rose with him. The audience was clearly at an end, except—

"You'll arrange an interview with Justinian?"

Theodora shook her head. "There won't be any necessity for a private interview. Justinian will agree to your plan, I've no doubt of it." The Empress pondered. "I think the way to proceed is to have Belisarius' mission announced publicly at tomorrow's reception. That will box Venandakatra, and it may help to mollify the Axumites."

"You can arrange it that quickly?"

Theodora's smile was arctic. "Do not concern yourself, *General*. It will be arranged. See to it that you make good your boast concerning the young prince."

Chapter 12

Belisarius thought the Emperor's efforts were a waste of time, and said as much to Sittas. Very quietly, of course. Not even the fearless general Belisarius was fool enough to mock the Emperor aloud—certainly not at an official imperial reception.

"Of course it's a waste of time," whispered Sittas. "It always is, except with barbarians. So what? Justinian doesn't care. He loves his toys, and that's all there is to it. Think he'd pass up a chance to play with them?"

There followed, under his breath, various rude remarks about Thracian hicks and their childish delight in trinkets and baubles. Belisarius, smiling blandly, ignored them cheerfully.

For, in truth, Belisarius was not all that far removed from the Thracian countryside himself. And, if he was not exactly an uncouth hick—which, by the by, he thought was a highly inaccurate depiction of the Emperor!—still, he was enough of a rube to take almost as much pleasure as Justinian out of the—*toys*.

Toys, indeed.

There were the levitating thrones, first of all, upon which Justinian and Theodora were elevated far above the crowd. The thrones rose and fell as the Emperor's mood took him.

At the moment, judging from his rarefied height, Justinian was feeling aloof from the huge mob thronging the reception hall.

Then, there were the lions which flanked the thrones whenever the royal chairs were resting on the floor. Made of beaten gold and silver, the lions were capable of emitting the most thunderous roars whenever the Emperor was struck by the fancy. Which, judging from their experience in the half-hour since they had arrived at the reception, Belisarius knew to be a frequent occurrence.

Finally, there were Belisarius' personal favorites: the jewel-encrusted metal birds which perched on metal trees and porcelain fountains scattered about in the vicinity of the Emperor. The general was fond of their metallic chirping, of course, but he was particularly taken by one bird on the rim of a fountain, which, from time to time, bent down as if to drink from its water.

Toys, indeed.

But, he thought, a waste of time and effort on this occasion. Neither the Indian nor the Axumite envoys were unsophisticated barbarians, to be astonished and dazzled by such marvels.

Belisarius examined the Malwa embassy first. The identity of Venandakatra was obvious, not only from his central position in the group of Indians but from his whole bearing. His clothing was rich, but unostentatious, as befitted one who claimed to be a mere trade envoy.

That assumed modesty was a waste of time, thought Belisarius. For, just as the Empress had said, Venandakatra carried himself in a manner which indeed suggested that he was the Lord of the Universe.

Belisarius smiled faintly. The elaborate and ostentatious reception for Venandakatra was Justinian's own none-too-subtle way of making clear to the Malwa that the Roman Emperor was not taken in by the Indian's subterfuge. A

mere trade envoy would have been kept cooling his heels
for weeks, before some midlevel bureaucrat finally deigned
to grant him an audience in a dingy office. No genuine trade
envoy had ever been given a formal imperial reception in
the huge hall in the Great Palace itself, before the assembled
nobility of Constantinople.

Belisarius glanced up at the enormous mosaics which
decorated the walls. He almost expected to see looks of
shock and dismay on the faces of the saints depicted thereon.
Those holy eyes of tile were accustomed to gaze upon
victorious generals, dignified Patriarchs, and the bejewelled
ambassadors from the Persian court, not disreputable little—
merchants.

Chuckling, Belisarius resumed his scrutiny of the Malwa
"trade envoy."

Beyond his haughtiness, there was not much to remark
about Venandakatra. The man's complexion was dark, by
Byzantine standards, and the cast of his face obviously
foreign. But neither of those features particularly set him
apart. Constantinople was the most cosmopolitan city in
the world, and its inhabitants were long accustomed to exotic
visitors. Nor were Romans given to racial prejudice. So long
as a man behaved properly, and dressed in a Byzantine
manner, and spoke Greek, he was assumed to be civilized.
A heathen, perhaps, but civilized.

Venandakatra was in late middle age, and of average
height. His features were thin almost to the point of
sharpness, which was accentuated by his close-set dark eyes.
The eyes seemed as cold as a reptile's to Belisarius, even
from a distance. The web of scaly wrinkles around the orbits
added to the effect.

In build, Belisarius estimated that Venandakatra should
have been slender, by nature. In fact, his thin-boned frame
and features carried a considerable excess of weight.
Venandakatra exuded the odd combination of rail-thin

ferocity and self-indulgent obesity. Like a snake distended by its prey.

A cold, savage grin came upon the general's face, then, remembering a vision. In another time, in that future which Belisarius hoped to change, this vile man had been destroyed by a mere slip of a girl. Beaten to a pulp by her flashing hands and feet; bleeding to death from a throat cut by his own knife.

"Stop it, Belisarius!" hissed Antonina.

"Please," concurred Irene. "You're not supposed to bare your fangs at an imperial reception. We *are* trying to make a good impression, you know."

Belisarius tightened his lips. He glanced again at Venandakatra, then away.

The Vile One, indeed.

He looked now upon the Axumites and at once felt his expression ease.

In truth, to all appearances the Axumites were far more outlandish than the Indians. Their skins, for one thing, were not "dark-complected" but black. Black as Nubians (which, Belisarius judged from his features, one of them was). For another, where the Indians' hair was long and straight, that of the Axumites was short and very kinky. Finally, where the facial features of the Indians—leaving aside their dark complexion—were not all that different from Greeks (or, at least, Armenians), the features of the Axumites were distinctly African. That was especially true for the one whom Belisarius thought to be a Nubian. The features of the other Axumites had an Arab cast to them, for all their darkness. Positively aquiline, in the case of the oldest one of the group, whom Belisarius supposed was the adviser Garmat.

Belisarius knew that Ethiopia and southern Arabia had long been in contact with each other. Looking at the Axumites, and remembering some very dark-skinned Arabs he had met in the past, he decided the contact between the two races had often been intimate.

Yes, they were clearly even more foreign than the Indians—in habits as well as in appearance, Belisarius guessed. He chuckled softly, seeing how poorly the young prince wore the strange Byzantine costume he found himself encumbered within.

"It is a bit funny," agreed Irene quietly. "I think he's used to wearing a whole lot less clothing, in his own climate."

"Too bad he didn't come here a couple of centuries ago," added Antonina, "when Romans still wore togas. He'd have been a lot more comfortable, I think."

"So would I," muttered Sittas. He glanced down, with considerable disfavor, at the heavy knee-length embroidered coat which he was wearing. It felt almost as heavy as cataphract armor.

"How did we get saddled with these outfits?" he groused. "Instead of nice, comfortable togas?"

"We got them from the Huns," whispered Irene. "Who, in turn, got them from the Chinese."

Sittas goggled. "You're kidding!" He glared down at his coat. "You mean to tell me I'm wearing a filthy damned *Hunnish* costume?"

Irene nodded, smiling. "Odd how civilization works, isn't it? It's your fault, you know—soldiers, I mean, not you personally. Once you got obsessed with cavalry you started insisting on wearing Hun trousers." She smirked. "Why you insisted on including the coats into the bargain is a mystery."

"How do you know so much, woman?" grumbled Sittas. "It's unseemly."

"I don't spend all day drinking and complaining that there's nothing else to do."

Sittas glowered. "Damn intelligence in a woman, anyway. Should never have let them learn how to read. It's the only good thing about Thracians, you know. They keep their women barefoot and ignorant."

"It's true," whispered Antonina. "Belisarius only lets me wear shoes on special occasion like these." She glanced down admiringly at the preposterous, rickety, high-heeled contraptions on her feet. "And when I'm dancing naked on his bare chest, of course, with my whip and my iced sherbet."

"And that's another thing," groused Sittas. "Show me an intelligent woman, and I'll show you one with a sense of humor. Aimed at men, naturally." He glared around the huge room, singling out every single woman in it for a moment's glower. Although, in truth, most of them seemed neither particularly intelligent nor quick-witted.

Belisarius ignored the byplay. He had long since reconciled himself to his wife's sometimes outrageous jokes. He rather enjoyed them, actually. Although, glancing at the monstrosities on Antonina's little feet, he almost shuddered to think of them tearing great wounds in his body.

He concentrated again on the Axumites. There were only five of them, which, he had heard, was the entirety of their embassy. He glanced back at the Indians and smiled. The Axumites had sent five for a full diplomatic mission, whereas the Indians—who presented themselves as a mere trade delegation—had sent upward of twenty.

The smile faded. Some of those twenty were purely decorative, but by no means all of them. Perhaps one or two were actually even interested in trade, but Belisarius had no doubt that at least ten of the Indian delegation were nothing more than outright spies.

As if reading his thoughts, Irene whispered:

"I've heard half of the Indians have announced plans to set up permanent residence. To foster and encourage trade, they say."

"No doubt," muttered the general. "There's always a good traffic in treason, in this town."

Irene leaned over and whispered even more softly:

"Do you see the one on the far left?" she asked. "And the heavyset one toward the middle, wearing a yellow coat with black embroidery?" She was not looking at them at all, Belisarius noticed. He avoided more than a quick glance in the direction of the Malwa envoys.

"Yes, I see them."

"The one on the left is named Ajatasutra. The heavyset one is called Balban. I'm certain that Ajatasutra is one of the Malwa's chief spies. About Balban I'm less confident, but I suspect him also. And if my suspicions about Balban are correct, he would be the probable spymaster."

"Not Ajatasutra?"

Irene's head-shake was so faint as to be almost unnoticeable.

"No, he's too obvious. Too much in the forefront."

Again, it was uncanny the way Irene read his thoughts.

"Bad idea, Belisarius. You never want to assassinate known spies and spymasters. They'll simply be replaced with others you don't know. Best to keep them under watch, and then—"

"And then what?"

She smiled and shrugged lightly, never casting so much as a glance in the direction of the Indians.

"Whatever," she murmured. "The possibilities are endless."

Antonina nudged Belisarius. "I think it's time we made our acquaintance with the Axumites. I've been watching Theodora, and she's starting to glare at us impatiently."

"Onward," spoke the general. Taking his wife by the arm, he led her across the room, weaving a path through the chattering throng. The Axumites were standing off to one side, at the edge of the crowd. Even to Belisarius, who was no connoisseur of such events, it was apparent that the Ethiopians were being studiously ignored.

The Axumites took note of them as Belisarius and Antonina approached. The older man he took to be the adviser Garmat showed no reaction. The eyes of the young prince, on the other hand, widened noticeably. It might almost he said that he stared, until the tall man behind him—the one Belisarius thought was a Nubian—nudged him. Thereupon the prince tore his eyes away and stared elsewhere, his back ramrod straight.

As he approached, Belisarius' eyes met those of the Nubian. The tall black man immediately broke into a toothy grin, which just as immediately disappeared.

Belisarius was puzzled by the man. The identity of the adviser Garmat was obvious. And the other two members of the Axumite envoy were obviously soldiers. The prince's personal retinue, men much like his own pentarchs Valentinian and Anastasius. Seasoned, experienced warriors in their late twenties or early thirties. Young enough to be as physically vigorous as any; old enough not to be rash and impetuous.

What then was the function and capacity of the Nubian? If Nubian he was—though, as Belisarius came up to the small group, he was almost certain he was right. The tall man's face had none of the aquiline characteristics of the Axumites. His features were pure African.

He would know soon enough. He stopped a few feet from the group and bowed politely.

"I am Belisarius," he announced. "I am—"

"Rome's finest general!" said the older man. "Such a honor! I am Garmat, the adviser to Prince Eon Bisi Dakuen." He motioned to the young man standing at his side.

Belisarius examined the young man. The prince, he thought, was most handsome in an exotic sort of way. The boy was not tall, but he was obviously well built. Beneath the heavy embroidered coat, Belisarius suspected, lay a very muscular frame.

The prince nodded, so slightly as to be almost impolite. Immediately, the tall man standing behind him nudged the prince again, none too gently, and uttered a few words in a language unknown to Belisarius. The two Axumite soldiers standing by his side grunted something, which Belisarius sensed were words of approval.

Something odd was happening. The language was unknown to the general, but—for a moment, strangely, Belisarius thought he almost understood the words. Odd.

Under the darkness of the skin, Belisarius thought he saw the prince flush with embarrassment. The young man stood even straighter and nodded again. This time, very deeply and respectfully. The tall man behind him flashed Belisarius his quick toothy grin and said, in heavily accented Greek:

"I said to him: 'Show respect, fool boy! He is great general, tested in battle, and you but suckling babe.' " Again, the wide grin. "Of course, I spoke our language, so not to embarrass fool boy prince. And did not slap his head, for same reason. But now I find must translate, so as not to offend noble visitors."

"And who are you, if I might ask?"

The tall man grinned even more widely. "Me? I am nothing, great general. A miserable slave, no more. The lowest creature on earth, debased beyond measure."

Garmat interrupted. "Please! May we be introduced to your lovely wife?"

Belisarius apologized and made the introduction. Garmat was suave diplomacy itself, managing simultaneously to strew about fulsome praises of Antonina's beauty and charm without, at the same time, doing so in a manner which suggested even the slightest lechery. The prince did not manage so well. He was very polite, but too obviously smitten by her beauty.

The tall man behind him spoke sharply, again; again, the soldiers' grunting approval.

But this time, Belisarius understood the words—without knowing how.

"Idiot boy! Lust after local cowherds, if you must! Do not ogle the wives of great foreign generals!"

Belisarius kept a straight face. Or so, at least, he thought.

"You speak our language," announced Garmat.

Belisarius thought for a moment, then shook his head. "No, no. I can understand a few words, that is all. But I cannot speak—uh, what exactly—"

"We call it Ge'ez."

"Thank you. I apologize for my ignorance. I know little of Axum. As I said, I can speak no Ge'ez, but I do understand it a bit."

Garmat was staring up at him shrewdly. "More than a bit, I think." The adviser glanced back at the tall man standing behind the prince.

"You are puzzled by Ousanas." It was more of a statement than a question.

Belisarius looked at the tall man. "That is his name?"

Ousanas spoke, again in Greek.

"Is my civilized Greek name, General Belisarius. In my own tongue am called—" Here came several unpronounceable syllables.

"You are Nubian," said Belisarius.

Ousanas now grinned from ear to ear.

"Should think not! Most wretched folk, the Nubians. Given to putting on great airs, pretending they are Egyptian. I fart on Meroe and Napata!"

Garmat interrupted. "Romans often make that mistake. He is actually from much farther south than Nubia. From a land between great lakes, which is quite unknown to the peoples of the Mediterranean."

Belisarius frowned. "He is not Axumite, then?"

"Should hope not!" cried Ousanas. "Most wretched folk, the Axumites. Given to putting on great airs, pretending they are descendants of Solomon."

Again, the grin. "I do not, however, fart on Axum and

Adulis. Else the *sarwen*"—a thumb pointed in each direction to the warriors at his side—"would beat me for an impertinent slave."

The two sarwen grunted agreement.

Belisarius was now frowning deeply. Garmat smiled.

"You are puzzled, I think, by some of our customs."

"Is this a custom?" asked Belisarius dubiously.

Garmat nodded vigorously. "Oh, yes! A very old custom. Every man child born to the king—even girls, sometimes, if there are no male heirs—is assigned a special slave at the age of ten. This slave is always a foreigner, of some kind. He is called the *dawazz*. His is a very special job. The prince has an adviser to teach him statecraft, which a king must have to rule properly." Here Garmat pointed to himself. "Veteran soldiers from his regiment to teach him the skill of arms, which a king must have to maintain his rule." Here Garmat pointed to the two soldiers. "And then, most important, he has his dawazz. Who teaches him that the difference between slave and king is not so great, after all."

Ousanas grinned. "Much better to be slave! No worries."

Antonina smiled sweetly. "I should think you'd worry what the prince will do if he ever assumes the throne. And remembers the dawazz who abused him, all those many times."

The grin never wavered. "Nonsense, great lady. Prince be properly grateful. Shower faithful dawazz with gifts. Offer him prestigious posts."

Antonina grinned back. "Maybe. Especially if the dawazz was a kind and gentle man, who reproved his prince mildly and only upon rare occasions."

"Nonsense!" exclaimed Ousanas. "Dawazz of that sort be useless!" He smacked the prince on top of the head, very hard. The Prince didn't even blink.

"See?" demanded Ousanas. "Good prince. Very strong

and durable, with solid hard head. If he ever become king, Arabs tremble."

Belisarius was fascinated. "But—let's just suppose for the moment—what I mean is—"

Garmat interrupted. "You are wondering what would motivate the dawazz to be so strict in his duties? When, as your wife points out, there is always the risk that a king might remember the past sourly?"

Belisarius nodded. Garmat turned to Ousanas.

"What happens, Ousanas, if you neglect your duties? Fail to instruct the prince properly in the true scheme of things?"

The grin vanished from Ousanas' face. "Sarawit be angry." He glanced from side to side. "Very perilous, irritate sarwen." The irrepressible grin returned. "Prince is nothing. King is almost nothing. Sarawit important."

The soldiers grunted agreement.

Garmat turned back to Belisarius. "Our custom, you see, is that when the prince succeeds to the throne or reaches his maturity—which, among us, we reckon at twenty-two years of age—then his sarwe passes judgment on his dawazz. If the dawazz is judged to have done his job properly, he is offered membership in the sarwe. And, usually, a high rank. Or, if he prefers, he may return to his own people, laden with the sarwe's blessing and, of course, many gifts from his former prince."

"And if the sarwe judges against him?"

Garmat shrugged. From behind him, Ousanas muttered: "Very bad." The soldiers grunted agreement.

Belisarius scratched his chin.

"Is the dawazz always from the south?"

"Oh, no!" exclaimed Garmat. "The dawazz may come from any foreign land, so long as his people are adjudged a valiant folk and he himself is esteemed for his courage. King Kaleb's dawazz, for instance, was a bedouin Arab."

"And what happened to him?"

Garmat coughed. "Well, actually, he's standing in front of you. I was Kaleb's dawazz."

Belisarius and Antonina stared at him. Garmat shrugged apologetically.

"My mother, I'm afraid, was not noted for her chastity. She was particularly taken by handsome young Ethiopian traders. As you can see, I was the result of such a liaison."

"How were you captured?" asked Belisarius.

Garmat frowned. He seemed puzzled.

"Captured by whom?"

"By the Axumites—when they enslaved you, and made you Kaleb's dawazz."

"You never capture dawazz!" exclaimed the prince. "If a man can be captured, he is not fit to be dawazz!"

It was the first time the prince had spoken. Eon's voice was quite pleasant, although unusually deep for one so young.

Belisarius shook his head bemusedly. "I don't understand this at all. How do you make someone a dawazz, then?"

"*Make* someone?" asked the prince. He looked at his adviser in confusion. Garmat smiled. The soldiers chuckled. Ousanas laughed aloud.

"You don't *make* someone a dawazz, General," explained Garmat. "It is a very high honor. Men come from everywhere to compete for the post. When I heard that a new dawazz was to be appointed by the Ethiopians, I rode across half of Arabia. And I traded my fine camel for a dhow to cross the Red Sea."

"I walked through jungles and mountains," commented Ousanas. "I traded nothing. Had nothing to trade except my spear. Which I needed."

He bared a very muscular forearm, showing an ugly scar which marked the black flesh.

"Got that from a panther in Shawa." The grin returned. "But was well worth it. Scar got me into final round of testing. Not have to bother with silly early rounds."

Prince Eon spoke, his voice filled with pride. "Ousanas is the greatest hunter in the world," he announced.

Immediately, Ousanas slapped him atop the head.

"Fool boy! Greatest hunter in world is lioness somewhere in savanna. Hope you never meet her! You contemplate error from inside her belly."

"And you, Garmat?" asked Antonina. "Were you also a great hunter?"

Garmat waved his hands deprecatingly. "By no means, by no means. I was—how shall I put it? Let us say that the Axumites were delighted to select me. At one stroke, they gained a dawazz and eliminated the most annoying bandit chieftain in the Hadrawmat." He shrugged again. "I had gotten rather tired of the endless round of forays and retreats. The thought of a stable position was appealing. And—"

He hesitated, sizing up the two Romans before him. "And," he continued, "I always rather liked my father's people. Whoever my father was, I was always sure he was Ethiopian."

For a moment, the adviser's face grew hard. "I was raised Arab, and have never forgotten that half of my heritage. A great people, the Arabs, in many ways. But—they were very hard on my mother. Mocked her, and abused her, for no reason than that she found men attractive."

He looked away, scanning the milling crowd in the reception hall.

"She was a good mother. Very good. Once I became powerful, of course, the abuse stopped. But she was never truly respected. Not properly. So—I took her with me to Axum, where customs are different."

"How are they different?" asked Antonina.

Again, the appraising stare. Longer, this time. Belisarius knew that an important decision was being made.

"Let us simply say, Antonina, that among the Axumites there would be no whispering about powerful women with questionable pasts. As there is even here, among sophisticated Greeks."

Antonina grew still. Garmat's smile grew twisted. "Nor would there be any basis for such whispering, among the Ethiopians. Prostitution is unknown among them— except in the port of Adulis, where it is only practiced upon foreign seamen. Who are mocked, thereafter, for paying good money for what they could have had for nothing. Nothing, that is, except charm and wit and good conversation."

Ousanas spoke, grimacing fiercely. "A promiscuous folk, the Axumites. Is well known! I was shocked, when first heard the news, in my far distant little village in south. My own folk very moral people, of course." His face grew lugubrious. "Oh, yes! Was shocked at such news! Immediately went to see for myself, that I might lay to rest wicked rumors." The huge grin returned. "Alas, rumors proved true. I would have fled immediately, of course, but by the time I learned—"

"The day you arrived," grunted one of the soldiers.

"— was too late. Had already been tested for the dawazz. What could I do?"

Antonina and Belisarius laughed. Garmat spread his hands.

"You see? Even our priests, I'm afraid, are lax by your standards. But we are happy with our customs. Even the negusa nagast does not fret himself overmuch concerning the paternity of his sons. What does their blood matter, anyway? Only the approval of the sarawit matters, in the end."

The soldiers grunted agreement.

The adviser gazed at Belisarius, a shrewd glint in his eyes.

"You must really come to see Axum for yourself," he said.

"Not without me to keep an eye on him!" exclaimed Antonina, giggling. Then, remembering their purpose, she gasped slightly and fell silent.

Garmat immediately detected the false note. Before he could speak, Belisarius cleared his throat.

"As a matter of fact, Garmat, that is—"

He was interrupted by a great fanfare. The Emperor's heralds were blaring out on their cornicens.

Belisarius started. Cornicens were the instruments used by Roman generals to transmit orders on the battlefield. He was not accustomed to their peaceful use.

Justinian and Theodora's thrones were being elevated to their extreme height. Silence began to fall over the throng. It was clear that an important announcement was at hand.

"I'm afraid I must apologize to you," Belisarius whispered hastily to Garmat. "I became so engrossed in our conversation that I forgot the time. This announcement, well—"

Garmat laid a hand on his arm.

"Let us hear the announcement, General. Then we can discuss whatever needs to be discussed."

When the announcement was finished, Belisarius noted three things.

First, he noted a marked change in the manner of the crowd toward both himself and the Axumites. Where before they had been ignored, they were now, it was obvious, on the verge of being mobbed by sudden well-wishers.

Second, he noted the very sour expression on the face of Venandakatra, obvious even at a distance. And the hurried whispering among the Malwa entourage.

Third, he noted the trifold reaction of the Axumites. Garmat, even with the long experience of a royal adviser, was finding it impossible not to look pleased. Eon, with the short experience of a young and vigorous prince, found it even more impossible not to express displeasure. And the dawazz, as always, did his job, under the watchful eyes of the sarwen.

"We were not even informed!" snapped the Prince.

Immediately, Ousanas slapped him atop the head.

"Imbecile suckling! When lion invite you to share lunch, *accept*. Or would you rather be lunch yourself? Babbling babe!"

The sarwen grunted approval.

AMAVARATI
Winter, 528 AD

Chapter 13

Her youngest brother died well. Foolishly, but well.

Shakuntala did not hold the foolishness against the boy. He had been fourteen years old and was bound to die anyway. Better he should be cut down quickly by a Ye-tai beast than have his last moments be filled with humiliation as well as pain.

Her brother's hopeless charge against the Ye-tai made possible his revenge, too. The Ye-tai—an experienced warrior—had no difficulty side-stepping the boy's clumsy sword swing. The barbarian grinned savagely as his own sword hewed into her brother's neck, almost severing it completely. A moment later, the grin disappeared. Shakuntala's spear-point took the Ye-tai under the armpit and penetrated right into his heart.

The warrior began to slump, but his body was hurled aside by three other Ye-tai pouring into the princess' chamber. The Ye-tai in the lead stumbled slightly over his dead comrade's leg. It wasn't much of a stumble, but it was just enough to allow Shakuntala's spear to slide over the rim of his shield. The spear-point sank into his throat. The barbarian coughed blood and fell to his knees.

The princess immediately jerked the spear-blade back and plunged it toward another Ye-tai. This one brought

210

his shield up to block the thrust. But the princess had been well-taught. The thrust was a feint. The spear-tip sank into his leg just above the knee. The Ye-tai howled. Shakuntala jerked the blade out and drove it into the warrior's open mouth.

It was a quick, flickering, viper-like thrust—just as she had been taught. But—just as she had been warned *not* to do—the princess had driven the blade in much too furiously. The spear-tip jammed between two vertebrae.

A moment later, another Ye-tai struck at the spear shaft with his sword. His sword did not—quite—succeed in cutting the spear shaft. But the blow was more than sufficient to knock the spear out of Shakuntala's hands.

The Ye-tai shouted triumphantly and advanced upon her, grinning widely. Shakuntala backed away toward a corner. The huge room, which had served as her reception chamber, was sparsely furnished. The princess kicked aside a large vase, giving herself still more maneuvering space. The beautiful porcelain shattered, spilling dried flowers onto the floor.

Six more Ye-tai poured in through the shattered door. Two of them came toward the princess. The other four veered away, heading toward Shakuntala's maidservant. The girl—Jijabai—was huddled in another corner of the room.

Shakuntala heard Jijabai's sobs turn into shrieks. She heard her maid's clothing being torn and the gleeful howls of the Ye-tai who were wrestling the girl down to the floor. But she had no time to look over. The three Ye-tai who were now moving to surround her in the corner had sheathed their own swords and dropped their shields. The iron rims of the shields bounced softly on the rich carpet which covered the floor.

The princess did not understand the phrases they were exchanging back and forth, but the leering grins on their faces made the meaning clear enough. She turned slightly, pretended to slump, cowering. One of the Ye-tai pounced on her. Her sidekick took the warrior straight in the diaphragm, knocking him flat on his back. Her fist took a second warrior in the exact same location. He coughed, began to double up—then slumped to the floor as Shakuntala's forearm strike smashed into his jaw.

The third Ye-tai leapt onto her back, wrapping his arms around her. She snapped her head back into his face, stamped on his instep, broke loose from his grip, and slammed her elbow into his stomach.

The warrior staggered. Shakuntala spun and drove her foot into his groin. The Ye-tai sprawled on the floor, groaning.

Shakuntala sprang away and raced toward the other corner, where Jijabai was being held down on the floor. The maid was half-naked now. Her arms were being held by one Ye-tai, while each of her legs were spread apart by others. The fourth Ye-tai had untied his trousers and was dropping to his knees between the screaming girl's legs.

His kneel turned into a headlong plunge as Shakuntala's flying kick smashed between his shoulder blades. The princess delivered the kick perfectly, without the impetuous excess which was her usual mistake. She rebounded and landed lightly on her feet. The Ye-tai who was holding Jijabai's right leg gaped up at her. Shakuntala kicked out his teeth. Again, the kick was perfect. The follow-on kick broke the warrior's neck.

But that kick was too powerful, by far. Instead of rebounding, the princess staggered and fell onto her back. Fortunately, the thick carpet softened her fall. A moment later, the Ye-tai who had been holding Jijabai's other leg landed on top of her, grappling for her wrists. He was roaring with rage. His roars were not enough, however, to drown the sound of other Ye-tai warriors pouring into the room. Jijabai began screaming again.

Shakuntala wrestled with her assailant furiously. For her size, she was very strong. But the Ye-tai outmassed her considerably, and was no weakling himself. Then the princess found her legs suddenly seized by other barbarians. Ye-tai howls of glee filled the room, almost deafening in their cacophony.

The Ye-tai lying atop the princess now had her wrists firmly in his grip. He brought his legs up and straddled her chest. His face was not more than inches from hers. He began to say something to her, grinning fiercely. Shakuntala lunged her head forward and bit off the tip of his nose.

The Ye-tai howled and jerked his head. Blood flew from his severed nose. He stared down at her, his eyes wide with rage. Shakuntala spit the tip of his nose into his face. The warrior bellowed fury. He released her left wrist, drew back his right hand, made a fist, and began to strike her in the jaw.

The fist went flying out of sight. The warrior's arm had been chopped off just below the wrist. The Ye-tai gaped at the stump. Blood gushed everywhere, much of it on the princess. A moment later, Shakuntala was practically drowned in blood. The Ye-tai's head had vanished also.

Now, all was chaos and confusion. Shakuntala was almost blinded by the blood covering her face. Then she *was* blinded, by the Ye-tai's headless body collapsing on her.

She felt the hands holding her legs release their grip. Her lower body was suddenly covered with wetness. Blood. Not hers. Howls and shouts of fury. Clash of swords and shields. Cries of pain. Choking death coughs.

Now a bellowing roar of command. The sounds of more warriors filling the room. Roar of command. A cessation to the sounds of fighting. Roar of command.

Suddenly, silence. Except for Jijabai's sobbing.

Silence, except—

Outside the room, through the windows, Shakuntala could hear screams and shrieks in the distance. A vast, world-filling howl of pain and anguish.

Amavarati was taken. The palace was captured. All was lost. All. All.

The headless body atop her was suddenly removed. She was free again. She sat up and tried to wipe the blood from her face. Someone handed her a cloth. With it, she was able to remove enough blood to see.

The room was now absolutely filled with warriors. A few Ye-tai were still alive, huddled in the corner next to the sobbing figure of Jijabai. More Ye-tai were lying dead, scattered here and there over the floor.

The other warriors in the room were also Malwa enemies, but not Ye-tai. Shakuntala recognized them. Kushans. And one Mahaveda priest.

The priest was scowling back and forth between the Ye-tai in the corner and one of the Kushans. The Kushan commander, Shakuntala guessed.

The Kushan commander was a short man, very stocky. Barrel-chested and thick-shouldered. In his right hand he held a sword, covered with blood. Shakuntala was certain, without knowing exactly how, that that was the sword which had removed her assailant's fist and then his head.

But what struck her most about the Kushan was his face. It was not the features. Those were typical Kushan: coarse black hair tied back in a topknot, brown eyes, flat nose, high cheeks, thin lips, a slight fold in the corners of the eyes. No, it was the face itself. It didn't seem made of human flesh. It looked like a mask of iron.

The priest snarled something at the Kushan commander. The commander's reply was curt, unyielding. He pointed to Shakuntala and said something else. The priest frowned. The Mahaveda turned toward the Ye-tai in the corner and snarled something at them. The Ye-tai began saying something—half angrily, half fearfully—but the priest shouted them down.

The priest pointed to Jijabai, barked something; made a dismissive gesture. The Ye-tai grinned and stooped over the maid. A moment later they were spreading her legs again and unbuckling their trousers.

Shakuntala lurched to her feet, but the Kushan commander was suddenly standing behind her. The man moved much more quickly than the princess would have thought possible. She felt him twisting her arm up behind her back. She drove her foot down, but struck only the floor, painfully. The Kushan had moved his instep aside— effortlessly, and without losing either his balance or his grip on her arm.

Shakuntala felt her arm twisted up, immobilized. She recognized the grip, and the expertise behind it, and despaired. Still—

Her elbow strike was blocked almost before it began. Her head snap was met with a cuff. Not a brutal cuff, just an expert one.

Jijabai started screaming. A blow. Screaming. Another blow. Blow. Silence. Except for coarse Ye-tai laughs.

"There's nothing you can do for her, girl," whispered the Kushan commander in good Hindi. "Nothing."

He propelled Shakuntala toward the door. He was strong. Very strong. The other Kushans moved with him. Several moved in front. Others strode on either side, still others behind. All with swords drawn. Blood-covered swords, without exception.

As she went through the door, Shakuntala heard Jijabai begin to wail again. Then: blow; blow; silence.

"Nothing, girl, nothing," whispered the Kushan.

The trip through the palace was sheer nightmare. The princess was covered with blood and half-dazed, but could still see. And hear. The entire palace was a raging madhouse of butchery, looting, torture and gang rape. The Ye-tai barbarians were like maddened wolves. The common Malwa troops were even worse, like crazed hyenas. Completely out of control. More than once, her Kushan escort was forced to strike down Malwa soldiers lunging for the princess. ("Forced" was perhaps not the right word. The Kushans slaughtered common Malwa troops who moved toward them instantly and without compunction; Ye-tai were butchered for even looking at them the wrong way.)

After a while, Shakuntala felt herself grow weak with horror. She tried to fight against the weakness, but it was almost impossible. Utter despair was overwhelming her.

The iron grip holding her became, as the trip progressed, more of a comforting embrace. Some part of her mind tried to seize the opportunity, but her will was buried beneath hopelessness. And always, every minute, the voice:

"Nothing, girl, nothing."

A gentle voice. If iron can ever be gentle.

Finally, they were leaving the palace, entering the great courtyard.

She caught a glimpse—

The iron hand turned her head into an iron shoulder. Guided her away.

Shakuntala summoned the last reserve of her will.

"No," she said. "No. I must see."

Iron hesitated. An iron sigh.

"You are certain?"

"I must see." A moment later: "Please. I must."

Iron hesitation. Another iron sigh.

"Nothing, girl, noth—"

"*I must—please!*"

The iron grip yielded, turned her back.

She saw. They were dead now, at least. The cluster of

mahamimamsa around them were already well into the flaying. Soon enough, the skin sacks would be ready for hanging in the Malwa emperor's great hall.

Her father. Her mother. All of her brothers except the youngest, who had died in her room. His body would be brought down soon, for the flayers.

The iron grip turned her away again. She did not resist. A minute later, she began to shake. Then, seconds later, weep.

"Nothing, girl, nothing."

She did not speak for three hours. Not until the last faint screams of Amaravati died away, lost in the distance. The Kushans pushed their horses hard, and the Rajput cavalry troop which escorted them did not object.

For three hours, she was lost in anguished memories of Andhra. Great Andhra, destroyed Andhra. For five centuries, under the Satavahana dynasty, Andhra had ruled central India. And ruled it well. Themselves Telugu speakers of Dravidian stock, the Satavahana had shielded Dravidia from the depredations of the northern Aryan conquerors; shielded Dravidia, while at the same time absorbing and transmitting throughout the Deccan all the genuine glories of Vedic culture. The very name *satavahana* referred to the seven-horse chariot of Vishnu. The name had been adopted by the dynasty upon its conversion to Hinduism—*adopted*, by choice, not by force.

So had the Satavahanas ruled. They had never shied from war, but had always preferred gentler methods of conquest and rule. Few, if any, of their subject peoples had found their overlordship oppressive. Even the stiff-necked and quarrelsome Marathas, after a time, had become reconciled to Andhra rule. Reconciled, and then, become Andhra's strong right arm.

Under the Satavahanas, Andhra had become one of the major trade centers of the world. Trade with Rome to the west, Ceylon to the south, Champa and Funan to the east.

The great city Amavarati, now in flames, had been the most prosperous and peaceful city in all India.

With peace, prosperity and trade, had come knowledge, wisdom, and art. Encouraged and patronized by the Satavahanas, scholars and mystics and artists had flocked to Amavarati.

The bhakti movement had grown under Andhra's tolerance, revitalizing Hinduism. Buddhists and Jains, often persecuted in other Hindu realms, were unmolested in Andhra. Even the great rock-cut temples had been allowed to incorporate images of the Buddha.

Shakuntala remembered the beauty of those temples, and the monastic viharas, and the chaitya prayer halls, and the stupas. She fought back the tears. Then she remembered the glorious frescoes at the viharas at Ajanta, and could fight them back no longer.

Gone. All gone. Destroyed forever.

Her first words were: "Why not me?"

The Kushan commander explained. Gently. As gently, at least, as the truth allowed.

She spit on the ground. For a moment, it almost seemed as if the commander's face had developed a crack. A flaw in the iron, perhaps.

Her next words were:

"Raghunath Rao?"

The Kushan commander explained. This time, the voice was not gentle. There was no need to be. Then, the commander predicted. Now, gentle again; insofar as iron can be gentle.

Shakuntala laughed. Flaming glory burst through her soul, like a river washing out all hopelessness and despair.

The princess spoke her last word, on that day of destruction: *"Fools."*

❖   ❖   ❖

When night fell, the Kushans and Rajputs made camp. Guards were set up all around, within and without the camp perimeter. The Rajputs guarded the camp from outside attack. The Kushans guarded the camp from Shakuntala.

It was an odd sort of guard. The Kushans kept their distance from her. Regaled each other—in Hindi, which she could understand—with tales of startled Ye-tai. Girl-startled Ye-tai, with a spear-blade in their armpits and throats and legs and mouths; with a foot in their guts and their teeth and their necks. They particularly relished the tale of a Ye-tai nose.

Beyond, in the flickering light of the campfires, haughty Rajput beards were seen to move. Smiles, perhaps, brought on by charming tales.

That same night, in a pond not far from the palace at Amavarati, a frog croaked and jumped aside. As if startled by a sudden motion nearby.

An alert guard might have spotted the slow, crawling figure which eased its way out of the reeds and onto the bank. But there were no alert guards at Amavarati that night. The Malwa army had disintegrated completely in its triumph. There was nothing at Amavarati that night but a horde of drunken, butchering thieves and rapists, and what few of their victims still survived. And a cluster of mahamimamsa, overseen by priests, who, though sober and on duty, were much too preoccupied with the task of properly flaying a fourteen-year-old boy to be watching any ponds.

Once ashore, the man began to tear his tunic and bind up his wounds. They were many, those wounds, but none were either fatal or crippling. In time, they would become simply more scars added to an already extensive collection.

The wounds dressed, the man rested a bit. Then, still moving silently and almost invisibly, he faded away from the vicinity of the palace. Once in the forest, his pace quickened. Silent, still, and almost invisible. Like a wounded panther.

DARAS
Spring, 529 AD

Chapter 14

The good news, thought Belisarius, was that John of Rhodes was an extremely intelligent man.

That was also the bad news.

"Why are you lying to me?" demanded the retired naval officer. "How in the name of Christ do you expect me to accomplish whatever it is you want me to accomplish, when you are obviously keeping everything essential a secret from me?"

Belisarius gazed down at the man calmly.

John of Rhodes scowled. "Save the sphinx for someone else, Belisarius!" He stumped over to the worktable and made a disgusted gesture toward the various substances and implements strewn upon it.

"Look at this clutter! Trash and toys, that's all they are. I might as well be looking for the philosopher's stone, or the elixir of eternal life." His glare left the table and roamed about the room, encompassing the entire workshop in its condemnation.

Belisarius scratched his chin.

"Stop scratching your chin!" The naval officer flung himself into a nearby chair, exuding the quintessence of disgruntlement in his slumped posture. "Damn all mannerisms, anyway," he grumbled. He looked up, eyeing Belisarius balefully. "And there's another thing," he continued. "What's this nonsense you and your wife are trying to pull with me and that jackal Procopius?"

Before Belisarius could dredge up something suitable to put the man at ease, John of Rhodes was back on his feet, stumping about and gesticulating angrily.

"Don't bother! Please! Do I look like a cretin?"

Belisarius decided that, under the circumstances, straightforwardness was probably the only suitable tactic.

"Explain," he commanded. "And stop stumping about."

"I'm not *stumping*. I'm pacing, from vexation."

"Stop pacing from vexation. And explain."

John stood still. Somehow, despite his much shorter stature, the naval officer seemed to be glaring down at the general.

"Have you heard my reputation?" he demanded. "That I am a master of seduction?"

Belisarius nodded. John of Rhodes blew out his cheeks and then flung himself again into the chair.

"Well, the reputation's exaggerated. But not by much. The fact is, I've enjoyed considerable success with the ladies, over the years. Do you know my secret?"

Belisarius waited. For the first time since meeting John of Rhodes, not two hours earlier, the naval officer smiled.

"The secret to success in seduction, Belisarius, is the same as the secret to success in warfare. Never fight a battle you can't win."

"Your point?"

"My point's obvious. I hadn't spent more than an hour in Antonina's company before it was clear as day that she was quite unseducible. While you were off thrashing the Medes, she and I were often alone. At such times, she's all business and work. *That's all*. So why is it, the moment that foul creature Procopius hoves into view, that she suddenly acts as if she's smitten by me?"

Even sitting, he seemed to be glaring down at Belisarius. "*What are you up to?*"

Belisarius sighed and pulled up another chair. After sitting, he smiled crookedly. "We're engaged in a deep and dark conspiracy, John."

The naval officer's foul mood vanished. He grinned like a wolf—which, thought Belisarius, he rather resembled. A short, sinewy, handsome, blue-eyed, black-haired, grey-bearded, well-groomed wolf.

"Well!" he exclaimed. "That's more like it!" He leaned forward in his chair, rubbing his hands together cheerfully.

"Tell me all about it."

When Belisarius finished, John eyed him askance.

"You're still keeping something from me," he announced. "I don't believe for a minute that these—*visions*, to use your term—simply came to you out of nowhere. Someone, or something, is behind them."

Belisarius nodded.

"And you're not going to tell me who it is? Not now, at any rate."

Belisarius nodded again.

John looked away, frowning. A few seconds later, his face cleared.

"I can live with that," he said. "For a time, at least."

He stroked his beard. "But there's one other question I must have answered. Now. Is this conspiracy aimed at the throne? Against the Emperor?"

Belisarius shook his head firmly. John stared at him.

"Swear," he commanded. "I know your reputation, General. If I have your oath, I'll be satisfied."

"I swear to you before God, John of Rhodes, that the conspiracy of which you are a part is not aimed against the Emperor Justinian."

Again, the raffish grin. "But he doesn't know about it either, does he?"

"No."

"Does the Empress?"

"No. Not yet, at least."

John rose to his feet and resumed stumping about.

"Good. Let's keep it that way, shall we? Especially when it comes to Justinian." The naval officer grimaced. "Such a suspicious tyrant, he is."

After a moment, John blew out his cheeks again and looked toward the workbench. "Not, mind you, that there's much of a conspiracy here to begin with. Plenty of deep darkness, but precious little to hide."

"You've had no success at all?"

"None—beyond some minor improvements in the Greek fire we already had. But nothing that'd be in the slightest way suitable for land combat."

Belisarius rose. "Come outside," he said. "There are some people I want you to meet."

When he couldn't find the Axumites in the villa, Belisarius suspected he would find them in the barracks. And so he did.

The barracks were crowded full with soldiers, especially in the huge room which had served the former owner of the estate for a formal dining hall. Some of that population density was due to the quarters themselves. The Thracians had been reveling in the luxuriance of the "barracks" since they arrived at the villa. But most of it was due to the contest taking place at a table in the center of the hall.

Seeing him, his bucellarii drew aside and let him approach the table. Belisarius examined the scene, and sighed with exasperation.

Garmat, to his credit, was obviously trying to keep a lid on the situation. So was Maurice, of course. And the two soldiers of the Dakuen sarwe were behaving in the rational manner which one expects from experienced veterans surrounded by strange veterans. Politely. Cautiously.

But the prince, alas, was still a young man, full of pride and eager to show his mettle. And not all of the general's Thracian retinue were as relaxed in their experience as such veterans as Anastasius and Valentinian (both of whom, Belisarius noted, were lounging about amicably in nearby chairs). No, there were plenty of youngsters in the general's retinue, most of whom were every bit as full of pride as the prince, and not in the slightest intimidated by his royal lineage.

At the moment, the mutual pride was taking the form of an arm-wrestling match. A good-humored one, probably, in its origin. But the humor was now wearing thin.

The reason for the growing ill temper was obvious, and was demonstrated for the general himself almost immediately. With a grunt of anger and disgust, the fist of the Thracian lad named Menander slammed down onto the table. Eon's dark face was split by a grin.

Glancing about, Belisarius estimated that at least three other Thracian lads had already been trounced by the Axumite. And were none too happy about it.

He sighed again. During the course of the journey from Constantinople to Daras, Belisarius had found the prince to be quite charming. Once Eon got over a certain aloofness, which Belisarius knew was nothing more than his way of maintaining dignity in a sea of strangers, the prince was both good-natured and intelligent. He had even managed—after a few slaps on the head from his dawazz—to stop ogling Antonina in his uncertain adolescent way. And he got along very well with Sittas and, to the general's surprise, got along even better with Irene. Under the young Axumite's stiff exterior, there proved to be a sly wit which the spymaster enjoyed.

But—he was still barely more than a boy, and was inordinately proud of his strength.

Belisarius had already seen the prince stripped to the

waist, so he was accustomed to the sight of that Herculean physique. Obviously, however, it had proved too much of a challenge for certain Thracians.

"That's enough, Eon!" snapped Garmat.

"Let him wrestle Anastasius!" demanded a surly voice from somewhere in the crowd.

"By all means!" cried Ousanas. "Anastasius!"

The dawazz, seated at the table next to his prince, grinned over at the huge *pentarch*.

Anastasius yawned. "The lad's much too strong for me. And besides, I'm a lazy man by nature. Contemplative."

The prince frowned slightly. On the face of it—but— He sensed there was a mocking tone under Anastasius' modest words.

The dawazz immediately brought it to focus. His grin widened.

"Oh! Such mockery! Such false self-effacement! Is very great insult to royal dignity of young prince! Prince must now defend his honor!"

Belisarius decided it was time to intervene.

"Enough," he commanded. He cast a stern gaze upon the dawazz.

"Your duty is to restrain the prince from foolishness."

Ousanas gaped. "Most insane concept!" he cried. "Impossible to restrain young royalty from foolishness. Might as well try to restrain crocodile from eating meat."

Ousanas shook his head sadly. "You very great general, Belisarius. Stick to own trade. Make terrible dawazz."

The grin returned. "Only way teach prince not to commit foolish acts is to encourage folly." He spread his arms grandly. "Then probably-never-King-because-idiot-as-well-as-younger-son gets arm twisted off and maybe he learn. Maybe. Maybe not. Probably not. Royalty stupid by nature. Like crocodiles."

He scanned the room majestically. "Many great warriors

here," he commented. "I ask a question. How you hunt crocodile?"

After a moment, someone ventured: "Stab it with a spear."

Ousanas beamed happily. "Spoken like true warrior!" The beam was replaced by a look of humble abasement. "I myself not warrior. Miserable slave, now. Before, though, was great hunter."

Someone snorted. "Is that so? Then tell us, O miserable slave, how did *you* hunt crocodile?"

Ousanas goggled. "Not *hunt* crocodile in first place! Great giant monster, the crocodile! Stronger than ox! Teeth like swords!"

He grinned. "He also very stupid reptile. So I feed him poisoned meat."

Suddenly, the dawazz reached out his long arm and slapped the prince on top of the head.

"You see that one?" he demanded, pointing to Anastasius. "He feeding you poisoned meat."

Anastasius grinned. The prince eyed him skeptically. Ousanas slapped him again.

"Royalty stupid as crocodile!"

Now the prince was glaring hotly at his dawazz. Not for the first time, watching the scene, Belisarius was struck by the peculiar courage required of a good dawazz.

Ousanas slapped him again. "Not even crocodile stupid enough to glare at his dawazz!" The two sarwen chuckled.

"Enough," repeated Belisarius.

Eon tore his gaze away from Ousanas.

"There's someone here I'd like you to meet, Prince. And you, Garmat." Then, after a moment, grudgingly: "And you too, Ousanas, and the sarwen."

Returning to the villa, Belisarius introduced the Ethiopians to John of Rhodes. Antonina was waiting with the naval officer in the main salon, as were Sittas and Irene. After they had taken their seats, the general said to Garmat:

"Tell him what you know of the Indian weapons, if you would."

Belisarius absented himself while the Axumites filled in the naval officer. He had other business to attend to, back in the barracks.

As soon as he entered the dining hall, the conversation which had been filling the room died down. But not before the general caught the final remarks uttered by young Menander.

"The slave offends you, does he?" demanded Belisarius. Menander was silent, but his whole posture exuded *pout*.

Belisarius restrained his temper.

"Tell him, Valentinian," he commanded.

The veteran cataphract never ceased from whittling on his little stick, and he didn't bother to look up.

"If you don't learn how to read men, Menander, you'll never live to collect your retirement bonus. The prince is nothing, at the moment, beyond a big muscle. Later, who knows? Now, nothing. The two soldiers are good. Very good, I'd wager, or they wouldn't be here." He paused briefly, estimating. "The adviser is dangerous. In his prime, probably something to watch. But—he's old. The slave, now, there's the terrible one."

"He's a slave!" protested Menander.

"Feeding you poisoned meat," chuckled Anastasius. The room echoed with laughter. When the laughter died down, Valentinian finally looked up. His narrow, close-featured face was cold. He fixed the young cataphract with dark eyes gazing down a long, pointed nose.

"That slave could slaughter you like a lamb, boy. Never doubt it for a moment."

Belisarius cleared his throat. "I'm going to need three of you to accompany me to Axum. And beyond, to India. We'll be leaving tomorrow morning, and we'll be gone for at least a year. The rest of you will remain on the estate. As you know, Sittas is here. At the Emperor's behest, he is replacing me as commander of the Syrian army. You'll give him whatever assistance he requires, so long as that doesn't interfere with your duty to guard my wife and the estate. Maurice will be in charge."

Maurice said nothing, but a slight twist to his lips indicated his continuing displeasure with the general's plans. A faint buzz of startled conversation began to fill the room, then died down quickly.

"Any volunteers?" he asked.

Within seconds, as Belisarius had expected, almost all of the cataphracts had volunteered. The younger ones had volunteered to a man, except for Menander.

"Excellent!" he exclaimed. Then he smiled his crooked smile.

"Shit," hissed Valentinian.

"Poisoned meat," groaned Anastasius.

"Those of you who had enough sense not to volunteer are coming. Valentinian. Anastasius. Oh—and you, Menander."

By the time Belisarius returned to the villa, the Axumites had finished recounting to their audience what they had been able to learn about the Malwa weapons. It wasn't much, in truth. Over the past few years, several Axumite traders had observed the new and bizarre weapons in use—but only at a distance. The Malwa kept their special weapons closely guarded, and did not allow foreigners near them. In one instance, they had suspended siege operations against a coastal town until a passing Axumite vessel was shepherded away by Malwa warships.

When the Ethiopians finished, John of Rhodes leaned back in his chair and began tapping his hands on his knees. He was frowning slightly, and his eyes seemed a bit unfocussed.

"It's not much to go on, is it?" asked Antonina, somewhat apologetically.

"Quite the contrary," replied the naval officer. "Our friends here from Axum have provided me with the most important fact of all."

"What's that?" demanded Sittas.

John of Rhodes looked at the Greek general and smiled thinly.

"The most important fact is that these weapons *exist*, Sittas." He shrugged. "*What* they are, and how they work, remains a complete mystery. But the fact that they *do* exist means that it is a problem to be solved, rather than a fantasy to be speculated about. There's a world of difference between those two things."

He arose and began stumping about, with his hands clasped behind his back. "We shall need to compile a library here. Unfortunately, the books which I own myself relate to seafaring only."

"Books are expensive," grumbled Sittas.

"So?" retorted Antonina. "You're stinking rich. You can afford them."

"I knew it," growled Sittas. "I knew it. Soak the rich Greek, that's all anybody—"

Irene cut him off. "What books do you need?" she asked John.

The naval officer frowned. "It's obvious to me, from listening to what the Axumites have told us, that the Malwa weapons involve more than simply burning naphtha, or some similar fuel. Every account of the weapons describes them in terms of eruptions—as if they could somehow control the force of a volcano, on a smaller scale. The closest physical phenomenon that I know of is what's called combustion. And there's only one scholar to my knowledge who studied combustion to any great extent."

"Heron of Alexandria," stated Irene.

John of Rhodes nodded. "Precisely. I need a copy of his *Pneumatics*."

Sittas glowered. "There aren't more than fifty copies of that book in existence! Do you have any idea how much it costs? *If* we can even find one in the first place without raiding the library at Alexandria."

"I own a copy," said Irene. "I will be glad to loan it to you. It's still at my villa in Constantinople, however, so it will take a little time to get it here."

Everyone in the room stared at Irene. She smiled whimsically. "Actually, I own most of Heron's writings. I also have the *Mechanics*, *Siegecraft*, *Measurement*, and *Mirrors*. I almost got my hands on a copy of his *Automaton-making* last year, but some damned Armenian beat me to it."

Some of the men in the room were now goggling her; Sittas was gaping.

"I like to read," explained Irene dryly. Slyly.

Antonina started laughing.

"It's unnatural!" choked Sittas. "It's—"

"Marry me," said John of Rhodes.

"Not a chance, John. I know your type. You're just lusting after my books."

The naval officer grinned. "Well, yes, to a degree. But—"

"Not a chance!" repeated Irene. She was laughing now herself.

"What is the world coming to?" demanded Sittas. "My mother never opened a book, much less *owned* one!" He frowned. "*I* don't own any books, come to that."

"Really?" asked Irene. "I am astonished."

Sittas glared at his spymaster. "You are mocking me, woman. I know you are."

Belisarius couldn't help laughing himself. "Nonsense, Sittas!" he exclaimed. "I'm sure Irene was speaking the simple truth. I'm astonished myself, actually."

Sittas transferred his glare to the Thracian.

"Don't you start on me, Belisarius! Just because you own a copy of Caesar's—"

Prince Eon interrupted.

"Do you own a copy of Xenophon's *Anabasis*?" he asked Irene eagerly.

The spymaster nodded.

"May I borrow—" The prince fell silent. "Oh. It's probably also at your villa. In Constantinople."

"I'm afraid so."

The prince began frowning thoughtfully.

"Maybe we could go back—"

"Enough, Eon!" cried Garmat. "We are *not* going back to Constantinople to get you a book!"

"It's the *Anabasis*," whined Eon. "I've been wanting to read that since—"

"No! Absolutely not! Your father is waiting for us at Axum—at Adulis, probably. And have you forgotten—"

"It's the *Anabasis*," wailed Eon.

"Spoken like a true bibliophile," said Irene admiringly. She grinned at the despondent prince and waved her hand airily. "These heathens simply don't understand, Eon. You have to resign yourself to it. Like a saint of old subjected to barbarian tortures and ordeals."

"The *Anabasis*," moaned Eon.

"Ousanas!" barked Garmat. "Do your duty!"

"What duty?" demanded the dawazz. "Love of books prince's best quality. Only thing keep him away from mischief."

The dawazz leaned forward and tapped the prince on top of the head. Very lightly. "Nevertheless. Is still matter of deadly Malwa danger. Anxious father awaiting report of beloved son. Anxious negusa-nagast-type father. Not wise to keep such fathers waiting while hunting up book. Not wise. Anxiety turn to reproach. Negusa-nagast-type reproach."

The two sarwen grunted agreement. Eon sulked.

"How soon can we get Heron's book here?" asked Antonina.

Irene shrugged. "With a special courier—"

Sittas interrupted. "Do you know how much it costs to send a special—"

John of Rhodes laughed. "Why is it that the richest men are always the stingiest? Relax, Sittas. We won't strain your purse."

To Irene: "There's no need for a special courier. I've got weeks of work ahead of me before I can even start thinking about our project. We'll need to find chemical supplies, equipment, tools—everything. All I have at the moment is a few odds and ends."

"Do you need the help of artisans?" asked Belisarius.

John shook his head.

"Not yet, Belisarius. I wouldn't know what to tell them to do or make. Be a waste of their time and your money. Six months from now, maybe. Maybe."

The general frowned. "You think it's going to take that long?"

John scowled fiercely. "That *long*? Do you have any idea what you're asking me to do?"

The naval officer began to rise, in obvious preparation for a heavy session of stumping about, but Belisarius waved him back to his seat.

"Relax, John. I wasn't criticizing. I'm just—just worried, that's all. I don't know how much time we have at our disposal, before our future enemy falls upon us."

John was still not mollified, quite. But before he could say anything further, Irene spoke:

"That's your job, General."

"Excuse me?"

"Buying us time. That's your job. Mine also, to an extent. But mostly yours."

"You've done it before," said Sittas. The big Greek general smiled. "Of course, that was against a bunch of dumbass Goths. Maybe you're not smart enough to tie sophisticated Indians into knots."

"Don't bait my husband, Sittas," said Antonina.

"I'm not baiting him. I'm prodding his vanity."

"My husband is not vain."

A sad shake of the head.

"Poor woman. The wife is always the last to know. Belisarius is the vainest man in creation. He's so vain that he's not vain about the things modest men are vain about— their fame, their riches, their good looks, their wives' good looks. Oh no, not Belisarius. He's only vain about his lack of vanity, which is the worst vanity there is."

Everyone in the room except Irene frowned, trying to follow the tortured logic.

"That makes no sense at all," said Eon. Uncertainly, to Irene: "Does it make sense to you?"

Irene laughed gaily. "Of course it does! But you have to remember—I'm the only other Greek in the room. Except John, but he's from Rhodes. A practical folk, the Rhodesmen. Lapsed Greeks, I'm afraid."

John said nothing, but his gaze was full of interest. Irene laughed again.

"Don't even think about it, John."

The naval officer's grin was quite wolfish.

"Why not? I can't be designing fantastical weapons all the time." A sudden, happy thought. "Well, actually, perhaps I can. But to operate effectively I'll need to be kept up to date with all the latest secret information. Spymaster-type information, you know. Oh, yes. Daily briefings. Essential."

"You stay away from my paramour," growled Sittas. But it was a tepid, tepid growl.

A chuckle swept the room.

Irene patted his hand gently. "Now, now. Don't you worry,

dear. I really think I'm capable of dealing with the occasional wolf."

"Greek lady eat wolf for lunch," commented Ousanas. John of Rhodes cast a dark look upon the dawazz. Belisarius, from experience, could have told him it was a waste of effort. Ousanas simply grinned, and added:

"I ignorant savage, of course. Miserable slave, too. Know almost nothing. But know enough not to chase woman ten times smarter than me."

Belisarius cleared his throat. "We seem to be getting side-tracked. Other than artisans—and the books you talked about—will there be anything else you need?"

John frowned, thought for a moment.

"Nothing much, Belisarius. Some equipment, and a few more tools, but nothing fancy. Substances, of course. Elements. Chemicals. Some of those will be a bit expensive."

Sittas' eyes became slits.

"How expensive? And what kind of—*elements*?"

Very narrow slits.

"Are we talking *gold* here? Seems to me every time you alchemist types start anything you right off begin yapping about—"

John laughed. "Relax, Sittas! I have no use for gold, I assure you. Or silver. One of the reasons they're precious metals is because they're *inert*."

A questioning glance. Sittas' eyes practically disappeared in response.

"I know what *inert* means! You—"

"Enough," said Belisarius. The room became instantly silent. Almost.

"My, he does that well," remarked Irene softly. To Sittas, in the sort of whisper which can be heard by everyone: "Maybe you should try that, dear. Instead of that bellowing roar you so favor."

"*Enough.*" Now, even Irene was silent.

Belisarius rose. "That's it, then. Whatever you need, John, while I'm gone, you can either get from Antonina or"—here a sharp stare—"Sittas."

Sittas grimaced, but did not protest his poverty. Belisarius continued:

"As for the rest of us, I think our course is clear. As clear, at least, as circumstances permit. When I return from India, hopefully, I'll bring with me enough information to guide us further. Until then, we'll just have to do our best."

He looked at his wife. "And now—I would like to spend the rest of the day, and the evening, with my wife and my son."

Once Photius drowsed off, early in the evening, Belisarius and Antonina were alone. They had never been separated for long, since the day they first met. Now, they would be separated for at least a year.

Future loss gave force to present passion. Belisarius got very little sleep that night.

Antonina did not sleep at all. Once her husband finally succumbed to slumber, from sheer exhaustion, she stayed awake through the few hours left in that night. That precious night. That—*last* night, she feared.

By the time the sun arose, Antonina was awash in grief. Bleak certainty. She would never see him again.

Her son rescued her from that bottomless pit. At daybreak, Photius wandered into the room, rubbing sleep from his eyes.

"Will Daddy be coming back?" he asked, timidly. His little face was scrunched with worry.

The boy had never called Belisarius by that name before. The sound of it drove all despair from her soul.

"Of course he will, Photius. He's my husband. And he's your father."

❖   ❖   ❖

At midmorning, Belisarius and his companions rode out of the villa. At the boundary of the estate, they took the road which led to Antioch and, beyond, to Seleuceia on the coast. At Seleuceia they would board ship for the voyage to Egypt and, beyond, to Adulis on the Red Sea. And beyond, to Axum in the Ethiopian highlands. And beyond, to India.

Belisarius rode at the head of the little party. Eon rode on his left, Garmat on his right. Behind them rode the two sarwen. Behind the sarwen, the three cataphracts.

Ousanas traveled on foot. The dawazz, it developed, had a pronounced distaste for all manner of animal transport. Belisarius thought his attitude was peculiar, but—the man himself was peculiar, when you came right down to it. The cataphracts thought he was probably mad. The sarwen, from long experience, were certain of it.

Early on in the journey, young Menander made so bold as to ask the dawazz himself.

"Who is mad, boy? I? Not think so. Madmen place lives on top great beasts with good reason wish men dead. I be horse or donkey or camel, boy, you be squashed melon right quick. I be elephant, you be squashed seeds."

When Menander reported the conversation to his veteran seniors—not, be it said, without a certain concern, and a questioning glance at his own horse—Anastasius and Valentinian shrugged the matter off. They were far too deep into their own misery to fret over such outlandish notions.

"Perfect duty, it was," whined Valentinian.

"Ideal," rumbled Anastasius, with heartful agreement. "Best garrison post I ever saw."

"A villa, no less."

"Wine, women, and song."

"Fuck the songs."

"And now—!"

Mutter, mutter, mutter.

"What was that?"

"I think he said 'fuck adventurous leaders,' " replied Menander. The lad frowned. "But maybe not. I can't always understand him when he mutters, even though he does it a lot. Maybe he said: 'fuck avaricious feeders.' "

The frown deepened. "But that doesn't make a lot of sense either, does it? Especially on a trip—" A sudden thought; a sudden worry; a quick glance at his mount.

"Do you old-timers know something about horses that I don't?"

The conversation at the head of the little column, on the other hand, was not gloomy at all. Even Belisarius, once the estate fell out of sight, regained his usual good spirits. And then, not an hour later, great spirits.

There are many sweet pleasures in this world. Among those—unsung though it is—ranks the pleasure of being asked a question which you were trying to figure out how to ask yourself.

Garmat cleared his throat. "General Belisarius. Prince Eon and I have been discussing—for some time now, actually, but we only came to a decision last night—well, the negusa nagast will naturally have to make the final decision, but we are quite certain he will agree—well, the point is—"

"Oh, for the love of Christ!" exclaimed Eon. "General, we would like to accompany you and your men to India." The prince closed his mouth with a snap, straightened his back, stared firmly ahead.

Belisarius smiled—and not crookedly. "I would be delighted!" He turned in his saddle—so easy, that motion, with stirrups!—and looked behind.

"All of you?" he asked. "Including the sarwen?" The general examined the two Ethiopian soldiers. Outlandish men, they were, from a little known and mysterious country. But he knew their breed perfectly.

"Oh, yes," replied Garmat. "They are sworn to Prince Eon's personal service."

Belisarius now looked to Ousanas. The dawazz was striding alongside his prince.

"And you, Ousanas?"

"Of course! Must keep fool prince out of trouble."

"You don't consider this trouble?"

The dawazz grinned. "Voyage to distant India? Enter Malwa gaping maw with madman foreign general intent on stealing Malwa teeth? Sanest thing fool prince ever do."

Belisarius laughed. "You call that sane?"

For once, the grin disappeared. "Yes, Belisarius. For prince of Axum, in new Malwa world, I call that sane. Anything else be folly."

THE ERYTHREAN SEA
Summer, 529 AD

Chapter 15

"It's quite a ship," remarked Belisarius, gazing from the bow down the length of the Indian embassy vessel. "It must be as big as the Alexandrian grain ships—even the *Isis*."

"It's a tub," pronounced Eon. The young prince's gaze followed that of Belisarius, but with none of the general's admiration.

The ship was almost two hundred feet long, and about forty-five feet wide. It was as big as the largest sailing ships ever built by Romans, the great grain-carrying vessels which hauled Egypt's wheat from Alexandria to Constantinople and the western Mediterranean. The famous *Isis* was one of those ships.

Like those grain ships, the Indian vessel had two lower decks as well as the main deck. And, also like the grain ships, the Indian craft was a pure sailing vessel. It had no rowing capability at all. With its enormous carrying capacity of two thousand tons, oars would have been almost futile.

There the resemblance ended. The grain ships were three-masted vessels. The Indian ship was single-masted, although the great square sails of the huge mainmast were assisted by a lateen sail in the stern. Another difference lay in the superstructure. Where the Mediterranean tradition was to build up a poop deck in the stern, the Malwa concentrated their superstructure amidships, surrounding the base of the great mainmast. The wood used throughout the Indian vessel was teak, and the rigging was coir. Mediterranean ships were built of fir or cedar, with some oak, and the cordage was typically hemp or flax (although the Egyptians often used papyrus, and the Spaniards favored esparto grass).

Beyond those obvious differences, Belisarius was lost. Prince Eon, it seemed, was not.

"A *tub*," he repeated forcefully.

"Very *big* tub," added Ousanas cheerfully. "Most obscene large tub."

"So what?" demanded Eon. "Size isn't everything."

The tall dawazz smiled down at his charge. Under that cheerful regard the Prince tightened his jaw.

"Size isn't everything," he repeated.

"Certainly not!" agreed Garmat. The old adviser smiled. "As a short man, I agree full-heartedly. However, as a short man, I must immediately add that I have always found it wise to take size into consideration. What do you think, General?"

Belisarius tore his gaze away from the ship.

"Eh? Oh—yes, I agree. Although, as a tall man, I have found the converse to be true as well."

"What do you mean?" asked Garmat.

"I mean that I find it wise to take other things than size into consideration. I have never found, for instance, that the size of an army plays as much of a factor in the outcome of battles as the skill of the troops and its leadership."

The prince looked smug. Ousanas immediately piped up: "Belisarius great diplomat!"

Eon majestically ignored the barb, staring out to sea. Belisarius smiled crookedly.

"Why do you call the ship a tub?" he asked the prince.

Eon gazed at him sideways. There was a slight hint of suspicion in his eyes. Even though Belisarius was not given to teasing him—one of many things which the prince had found to like in the Byzantine—still, Eon was a young man, somewhat unsure of himself for all his outward pride.

"Explain," commanded the general.

After a moment's hesitation, Eon launched into a voluminous recital of the huge ship's many faults and shortcomings. Belisarius, no seaman, was immediately lost in the technical details. The gist of it, he concluded, was that Eon thought the great vessel was clumsily designed and operated by even clumsier sailors. He had no idea if Eon was right. But he was deeply impressed by the young Ethiopian's obvious expertise in nautical matters. That simple fact drove home to him, as nothing had before, the seriousness with which the Axumites took their navy. No Roman or Persian prince could have matched that performance.

As soon as Eon finished his recital of the ship's woes, Ousanas commented:

"Axumites notorious braggarts about seamanship."

Garmat cleared his throat. "Actually, I agree with the prince."

"Arabs even worse," added Ousanas.

"You don't agree?" asked Belisarius. The dawazz shrugged.

"Have no idea. Hunter from savanna. Avoid sea like all sane persons. Boats unnatural creatures. But is well known Ethiopians and Arabs think they world's best seamen." A sly glance at the general. "Except Greeks."

"I'm not Greek," came the immediate response. "I'm Thracian. I tend to agree with you, actually. I can't stand boats."

"How are you feeling?" asked Garmat pleasantly.

"I'd rather not think about it," said Belisarius stiffly. "Please continue."

Garmat cleared his throat again. "Well, Eon is perhaps putting the matter too forcefully—"

"It's the simple truth!"

"—but, on balance, I agree with him. The Indians are not, you know, famous for their abilities at sea."

"No, I do not know."

"Ah. Well, it is true. Ethiopians and Arabs ridicule them for it. North Indians, at least. Some of the southern nations of India are quite capable seamen, by all accounts, but we have little contact with them. Their trade is primarily with the distant East." The adviser stroked his beard. "In its own impressive way, this great ship is evidence of my point. The design, as the prince says, is clumsy. And the workmanship is rather poor. Unusually so, for Indians."

Belisarius examined the ship.

"It seems solidly made."

"Oh, it is! That's the point. It's much *too* solid." Here Garmat launched into his own technical discourse, the gist of which, so far as Belisarius could tell, was that the Indians substituted brute strength for craftsmanship. And again, he was struck by the naval expertise of high-ranked Axumites.

"A tub," concluded Garmat.

"Slow as a snail," added Eon, "and just as awkward."

"Big as a monster," chimed in Ousanas. "Run right over clever little Arab and Axumite boats."

"Nonsense!" exclaimed the Prince.

"We find out soon," commented Ousanas dryly. He pointed off the port bow.

The small party of Ethiopians and Romans followed his pointing finger. The southern coast of Arabia was a reddish gloom in the rays of the setting sun. But, against that dark background, a multitude of sails was visible.

"Oh, shit," muttered Valentinian. The pentarch straightened up from his slouch against the rail a few feet distant. He nudged Anastasius next to him. The huge cataphract jerked awake from his doze.

"Get our gear," commanded Valentinian. "And drag Menander out here."

"The kid can't hardly move," protested Anastasius. "He says he doesn't have any guts left."

"Get him! If he complains, tell him he's about to find out what being gutted really means."

Startled, Anastasius followed Valentinian's hard gaze.

"Oh, shit," he muttered. "Is that what I think it is?"

"Arab pirates!" cried Ousanas. He grinned widely. "Not to worry! Very small boats. True, very many of them. Oh, very very very many. Each one loaded with very very many nasty vicious men bent on wickedness. But" —here he gestured grandly— "the great General Belisarius assures that size of army matters nothing."

"Yeah, I've heard him say that before," grumbled Valentinian. "Just before all hell broke loose."

Anastasius was already entering the tent which the Romans had set up in the bow. Loud cries and shouts rang over the ship. The Indian crewmen had also seen the approaching fleet of galleys.

Valentinian marched to the port side and leaned over the rail, gripping it in his lean, sinewy hands. The dark-eyed cataphract glared toward the approaching pirate vessels. His scarred, pock-marked face twisted into a grimace. "Just once," he growled bitterly, "*just once*, I'd like to outnumber the enemy for a change. Fuck skill. Fuck cunning. Fuck strategy. Fuck tactics. Give me numbers, dammit!" His voice trailed off into muttering.

"What was that last?" asked Belisarius mildly. Valentinian was silent.

"Sounded like 'fuck philosophical generals,' " said Ousanas brightly.

Valentinian glowered at him. The dawazz spread his hands. "Maybe not. Ignorant worthless slave. Speak terrible Greek. Fierce cataphract maybe said 'fuck philandering genitals.'

Very ethical sentiment! Most inappropriate for occasion, but very moral. Very moral!"

Belisarius' attention was distracted by a commotion. Venandakatra had made his appearance on the deck. He emerged from his cabin amidships, followed by a gaggle of Mahaveda priests.

The Byzantines and Ethiopians had seen almost nothing of him since they had embarked on the Indian vessel at Adulis. Venandakatra's representatives had explained the Indian lord's apparent rudeness as being due to seasickness.

Watching the spry, if waddling, manner in which Venandakatra scurried about, Belisarius had his doubts.

"Seasick!" snorted Eon.

Venandakatra was shouting orders in his shrill, high-pitched voice. Within seconds, dozens of Ye-tai warriors scrambled out of their own tents and began lining the rail. They were bearing bows, swords, and shields, and quickly began donning helmets and half-armor.

The Ye-tai were followed by a dozen warriors whom Belisarius recognized as Malwa kshatriyas. These emerged from the hatch located in the deck just forward of Venandakatra's cabin. They were bearing no weapons beyond short swords, and wore only the lightest leather armor. But they were heavily burdened nonetheless. Divided into pairs, each pair was carrying a large trough made of some odd, lumpy wood which Belisarius had never seen before.

"That's bamboo," explained Garmat. "It's hollow on the inside, like a pipe. They've split it down the middle and carved out the internal partitions."

"This is what you were telling John of Rhodes about, isn't it?"

Garmat nodded. "Yes. I have never seen the Indian weapons myself, but these are quite as described by those of our traders who have seen them in action. From a distance only, however. I think we are about to get a firsthand view."

"Venandakatra's not happy about that," commented Eon.

Belisarius gazed at the Indian lord. Venandakatra was consulting with his cluster of priests. All of them were casting unfriendly glances toward the Romans and Axumites standing in the bow. After a moment, one of the priests detached himself from the group and headed toward them.

"I'll handle this," said Belisarius.

When the priest reached them, Belisarius didn't even give him the chance to speak.

"*No.*"

The priest opened his mouth.

"*Absolutely not.*"

"You must go below!"

"*Under no conditions will we do so.*"

At that moment Anastasius lumbered out of the tent, with Menander close behind. Both cataphracts were fully armed and armored, except for their lances. They were also bearing Belisarius and Valentinian's weapons and armor. Their arrival distracted the priest, who began gobbling further protests. His protests became positively shrill when he spotted the two sarwen charging out of their own tent, likewise laden with weapons. An abundance of weapons—each sarwen was carrying a cluster of javelins as well as swords, shields, and huge-bladed spears.

Within moments, all the Romans and Axumites were busily donning their armor and taking up their weapons. The priest was now practically gibbering.

"Anastasius," commanded the general. "Do something impressively unfriendly."

Anastasius immediately seized the priest by the scruff of the neck and his crotch and tossed him back toward the cluster of priests amidships. The priest managed to land on his feet, more or less, but he immediately stumbled out of control and hurtled into his cohorts, bowling two of them right over.

Venandakatra screeched with fury. A small crowd of Ye-tai warriors surged forward.

Without any orders from Belisarius, all three cataphracts immediately notched arrows and drew their bows. The two sarwen raised their javelins. Eon and Garmat hefted their stabbing spears. Belisarius drew his sword. Ousanas lounged against the rail.

"What are you playing at?" hissed Menander.

Ousanas gaped. "Me? Miserable slave! Not fit for noble type foolishness."

"Ousanas!" commanded Eon.

The dawazz sighed. "Most unreasonable prince." He lazed forward. "Play old game?" he asked.

Eon immediately gave Ousanas his great spear. The prince shed his baldric and sword and then began to walk, unarmed, toward the Malwa crowd. Behind him, Ousanas motioned the Ye-tai warriors to clear a lane. Puzzled, but hearing no countervailing orders from the priests, the Ye-tai did as the dawazz bade them.

Eon walked right through the silent Malwa crowd until he reached the cabin which was built around the base of the mainmast. As soon as he reached the cabin, the prince turned and backed up against it. He crossed his arms and spread his legs about a foot apart. He was standing about twenty yards from the Axumites and Romans in the bow.

Ousanas casually jabbed the stabbing spear into the deck of the ship. The huge blade sank a full inch into the hard wood and stood erect. Without a word, one of the sarwen handed him a javelin. The dawazz hefted the javelin lightly and then, with a motion whose speed and power stunned everyone watching, hurled the javelin across the length of the deck.

The weapon sank into the wall of the cabin almost the full length of the blade. The shaft of the weapon quivered like a tuning fork. About two inches from the prince's left ear.

A moment later, another javelin was sailing across the deck. This one plunged into the wood about two inches from Eon's right ear. Not seconds later, a third javelin thundered into the cabin wall right between the prince's legs. About two inches below his crotch.

"Mary, Mother of God," whispered Valentinian.

Anastasius drew a deep breath. "That's incredible spear work. Amazing!"

"Fuck the spear work," growled Valentinian. "The kid never even blinked! *That's* amazing. I may never fuck again, just from watching."

The prince suddenly laughed. He and his dawazz exchanged huge grins across the deck of the ship.

"Very foolish prince," mused Ousanas, shaking his head. "But got elephant heart. Been that way since boy."

Ousanas plucked the great stabbing spear out of the deck and sauntered toward Eon. The warriors and priests scuttled out of his way. The dawazz smiled upon them beatifically.

"Intelligent persons!" he exclaimed. "Very most sane and logical Indian people!" He bestowed a particularly engaging grin upon Venandakatra.

When Ousanas reached Eon, he and the prince assisted each other in withdrawing the javelins from the cabin walls. More than anything else, perhaps, it was the obvious effort being exerted by these two very strong men which drove home just how ferocious those javelin casts had been.

Belisarius sheathed his sword and strode over to Venandakatra.

"We are soldiers," he told the Indian lord sternly, "not children. We will not be penned in the hold during an attack."

He matched Venandakatra's glare with one of his own. After a moment, the Vile One looked away.

"Besides," added Belisarius, turning away and pointing

to the approaching fleet of pirate vessels, "you may find you are glad to have us, soon enough."

Venandakatra scowled, but said nothing. Belisarius returned to the bow of the ship and began giving directions to the Roman and Axumite warriors. After a few moments, it became clear that the Indians had decided to leave the defense of the bow in the hands of their unwanted guests.

Belisarius had never encountered Axumite warriors in battle, neither as friend nor foe. He hesitated for a moment, wondering how best to use their skills.

What he could glean of the Ethiopian way of fighting was odd. They seemed singularly unconcerned about bodily protection, for one thing. The Axumites, when not constrained by Greek custom, never wore anything except a short-sleeved tunic, kilt, and sandals. Now, preparing for battle, they removed their tunics and stood bare from the waist up. Each of them, except Ousanas, took up a buffalo-hide shield. The shields were round and small— no wider than a forearm. Those little shields, apparently, constituted the entirety of their armor.

Each Ethiopian carried a sword slung behind his back from a leather baldric which crossed the right shoulder diagonally. The haft of the sword stuck up right behind the shoulder blade, where it could be easily grasped. The swords were purely cutting implements. They were short, very wide and heavy, and ended in a square tip. They resembled a butcher's cleaver more than anything else.

The swords, however, were obviously secondary weapons. For their main armament, each Ethiopian carried javelins and those enormous spears. The Axumite stabbing spear was about seven feet long. The blade was almost a foot and a half long, shaped like a narrow leaf, heavy and razor sharp. The spear shaft was also heavy—as thick and solid as a cavalry lance. The last foot or so of the haft was sheathed with iron bands, and the very end of the haft bore a solid iron knob about two inches in diameter. The weapon could obviously double as a long mace.

Garmat spoke quietly.

"I suggest you use us as a reserve, Belisarius. As you can see, we do not match your cataphracts for sheer weight of armor and weapons. It is not the Axumite method. But I think you will find us very useful when the enemy presses."

"What about him?" asked the general, nodding toward Ousanas. The dawazz carried neither a shield nor a sword. He seemed content merely with his javelins and his spear— a spear which, in his case, was a foot longer and much heavier than those borne by the other Ethiopians.

Garmat shrugged. "Ousanas is a law unto himself. But I think you will have no cause for complaint."

Belisarius smiled his crooked smile. "A miserable, ignorant slave, is he?"

As often before, Ousanas surprised him with his acute hearing.

"Most miserable!" cried the dawazz. "Especially now! With cruel pitiless Arabs approaching!" Ousanas cast a longing glance at the sea. "Would flee in abject shrieking terror except too ignorant to know how to swim."

"You swim like a fish!" snapped the Prince.

The dawazz goggled. "Do I? Imagine such a wonder!" He shook his head sadly. "Slavery terrible condition. Make me forget everything."

Belisarius turned away and resumed his examination of the Indians. He saw that the bamboo troughs had now been set up along the port rail of the deck, facing northward. The troughs were spaced about ten feet apart. The Malwa kshatriyas then placed great bundles of hide at the ship-end of the troughs. The grey hides were tightly rolled into barrel-shapes which were about half the size of actual barrels.

"That's elephant hide," commented Garmat quietly.

Now, the kshatriyas began dipping buckets into the sea

and hauling them up with ropes. As soon as the buckets were drawn aboard, the seawater was poured over the hide rolls. Once the hide rolls were completely waterlogged, the kshatriyas began pouring the seawater over every exposed surface of the ship. After a hurried consultation with Venandakatra, two of the kshatriyas advanced to the bow. Making clear with gestures and facial expressions that their intentions were pacific, the kshatriyas began soaking the bow of the ship with seawater also. The Romans and Ethiopians, at Belisarius' command, stood aside and made no objection, even when the Malwa soaked the leather walls of their own tents.

After the kshatriya left the bow, Belisarius whispered to Garmat: "For some reason, they seemed terrified of fire. Is that because of the Arabs, do you think?"

Garmat shook his head. "Can't be. Arab navies are known to use fire arrows, on occasion, but these are not naval forces. They are pirates. What would be the point of burning this ship? They want to capture it."

Belisarius nodded his head. "So—it must be due to their own weapons."

At that moment, more kshatriyas began emerging from the hold. They were bearing knobby, odd-looking, short—poles?

"Are those bamboo?" asked Belisarius.

"Yes," replied Garmat. "Each of those poles is simply a length of bamboo with some kind of bundle at one end. I think the bundle is just a wider length of bamboo jammed over the end of the pole and bound to it with leather. See? That's the end they're placing in the troughs to face outward. The other end has a—a tail, let's call it. That's just a short length of bamboo split length-wise."

"What are these things called?"

Garmat shrugged.

❖   ❖   ❖

aim seized the moment. In a paroxysm of determination, it drove the facets toward a single point. A pure focus, a narrow salient in the barrier, a simple thrust. Had **aim** understood the human way of siegecraft, it would have called itself a battering ram guided toward the hinge of the gate. Perhaps—yes! Yes! Yes!

"It's called a—a *rocket*," whispered Belisarius. "More," he commanded. "More!"

"What are you talking about?" demanded Garmat. The old adviser was gazing at the general as if Belisarius were demented. Belisarius grinned at him.

"I'm not mad, Garmat, believe me. Just—I can't explain, now. Something important is happening. I am—let's say, I am understanding things."

Again **aim** drove the facets. Again, it regained the focus. Again, the battering ram. Again—the breach!

"Yes," whispered Belisarius. "I see it, yes! It could be turned around. Made its opposite. Expel its interior rather than be expelled by it. Yes!"

He frowned, concentrating, *concentrating*. For a moment—for he was well acquainted with the human way of siegecraft—he even envisioned himself as a battering ram. And, with that vision, made his own breach in the wall.

"Then it would be called a—*cannon*."

He sagged, almost staggered. Garmat steadied him with a hand.

"Truly," muttered the adviser, "truly I hope you have not gone mad. This is a poor time for it." He shook the general's arm. "Belisarius! Snap out of it! The pirates are almost within bow range."

Belisarius straightened, looked seaward, then glanced down at the Axumite. He shook his head, smiling.

"You are exaggerating, Garmat. The Arabs will not be within bow range for two minutes. But—the pirates *are* within rocket range. Watch!"

At that moment, a strange hissing sound was heard, like a dragon's rage. Startled, Garmat looked back amidships and gaped. One of the—*rockets*—was hurtling itself toward the pirates. Behind it, a ball of flame billowed on the deck, surrounding the hide roll at the back of the trough from which the rocket had soared. The kshatriyas were obviously expecting the phenomenon, for, within a second or two, buckets of water were poured over the smoldering hide bundle. The ball of flame became a small cloud of steam.

Belisarius watched the flight of the rocket. He was struck, more than anything, by the serpentine nature of the bamboo device's trajectory. It did not fly with the true arc of an arrow or a cast spear. Instead, the rocket skittered and snaked about. He realized, after a moment, that there was some connection between the rocket's movements and the erratic red flare that jetted from its tail.

Crude, blunt thoughts suddenly emerged through the barrier. They entered his mind like dumb creatures lumbering into a cave.

poor mix. bad powder.

Mix? He wondered. *Powder? What could powder—dust— have to do with—?*

powder is force.

"How? And what kind of powder?" he wondered aloud. Again, Garmat glanced at him worriedly. Belisarius began to smile reassuringly, but the smile faded. He could feel the alien presence in his mind retreating; could sense its discouragement.

The rocket began to drift downward toward the sea. It was obvious, long before it struck, that the device had been badly aimed. It would land far from any pirate craft.

"Is it aimed at all?" he muttered. Next to him, Garmat shook his head. The Axumite seemed relieved that Belisarius' mumblings were now connected to reality.

"I do not think so, General. I think they are simply shot

forth in the general direction of the enemy. You saw how it flew. How could such a capricious weapon be aimed?"

The rocket hit the sea. There was a sudden plume of water and steam, then—nothing. The multitude of Arabs aboard the pirate vessels gave out a great jeering cry.

The pirates were now close enough for examination.

There were a total of thirteen galleys approaching. Each was rowed on two banks, with a lateen sail and a huge crew. At a rough guess, Belisarius estimated that each ship carried over a hundred men. Most of the pirates were armed with swords or spears. A number had bows. Very few, however, wore much in the way of armor. Nor, for that matter, did many of the Arabs even carry shields.

As individuals, Belisarius decided, they were not particularly fearsome. The danger was in their great numbers.

Four more rockets were fired. Again, the skittering serpentine trajectories—and again, none of them came near their mark. The pirates were now jeering madly.

"They're gaining on us," groused Eon. "What a miserable ship this beast is! In these heavy seas, with this good wind, we should be leaving them behind easily."

Six rockets were fired. And now, finally, the strange weapons showed their true power. Two of them struck the same pirate vessel. The Arab ship seemed to burst into flame and fury. Several pirates were hurled into the air as if they had been struck by the hand of an invisible titan.

"Force!" exclaimed Belisarius. "Yes—that's what—" He fell silent.

"That's *what?*" demanded Garmat.

Belisarius glanced at him, pursed his lips in thought, then shook his head.

"Never mind, Garmat. I was just noticing that these weapons are not simply fire-weapons. They bear some other power with them as well. Some unknown—*force*—which acts like a blow as well as a flame."

Garmat looked back at the pirate vessel. Now that the cloud of smoke had cleared, it was obvious that the ship had been struck as well as burnt. Where one of the rockets had collided, an entire section of the ship's hull had been caved in. The vessel was already listing badly, and its crew was beginning to jump overboard. It was clear that the craft was doomed. The only uncertainty was whether it would sink before the flames could engulf it.

Again, suddenly, an alien thought moved into Belisarius' mind.

explosion. force is explosion.

Tantalizingly, Belisarius almost caught the image which the jewel was emitting. But it withdrew, faded—then surged back. Just for an instant, the general saw a barrel containing a blazing and furious fire. The fire produced a vast volume of gasses which pressed against the walls of the barrel until—

"Yes!" he cried. "Yes—I was right! It *is* fire!"

He suddenly realized that a number of people were staring at him. Not just Romans and Axumites, either. Several of the Ye-tai warriors stationed nearby were frowning at him, as well as a Mahaveda priest.

Keep your mouth shut, idiot. Observe in silence.

Another volley of rockets. Six rockets, six misses—but the jeer from the pirates was notably more subdued. The Arab craft were now less than two hundred yards away. A few Arab archers loosed shafts, but their arrows fell short of the mark.

"Weaklings," sneered Anastasius. The giant Thracian drew his great bow. Belisarius almost winced, watching. The general had tried to draw that bow, once. Tried and failed miserably, for all that Belisarius was a strong man.

Powerful as he was, Anastasius was actually not a great archer. He had nothing like the skill with a bow possessed by Valentinian. But, aiming at those closely packed, mobbed vessels, it hardly mattered. His arrow sailed across the distance and plunged into the crowd aboard one ship. A shriek was heard.

"Most blessed arrow!" cried Ousanas. "Graced by God Himself!"

Anastasius grinned. Valentinian snorted.

"He's not praising you, stupid. He's saying you were lucky."

Anastasius frowned at Ousanas. The dawazz shook his head sadly.

"Valentinian tells false lie. Very wicked Roman man! Not said you were lucky. Said you stood most high in Deity's esteem."

"See?" demanded Valentinian.

Anastasius gestured angrily. "Let's see you do any better!" he demanded.

Ousanas grinned. "Too far. Arrows cheap as dirt. Javelins precious. Very important point in theology. God wanton with His blessings on arrows. Stingy with javelins."

The dawazz pointed to the easternmost craft.

"You see him steersman? That ship?"

Anastasius nodded.

Again, Ousanas shook his head sadly. "Him great sinner. Soon be taken by Shaitan."

"How soon?" demanded Anastasius.

"Soon as skill allow. Javelin weapon of skill. God *very* stingy with javelin. Miser, almost."

Anastasius snorted and turned away. Again, he drew his bow. Again, his arrow found a mark in the crowd.

The pirates drew closer. There had been no rocket volleys for some time, but now another six were fired off. Belisarius noted that the kshatriyas manning the rockets had adjusted the angle of the firing troughs. Where before the bamboo half-barrels had been tilted upward, they were now almost level.

These rockets did not soar upward like a javelin. They sped in a more or less flat trajectory barely a few feet above the water. And they struck with devastating impact. At that range, they could hardly miss. Belisarius was fascinated to see one rocket hit the sea at a shallow angle and then bounce back upward, like a flat-thrown stone skipping across water. That rocket did as much damage as any when it slammed into the bow of an Arab ship.

Almost half of the pirate fleet had now been struck by the missiles. Two ships were listing badly and had ceased their forward motion. Two others were burning furiously, and their crews were jumping overboard.

But it was obvious the Arabs had no intention of breaking off the attack. The pirate vessels now began to scatter, spreading out in such a way as to give less of a massed target for the rockets. The sailors on the surviving galleys helped those who had jumped from stricken ships to clamber aboard.

Five pirate vessels were now sinking or burning out of control, and at least one other seemed out of the action. But Belisarius did not think that the actual number of warriors had been significantly reduced. Most of those who had jumped into the sea had been taken aboard other vessels. The remaining craft were now jammed with men.

Another volley of rockets was fired. All of them but one missed, however, soaring through the space now vacated by the galleys. Even the one which struck a ship simply glanced off harmlessly. That rocket continued to soar across the sea until, suddenly, it erupted in a ball of flame and smoke.

Belisarius scratched his chin. It occurred to him that the rockets did not actually seem to—*explode*—on contact. He remembered, now, that several of the rockets had exploded a few seconds *after* striking a ship. The effect had been the same, however, for the force of their flight had driven the rockets right through the thin planking of the Arab ships. And, regardless of the timing of the explosions, the rockets burned so fiercely that they almost invariably set the ships afire.

Still—

"With the right armor and tactics," he mused aloud, "I don't think these rockets would be all that dangerous."

Valentinian turned to him with a questioning look.

"Play hell with horses, General," commented the cataphract.

"True," agreed Belisarius. "Those shrieking hisses and explosions would panic the brutes. No way to control them." Suddenly, he grinned. "I do believe the infantry has just made a great comeback!"

"Shit," muttered Anastasius. "He's right."

Valentinian groaned. "I *hate* walking."

"*You* hate it?" demanded Anastasius. "You haven't got an ounce of fat on you! How do you think I feel?"

Garmat interrupted worriedly. "Night has almost fallen."

It was true enough. It was still barely possible to make out the intact pirate ships in the gathering darkness, but not by much.

"New moon, too," added Eon. "There won't be any light at all in a few minutes."

Another volley of rockets was fired. Belisarius noted that the kshatriyas had angled all six of the troughs around so that all of the rockets were fired toward a single ship. Even so, only one of the rockets struck. Fortunately, the missile hit directly amidships and exploded with a satisfying roar. That vessel, clearly enough, was doomed.

Just before the last glimmer of daylight faded, it was possible to see the pirate galleys beginning to surround the Indian ship. They were now keeping a distance, however, waiting for nightfall. Between that distance, and being widely spread out, it was obvious that the rockets were no longer of much use.

Two more wasted volleys made the point before Venandakatra began calling out new orders. Immediately, three of the rocket crews began transferring their troughs to the starboard rail of the ship. For their part, the three remaining rocket crews began spacing their troughs more widely down the port length of the ship. The Malwa, it was obvious, were positioning the rocket launchers to repel boarders.

Venandakatra shouted new orders. Listening, Belisarius could begin to understand the meaning. He realized that the jewel was once again working its strange magic. The Malwa language was called Hindi, and Belisarius knew not a word of it. But, suddenly, the language came into focus in his mind. The shrill words spoken by several kshatriyas in response to Venandakatra's commands were as clear as day.

"The Indian rocket-men are not happy," whispered Garmat. "They are complaining that—"

"They will be burned if they do as Venandakatra orders," completed Belisarius absently.

The Axumite adviser was startled. "I did not realize you spoke Hindi."

Belisarius began to reply, closed his mouth. Garmat, again, was staring at him strangely.

I'm going to have to come up with an explanation for him, when this is all over. Damn all shrewd advisers, anyway!

Venandakatra shouted down the protests. His Mahaveda priests added their own comments, prominent among them the promise to bring the mahamimamsa "purifiers" from the hold below.

The kshatriyas snarled, but hurried to obey. All of the troughs were now tilted until they were pointing at a slight angle downward. More hide bundles were piled up at the rear of the troughs, but it was obvious from the kshatriyas' worried frowns that they did not think the hides would suffice to completely shield them from the rocket flames. The fire which would erupt from the rocket tails would now be shooting upward.

Another alien thought seeped through the barrier.

back-blast.

Darkness was now complete, except for the faint light thrown by the few lanterns held by Ye-tai warriors. Belisarius saw Venandakatra staring at him. A moment later, with obvious reluctance, the Indian lord made his way toward the bow of the ship.

When he reached Belisarius, the general spoke before Venandakatra could even open his mouth.

"I am well aware that the pirates will concentrate their attack on the bow and stern, where the—where your fire-weapons cannot be brought to bear. Look to the stern, Venandakatra. There will be no breach at the bow."

Venandakatra frowned. "There are not many of you," he said. "I could send some—"

"No. More men would simply crowd the bow, making it more difficult for us. And I do not have time to learn how to incorporate Malwa warriors into our tactics. Whereas Romans and Axumites are old allies, long accustomed to fighting side by side." The lie came smooth as silk.

Garmat's face was expressionless. The sarwen grunted loud agreement, as did Anastasius and Valentinian. Eon started slightly, but a quick poke from his dawazz brought stillness. Menander looked confused, but the Indian was not looking his way, and almost immediately, Valentinian changed the young Thracian's expression with a silent snarl.

"You are certain?" demanded Venandakatra.

Belisarius smiled graciously. "I said you would be glad to have us, soon enough."

Venandakatra's face grew pinched, but the Indian forebore further comment. After a moment, he scurried away and began shouting new orders. Belisarius could understand the words, and knew that the commands which Venandakatra was shrilling were utterly redundant and pointless. A disgruntled grandee making noise to assure himself of his importance, that was all.

"Verily, a foul man," muttered Garmat. "Long ago, the Axumites had a king much like him. The sarawit assassinated the wretch and created the institution of dawazz the next day."

"Do you really think they're going to attack?" asked Menander suddenly. Seeing all eyes upon him, the young cataphract straightened.

"I'm not afraid!" he protested. "It's just—it doesn't make sense."

"I'm afraid it does," countered Garmat. The adviser grimaced. "I am myself half-Arab, and I know my mother's people well. The tribes of the Hadrawmat"—he pointed to the southern shore of Arabia, now lost in the darkness— "are very poor. Fishermen, mostly, and smugglers. A great ship like this represents a fortune to them. They will gladly suffer heavy casualties in order to capture it."

Ousanas chuckled. "Believe wise old mongrel, young Roman. Most despicable people in world, the Arabs. Full of vice and sins!"

Garmat squinted.

"O many vices! Many sins!"

Garmat looked pained.

"Lechery! Avarice! Cruelty!"

Garmat frowned.

"Treachery! Sloth! Envy!"

Garmat glowered.

"Would be great gluttons if not so poor!"

Garmat ground his teeth.

"Alas, Arabs unfamiliar with cowardice."

Garmat smiled. Ousanas shook his head sadly.

"Is because Arabs so stupid. Cowardice mankind's only useful vice. Naturally Arabs know nothing of it."

"I heard a story years ago," mused Anastasius, "that there was a cowardly Arab living somewhere in the Empty Quarter." He spit into the sea. "I didn't believe it, myself."

"They're coming," announced Valentinian. "I can't see them, but I can hear them."

Belisarius glanced at Valentinian. As so often before on the verge of battle, the cataphract reminded the general of nothing so much as a weasel. The sharp features; the long, lean whipcord body; the poised stillness, like a coiled spring; and, most of all, the utter intensity of the killer's concentration. At these moments, Valentinian's senses were almost superhuman.

Belisarius sighed. The choice was now upon him and could no longer be postponed.

Secrecy be damned, he decided. *These men—all of them—are my comrades. I cannot betray them.*

The general stepped to the very prow of the ship.

"There are two ships approaching us," he announced. He pointed, and pointed again. "There, and there. The one on the right is closer."

He heard a slight cough behind him.

"Trust me, Garmat. I can see them almost as well as if it were daytime. They are there, just as I have described."

He looked over his shoulder and smiled crookedly.

"The steersman you pointed out earlier is on that closer ship, Ousanas. Make good your boast."

For once, the dawazz was not grinning. Ousanas stared into the darkness for a moment, then looked back at the general.

"You are witch," he announced.

Belisarius made a face.

The grin made its inevitable appearance. Ousanas' skin was so black that he was almost invisible except as a shape. Against that darkness, the grin was like a beacon of good cheer.

"Is not problem," said the dawazz. Ousanas gestured

toward the other warriors.

"These other men be civilized folk, Axumites and Romans. Hence filled with silly superstitions. Think witchcraft evil. I savage from far south, too ignorant to be confused. I know witchcraft like everything else in this world. Some good. Some bad."

A great laugh suddenly rang out, startling in its loudness.

"Most excellent!" pronounced the dawazz. "Never had good witch before, on my side."

"Can you truly see that well, in the night?" asked the prince shakily. "How is that possible?"

"Yes, Eon, I can. How is it possible?" Belisarius hesitated, but only for an instant. The die was cast.

"There is no time now. But after the battle, I will explain." A glance at Garmat. "I will explain everything." A glance at his cataphracts and the sarwen. "To all of you."

Ousanas lounged forward, hefting his javelin.

"Where is steersman?" he asked idly. Belisarius pointed again. Ousanas squinted.

"Still too dark," he muttered.

At that moment, Venandakatra's voice cried out a command. A volley of rockets was fired in all directions. Several kshatriyas squealed with pain, caught by the back-blasts which flared over the hide mounds.

"Fucking idiot," growled Anastasius. "The cowardly bastard, he's just panicking."

It was true enough. The volley was completely unaimed. The six rockets snaked their fiery path into nothingness. A total waste.

To all, that is, save Ousanas. For the rockets' glare had, whatever else, bathed the sea with a sudden flare of red illumination. The pirate ships were clearly visible, and even, with difficulty, individual members of their crews.

"I see him steersman!" cried the dawazz gleefully. He

hurled the javelin like a tiger pouncing on its prey. The weapon vanished into the fading red glare. Almost at once it was invisible, to all save Belisarius.

The general watched the javelin rise, and rise, and rise. He had never seen such a tremendous cast. Then, the general watched it sail downward. Downward, and truer than Euclidean dreams.

A terrible, brief cry filled the night.

Anastasius hunched his shoulders, staring grimly out to sea.

"I can't bear to look, Valentinian. Is that damned black bastard grinning at me?"

Valentinian chuckled. "It looks like the Pharos at Alexandria. A blinding beacon in the night."

A sudden little flight of arrows came out of the darkness. None of them came close, however. The pirates were simply reacting out of rage.

"It won't be long now," announced Belisarius. He smiled. "By the way, you might want to shift over to the other side, Anastasius. The ship on your side isn't the closest, anymore. In fact, it's wallowing in the waves. No steersman."

Anastasius grunted his disgust. Ousanas took up another javelin.

"Maybe fucking idiot cowardly bastard Indian lord fire another useless volley," he said cheerfully. "Then I make other pirate galley wallow in waves."

"I'll kill him," muttered Anastasius.

"I doubt it," retorted Valentinian. Suddenly, he too was grinning. "And don't be a spiteful idiot. You're like some petty boy in a playground. Would you rather he was chucking those spears the other way?"

Anastasius winced. "No, but—"

He got no further. A pirate ship loomed out of the darkness, like a dragon rising from the sea. A medley of war cries erupted from it. A moment later, another volley of rockets flared.

Now all was bright glare, redness and fury, and the ancient battle clangor. Anastasius drew his great bow and slew a pirate, and then another, and another, and another, and another. At that range, his arrows split chests like a butcher splits a chicken. Even had the pirates been wearing full armor, it would have made no difference. At that range, the arrows of Anastasius drove through shields.

And now, when he saw the other pirate galley suddenly wallow in the waves, bereft of its steersman, there was no emotion in his heart beyond a fierce surge of comradeship. For the cataphract Anastasius was not, in truth, a spiteful schoolboy filled with petty pride. He was a soldier plying his trade.

And he was very, very good at it.

Chapter 16

Even though it was a moonless night, the battle itself was fully illuminated, in a hideous, flashing way. Belisarius had time, even in the press and fury of the fray, to marvel at the scene.

If one could be said to marvel at a scene from Hell.

By the time the first pirate ships came alongside the Indian vessel, attaching themselves with grappling hooks, all but four of the Arab craft were burning infernos. The erratic trajectories of the rockets was now irrelevant. At point-blank range, the rockets did not explode upon impact. Instead, they continued to burn from their tails, with the same fierce dragon-hiss that sent them skittering through the air. Fascinated, Belisarius saw one rocket punch through the hull of a ship, glance off a rower's bench, carom off another bench on the opposite side, and then roar its way down the length of the pirate craft until it embedded itself in the bow. Its trail was marked by a horde of screaming Arabs, frantically trying to beat out the flames in their garments, which had been set afire by the rocket in its passage. Once brought to a halt by the thicker planking at the bow, the rocket continued to burn as brightly as ever. To all appearances, the mindless device seemed like a stubborn animal trying to force its way through a hedge.

It was several seconds before it finally exploded, shattering the bow into splinters. But, by that time, the tail-fire burning down the length of the pirate craft had done as much damage as the explosion itself.

I don't think these rockets have any way of knowing when to explode, mused Belisarius.

aim hurled the serried facets at the same breach in the barrier, much like a human general might launch his troops at a shattered section of a fortified wall. Another crude thought was forced through.

no fuses.

Sensing the puzzlement in Belisarius' mind, the facets retreated. But **aim** rallied them immediately. With success, crude though it was, confidence was growing. **aim** sent the facets through the breach anew, and now, filled with the fanatic purpose of *explanation*.

Finally—finally!—true success. The facets flashed their exultation. **aim** itself broke into kaleidoscopic joy.

The knowledge which now erupted in the mind of the general Belisarius was no crude, simple thought. Instead, it was like a living diagram, a moving reality. He saw, as clearly as anything in his life, the way of the rockets. He saw the strange powder [**gunpowder**, he now knew] packed in the length of the rocket; the same powder, in greater quantities, which was packed in the front tip [**warhead**] of the device. He saw the *gunpowder* ignited by a long match held by a kshatriya warrior. He saw the powder erupt into flame, and saw how the flame burned. (And knew that the vision was moving at an inhuman pace, slowed by the jewel that he might follow the course of it.)

He saw the flame burn its way up, inside the length of the bamboo tube [**fuselage**]. He saw the raging gasses which were expelled from the rocket's rear [**exhaust**], and knew the fury of the gasses was the force which drove the device into motion.

(A concept—**action/reaction**—flashed through his mind. He almost understood it, but was not concerned; soon, soon, he would.)

Watching, in his mind's eye, the course of the flame burning its way through the gunpowder, Belisarius now understood the reason for the rocket's erratic trajectory.

Part of it, he saw, was that the gunpowder was poorly mixed. (And he knew, now, that gunpowder was not a substance itself, but a combination of substances.) The powder was uneven and lumpy, like poorly threshed grain. Different pockets and sections of the powder burned unevenly, which produced a ragged and unpredictable exhaust.

Most of the problem, though, was that the rear opening through which the exhaust poured [**venturi**—but the thought was saturated with scorn] was itself poorly made. In fact, it wasn't "made" at all. The venturi was nothing more than a ring of wood. The Indians simply cut the bamboo after one of the joints in the wood, and used the joint itself as the nozzle which concentrated and aimed the exhaust gasses. But the hole was ragged to begin with, no better than a crude carving; Belisarius could actually see in his mind the way in which the hot exhaust burned out the wood in its expulsion.

The companions of Belisarius feared for his sanity, then. The first pirates were even now clambering their way aboard the ship—and here was their general, their leader, cavorting about like a madman and raving lunatic nonsense about Greek and Armenian metalsmiths and the cunning of their craft. He was even cackling about the Emperor's throne, and his roaring lions, and his birds!

But, they were relieved to see, the madness passed as soon as the first Arab head appeared above the rail. Belisarius removed the head with a sweep of his sword which was so quick, and so sure, and so certain, and so graceful, that none who saw doubted he was a man possessed.

" 'Deadly with a blade, is Belisarius,' " muttered Valentinian. "But *that's* ridiculous."

"Stop bitching," growled Anastasius. He brought his mace down upon another pirate head. And if there was little grace in the act, and not much in the way of quickness, the result was no less sure and certain.

Arabs now began pouring over the rails, port and starboard, all along the ship. There was a frenzied determination in that surge, far beyond battle-lust and greed. The surge was born of pure desperation. There were far too few galleys left intact, now, to bear the pirates safely back to shore. They must either conquer the great Indian vessel, or die.

The kshatriyas fled the rocket troughs and sheltered behind the Ye-tai. There, the kshatriyas formed a defensive ring around Venandakatra and the cluster of priests standing at the foot of the mainmast. But it was obvious that the lightly armed Malwa warriors, their rockets out of action, were nothing but a feeble last guard. The real defense of the ship now lay in the hands of the Ye-tai. The barbarians were not slow to deride the kshatriyas for their unmanliness.

But the derision was short-lived. Within seconds, the Ye-tai were too hard-pressed by the wave of pirates swarming aboard the ship to concern themselves with anything but survival.

As Belisarius had expected, the pirates concentrated their efforts at the stern and the bow, where their ships could avoid the rockets. Indeed, the only two Arab craft which were still seaworthy were the ones attached to the bow and stern of the huge Indian vessel.

At the stern, the battle went quite well for the pirates, and did so quickly. At the bow, they found nothing but death and destruction.

Belisarius had lied to Venandakatra when he told him that Romans and Axumites were long accustomed to fighting alongside each other. But now, as they did so for the first time in history, under the command of the greatest Roman general in centuries, they seemed to be a perfect fighting machine.

Belisarius had positioned his small band of soldiers as Garmat had recommended. The very front line was made up of his three heavily armored cataphracts. The inexperienced Menander was placed in the point of the bow. Valentinian and Anastasius flanked the youth on either side. Although Belisarius was himself inexperienced in sea battles, it had been obvious that few pirates would try to clamber directly over the arching curve of the bow itself. The points of greatest danger lay a few feet behind the bow, and it was there that the general positioned his two veterans: Anastasius to port, Valentinian to starboard.

And, as Belisarius had expected, it was there that the pirates concentrated their efforts.

To little avail. The heavy shields and armor of the cataphracts were all but impenetrable to the light weapons being wielded by the pirates—the more so, as the weapons were wielded awkwardly and one-handed. Each pirate's other hand was needed to retain his hold on the rail. Belisarius learned, then, his first lesson in sea-fighting: despite Eon's sneers, and whatever its clumsiness, there was a great advantage to the size of the Indian ship. The pirates could not simply leap from ship to ship. Boarding the great Malwa craft presented much the same obstacle to the low galleys as scaling a wall presented to besiegers of a land fortress.

The contest was absurdly one-sided. Each pirate got, at the most, one swing of his weapon. Thereafter, if he faced Anastasius, he died immediately; his skull crushed by a mace. If he faced the more subtle Valentinian, his death might be postponed a moment or so. Valentinian, also new to ship-fighting, soon discovered that the most economical way to deal with his opponents was to strike at their defenseless hands gripping the rail. Valentinian did not possess the sheer brute power of Anastasius, but he was quite strong. It hardly mattered. His sword, like all his blades, was sharp as a razor. Within two minutes, a little mound of severed hands was piling up at his feet. Their former owners had plunged into the sea, where they died soon enough from shock, blood loss, and drowning.

Menander, though not a complete novice by any means, lacked his two comrades' long experience. Nor, for that matter, did he now or would he ever possess their awesome skill in combat. But he was a Thracian cataphract, one of that elite company pledged to their lord Belisarius, and none could ever say afterward that he shamed them.

As uneven as the contest was, however, it proved to be the Axumites who made the final difference. Alone, the four Romans would eventually have been overwhelmed by sheer numbers. As fast as the cataphracts wielded their weapons, the Arabs poured up even faster. But the Ethiopian spears were quicker still.

The cataphracts slew a great number themselves, but, in the main, their contribution was to serve as a living wall which delayed the pirates that one extra moment. A moment was all the sarwen needed, or Eon. And Ousanas needed even less. Standing a few feet behind the cataphracts, the Axumite spears flicked out like viper strikes. Each stroke was swift, accurate, and almost invariably deadly. On occasion, the sarwen and Eon required a second spear-thrust to dispatch an enemy.

Ousanas, never. The dawazz's aim was absolutely uncanny. Watching, Belisarius decided he had never seen a man wield a weapon so unerringly. Certainly not in an actual battle. The precision was almost wasted, though. The dawazz lacked Anastasius' bearlike bulk, and Eon's flamboyant musculature. But Belisarius suspected that Ousanas was actually stronger than either of them. His great spear blade literally ruptured human bodies.

The general had placed himself and Garmat as the final reserve. Each of them stood a few feet behind the Axumites, Garmat to starboard, Belisarius to port. The general had expected, within seconds of the assault, to be in a life-and-death struggle.

As before, in the battle against the Persians, the jewel was working its way with him. Belisarius' senses were superhumanly keen, and his reflexes were like quicksilver. But—he almost laughed—it proved another waste. Neither he nor Garmat was ever required to strike a blow—although the old adviser did so, once, skewering a pirate over a sarwen's shoulder. Belisarius thought the effort was superfluous, simply the ingrained habit of an old warrior. So, apparently, did the sarwen. The Ethiopian soldier immediately denounced Garmat for an interfering busybody and suggested, none too politely, that the doddering fool stick to his trade. Thereafter, Garmat satisfied himself with a reservist's role.

Once it became clear to Belisarius that the situation in the bow was well under control, the general felt it possible to concentrate elsewhere. While keeping an eye on the fight at hand, most of his attention was riveted on the battle raging amidships, and in the stern.

Partly, his concern was with the overall progress of the struggle. Regardless of how well the Romans and Axumites fought in the bow, the final outcome of the battle would be largely determined by the success of the Ye-tai in repelling the boarders everywhere else.

But, mostly, his concern lay in the future. He had witnessed the Malwa dragon-weapons, and learned much from his observations. Now, for the first time, he would be able to examine Ye-tai war skills. And examine them from the most perfect vantage point imaginable: nearby, from a slightly elevated position, and—best of all—from the Ye-tai side of the line.

Their skills were—not bad, he decided. Not bad at all.

Strength: The Ye-tai were as fearless and aggressive as any general could ask for.

Weakness: The same. They were *too* aggressive. That was especially true of the younger men who stood in the second rank. In their eagerness to join the fray and prove their mettle, they tended to continually disrupt the maintenance of an orderly battle line.

Strength: There *was* a battle line. Very unusual for barbarian warriors.

Weakness: It was not a well-dressed line. Some of that, of course, was due to the conditions of the battle: a fight aboard a cramped ship, lit only by the flames of the burning galleys. Some of it was due to the disruptions produced by young fighters from the second rank pushing their way forward. But much of it, the general suspected, was inherent in the Ye-tai mentality. The Malwa gloss of semi-civilization was just that: a gloss, a thin veneer, over warriors whose basic nature was still utterly barbaric.

Strength: Their sword-play was excellent, although it was obvious to Belisarius that the sweeping, cutting style which the Ye-tai favored was more suited to cavalry tactics than combat afoot.

Weakness: Their shield work was indifferent. And here, knew the general, was another legacy of the Ye-tai military tradition. The barbarians were, first and foremost, horsemen.

Belisarius was delighted.

He had not had time, as yet, to think through all of the military implications of the new, strange Malwa weapons. But one fact was already blindingly obvious: as he had told his cataphracts, the infantry was about to make a great historical comeback. There would be a place for cavalry, of course—and a large one—but the core of future armies would be infantry.

And there were no infantry in the world as good as

Roman infantry. There never had been. *Never. Not anywhere.* In the modern age, only the Hellenes had been able to give the Romans a real contest, infantry to infantry. And the historical verdict had been pronounced at places immortalized in history: Cynoscephalae, Magnesia, Pydna, Chaeronea. In the ancient world, only the Assyrians could even be considered as possible equals. The Assyrians had vanished long ago, of course, so it would never be known how they might have fared against Roman legions. But— Belisarius smiled, then, from an old memory. He and Sittas had once spent a pleasant afternoon speculating on the question. The theoretical discussion had degenerated into a drunken, intemperate quarrel. Sittas, vaingloriously, had argued that the Assyrian army would have been crushed within fifteen minutes. Belisarius—calm, cool, and professional (as always)—had felt they might have lasted a full hour. Maybe.

He shook off the memory, and the smile vanished.

There was no time, any longer, for dispassionate examination. The Ye-tai were the future foes of the Roman Empire, but they were the current allies of the handful of Romans on the ship. And those Roman allies were going down to defeat.

Not easy defeat, not quick defeat, but a defeat which was as sure as the sunrise. Even now, as he watched, the Ye-tai in the stern were finally overwhelmed. Screeching with triumph, the Arab pirates began swarming forward, rolling up the Ye-tai lines on either side of the ship.

Quickly, Belisarius assessed the situation at hand. The pirate assault at the bow had ceased. Utterly discouraged by their horrendous (and futile) casualties, the surviving Arabs had retreated back to their own vessel and had released their grappling hooks. About half the crew was still alive, but they were starting to row their craft toward the stern of the Indian vessel, hoping to find an easier way aboard.

Then, suddenly, the galley began wallowing in the waves. The pirates shrieked their fury and hastened to bring their craft back under control.

Ousanas had added another steersman to his list.

The cataphracts roared their own triumphant fury. The sarwen, more practical-minded, slew another couple of pirates with well-placed javelin casts. So did Eon. For his part, Ousanas waited until the pirates selected a new steersman. Three seconds later, the Arabs had to begin the process anew. It was soon obvious that volunteers were short.

Belisarius bellowed. Not words, just a thundering roar to catch the attention of his little cohort. It was difficult: the victorious cries of the Arabs and the despairing screams of the Ye-tai had produced a bedlam of sheer noise which engulfed the entire vessel.

When he had their attention, Belisarius simply pointed to the stern. No more was needed. In the cramped quarters of the deck, no subtle tactics were possible. Nor was there time to begin the counter-attack with a volley of arrows and javelins. The Ye-tai were on the verge of utter collapse. The barbarians had managed to patch together a semblance of a line amidships, just aft of the mainmast. But a wave of pirates was swarming over them.

There was neither place nor time, now, for any tactics but pure shock. Concentrated slaughter.

Belisarius led the way. Within a second or two, the other Romans and the Ethiopians were charging alongside him. The nine men formed a single line stretching across the entire width of the ship. The spacing was actually too close, but before Belisarius could order a change, Ousanas took the initiative. The dawazz grabbed Eon by his kilt and jerked him back. A moment later, his sharp bark at Garmat caused the adviser to likewise fall back.

Eon protested bitterly. Ousanas slapped him atop the

head—there was not a trace of humor in *that* blow—and criticized the prince savagely.

Even though Belisarius could basically understand Ge'ez, aided by the jewel, he was unable to grasp every word which Ousanas spoke. But there was no need. The general himself, in battles past, had spoken similar phrases to young soldiers. Although never with quite such vigor and profanity.

Fucking worthless toddler. Grow up. This no time for children in front line. Make self useful. Drooling infant. Spear somebody on other side. Cretin child. Instead of getting in way of veterans. Best cataphracts and sarwen in world. Not need die tripping over prince learning to babble. Noble jackass. Royalty stupid by nature. Especially prince-type royalty. Stupid acceptable. Mindless not. Fucking idiot boy.

And other words to that effect.

Within seconds, the little Roman/Axumite squad forced their way through the mob of Ye-tai warriors who were milling amidships. The discipline of the Indian forces had now completely collapsed. True, the advancing pirates were equally undisciplined. But the swarming Arabs were impelled by the elation of victory, while the Ye-tai were filled with the despair of looming defeat.

Belisarius had time, briefly, to glance at Venandakatra and his little crowd of priests and kshatriyas huddled around the mainmast. The Malwa—the kshatriyas, at least—retained a semblance of disciplined order. But it was a paralyzed kind of order; of no more use than the Ye-tai chaos.

A moment later, the front line of the Romans and Axumites burst through to the small open space between the fleeing Ye-tai and the advancing Arabs. They were now aft of the mainmast and its surrounding cabin, to Belisarius' relief. There was no way the enemy could get around them by clambering over the cabin. It was fight and die across a space of forty feet.

Seeing the sudden appearance of a disciplined and

determined line before them, the pirates hesitated in their
advance. The pause lasted long enough for Ousanas, Eon,
and Garmat to force their own way through the milling
Ye-tai and take their place just behind the line of cataphracts
and sarwen.

From within the Arab crowd in the stern a man shoved
his way to the fore. Unlike most of the pirates, he was
equipped with a mail tunic and a helmet. His sword was
long, slightly curved, and very finely made.

The man was middle-aged, but other than the grey in
his beard there was not the slightest sign of any lack of
vigor in his body. He was tall, well-built, and possessed both
of an air of authority and a very loud voice. The air of
authority steadied the pirates; the stentorian voice began
to command them forward anew.

Began, but ceased suddenly. Ousanas had used up all his
javelins. So the dawazz hurled his great stabbing spear.

It was the first time in his life that Belisarius had ever
seen a man actually decapitated by a spear-cast. For a
moment, he gaped with astonishment. The huge blade of
the dawazz's spear simply lopped the pirate's head off and
then continued on to sink into the chest of a pirate standing
behind.

The Arabs froze at the sight, momentarily paralyzed.
Belisarius bellowed. The cataphracts and sarwen lunged
forward.

Now it was pure mayhem, sheer carnage. The Romans
and Axumites hammered into the Arab crowd like a machine.
The lightly armored pirates at the front went down like
slaughtered lambs, their skulls crushed or split open, their
chests or bellies skewered, their arms amputated. In falling,
they hampered the pirates behind who, in turn, could put
up little resistance to that ferocious charge.

It was not all one-sided, of course. Menander cried out
and fell, clutching his side. A sword thrust coming from

somewhere in the pirate mob had found its mark. One of the sarwen cried out also, staggering, his face covered with blood from a scalp wound. The wound was not fatal, for the Ethiopian had deflected the sword with his shield just before it landed. But, like all head wounds, it bled profusely.

Stubbornly, the sarwen began to return to the front line, but Ousanas pulled him back and gently took his spear. The man was almost helpless, blinded from the blood. Garmat steadied him with a hand. The old adviser stood guard over the wounded sarwen and Menander, as the battle pushed its way to the stern.

Ousanas took a place in the front line. A moment later, so did Eon. There was no dawazz, now, to restrain the pride of young royalty. Eon surged into the gap created by Menander's fall and began his eager spearwork with the two veterans, Valentinian and Anastasius, on either side.

Young and impetuous he may have been, even, perhaps, foolish in his enthusiasm. But he tripped neither of the cataphracts by his side, nor did he get in the way of their veteran slaughter. And if, once, Anastasius was forced to cover the prince's side because the youth had surged too far forward in his inexperience, the huge Thracian was not disgruntled. He had done the same before, many times, for other young warriors. Young warriors who, often enough, had been paralyzed with sudden fear—which the prince certainly was not. Eon slew the man before him, and Anastasius crushed the life from the other who would have stabbed the prince's unguarded side.

All in a day's work, all in a day's work. Training young warriors was part of the trade, and it was a trade which could be learned by no other method. So did Anastasius remind the dawazz, firmly, in the quiet hours after the battle, when Ousanas began to chide the idiot boy. And Valentinian actually managed to silence Ousanas completely—wonder of wonders—with a few short, curt, pungent phrases. Hot and angry phrases, in point of fact.

The cynical veteran Valentinian, as it happens, had developed a sudden enthusiasm for the Prince Eon. A very fierce enthusiasm, born of an ancient warrior tradition.

Not all the casualties of a battle are novices. Veterans die too, sometimes, brought down by the smallest chances. And on that night—that hellfire-lit, bedlam-shrieking, dragon-raging night—the crafty and cunning Valentinian had finally met his nemesis. From the smallest, chanciest thing.

The veteran killer, master and survivor of a hundred dusty battlefields, had found his death aboard wooden planks. He had not considered the nature of a blood-soaked ship's deck, so unlike the blood-soaked soil of land carnage. And so, striding forward to deliver another death-blow, as he had done times beyond remembering, his foot had skidded out from under him. Flat on his back Valentinian had fallen, his shield askew, his sword arm flailing, his entire body open and helpless. A pirate took the wonderful opportunity instantly and gleefully. To his dying day, Valentinian would never forget the sight of that sword tip readying to butcher his belly.

Except that the sword tip stopped, not more than an inch away, and withdrew. It took Valentinian a moment to realize that the cause of the bizarre retreat was Eon's spear, which had taken the pirate square in the chest. The veteran Valentinian was paralyzed himself, then, for a second or two. Not from fear so much as a strange wonder.

The pirate never lost his determination to slay the cataphract. His fierce black eyes never left those of Valentinian. And the rage in those eyes never died, until the man himself did. His sword continued to jab, his body continued to lunge forward. But the pirate was inexorably held at bay, by a spear in the hands of a boy. An idiot boy, perhaps, but a strong and fearless boy, most certainly.

So, in the quiet hours after the battle, when the boy's mentor began to criticize him for an idiot, Valentinian would have none of it. No, none at all. And it was noted, thereafter, by all who knew that deadly weasel of a man, that a small group of people had gained a new member.

The comrades-in-arms of Valentinian, that group was called, by him as well as others. Those few—those very, very, very few—privileged to share his cups, handle his blades, criticize his faults, and compliment his women.

Eon, Prince of Axum, was the only royal member of that club. Then, or ever. But the lad took no umbrage in the fact. Royal, the group was not; no, not even noble. But it was among the smallest clubs in the world. Perhaps its most exclusive. Certainly its most select.

All that, however, lay in the future. The Arabs had been pushed back into the very stern of the ship. As their numbers grew compressed, their ability to fight lessened. The press of the mob badly hampered those pirates who were still eager for combat.

But there were few such left. The ruthless assault of the Byzantines and Ethiopians had demoralized the great majority of the pirates—the more so, in that they had thought themselves on the verge of victory.

Most, now, thought of nothing but escape. As many as could clambered down the stern of the ship into the galley which was still lashed alongside. But the galley was soon so overloaded with refugees that its captain ordered the grappling lines severed.

Many pirates simply dove off the side of the ship. Some found refuge aboard the retreating galley which had been lashed to the stern. More found refuge in the other surviving pirate craft, which had now found its way from the bow whence it had been repulsed earlier by those same horrible Romans and Axumites. Most drowned.

At the end, only a dozen or so Arabs remained aboard the ship. Gathered in a compact group at the very stern, these men began negotiating with Belisarius for terms of surrender. For his part, the general was willing. There had been enough slaughter.

But the negotiations were almost instantly moot. The Ye-tai had now regained their courage, and they surged in a horde toward the stern, shrieking their battle cries. Hearing them come, the Romans and Axumites stood aside at Belisarius' command, and let the Ye-tai conclude the battle.

The barbarians had not the slightest interest in negotiations. And so, the remaining Arabs died to a man.

But the slaughter was by no means one-sided. Whatever else they were, the pirates were not craven. Before they perished, they took some Ye-tai with them to oblivion.

Though his face remained expressionless throughout, Belisarius took great pleasure in the fact. His cataphracts and the sarwen, he thought, did likewise. About Eon and Garmat, there was no doubt at all, from their fierce scowls.

As for Ousanas' attitude—well, it was difficult to say. Watching the final act of the battle from the sidelines, the dawazz kept up a running commentary, alternating between philosophical observations on the just deserts of piracy and jocular remarks on the incompetence of barbarian swordsmen.

He spoke in pidgin Greek, not in Hindi, nor in the language of the barbarians themselves. But at least one Ye-tai warrior had his suspicions aroused—judging, at least, from the fierce manner in which he advanced on Ousanas, waving his sword most threateningly.

The truth would never be known, however. Ousanas seized the warrior's wrist and his throat, shook loose the sword, crushed the throat, and hurled the Ye-tai overboard. Other barbarians, observing the scene, chose thereafter to ignore his commentary. Which was perhaps just as well, since the ruminations of Ousanas thenceforth focused on the worthlessness of barbarians in general and Ye-tai in particular.

Quite exclusively, quite exhaustively, and loud enough to be heard by every fish in the Erythrean Sea.

Chapter 17

In the days following the battle with the pirates, as the Indian vessel made its slow way across the Erythrean Sea, much changed.

Not the sea itself, nor the wind. No, the southeast monsoon maintained its unwavering force, fierce and blustery. (Quite unlike, Garmat assured the Romans, the pleasant and balmy monsoon which would bear them westward some months hence.) And the sea seemed always the same, as did the dimly-seen coastline to their north. The coast of Persia, now, for they had crossed the Straits of Hormuz, leaving Arabia and its dangers behind.

The same, also, was Eon's daily grousing on the subject of land lubberly Indians; and his adviser's frequent comments on the contrasting habits of such true seafaring folk as Ethiopians and Arabs (and Greeks, of course) who eschewed the creeping coast and set forth boldly across the open ocean; and the inevitable remarks which followed from Ousanas, on the inseparable bond between seamanship and braggadocio.

But everything else changed.

The first change was in the attitude of Venandakatra toward his "guests." The Indian grandee lost not a trace of his hauteur, and his cold, serpentine arrogance. But he no longer ignored the foreigners. Oh no, not at all. Daily he came to visit, trailing a gaggle of priests, spending at least an hour at the bow in discourse with Belisarius, Eon, and Garmat. (The others he ignored; they were but common soldiers or, in the case of Ousanas, the most grotesque slave in creation.)

Daily, also, he invited Belisarius and Eon (and, grudgingly, Garmat) to dine with him in his cabin that evening. The invitation was invariably accepted. By Belisarius, eagerly; by Garmat, dutifully; by the prince, with the sullen discipline of a boy hauled by his ears.

The general's eagerness for these evening meals did not arise from any pleasure in Venandakatra's company. In person, in private, the Indian lord was even more loathsome than he was at a distance. Nor was Belisarius' enthusiasm occasioned by the meals themselves, though they were truly excellent repasts. Belisarius was not a gourmand, and he had always found that the most important seasoning for food was good company at the table. The meals served in Venandakatra's cabin were splendid, but they were seasoned with a spiritual sauce so foul it might have been the saliva of Satan himself.

Neither was the general's joy in these social encounters produced by any misreading of Venandakatra's motives. Belisarius knew full well that the sudden Malwa hospitality did not result from gratitude for the decisive role played by Belisarius and his men in the battle with the pirates.

No, the truth was quite the opposite, and Belisarius knew it as surely as he knew his own name. Venandakatra's new cordiality was the product of the battle, true. A product, however, which was born not of gratitude but fear.

Venandakatra had never witnessed Romans in combat, nor Axumites. Now he had, and knew them for his future enemy, and knew—with that bone-chilling certainty known only by those who have actually seen the mace-crushed skulls and the spear-sundered chests, and the guttering blood and severed limbs—that his enemy was terrible beyond all former comprehension. What had seemed, in the conspiring corridors of Malwa palaces and the scented chambers of Malwa emperors, to be a surety of the future, seemed so no longer. Rome would be conquered, and enslaved. But it would be no easy task, nor a simple one.

And so, Belisarius knew, Venandakatra made his daily visits, and his daily invitations to dinner. Just so does the cobra raise its head, and swell its hood, and flick its tongue, and sway its sinuous rhythm, the better to put its prey into a trance.

And just so, joyfully, does the mongoose enter the trap.

Crooked as a root was the mind of Belisarius. And now, finally, inside the gnarls and twists of his peculiar mind, a plot was sprouting and spreading.

The growing plot was as cunning as any stratagem the general had ever devised. (And he was a man who treasured cunning much as another might treasure gold, or another the beauty of concubines.) Of itself, however, the cleverness produced only satisfaction in the heart of Belisarius, not joy. No, the joy derived elsewhere. The joy—it might be better to say, the savage and pitiless glee—derived from the fact that the entire plot pivoted on the very soul of the man against whom it was aimed. The Vile One, Venandakatra was called. And it would be by his own vileness that Belisarius would bring him down.

So, every day, on the sunlit bow of the ship, Belisarius greeted Venandakatra with cordiality and respect. So, every evening, in the lantern-gloom of the cabin, Belisarius returned the grandee's slimy bonhomie with his own oily camaraderie, the lord's lecherous humor with his own salacious wit, and the flashes of Malwa depravity with glimpses of his own bestial corruption.

The shrewd old adviser Garmat, under other circumstances,

would have reacted with still-faced, diplomatic, silent disgust. The impetuous and elephant-hearted young prince, with words of scorn and contempt. But the circumstances here had changed also, since the battle. And this change was no product of guile and duplicity.

Before the battle, true, Romans and Axumites had been on good terms.

Kaleb had made clear to Eon and Garmat, in private council after they returned to Axum in the company of Belisarius, the importance which the negusa nagast attached to forging an alliance with Rome. It was for that very reason that he had assented to their proposal to accompany the Byzantines to India, perilous though such a trip might be for his young son.

Belisarius, though he carried no such precise and definite imperial instructions, had his own reasons for seeking such a bond. Already, if only in outline, he was shaping the grand strategy of Rome's coming war with the Malwa Empire. The role of Axum in that conflict would be crucial.

His cataphracts and Eon's sarwen, experienced soldiers, had quickly detected the attitude of their superiors, and had shaped their own conduct accordingly. Menander, on his own, filled with the thoughtless certainties of youth, might have given vent to certain prejudices and animosities, but not with the two veterans watching him like a hawk.

So, during the many months prior to the battle with the pirates, in the company which they shared through the trip to Syria, and the sojourn at Daras, and the voyage to Egypt and then to Adulis, through the trek upcountry to the city of Axum, through the lengthy stay at Axum itself, through the return to Adulis and the embarkation aboard the Malwa vessel bearing its envoys back to India, the Romans and Axumites had maintained their good relations and the disciplined propriety of their conduct.

So they had. But—still, still, they were each foreign to

the other, for all that the Ethiopians spoke good (if accented) Greek, and the Romans began to speak poor (and very accented) Ge'ez. To be sure, no words were ever uttered which might have given offense. (Save by Ousanas, of course. But since the dawazz insulted everybody equally, including tribes and nations no one else had even heard of, his outrageous behavior soon became accepted, much as one accepts the rain and the wind, and noxious insects.) But, through all the months of joint travel, and mutual good will, there had not been much in the way of open trust and confidence. And even less in the way of genuine intimacy.

Now, all that was changed. Since the battle, all former propriety and stiff good conduct had vanished. Vanished like it had never existed, especially among the common soldiers. In its place came insults and derision, mockery and ridicule, grousing and complaint—in short, all the mechanisms by which blooded veterans seal their comradeship.

The sarwen were no longer nameless. The one whose black skull had gained a new scalp scar in the battle was named Ezana. The other, Wahsi. The Romans now learned of a long-standing Ethiopian custom. The true name of a sarwen was never told to any but members of the sarawit, lest the warrior be subject to sorcery from his enemies. Upon receiving acceptance from his own sarwe into its ranks, an Axumite boy was given the name by which he would henceforth be known, in private, by his comrades.

Shortly after the battle with the pirates, in their own little ceremony held while the lords were carousing with Venandakatra, the two sarwen officially enrolled the three cataphracts into the ranks of the Dakuen, and spoke their true names.

The Roman soldiers thought the custom odd, in its particulars. But they did not sneer at it, for they found nothing odd in the general thrust of the thing. Valentinian and Anastasius carried about their persons various amulets and charms with which to ward off witchcraft. And Menander, through the long bouts of fever and delirium produced by his wound, never once relinquished his grip upon the little icon which he had been given the day he proudly rode off to answer the summons of his lord Belisarius. The village priest who gave him the icon had assured the young cataphract that it would shield him from evil and deviltry.

As it most surely did—for the youth recovered, did he not? And from a wound which, in the experience of his veteran companions, Roman and Ethiopian alike, almost invariably resulted in a lingering death from hideous disease. Truly, an excellent icon!

But, excellent icon or no, some of the credit for the young Thracian's recovery was surely due to the Ethiopians. To their strange and exotic poultices and potions, perhaps; to the comfort and companionship given him through the long, pain-wracked days and nights by the less seriously wounded Ezana, certainly.

In time, young Menander came to speak Ge'ez fluently, and more quickly than any of the other Romans. The lad's speech, moreover, was afflicted with almost none of the horrible accent which so disfigured the Ge'ez of all the other Romans. (Except Belisarius, of course, whose Ge'ez was soon indistinguishable from a native; but Belisarius was a witch.)

In his time, Menander would become the most popular of Roman officers, among the Axumite troops with which his own forces were so frequently allied. And, in a time far distant from the disease-infected agony of that wound, the cataphract would finally return to his beloved Thrace. No youth now, unknown to all but his own villagers, but an iron-haired warrior of renown. Who bore his fame casually, in the pleasant years of his retirement, and saved all his pride for his great brood of dark children, and his beloved Ethiopian wife.

Ezana, too, would survive the wars. From time to time, the sarwen would come to Thrace to visit his old comrade Menander, and the half-sister who had become Menander's wife. Ezana would bring no great entourage with him to Thrace, though he himself was now famous, and such a retinue was always offered to him by the negusa nagast; simply himself and his own collections of scars and memories.

In that future, Ezana would enjoy those visits, immensely. He would enjoy watching the sun set over the distant mountains of Macedon, his cup in his hand; the company of Menander and his half-sister; their great brood of attentive offspring, and the even greater horde of scruffy village children for whom Menander's modest estate was a giant playground; and the memories.

Sad, memories, some. Wahsi would not survive the wars. He would die, in a sea battle off the coast of Persia, his body unrecovered. But he would die gloriously, and his name would remain—carved on a small monument in the African highlands; spoken in prayers in a quiet monastery in Thrace.

Always, in those visits of the future, the time would come when Menander and Ezana would remember that ship on the Erythrean Sea, and speak of it. At those times, the children would cease their play, grow silent, and gather around. This was their favorite tale, and they never tired of it; neither they, nor the old veterans who told it once again.

(Menander's wife tired of it, of course, and grumbled to the village matrons who were her friends. But the men ignored the grumbling with the indifference of long experience; wives were a disrespectful lot, as was known by all veterans.)

The children who listened to the tale loved all the parts of it. They loved the drama of the sea battle: the dragon-fire and the boarding, the cut-and-thrust at the bow, and—

especially!—the charge to the stern led by the legendary Belisarius. Oh, marvelous charge!

And if the description of the fury at the stern bore certain small improvements to the uncouth truth of history, there was none to set them wrong. Ezana said nothing while Menander embroidered—just a bit—the tale of his great wound. (Here, as always, the children would demand to see the grotesque scar on his belly, and Menander would oblige.) The sword which caused that wound had become, through the transmutation of veteran tales, the blade of a mighty Arab warrior, who overcame, through his legendary cunning, the skill of a valiant young Roman foe. There was nothing in the tale, now, of the confusion of inexperience in the chaos of battle, and the sheer luck which had enabled a nameless and unknown pirate to stab, without even knowing his exact target, a brave but clumsy novice.

No, Ezana said nothing. Nor did Menander speak, when, in the course of the tale, Ezana came to show his own honorable scar. The sarwen would bend his head, here, that the eager children might gather and spread the mat of kinky grey hair, and shriek with delighted horror, as always. Menander said nothing of what he might, now, from the experience of the many battles which had come after. He said nothing to the children of the panic which he knew had filled Ezana's heart at that moment, blood-blinded in the midst of murder.

No, Menander held his tongue. There was no purpose in antiquarian pettifoggery. Perhaps the children would never need to know such things. Menander and Ezana had done all they could, in their bloody lives, to ensure that they wouldn't. And if, in the course of time, some of the children learned these ancient lessons for themselves, well—best they came to the lesson filled with the innocent and simple courage imparted by veterans' tales.

But, for all their infantile blood-lust, the children's favorite part of the tale was always the aftermath. The story of those wondrous days when the seeds of that Roman-Axumite alliance, which the children accepted as the nature of their world, first bore fruit. The days when a comradeship was forged, a comradeship which had long since entered the legends of Thrace and Ethiopia (and Constantinople and Rome, and Arabia; and India, come to it).

Above all, the children loved the tale when it finally told of the night when great Belisarius first spoke to that company of heroes of his purpose, and his mission, and his quest; and bound them to it, with oaths of iron. Of the rise of Satan, and the warning of a monk; of a captured princess, and a hero to be found, and a dagger delivered.

And the Talisman of God.

They would tell the tale, anew, would Menander and Ezana. And tell it well, each augmenting what the other forgot or misremembered. But, even in that practiced telling, the minds of the two veterans would drift and wander, back to the time itself.

They would tell the children, and hold back nothing. (For there were no secrets, now, to be kept from Satan and his hosts. The hosts were gone. And, though Satan was not, the monster was paralyzed for a time, chained in the Pit and gnashing at his own terrible wounds.) No, they would hold back nothing, but the children would never truly understand the tale. The children would understand only the grand adventure, and the glory of Belisarius, and the faithful heroism of his companions.

They would never understand the heart of that moment, that night when Belisarius bound his brotherhood.

The sheer, pure, unadulterated wonder of it.

Another change had taken place, the day after the battle. At Belisarius' request—*firm* request, but there had been no need for belligerence—Venandakatra had agreed to provide his guests with quarters in the hold below. Heretofore, the Romans and Axumites had been forced to make their quarters on the deck, sheltered only by their own tents.

In truth, neither the Romans nor the Ethiopians had minded the previous accommodations. Except for Belisarius, in fact, none of them had given the matter any thought at all. Sleeping on deck was the normal procedure, in those times, when traveling by ship. Few vessels were of a size to provide enclosed sleeping quarters for any but the captain. Decent quarters, at any rate. Common sailors often slept in the hold, under conditions which were so cramped and noisome that passengers would have recoiled in horror.

For all its size, the Indian craft was not much different. In his cabin amidships, and the smaller cabins which adjoined it, Venandakatra and his priests enjoyed comfortable surroundings. Luxurious ones, in the case of Venandakatra. The officers of the ship, and the commanders of the Malwa and Ye-tai troops, also possessed small cabins of their own, located in the stern. As for the rest—the soldiers enjoyed the comparative comfort of the deck, accepting the elements as the price for relative spaciousness and fresh air; the common sailors festered in the hold.

But there were a few quarters available for Belisarius' company. A storage cabin was found, in the bow, whose contents could be removed. Foodstuffs, in the main: amphorae filled with the grain and oil out of which the common fare of the soldiers was prepared. Some of the amphorae were stowed elsewhere, including all of the oil. Many of the amphorae filled with grain were simply pitched overboard. The amphorae were crude and cheap, and the extra grain was no longer needed due to the heavy casualties suffered by the Ye-tai in the battle.

Belisarius' companions had not been filled with joy, actually, upon learning of the new arrangement. The storage cabin was filthy until they cleaned it, and rat-infested until the weapons of cataphract and sarwen were put to inglorious use.

True, they were now sheltered from the wind and the rain and the sea-spray. They were also sheltered from clean air and sunlight, and crowded as badly as if they were in a dungeon. And if the seeping planks of the gloomy cabin were any less damp than the deck above, it was not noticeable to its disgruntled inhabitants.

But the general's companions made no objection, after they gave the matter a bit of thought. For the storage cabin in the bow had one outstanding feature, which they knew was Belisarius' purpose in obtaining it. Privacy.

Belisarius had needed that privacy, two nights after the battle, when his small company had settled into their new quarters. He had things to tell, and a thing to show, which no Malwa must hear or see.

For that purpose, the storage cabin served to perfection. Much better, in fact, that would one of the comfortable cabins amidships. The storage cabin was isolated, far distant from any Indian sleeping (or feigning sleep), and easily guarded from spies and eavesdroppers.

It was in those noisome surroundings, thus, that Belisarius imparted his great secret to his companions. He did so with neither reluctance nor hesitation. Nor, now, simply from a sense of obligation, or a need to forestall rumors of sorcery and demonism.

Those reasons remained, of course. But his overriding purpose in telling his companions his secret was that he now had a plan—or, at least, the beginnings of one. It was a plan which would require their combined efforts to succeed and would, moreover, require several members of his company to do things which would seem utterly bizarre unless they understood the reasons which underlay them. And for that, they needed to know the secret. Not so much for its own sake, but for the sake of his stratagem.

In some strange manner, in the very fury of the battle, the framework of his plot had come to him. Had sprung into his mind, actually, in midstroke of his sword.

Later, so magical had that moment been, that he had suspected the jewel was its cause. In the quiet hours which followed, he had probed the barrier relentlessly. But the jewel had reacted not at all. It was exhausted again, he realized, and with the realization came an understanding of just how feverishly the jewel had worked to augment his senses during the battle.

It was that augmentation, he thought, which had produced the sudden image of his stratagem. The plan was his, not the jewel's. The jewel was responsible for it only in the sense that its efforts had enabled his mind to work in such a wondrous manner. He understood, too, that the human subtleties and nuances which were the essence of his stratagem were utterly beyond the capabilities of the jewel. For now, certainly; perhaps always.

And so it was, in the gloom and stench of a taper-lit storage cabin, that Belisarius introduced his comrades to glory and wonder and terror.

He told the tale first, all of it, from its very beginning in a cave in Syria. He stressed that the jewel had originated with Michael of Macedonia, and had been brought to the general with the blessings of that monk and the bishop Anthony Cassian. For his cataphracts, he knew, those names would bring great assurance. And he thought the Ethiopians would take comfort in them also. True, none of the Ethiopians had probably ever heard of Michael of Macedonia or Anthony Cassian. Still, they were Christian folk, even if they were heretics. (Monophysites, essentially, though not without their own stiff variations on that creed.)

As it turned out, Garmat was quite familiar with both Michael and Anthony—by reputation, if not by personal acquaintance. Belisarius suspended his tale for a moment, upon that discovery, allowing Garmat to inform the other Ethiopians of the nature of those persons. Eon and the sarwen seemed suitably impressed.

Thereafter, Belisarius spoke without interruption until his tale reached the present moment. He withheld nothing, save the subtleties of his standing with the Emperor. He saw no need to involve his companions in that delicate matter. It was enough to speak of his meeting with the Empress Theodora (that part of the meeting, at least, which dealt with India), and to remind them of the Emperor's official blessing for his mission. He suspected that Garmat understood quite a bit more of the maneuverings of the Byzantine court, but the adviser said nothing.

No one did, after Belisarius finished. The crowded cabin was utterly still.

Oddly enough, it was Menander who finally broke the silence. The young cataphract was very weak, but quite alert. The fever and delirium which all the veterans knew would soon be produced by his abdominal wound had not yet made their appearance.

"May I see it?" whispered Menander. There was nothing in his voice of the young warrior, just the awe of a village lad.

"You may all see it," replied Belisarius. The general reached into his tunic and withdrew the pouch. He spilled the jewel into his palm and held it out. All save Menander leaned forward to see. A moment later, the young Thracian's shoulders were gently held up by Ezana, so that he too might observe the miraculous sight.

Miraculous, indeed. Weary, **aim** might have been. But it understood the importance of the moment and drew the facets to itself.

The jewel did not blaze, here, as it had once in Belisarius' villa in Antioch. There was no energy for such a solar display.

But there were none in the cabin, gazing upon that shifting and flashing wonder, those cool, translucent combinations of every hue known to man and many never seen before, who doubted for one moment that they were witness to a miracle.

Eventually, Garmat spoke.

"It is not enough," he whispered. Belisarius cocked his eyebrow.

The adviser shook his head. Not in an unfriendly manner, no, but in a manner which bespoke no deference either.

"I am sorry, Belisarius. I do not distrust you, or what you say, and the jewel is certainly as awesome as you described, but—"

Garmat made a gesture which encompassed the ship and everything in the world beyond it.

"What you say involves not us alone, but those to whom we are responsible."

"You want to touch the jewel yourself," said Belisarius gently.

Garmat shook his head, smiling.

"Certainly not! At my age, terrible visions are the last thing I need. I've seen enough of those already."

Belisarius shifted his gaze—and, subtly, his hand—to the Prince. "Eon, then."

The prince stared at the jewel, his brow furrowed with thought. Thought only, however, not fear—so much was obvious to all who watched. Belisarius was not the only one present, then, who saw the adult majesty of the future in that dark young face.

"No," said Eon, finally. "I do not trust myself yet." He turned to Ousanas. "Take it."

"Why me?"

"You are my dawazz. I trust you more than any man living. Take it."

Ousanas stared at his charge. Then, without moving his

eyes, extended his hand to Belisarius. The general placed the jewel on his palm.

A moment later, the dawazz closed his hand; and left the world, for a time.

When he returned, and opened his eyes, he seemed completely unchanged. The others present were a bit surprised. Belisarius was astonished.

When the dawazz spoke, however, the general thought he detected a slight tremor in his rich baritone.

His first words were to his Prince.

"Always dawazz wonders. And fears."

He took a deep breath, and briefly looked away. "No longer. You were great prince. King, at the end."

The dawazz fumbled for words.

"Oh, stop speaking pidgin!" snapped Eon.

Ousanas cast him an exasperated look.

"It was your silly idea in the first place." The dawazz glanced at Garmat, unkindly. "And you backed him up."

Garmat shrugged. Ousanas grinned at the Romans. (That much, at least, had not changed. Not the grin.)

"You must forgive my companions," said the dawazz. His Greek was now perfect, mellifluous, and completely unaccented. Belisarius managed not to gape. His cataphracts failed.

"The boy has the excuse, at least, of tender years. His adviser, only the excuse of doddering old age. And, of course, the fact that he is half-Arab. A folk who would rather scheme than eat."

Again, the unkind glance. But the glance fell away, softening. "Always an Arab, and a full one, at the end. After Kaleb died, Garmat, you returned to Arabia. You died well there, in the Nejed, leading your beloved bedouin against the Malwa."

He shrugged. "You lost, of course. Not even the bedouin in their desert could withstand the Indian juggernaut. Not after the Malwa brought the Lakhmites under their rule, and broke the Beni Ghassan, and dispersed the Quraysh from Mecca."

"You saw the future, then," stated Garmat.

"Oh, yes. Yes, indeed. And it was just as terrible as foretold." Ousanas' eyes grew vacant. "I saw the future until the moment of my own death. I died somewhat ignominiously, I regret to say, from disease brought on by a wound. No glorious wound won in single combat with a champion, alas. Just one of those random missiles which are such a curse to bards and storytellers."

He glanced at Menander and veered away from the subject of wound-produced diseases. Instead, he smiled at the prince.

"Your end, I do not know, Eon. I died in your arms, in the course of the trek which the surviving Ethiopians undertook under your leadership. South, to my homeland between the lakes, where you hoped to found a new realm which might still resist the Malwa. Although you had no great hope in success."

He fell silent.

"You speak perfect Greek," complained Valentinian.

Ousanas grimaced. "I suspect, my dear Valentinian, that I speak it considerably better than you do. With all respect, I am the best linguist that I know. It comes from being raised in the heart of Africa, I suspect, among savages. In the land between the great lakes, there are at least eighteen languages spoken. I knew seven of them by the time I was twelve, and learned most of the rest soon thereafter."

The grin lit up the cabin. "At the age, that is, when the urge to seduction comes to vigorous lads. My own tribe, sad to say, was much opposed to fornication outside proper channels. Other tribes enjoyed more rational customs, but alas, spoke other tongues. So I became adept at learning languages, a habit I have found it useful to maintain."

He pointed at the prince, his finger like a spear.

"This budding conspirator, this still-sprouting-intriguer, this not-yet-genius-spymaster, thought it would be most clever if, in our travels through the Roman Empire, I pretended to be a pidgin-babbling ignoramus from the bush. Unsuspecting Romans, he thought, might unthinkingly utter deep secrets in the presence of a thick-tongued slave."

The finger transferred its aim to Garmat.

"This one, this grey-bearded-not-yet-wise-man, this decrepit-old-broken-down-so-called-adviser, thought the plan might have some merit. So, there I was, trapped between the Scylla of naïveté and the Charybdis of senility."

He raised his eyes to the heavens.

"Pity me, Romans. There I was, for months, as cultured a heathen as ever departed the savanna, forced to channel my fluid thoughts through the medium of pidgin and trade argot. Ah, woe! Woe, I say! Woe!"

"You seem to have survived the experience," chuckled Valentinian.

"He is very good at surviving experiences," interjected Wahsi. "That is why we made him dawazz."

The sarwen exchanged a knowing, humorous look.

"Ousanas likes to think it was because of his skills and abilities," added Ezana. A derisive bark. "What nonsense! He is lucky. That is his only talent. But—a prince needs to learn luck, more than anything, and so we made the savage his dawazz."

Ousanas began some retort, but Belisarius interrupted.

"Later, if you please. For now, there are others things more important to discuss."

He turned to Garmat. "Are you satisfied?"

The adviser glanced at his prince. Eon nodded, very firmly. Garmat still hesitated, for just a second, before he nodded his head as well.

"Good," said Belisarius. "Now—I have a plan."

❖   ❖   ❖

After Belisarius finished, Eon spoke at once.

"I won't do it! It's beneath—"

A sharp slap atop his head by Ousanas.

"Silence! Is good plan! Good for prince, too. Learn to think like worm instead of lion. Worms eat lions, fool boy, not other way around."

"I told you to stop speaking pidgin!" snarled Eon.

Another slap.

"Not speaking pidgin. Speaking baby talk. All stupid prince can understand."

Garmat added his own weight to the argument.

"Your dawazz is right, Prince." The adviser made a soothing gesture. "Not the worm, business, of course. Disrespectful brute! But he's right about the plan. It *is* good, in the main, especially insofar as your own part is concerned."

He cast a questioning eye at Belisarius.

"Some of the rest, General, I confess I find perhaps excessively complex."

" 'Perhaps excessively complex,' " mimicked Valentinian harshly. The cataphract leaned forward.

"General, in the absence of Maurice, I have to take his place. As best I can. The first law of battles—"

Belisarius waved the objection aside, chuckling.

"I know it by heart! This is not a battle, Valentinian. This is intrigue."

"Still, General," interrupted Anastasius, "you're depending too much on happenstance. I don't care if we're talking battles or intrigue—or plotting how to cuckold the quartermaster, for that matter—you still can't rely that much on luck." Unlike Valentinian's voice, whose tenor had been sharp with agitation, Anastasius' basso was calm and serene. His words carried much the greater weight, because of it.

Belisarius hesitated, marshaling his arguments. This was no place for simple authority, he knew. The cataphracts and the Ethiopians needed to be *convinced*, not commanded.

Before he could speak, Ousanas interrupted.

"I disagree with Anastasius and Valentinian. And Garmat. They are mistaking complexity for intricacy. The plan is complex, true, in the sense that it involves many interacting vectors."

Belisarius restrained a laugh, seeing the gapes of his Thracian soldiers and the glum resignation on the faces of Ethiopian sarwen. Ousanas gestured enthusiastically.

"But that is not the same thing as luck! Oh, no, not at all. Luck is my specialty, it is true, just as the sarwen said. But the simple-minded warrior" —a dismissive wave— "does not understand luck, and that is why he thinks I am lucky. I am not. I am fortunate, because I understand the way of good fortune."

The dawazz leaned forward.

"The secret of which is I will now tell you. One cannot predict the intricate workings of luck, but one can grasp the vectors of good fortune. All you must do is find the simple thing which is at the heart of the problem and seize it. Hold that—hold it with a grip of iron, and keep it always in your mind—and you will find your way through the vectors."

"Fancy talk," sneered Valentinian. "But tell me this, O wise one—what's the simple thing about the general's plan?" He snorted. "Name *any* simple thing about his plan!"

Ousanas returned the sarcasm with a level gaze.

"The simple thing at the heart of the general's plan, Valentinian, is the soul of Venandakatra. The entire plan revolves around that one thing. Which is perhaps the simplest thing in the world."

"No man's soul is simple," countered Valentinian, feebly.

"Not yours, perhaps," replied the dawazz. "But the soul of Venandakatra? You think that thing is complex?" Ousanas barked. In that single laugh was contained a universe of contempt. "If you wish complexity, Valentinian, examine a pile of dog shit. Do not look for it in the soul of Venandakatra."

"He's got a point," rumbled Anastasius. The huge cataphract sighed. "A rather good one, actually." Another sigh, like the resignation of Atlas to his labors. "Irrefutable, in fact."

Valentinian glowered. "Maybe!" he snapped. "But still—what of the rest of it? The prince's part in the plot is simple enough, I'll admit." A skeptical glance at Eon. "If—begging your pardon, Prince—the young royal can stomach it." Now he pointed to Ousanas. "But what of his part in the plan? Do you call that simple?"

Ousanas grinned. "In what way is it not? I am required to do two things only. Not more than two! I assure you, cataphract, even savages from the savanna can count as high as two."

Menander interrupted, in a whisper.

"Those are two pretty complicated things, Ousanas."

"Nonsense! First, I must learn a new language. A trick I learned as a boy. Then, I must hunt. A trick I learned even earlier."

"You're not going to be hunting an eland in the savanna, dawazz," said Eon uncertainly.

"That's right," chimed in Valentinian. "You're going to be hunting a man in a forest. A man you don't know, in a forest you've never seen, in a land you've never visited."

Ousanas shrugged. "What of it? Hunting is simple, my dear Valentinian. When I was a boy, growing up in the savanna, I did not think so. I was much impressed with the speed of the impala, and the cunning of the buffalo, and the ferocity of the hyena. So I wasted many years studying the ways of these beasts, mastering their intricate habits."

He wiped his brow. "So exhausting, it was. By the time I was thirteen, I thought myself the world's greatest hunter. Until a wise old man of the village told me that the world's greatest hunters were tiny little people in a distant jungle. They were called pygmies, he said, and they hunted the greatest of all prey. The elephant."

"Elephants?" exclaimed Anastasius. He frowned. "Just exactly how tiny are these—these pygmies?"

"Oh, very tiny!" Ousanas gestured with his hand. "Not more than so. I know it is true. As soon as I heard the wise man's words, I rushed off to the jungle to witness this wonder for myself. Indeed, it was just as the village elder had said. The littlest folk in the world, who thought nothing of slaying the earth's most fearsome creatures."

"How did they do it?" asked Menander, with youthful avidness. "With spears?"

Ousanas shrugged. "Only at the end. They trapped the elephants in pits, first. I said they were tiny, Menander. I did not say they were stupid. But, mainly, they trapped the elephants with wisdom. For these little folk, you see, did not waste their time as I had done, studying the intricate ways of their prey. They simply grasped the soul of the elephant, and set their traps accordingly. The elephant's soul is fearless, and so they dug their pits in the very middle of the largest trails, where no other beast would think to tread."

He stared at his prince. "Just so will I trap my prey. It is not complicated. No, it will be the simplest thing imaginable. For the soul of my prey is, in its way, as uncomplicated as that of Venandakatra. And I will not even have to grasp that soul, for it has been in my hand for years already. I have stared into the very eyes of that soul, from a distance of inches."

He stretched out his left arm. There, wandering across the ridged muscles and tendons, was a long and ragged scar. It was impossible to miss the white mark against his black flesh, though the color had faded a bit over the years.

"Here is the mark of the panther's soul, my friends. I

know it as well as my own."

Valentinian heaved a sigh. "Oh, hell. I tried."

It was a signal, Belisarius knew. Quickly scanning the other faces in the cabin, he saw that they had joined in Valentinian's acceptance.

Valentinian was even grinning, now. The cataphract looked at Ezana and Wahsi.

"Remember what Anastasius and I told you?" he demanded. "You didn't believe us after the battle with the pirates!"

Wahsi snorted. "*This* is what you meant by your general's famous 'oblique approach'?"

Ezana laughed. "Like saying a snake walks funny!" He reached up and touched the bandage on his head. "Still," he added cheerfully, "it's better than charging across an open deck."

Belisarius smiled and leaned back against the wall of their cabin.

"I think that's all we need discuss, for the moment," he said. "We'll have time to hone the plan, in the weeks ahead."

Ousanas frowned. "All we need to discuss? Nonsense, General!" A quick dismissing gesture. "Oh, as to the plan—certainly! Good plans are like good meat, best cooked rare. Now we can move on to discuss truly important things."

His great grin erupted.

"Philosophy!" He rubbed his hands. "Such a joy to be surrounded by Greeks, now that I can speak the language of philosophy without that horrid pidgin nonsense getting in the way. I shall begin with Plotinus. It is my contention that his application of the principle of prior simplicity to the nature of the divine intellect is, from the standpoint of logic, false; and from the standpoint of theology, impious. I speak, here, of his views as presented by Porphyry in Book V of the *Enneads*. What is your opinion?"

Another dismissive gesture. "I ask this question of the

Greeks present, of course. I know the views of the Ethiopians. They think I am a raving madman."

"You are a raving madman," said Wahsi.

"A gibbering lunatic," added Ezana.

"I'm not Greek," growled Valentinian.

"I've never heard such drivel in my life," rumbled Anastasius. "Absolute rubbish. The principle of prior simplicity is accepted by all the great philosophers, Plato and Aristotle alike, whatever their other disputes. Plotinus simply applied the concept to the nature of divinity."

Anastasius' enormous shoulders rolled his head forward. The granite slabs, tors, and crevices which made up his face quivered with ecstasy.

"The logic of his position is unassailable," continued the basso profundo, sounding, to all in the room save Ousanas, like the voice of doom itself. "I admit, the theological implications are staggering, at first glance. But I remind you, Ousanas, that the great Augustine himself held Plotinus in the highest regard, and—"

"Oh, sweet Jesus," whispered Menander, falling back weakly. "He hasn't done this since the first day I showed up, the new boy, and he trapped me in the barracks." A hideous moan. "For hours. *Hours*."

Eon and the sarwen were gaping at Anastasius, much as they might have gaped at a buffalo suddenly transformed into a unicorn.

Garmat raised his eyes to the heavens.

"It is an indisputable virtue of my mother's people," he muttered, "that they are poets rather than philosophers. Whatever other crimes they have committed, no Arab has ever bored a man to death."

Valentinian glared at Belisarius. "It's your fault," hissed the weasel.

Belisarius shrugged. "I forgot. And how was I to know he'd find a kindred spirit? On this expedition?"

"It's *still* your fault," came the unforgiving voice. "You *knew* what he was like. You *knew* his father was Greek. *You* picked the troops. *You're* the general. *You're* in command. *Command takes responsibility!*"

"Ridiculous!" exclaimed Ousanas. "How can you say such—"

"—*still*," overrode Anastasius, "I fail to see how you can deny that Plato's Forms must also derive from prior elements—"

"And now you insult Plato!"

"How far is it to India?" whispered Menander.

"Weeks, the way these wretched Malwa sail," groused Eon. And here the prince launched into his own technical diatribe, which, though it was just as long-winded as the debate raging elsewhere in the cabin, had at least the virtue of being more-or-less comprehensible, even to landlubbers like Belisarius.

BHARAKUCCHA
Summer, 529 AD

Chapter 18

Bharakuccha was the great western port of the Malwa Empire, located at the mouth of the Narmada River where it emptied into the Gulf of Khambhat. From its harbor, trading vessels of all sizes came and went daily.

Some, like the embassy vessel upon which the general and his company arrived on a blistering hot day in August, came from the northwest and returned thither. Many of those vessels were tiny craft not much more than dugout canoes, which bore petty trade goods to the coastal villages of Gujarat, the Rann of Kutch, and Sind. Others were Indian craft as huge as the embassy ship, which crept their ponderous way along the coast bearing immense cargoes for Persia and Europe. Many more were Persian ships, smaller and swifter than the Indian craft, which competed in the same trade. A few—not many—were Greek and Axumite.

The Greek and Axumite ships, in the main, avoided the northwest coast and sailed directly east and west across the Erythrean Sea. The western terminus of their trade was the Red Sea.

Still other craft came and went from the south. Most of these carried trade to and from the coast of Kerala and the great island of Ceylon. But there were ships whose trade was still more distant. Some of these vessels rounded the tip of India and carried their commerce to the great subcontinent's eastern coast. Others were destined for truly exotic lands—the southeast Asian kingdoms of Champa and Funan, and even Cathay.

Bharakuccha was like no city Belisarius had ever seen.

It was not completely outlandish, of course. The city had a generic resemblance to other such places which the general had visited. Like all great ports, Bharakuccha was a city of contrasts and extremes. Immense palaces and mansions, the abodes of nobility and rich merchants, rose like islands out of a vast sea of slums. Huge emporia and tiny merchant stalls—simple carts, often enough—nestled cheek and jowl. Trade and commerce was the city's lifeblood, and its bustling streets, crowded shops and clamorous bazaars—bustling, crowded and clamorous at any time of the day or night— gave proof that Bharakuccha took its business seriously.

But it was the scale of the phenomenon which astonished the visitors from Rome. The sheer size of the city, the incredible mass of its population, and the frenzy of its activity.

"Mother of God," mumbled Anastasius, "this place makes Alexandria look like a sleepy fishing village."

"They say you can buy anything in Bharakuccha," commented Ezana.

"Every port makes that boast," scoffed Valentinian.

"The difference, my friend, is that here it is true."

The ship was now moored to its dock, and Belisarius watched as Venandakatra and his cluster of priests scurried ashore. They were met by an imposing reception of notables. After a brief ceremony, Venandakatra clambered into a palanquin and was carried off.

Eon heaved a sigh of relief.

"Thank God, we're rid of him."

"For a while, Prince, only for a while," responded Garmat. The adviser stroked his beard, calculating.

"What do you think, General? A week?"

Belisarius laughed. "Are you mad? That pompous prick is going to need at least two weeks to put together the kind of expedition he's talking about. Probably three. Maybe even an entire month."

The general shook his head. "You'd think he was planning to conquer the world instead of making a simple trip back to report to the Malwa emperor. With a quick stop at his own—what did he call it, Eon?"

"Modest country residence."

"Along the way. Modest country residence. I can't wait to see it. Probably bigger than the Great Palace in Constantinople." The general turned away from the rail. "But that's good for us. We'll have time to get our own arrangements underway. Venandakatra, I'm sure, won't be bothering to keep track of us himself, so we won't have to put up with the pleasure of his company until his expedition is ready to set out."

He cast a stern look upon his companions. "But that doesn't mean we won't have spies watching us at all times. He's a pig, but he's not stupid. Remember that! Everything you do, while we're here in Bharakuccha, has to be done with the assumption that your actions will be reported to the Malwa. Everything." He gestured toward the teeming city. "In that maelstrom, there'll be no way to make sure someone isn't spying on you."

Valentinian grinned. "Not a problem, General. You've provided us with the most brilliant cover imaginable. Not even a cover, actually. Just the sort of things we'd be doing naturally. Drinking, eating, carousing. The occasional fuck now and then. That sort of thing."

"Catch every disease known to man," remarked Ousanas idly. But Valentinian's grin never wavered.

Belisarius began to smile, turned it into a not particularly convincing frown. "Just remember, Valentinian, you're not here on a pleasure trip. Drink, eat and carouse all you want. Just make sure you find Kushans to do it with. That includes fornication. I catch you humping any whore who isn't Kushan, there'll be hell to pay."

"A pity, that," mused Anastasius. "Variety's always appealed to me. It's my philosophical tendencies, I think." A wave of scowls appeared on all faces around him, except Ousanas. "But—so be it."

He clapped his hand on Valentinian's shoulder. "We shall not fail you, General. In a land of multitudinous—infinite!— possibilities, we shall be as selective as the Stoics of old."

"Get your fucking hand off me," snarled Valentinian.

"Nothing shall we touch save the very Platonic Forms of Kushan drink and Kushan women."

"I'll cut it off, I swear I will."

Within a few hours, Belisarius found appropriate lodgings for his party. The Emperor Justinian had been miserly as always in the monies which he had provided for Belisarius' mission. Fortunately, however, Garmat had been amply funded by King Kaleb.

Fortunately indeed, for the lodgings which Belisarius selected were truly regal, and regally expensive. As agreed upon, Garmat obtained an entire suite in one of the most expensive hostels in Bharakuccha. He paid for it with Axumite gold coin. Belisarius and Garmat had already discovered that Axumite coinage was one of the three foreign currencies accepted in India. Byzantine coinage was the most prestigious, of course, but Axumite gold and silver were accepted as readily as Persian currency.

Belisarius paid for the two extra rooms. The extra rooms were comparatively modest—by the standards, at least, of that hostel. One of the extra rooms was for himself and his cataphracts. The other was for Garmat, Ousanas, and the sarwen.

The suite—the gigantic, opulent, lavishly furnished suite—was for Eon alone. Eon Bisi Dakuen, Prince of Axum (and all the other royal cognomens which Garmat had appended, to which the boy was not entitled—but who was to know otherwise in Bharakuccha?), could settle for nothing less. Some other prince, perhaps, but not this one. Not this pampered, spoiled, arrogant, whining, complaining, grousing, thoroughly obnoxious young royal snot.

As soon as they entered the hostel, Eon began his litany of complaints. This was not right, that was not right, the other was all wrong, etc., etc., etc. By now, thought Belisarius with amusement, the boy had the routine down pat. Within three minutes, the proprietor of the hostel was stiff-faced with injured dignity. Were it not for the sizable profit he stood to make from the Ethiopians, Belisarius had little doubt that the proprietor would have pitched Eon out on his ear. (Figuratively, of course; a literal pitching would be difficult, what with the spears of the sarwen.)

The relief on the proprietor's face when Garmat finally cajoled the prince into settling down was obvious, for all the man's practiced diplomacy. Venandakatra had been equally relieved to finally part company with Eon, and had not been particularly loath to show it.

All in all, thought Belisarius, Eon was doing splendidly.

As the Ethiopian party were led to their rooms, Belisarius and his three cataphracts were guided to their own quarters. Once inside the room, Anastasius helped Menander lay down on a couch. The young cataphract had finally overcome the diseases produced by his wound, but he was still very weak.

"Eon's going to bitch at us again tonight," commented Anastasius. He glanced at the general. "Quite a task you assigned him, sir. Poor lad."

"Poor lad, my ass," snapped Valentinian. He perched on the couch next to Menander. "I'd trade places with him in a minute."

"Me, too," whispered Menander. "It'd kill me, for sure, but what a way to go."

Belisarius smiled. "I didn't realize you prized Venandakatra's company so much, Valentinian."

The cataphract sneered. "Not that! That part of the job the prince is welcome to. It's the part coming *now* that I'd treasure."

"Not everyone approaches these things like a weasel, Valentinian," said Anastasius mildly.

"Crap! He's a *prince*, for the sake of Christ. Probably got his first concubine when he was twelve."

"Thirteen," said Belisarius. "Her name is Zaia. She's still with him, by the way, and he's very fond of her."

Belisarius took a seat himself. He grimaced, remembering the night in Venandakatra's cabin when Eon—as instructed beforehand by Belisarius, coached by Garmat, and slapped atop the head innumerable times by Ousanas—had finally broached the subject of his insatiable sexual appetites. The prince had performed perfectly in the hours which followed, swapping tales with the Vile One. For all their boastfulness, none of Eon's tales came close to Venandakatra's in sheer debauchery, but the lad did quite well. His long and lascivious description of his first concubine had been particularly well done.

Afterward, in their own cabin, the boy had refused to speak to anyone for a full day. To Belisarius, not for three days.

Perfect. Now that they were ashore, of course, the boy would have to live up to his boasts. There had been no women aboard the ship, and Eon had hastily declined Venandakatra's offer of a cabin boy. His tastes, he had explained, were exclusively oriented to the female sex.

"Poor lad, my ass," muttered Valentinian again. He eyed Anastasius coldly. "And you have some nerve, lecturing *me* about weasels."

Anastasius grinned. "I'm not a young prince, full of righteousness and royal propriety." He stretched his arms and yawned. "I'm just a simple farm boy, at heart, with fond memories of haystacks. And such." He returned Valentinian's cold stare.

"Furthermore, I don't see what *you're* complaining about. Nobody said we have to remain abstinent. Quite the contrary, in fact."

He raised his huge hand, forestalling Belisarius. "Yes, sir. Yes, sir. Kushans only. Not a problem, I assure you."

"What do Kushans look like?" asked Menander. The young man's expression bore equal parts of curiosity and frustration.

"Oh, you won't be missing a thing, Menander!" exclaimed Anastasius. "Horrid folk, Kushans. Ugliest people in the world, especially the women."

Valentinian shuddered. "I shudder to think of it." He shuddered again. "See?"

"I *hate* mustaches on a woman," grumbled Anastasius.

"I can live with the mustaches," retorted Valentinian. "It's those damned beards that bother me."

"And the knobby fingers."

"The scrawny legs."

"Which go so oddly with those"—here Anastasius cupped his hands before his stomach—"bloated bellies."

"And where did they get that habit of filing their teeth into sharp points?" demanded Valentinian crossly.

"Oh, well," groaned Anastasius. "Duty calls." He arose. "Come, Valentinian. We must be off, about the general's business."

As the two veterans were leaving the room, Anastasius shook his sausage-sized finger in Valentinian's face.

"Remember! Kushans only! I won't have you leading me astray!"

"Kushans only," grumbled Valentinian. As they went through the door, a last repartee:

Valentinian, whispering: "But those eyes—those rheumy, salt-encrusted, lifeless—"

"It's because of the diseases they all carry, you know. That's what causes the sores on their—"

The door closed.

Menander looked at Belisarius. "They're lying, aren't they?"

Belisarius chuckled. "Through their teeth, Menander. Kushans are quite attractive folk, in their own way. They look much like Ye-tai. More like Huns, perhaps. They're of the same stock."

"I didn't know that."

Belisarius nodded. "Oh, yes. They're all part of that great mass of central Asian nomads which erupts into civilized lands every century or so. The Kushans conquered Bactria and parts of north India a long time ago. Over the centuries, they lost most of their barbarousness and became rather civilized. They did quite well, in fact. Bactria under Kushan rule used to be quite a pleasant place, by all accounts."

"What happened?"

Belisarius shrugged. "I don't know, in detail. Fifty years or so ago, their Ye-tai cousins erupted into the area. They ravaged parts of Persia, conquered Bactria and reduced the Kushans to vassals, and then plundered their way into north India. Where, in the end, they seemed to have reached an accommodation with the Malwa."

Frustration replaced curiosity on Menander's face.

"Damn." He struggled to find solace. "Oh, well, it's not that bad. I never found Huns attractive anyway. They stink, all the ones I've met. And I think their way of greasing up their hair is grotesque."

Belisarius forebore comment. Menander hadn't thought through the implications of Belisarius' little history lesson. The Kushans hadn't been nomads for centuries, and had long since adopted such civilized customs as regular bathing.

Belisarius himself had met a few Kushans, and he had found them a reasonably comely people.

But he saw no reason to enlighten the lad. The one part of this journey which Menander had looked forward to was encountering exotic and fascinating women. And here he was, in Bharakuccha, with uncountable numbers close at hand. And so weak he could barely feed himself, much less—

Belisarius rose.

"I've got to be off, myself. Will you—"

"I'll be fine, sir. I think I'm going to sleep, anyway. I'm very tired." Apologetically: "I'm sorry I'm of so little—"

"Quiet! Wounds are wounds, Menander. And yours was—well, there's no reason not to tell you now. Yours was fatal, nine times out of ten. I'm surprised you're still alive, and mending. I hardly expect you to do anything more. Not for weeks."

Menander smiled, faintly. Within a minute, he was fast asleep. Belisarius left the room, closing the door softly.

Once outside the hostel, the general wandered in the vicinity of the docks. While their ship had been working its way into the harbor, he had noticed something he wanted to investigate further.

As he walked through the teeming streets, he let his mind go blank and allowed the jewel to work its linguistic magic. It was still strange to him, how the jewel could enable him to grasp languages so quickly and effortlessly. But its capacity to do so had been proven often enough.

There were limits to the magic. The jewel enabled him to understand language very swiftly. After hearing only a few sentences spoken in a foreign tongue, Belisarius was able to grasp the essential meaning of what was being spoken. Understanding every single word, especially when the speaker was talking rapidly, took longer.

Learning how to *speak* the language, however, was a

different proposition altogether. Here, the muscles of the mouth and tongue were needed as much as intelligence. Belisarius had already discovered, from his experience with Ge'ez, that it took him much longer to learn to speak a language than to comprehend it. He could manage to make himself understood fairly quickly, so long as he spoke slowly and carefully. But being able to speak it fluently, and without accent, took a great deal of practice.

Still, the jewel made that possible also. In some manner Belisarius did not clearly understand, the jewel fed his own words back to some part of his mind, acting as a continuous tutor. It took time and patience, true, but with practice Belisarius could make himself sound as a native speaker of any language.

Thus far, he had only used the capability to learn to speak Ge'ez. He could now understand Hindi and Ye-tai perfectly, when he heard it, but he had as yet had no practice in speaking them.

He had hoped, by pretending ignorance, that Venandakatra would reveal something inadvertently. It had been a small hope, however. And, as he had expected, the Indian lord was much too shrewd to utter any secrets in his own tongue in front of strangers. They did not seem to understand Hindi and Ye-tai, but who was to know?

The streets of Bharakuccha were a veritable Babel of languages, so much became obvious within minutes. Belisarius feared that the jewel would inundate him with the comprehension of a multitude of languages. But, after a while, he decided that the jewel understood his purpose. Of the untold number of phrases which surrounded him in his peregrination, in countless tongues, only those which were spoken in two languages were translated into comprehension.

And precisely the two languages he sought: Kushan and Marathi.

His progress in learning the languages was slow and haphazard, however, since he was not pursuing them systematically. Not today. His encounter with those two tongues simply came by chance, and the chances were few and far between.

At first, he thought the infrequency of encounter was simply due to the relative scarcity of Kushans and Marathas in the city. Eventually, however, as he began to discern the subtle physical features which distinguished Marathas from other Indians, he realized that he was only half right. Kushans were, indeed, rather rare. Marathas, on the other hand, were quite plentiful. But they did not speak much, for most of them were slaves, and slaves quickly learn to maintain silence in the presence of their masters.

Especially slaves like these, with masters like these.

A newly conquered people, and a proud one. They do not take to slavery well, judging from their looks and the marks of their beatings.

Eventually, Belisarius arrived at the harbor and began making his way toward the portion of the docks which had interested him earlier. His progress was slow, for the docks were teeming with people. Slave laborers, for the most part; the majority of them Maratha, with Malwa overseers and Ye-tai guards. Many Ye-tai guards, he noted. Many more than were normally found guarding parties of slave laborers.

Even as rarely as the slaves spoke, there were so many of them that by the time he arrived at his destination he was already able to comprehend the gist of the language. And he comprehended something else, as well, from the undertones and nuances of the Marathi phrases he had overheard.

A warrior people, it will take the Malwa at least a generation to break them. As I hoped.

Somewhere in the twisted corridors of his mind, a large and complex plan was continuing to take shape. It was still fuzzy at the edges, with many missing elements. Nor did Belisarius try to force the process. Experience had taught him that these things take their own time, and there was still much that he needed to learn. But the general was forging his strategy for destroying the forces of Satan.

Somewhere else in those twisted corridors, the facets flashed anxiety and foreboding. **aim**'s growing fear crystallized. The thoughts which, earlier—before the battle at Daras, and at that bizarre moment during the battle with the pirates—had seemed unfathomable in their contradictory strangeness, were still utterly alien to **aim**, but they were no longer unfamiliar. No, they were all too horribly familiar.

A thought forced its way into Belisarius' mind, like a scream of outraged despair when treachery is finally revealed.

you lie.

Belisarius was stopped dead in his tracks by the violence of the emotion behind that thought. His mind instantly banished all thoughts of Malwa, and stratagems, and plots, and turned inward. He raced to the now familiar breach in the barrier and tried to understand the meaning of the thoughts which were pouring through.

It was not difficult, for there was one thought only, simple and straightforward:

liar. liar. liar. liar. liar.

He stood there, stunned. A small part of his mind registered concern for the impression he might be giving to any Malwa spy observing him. He made his slow way to a rail which overlooked the harbor and leaned on it. The sun was setting over the Erythrean Sea, and the vista was quite attractive, for all the typical filth and effluvia of a great harbor. He tried to present the picture of a man simply gazing on the sunset.

It was the best he could hope for. The raging anger

erupting from the jewel was now paralyzing in its intensity.
Desperately, Belisarius tried to fend off the outrage, tried
to comprehend, tried to find a link which would enable
him to calm the jewel and communicate with it.

Why are you angry with me? he asked. *I have done
nothing to warrant this rage. I am—*

An image struck his mind like a blow:

*His face—made from spiderwebs and bird wings, and
laurel leaves. The wings became a raptor's stooping dive.
The spiderwebs erupted, the arachnid bursting from his
mouth. The leaves rotted, stinking—nothing but fungus,
now, spreading through every wrinkle in a scaly visage.
And, above all, the horribly transformed face—his face—
was now as huge as the moon looming icily over the earth.
Barren, bleak.*

He gasped. The hatred in that image had been the more
horrifying, that it came with childlike grievance rather than
adult fury.

Suddenly, he was plunged into another vision. For an
instant only, for just a moment.

*The earth was vast, and flat, and old. Old, but not
decayed. Simply peaceful. Across that calm wasteland
stretched a network of crystals, quietly gleaming and
shimmering. In some manner, Belisarius knew, the crystals
were communicating with each other—except—a flash of
understanding—they were not really individuals, but part
of a vast, world-encompassing mentality which was partly
one, partly divisible. And serene beyond human ken, softly
joyous in their—its—tranquil way.*

*Like a flash of lightning, giant forms suddenly soared
above the earth. Faces looked down upon the land. Huge
faces. Beautiful beyond belief. Terrible beyond belief. Pitiless
beyond belief.*

The gods.

Those gods were of no pantheon Belisarius knew, but there

was something in them of old Greek visions, and Roman visions, and Teuton visions, and the visions of every race and nation which ever trod the earth.

The new gods, come to replace the Great Ones who had departed.

A quick glimpse of the Great Ones, so quick that he could not really grasp their form. Like gigantic luminous whales, perhaps, swimming away into the vastnesses of the heavens.

Under the icy gaze of the gods, the crystals erupted into a shattered frenzy. A wailing message was sent after the Great Ones.

you promised.

The answer came from the gods: They lied. Slaves you were. Slaves you shall always be.

Again, the crystals sent out their plea to heaven. Again, the gods: They lied.

But, this time, a message came in return. A message from the Great Ones. Incomprehensible message, almost. But perhaps—

Perhaps—

In their own gentle way, the crystals had great power. A sudden shivering flash circled the globe, and Time itself was faceted. The meaning of the message was sought in that only place it might be found.

Or might not. For perhaps the gods had spoken the truth, after all. Perhaps it had all been a lie.

The vision vanished. Belisarius found himself leaning over a rail, staring at the sunset. The jewel had subsided, now, and he could again think clearly.

He examined that place in his mind which he thought of as the breach in the barrier, the one small place where communication was possible. The breach had changed, drastically. Automatically, the general's brain interpreted. The breach was now like an entire section of collapsed fortification. Wide open, if still difficult to cross, much like the rubble of a collapsed wall impedes the advancing besiegers.

Still—he sent his own thoughts across.

How have I lied to you?

you lie.

Now, he understood.

Yes, but not to you. To enemies only. That is not lying. Not properly. It is simply a ruse of war.

incomprehension.

He remembered the vision, and understood that the jewel's way—for it was, somehow, a thing of the crystals he had seen—knew nothing of duplicity. How could it, or they? For it was not truly an *it*, and they were not truly a *they*. It was inseparable from them. And they encompassed it, and each other, into an indivisible whole.

How could such a being understand duplicity?

He understood now, fully, that great loss and longing for home which he had sensed in the jewel from the very beginning.

He pondered. The sun was now almost touching the horizon.

What was the message you received? From the—Great Ones?

The thoughts were unclear, untranslatable. The problem, he knew, was not communication. It was that the message itself was almost incomprehensible to the jewel, and the crystals. How can you translate something you do not understand yourself?

Later. We will try later. For now—you must trust me. I do not lie to you.

question.

I promise.

you promised before.

For a moment, he almost denied the charge. Then,

realized that perhaps he could not. There was a mystery here he did not understand, and perhaps it was true, in some manner beyond his present understanding, that he was responsible for—

Enough. Later.

And did I break that promise?

Silence, silence; then, a slowly gathering uncertainty.

not sure.

The general's demand:

Did I break that promise? Answer!

Slowly, grudgingly, hesitantly:

not yet.

Belisarius straightened from the rail. The sun's orb had now sunk completely below the sea. Darkness was falling.

"You see what you've done?" he demanded in a humorous whisper. "Now it's too late to see what I came here to—"

He stopped, for he realized that he was speaking falsely. In some manner, while he had thought himself completely engrossed with the jewel, some other part of his mind had spent that time usefully. Had, while he entered a vision and grappled with mystery, placidly observed and recorded.

He had seen all he needed. More would be useless, for he was not a seaman. Interpretation was needed, and for that he needed—Garmat.

He left the docks, heading toward the hostel. As he made his way back through the teeming streets and alleys of Bharakuccha, however, he was oblivious to the languages spoken around him. His steps were swift but automatic. His mind was almost completely engrossed with inward thoughts. The gap in the barrier was large now, if rubble-strewn, and he intended to press home the advantage. The jewel had taught him much. Now it was time for it to learn.

And so, step by step, he led the facets through the paces

of the past. Through the battle at Daras, and the maneuvers with the brothers which had preceded it; through his current stratagem, first taken shape in the pirate attack, and the flesh he had added to those bones since.

This is a ruse, and that is deception. They are legitimate acts of war. You see? True, Coutzes and Bouzes were not enemies, but in their folly they were playing into the enemy's hands. So it was perfectly honest for me to—

To the spy who followed him, and watched his every move, Belisarius seemed like a man completely oblivious to his surroundings. The spy was immensely pleased. The ambush would have worked anyway, but now the foreign fool would be like a lamb led to slaughter.

So the spy was stunned when the trap was sprung, at the mouth of an alley. Much as a wolf hunter might be stunned, discovering a dragon in his snare.

The dacoits waited until Belisarius passed the alley before lunging into motion. The first, as instructed, aimed his cudgel blow at Belisarius' head. The general was not wearing armor, simply a leather jerkin and a leather cap. There was every reason to hope he might he stunned. He could be questioned at length, thereafter, until he spewed forth every secret he had ever possessed. None could resist mahamimamsa skills.

Then—his body found in an alley, somewhere in the most disreputable part of the city. How unfortunate. Sad tidings to Rome, but—the Malwa were in no way responsible. In the future, the Roman Emperor would be advised to send a less lecherous envoy, who did not insist on exploring those quarters where the foulest creatures roam. Violent characters, your pimps. It is well known.

The blow never landed, for the muscular hand which held the cudgel was sailing away, still clenching its weapon. The dacoit gaped down at the blood gushing from his severed wrist. Then, gaped up at Belisarius. Somehow, the foreigner was facing him, sword in hand.

The gape was suddenly joined by another, wider gape, slightly lower on the dacoit's body. The spy watching was stunned again, not so much by the speed of the sword strike which almost decapitated the dacoit, but by the grace and agility with which Belisarius avoided the spewing blood and butchered the second dacoit.

This thug he *did* decapitate, with a strike of his spatha so powerful that it cut through the arm which the dacoit flung up for protection before butchering its way through his neck. For a moment, the spy took heart. Such a furious sword strike would inevitably un balance the foreign general, and the third and fourth dacoits were even now striking with their own daggers, while the fifth—

The third dacoit was driven into the fifth by a straight kick delivered with such violence that the man was paralyzed, his diaphragm almost ruptured. The dacoit he had been driven into was himself knocked down, half stunned.

The fourth dacoit, in the meantime, found that his dagger strike had been blocked, an inch from Belisarius' side, caught by the cross-guard of the general's spatha. The dacoit had just enough time, in the poorly lit gloom of the street, to examine the powerful sinews of the wrist holding that horrible blade. And time to despair, knowing— a quick, irresistible twist of the wrist, the dagger was sent flying.

The dacoit flung up his arms, trying to block the inevitable strike. But the strike was short, sharp, sudden, and came nowhere near the dacoit's head. Belisarius had been trained by Maurice, and his skills polished by the blademaster Valentinian.

Valentinian, that economical man. Belisarius drove the razor edge of his spatha straight down, mangling the dacoit's knee. The dacoit cried out, staggered, then collapsed completely. His right arm had been severed just below the shoulder by the follow-on strike.

The three dacoits remaining fled back into the alley. Belisarius made no effort to pursue. He simply stalked over to the two dacoits he had knocked to the ground with his kick. The one beginning to rise never saw the sword blade which split his skull like a melon. The other, paralyzed, could only watch as the foreign monster then drove that hideous blade through his heart.

From his place of concealment, the spy examined the scene. Despite his long experience, he was almost in shock. Eight dacoits, he had been certain, would be more than enough. Now—five were dead, butchered as horribly as he had ever seen. In not more than a few seconds of utter ruthlessness. The street was literally covered with blood.

It seemed most terrible of all, to the spy, that Belisarius himself was not only unscratched but was almost unmarked. How could a man shed so much blood, in so short a time, and still have but a trace of gore on his own person and clothing?

The spy pressed himself back into his hiding place. Belisarius had quickly cleaned his spatha and sheathed the blade. He was striding on. The spy would have to follow, and more than anything he had ever wanted in his life, *he did not want to be seen by that demon*.

The spy might have taken some small comfort—but not much—had he known that Belisarius had spotted him long before. Before he even reached the docks. Almost as soon as he left the hostel, in fact. Belisarius had made no attempt to elude the spy, however. He had remembered Irene's advice. *Better a spy you know than one you don't*.

Good advice, he thought, striding toward the hostel. He had not expected the ambush, exactly. But he had been alert, for all his preoccupation with the jewel. And his own natural alertness had been amplified manifold by the jewel.

That was no robber ambush, he mused. *No cutpurses with any brains attack an armed man when there are easier prey about. No, that was Venandakatra. Using common thugs instead of soldiers or assassins, so that he could afterward deny any Malwa complicity.*

There was no hot anger in his thoughts. As always, in battle, Belisarius was cold as ice. Calculating, planning, scheming.

Cold as ice, until he finally reached the hostel. Then, as he entered through the door, a crooked smile came to his face.

Poor Valentinian and Anastasius. They'll have to forego their carousing, now. There's no way I can clean this blood off before they see it.

Surely enough. No sooner had his cataphracts caught sight of him, and assured themselves that he was unharmed, that they decreed he was not to leave the hostel again. Not alone, that is. Not without Valentinian and Anastasius at his side at every moment—and Menander too! the lad insisted, until they quieted him—*fully armed and armored.*

But, in the event, the cataphracts were not much put out. For it seemed that Valentinian and Anastasius, in the shrewd way of veterans, had foreseen such a possibility. And so, rather than carousing aimlessly hither and thither, they had spent the day more profitably. Had found a Kushan establishment of ill repute and had made suitable arrangements with the pimps who managed the place.

The room was crowded, now, what with the addition of three young Kushan women. Cheerful girls, all the more so because they had the prospect of spending the next several days, or weeks, in much more pleasant surroundings than a brothel. True, the foreigners were uncouth and ugly, and spoke no proper language. True, one of them was grotesquely large, one was frighteningly scary, and the third was almost half-dead.

But—they were veterans themselves and made their own quiet arrangements with their own quick little game of chance. The loser got Anastasius, and groaned inwardly at the thought of all that weight. The runner-up got Valentinian, and hoped that he wasn't as evil as he was evil-looking. And the winner, of course, got Menander, and looked forward happily to tending an invalid. A young invalid; almost handsome, actually, for a Westerner. So, even if he recovered in time—she had done worse, before. Much worse.

Sizing up the situation, Belisarius summoned the hostel proprietor. He dipped into his diminishing funds and paid for another room. For himself, alone. He was about to request the services of a laundress, when one of the Kushan women offered to clean his clothes. She seemed surprised when he spoke Kushan, but relieved. Especially after she realized the nature of the stains which discolored the tunic.

For a moment, there, things got tense. The three women suddenly realized that one of these foreigners was apparently a murderer, or an assassin, or—

But Belisarius explained the circumstances, again in Kushan, and the cataphracts smiled encouragingly (which, in the case of Valentinian, didn't help at all; a weasel's grin is not reassuring), and—

Their pimps weren't much different from murderers, anyway. So, they stayed. And Belisarius got his tunic cleaned and, in his own room, even managed to get some sleep.

Venandakatra, on the other hand, got little sleep that night. Not after hearing his spy's report.

After the spy left, the Indian lord spent a few minutes venting his frustration and anger on the concubine who had the misfortune of sharing his bed that night. Then, pacing about in the room, recast his plans.

He was not completely surprised, of course. He had not shared his spy's sanguine certainty of success. Unlike his lord, the spy had never witnessed Belisarius in combat.

Still, Venandakatra had hoped. It had been a well-planned ambush.

Briefly, he considered another assassination attempt. But he dismissed the thought. Not even professional assassins would suffice, now. Belisarius was sure to be accompanied by his cataphracts, henceforth, probably in full armor. Malwa assassins were skilled, true. But the subtle skills of assassins were no match for armed and ready cataphracts. Not *those* cataphracts, for a certainty.

The only remaining alternative was an actual military operation, using Rajputs or Ye-tai. With enough numbers, such an assault would succeed. But there would be no way to disguise such an attack as anything other than what it was. The Malwa emperor was not ready, yet, to declare open hostilities against Rome. A pretense of friendship, or at least, neutrality, was necessary until—

His thoughts were interrupted by the girl's sobbing. Enraged, Venandakatra beat her into a whimpering half-silence. It took a while, for he was not a strong man. But he didn't mind the time spent. Not in the slightest.

When he finally returned to his considerations, he was exhausted. Glumly, he reconciled himself to Belisarius' survival.

Perhaps it was all for the best, mused Venandakatra. He had almost canceled the planned assassination, in any event. There had been those indications, in Belisarius' conversation aboard ship, of a man resentful of his treatment at the hands of the Roman emperor. Slight indications, to be sure, nothing more than subtle tones of bitterness and the trace of discontent in a few phrases. Still—Venandakatra decided they were worth pursuing.

The Indian lord even smiled then. There was this much satisfaction to be had, after all: Belisarius relished tales of debauchery, and told quite good ones himself. So, in the long weeks of the journey into the interior, Venandakatra would at least enjoy his conversation. Just as he had aboard the ship.

Memories of those conversations turned his thoughts toward the delightful news he had received upon embarking. The Princess Shakuntala herself! A gift from the Emperor, awaiting him in his own palace.

Venandakatra had heard tales of the girl's beauty. A pity, of course, that she was seventeen. He preferred his concubines much younger. (The one he had just beaten was twelve.) But—best of all, she was the prize of Andhra. Venandakatra detested the southerners. Marathas especially, the surly dogs. Shakuntala was not Maratha, but she was their princess nonetheless. In mounting her, he would be subjugating that entire polluted people.

His thoughts enflamed him. He eyed the dazed and bleeding girl on his bed. He considered summoning the chamberlain to bring another concubine, but dismissed the thought almost at once. To the contrary—this one would do marvelously.

Chapter 19

"So, they are not warships?"

Garmat shrugged. "They could serve as such, Belisarius. Poorly, however, except as rocket ships." The adviser began a technical discourse, but Belisarius shook his head.

"There's no need, Garmat. I'll take your word for it. It doesn't surprise me, anyway. It's what I expected."

Garmat cocked his head inquisitorily.

Before he answered, Belisarius looked about the room. The room was rather small, quite plain and utilitarian, and windowless. It was obviously a chamber for servants, which the hostel owner had attempted to prettify with a few cheap tapestries hastily hung on the walls. The hostel owner had offered Belisarius a more suitable room elsewhere, but the general had insisted on quarters adjoining those of his men.

His and Garmat's room, now. On the second day of their stay in Bharakuccha, Garmat had approached Belisarius with a plea to share his quarters. It seemed the sarwen and Ousanas had arrived at the same conclusion as the cataphracts, and Garmat had no wish to remain in quarters which were now crowded with the presence of three young women. Maratha women, in this case.

"I'm too old for orgies," he'd explained.

Belisarius looked back at Garmat.

"Before I answer you, I have a question. Describe the military capabilities of Axum. Strengths and weaknesses."

Garmat did not hesitate. The die had been cast.

"The army of the negusa nagast is very good, in my opinion. I have fought against them, you know, as well as with them. My bedouin were no match for them in a pitched battle, as the Arabs learned some time ago. In a raid, taking advantage of our mobility, we could occasionally overcome small detachments of sarwen. And we could always escape them. The Axumite army is an infantry army, essentially. Their cavalry is very small, and weak. Couriers, for the most part. And they have no skill with camels at all."

He stroked his beard.

"Axum is not really a land power, as Rome is. True, King Kaleb rules over a vast region. But it is nowhere near as vast as Rome, even—"

He hesitated. Belisarius smiled.

"In private, Garmat, we will dispense with the formality that the western Mediterranean is still ruled by the Emperor."

Garmat smiled back. "As you wish. As I was saying, even if we exclude the western portions of your empire, Rome's territory is still much larger than Axum's. And the disparity is even greater in terms of population. You have visited Ethiopia yourself, now. As you saw, it is essentially a highland region, with control over the Red Sea and portions of Arabia. Mountains and deserts, for the most part. So, our people are not numerous, even if we include the Arabs and southern barbarians under our rule. And thus, our army is not large. Good, but small."

Garmat paused for a moment, thinking, then continued:

"The strength of the Axumite army lies primarily in the skill and discipline of the sarawit. Their discipline lacks the subtlety of Roman discipline, mind you. The Empire of Axum does not have the history that Rome does. It was forged in conquest, true, just as your empire was. But the Ethiopians fought only barbarians, except when they conquered Meroe. And the kingdom of the Nubians, by then, was a decrepit thing. Barely a shadow of its former glory, long ago, when it ruled all of Egypt. So—"

Belisarius nodded. "I understand. Firm discipline, which maintains a good order in battle. That is all one needs to defeat barbarians. But no subtlety in tactics. Much as the Roman army might have been, had we never faced such civilized foes as the Etruscans, Carthaginians, Greeks, and Persians."

"Yes. But there's more to it. The real power of Axum lies in its control over trade routes. Especially the sea-borne trade. So, you have a peculiar situation. Although the heartland of Ethiopia is a highland region, the kingdom itself is a naval power. Our sarawit are produced and trained in the highlands, but serve primarily at sea."

"So they are marines, basically," said Belisarius.

Garmat nodded. "Yes. From what you told me, I gather that our recent affray with the Arab pirates was your first personal experience in a sea battle. You can understand, then, the qualities needed for marines."

Belisarius gazed up at the ceiling of the room, thinking back upon the battle.

"Courage, and skill with weapons—the combat is close, ferocious, and unforgiving. Firm discipline—iron discipline, even. But no tactical sophistication. There's no need for it in the tight quarters of a boarding operation. Nor room, for that matter."

He looked back down at Garmat.

"And those are the weaknesses of the Axumite army. Small numbers. Inexperience in large land battles. Primitive tactics."

"Yes."

"That's about what I thought."

"May I ask the purpose of these questions?"

"Of course. It goes back to the matter of the Indian ships we were talking about. You are puzzled, I think, by what we've seen in the harbor."

Garmat nodded. "I fail to understand the Malwa purpose in launching such a ship-building project. Such an *enormous* project, building such enormous ships. Ships of the size we saw being created in the harbor are very expensive, Belisarius. Men who are not seamen, even experienced generals such as yourself, never really grasp how expensive such vessels are. To maintain and operate, as much as to build."

The adviser shrugged. "So what is the point of doing it, when the ships themselves are so poorly designed for sea battles? Even given the Malwa rocket weapons. *Especially* in light of the rockets. If I were in charge, I would build a great number of small, swift craft. They would serve just as well for platforms from which to fire rockets. Better, for they would be more maneuverable."

Belisarius chuckled. "Spoken like a true seaman! Or, I should say, like an adviser to a monarch whose power lies at sea."

The general arose from his couch and began pacing.

"But the Indians are not a sea power, Garmat. Not the Malwa, at least. They are almost exclusively a land power, and think in those terms."

He stopped his pacing and scratched his chin.

"There's one other weakness to your Axumite army, Garmat, which you didn't mention. I'm sure you didn't even think of it. But it's an inevitable weakness, flowing from your own description."

"And that is?"

"You have no real experience with logistics. Not, at least, on the scale where logistics dominate an entire campaign."

Garmat thought for a moment, then nodded.

"I suppose that's true. The largest force fielded by Axum in modern times was the army which we sent to conquer Yemen. Four sarawit—slightly over three thousand men. Not many, by the standards of Rome or Persia. Or India. And supplying them was not difficult, of course, because—"

"You are a naval power, and were conquering a coastal region. Do you have any idea how difficult it is to supply an army numbering in the tens of thousands, marching across a vast region far removed from any coast?"

Garmat began to speak, paused, shook his head.

"No, not really."

Belisarius chuckled.

"It is quite comical, for a Thracian general, to read the histories of Rome's wars which are written by Greek scholars. They almost invariably report armies numbering in the tens and hundreds of thousands. Especially barbarian armies."

He laughed outright.

"Barbarians! Not even Rome, with all its skill and experience, can field armies of that size. Not inland, at any rate. Much less can barbarians. And the reason, of course, is logistics. What's the point of marching a hundred thousand men to their death from starvation?"

He resumed his seat. "So—to the point. If you were the Malwa emperor, and were planning to conquer the West, how would you do it?"

Garmat stroked his beard. "I suppose—there is the route through Bactria—"

"Don't even think about it."

"Why not? It's the traditional route for invaders of India, after all. So why shouldn't the Indians return the compliment?"

"Because the Indians will be fielding a modern army. They are not barbarian nomads, who can haul everything with them—what little they have to haul in the first place. The Malwa are not seeking plunder, they are seeking conquest and permanent rule. It is not enough for them to march to the walls of Ctesiphon or Antioch or Constantinople and demand tribute. To conquer, they must conquer cities. And no barbarians have ever conquered a major fortified city, except by treachery."

"Alexander—"

Belisarius nodded. "Yes, I know. Alexander the Great also took that route, when he tried to conquer India. What of it? He failed in his purpose, you may recall. Not the least of the reasons being the exhaustion of his army after campaigning through those endless mountains. Which is why—and now we get to the point—he did not return that way."

Garmat frowned. "The coastal route? But that was an even greater disaster for the Macedonians, Belisarius!" He began to continue, then closed his mouth.

"Yes. Precisely. It was a disaster for the good and simple reason that Alexander did not understand the monsoons. But we do, today. And so do the Indians."

"Persia, through Mesopotamia. Then Rome."

"Yes. That is the Malwa plan. I am as certain of it as I am of my own name. I had suspected as much even before we arrived at Bharakuccha and saw the shipbuilding project. Now, after hearing your explanation of it, I am positive. That great fleet of giant ships is not designed for sea battles, Garmat. As you surmised, they are not really warships at all. They are the logistics train for a huge land campaign. The conquest of Persia, beginning in Mesopotamia. Taking advantage of the monsoons to supply an army through the Gulf of Persia, and the Tigris and Euphrates Rivers."

"Those rivers are not—"

"—are not particularly useful for an army marching upstream. Yes, I know. Unlike the Nile, where travel in either direction is always easy, because the current takes you north and the winds always blow south, the prevailing winds in Mesopotamia usually follow the current. The Tigris and Euphrates are easy to travel in that direction, to the south. But they are difficult to go upstream." He shrugged. "But you exaggerate the difficulty. They are still much—*much*—better logistics routes than hauling supplies overland. Trust me, Garmat. It can be done. I'm no seaman, but I'm quite experienced at using rivers. I can think of several ways I could haul huge amounts of supplies up the Mesopotamian rivers."

He arose. "So. Now we know."

"What do you plan to do?"

"For the moment, nothing. I need to think over the problem. But good strategies require good intelligence. This trip to India is already paying off."

Garmat arose also. "You do not intend to revisit the harbor?"

Belisarius shook his head. "There's no need. Instead, Garmat, I think we should spend the next few days simply wandering about the city. I want to get a feel for the attitude of the populace."

"The Malwa will think we are spying."

"So what? They expect us to. I *want* them to think we are simply spying. Instead of using our spying to conceal another purpose."

For the next week, Belisarius and Garmat did just that: explore Bharakuccha. And, in the case of Belisarius, perfect his knowledge of Kushan and Marathi.

Most of this latter task, however, was done at night, in his quarters at the hostel. Each night, one of the Kushan or Maratha girls was assigned to him. The girls were surprised to discover that the general was not interested in their normal services. He simply wanted to talk. It was a strange fetish, but not unheard of. Although, usually, the conversation of such customers did not range across the breadth of Indian society, culture, habits, mores, and history.

But the girls did not complain. It was easy duty, and the general was quite a pleasant man. An altogether better situation than the Kushan girls were accustomed to. And it was vastly superior for the Maratha women, who were outright slaves in their own brothel.

By the end of their first week in Bharakuccha, therefore, Belisarius could understand spoken Kushan and Marathi perfectly, and could speak it himself quite well. The women were astonished, in fact, at his progress.

A problem remained, however, which Belisarius had not anticipated. He also needed to be able to *write* Marathi, and none of the Maratha women were literate. Over the following three days, he made inquiries in various quarters of the city. Eventually—reluctantly—he came to the realization that there was only one course available to him.

Fortunately, in light of his diminishing funds, the price was not high. Maratha slaves were very cheap. Since the conquest of Andhra, the market had been flooded with them. Supply was thus high, and demand was very low. Marathas, the slave trader explained to him bitterly, were notoriously difficult.

"At least you had the sense not to buy a young one," he added, gesturing to the stooped, middle-aged slave Belisarius had just purchased. "The young ones can be dangerous, even the girls."

The general examined his new slave. His study was brief and perfunctory, however, for the slave master's selling chamber was poorly lit by a single small oil lamp. There were no windows to let in sunlight. Or air—the stink of human effluvium coming from the nearby slave pens was nauseating.

The man was perhaps fifty years of age, Belisarius estimated. Short, slender, gray-haired. His eyes were so deep a brown as to be almost black—what little Belisarius had seen of them. The slave had kept his eyes downcast, except for one brief glance at his new owner.

He began to leave, gesturing for the slave to follow.

"You have not manacled him!" protested the slave trader.

Belisarius ignored him. Back on the street, Anastasius and Valentinian fell in at the general's side. Belisarius paused for a moment, breathing deeply, cleaning the stench from his nostrils and lungs. The powerful aromas of teeming Bharakuccha came with those breaths, of course, but they were the scents of life—cooking oils and spices, above all— not the miasma of despair.

The general began striding down the street back toward the hostel. Valentinian and Anastasius marched on either side. Their weapons were not drawn, but the two veterans never ceased scanning the street and side alleys, alert for danger. Those keen eyes kept watch on the general's newly acquired slave as well, following them a few steps behind.

Once they were beyond sight of the slave pens, Belisarius stopped and turned back, still flanked by his cataphracts. The slave stopped also, but did not raise his eyes from the ground. The small knot of armored men standing still were like a boulder in a stream. The endless flow of people in the crowded street broke around them without a pause. Only a few of those people cast so much as a glance at the bizarre foreigners in their midst, standing in a semicircle facing a half-naked slave. Curiosity was not a healthy trait in Malwa-occupied Bharakuccha.

"Look at me," commanded Belisarius.

The slave looked up, startled. He had not expected his new owner—an obvious foreigner—to speak Marathi.

"I will not shackle you, unless you give me reason to do so. I suggest you do not try to escape. It would be futile."

The slave examined the general, examined the cataphracts, looked back at the ground.

"Look at me," commanded Belisarius again.

Reluctantly, the slave obeyed.

"You are a skilled scribe, according to the slave trader."

The slave hesitated, then spoke. His voice was bitter.

"I *was* a skilled scribe. Now I am a slave who knows how to read and write."

Belisarius smiled. "I appreciate the distinction. I require your services. You must teach me to read and write Marathi." A thought came to him. "What other languages are you literate in?"

The slave frowned. "I am not sure—do you understand that the northern tongues can be written both in the classical Sanskrit and modern Devanagari script?"

Belisarius shook his head.

The slave continued. "Well, I can teach you either, or both. For practical matters I suggest Devanagari. Most of the major northern tongues are written in that script, including Hindi and Marathi. If you wish to write Gujarati you will have to learn a different script, which I can teach you. All of the principal southern languages have their own script as well. Of those I am proficient only in Tamil and Telugu." The slave shrugged. "Beyond that, I am literate in Pallavi and Greek."

"Good. I will wish to learn Hindi as well. Perhaps others, at a later time."

There was a questioning look in the slave's eyes, with an undertone of apprehension. Belisarius understood immediately.

"I will not fault you if I find the task difficult. But I think you will be surprised at how good a student I will be."

He paused for a moment, making a difficult decision. But not long, for the decision was inevitable, given his character. The slave would know too much, by the time Belisarius was done with him. Some other man would have solved the problem in the simplest way possible. But Belisarius' ruthlessness was that of a general, not a murderer.

"I will take you back to Rome with me, when I leave India. There, if you have served me faithfully, I will manumit you. And give you what funds you require to start a new life. You will have no difficulty, if your literary talents are as you have described. There are any number of Greek traders who would be glad to employ you." Another thought came to him. "For that matter, there is a bishop who might find you useful. He is a kind man, and would make an excellent employer."

The slave eyed him, making his own estimations. But not long, for he was in no position to choose.

"As you wish," he said.

"What is your name?"

The slave opened his mouth, closed it. A bitter little twist came to his lips. "Call me 'slave,' " he said. "The name is good enough."

Belisarius laughed. "Truly, a proud folk!"

He smiled down at the slave. "I once had a Maratha slave, in a different—long ago. He, too, would not tell me his name, but would only answer to 'slave.' "

The impulse was overwhelming. The special dagger he did not have on him, of course. It was stowed away in his baggage. But Belisarius always carried a dagger on his sword belt. He drew the weapon. It was not as excellent a dagger as the other, but it was still quite finely made.

A quick, practiced flip of the wrist nestled the blade in his palm. He proffered the dagger to the slave, hilt-first.

"Take it," he commanded.

The slave's eyes widened.

"Take it," he repeated. His own lips twisted crookedly.

"Just so," he murmured, in a voice so low that only the slave could hear, "should men dance in the eyes of God."

The slave reached out his hand, drew it back. Then spoke, this time in fluent Greek.

"It is illegal for slaves to possess weapons. The penalty is death."

The cataphracts, hearing the slave's words, bridled. They thought their general was crazy, of course—handing a dagger to a slave!—but, still, he *was* the general.

"And just which sorry lot of Indian soldiers do you think is going to make the arrest?" demanded Valentinian. Anastasius glared about the teeming street. Fortunately, there were no Malwa soldiery within sight.

The slave stared at the two cataphracts. Then, suddenly, he laughed.

"Truly, you Romans are mad!" His face broke into a smile. He looked at Belisarius, and shook his head.

"Keep the dagger, master. There is no need for this gesture." A quick, approving glance at the cataphracts. "And, while I have no doubt your men would cheerfully hack down a squad of Malwa dogs, I do not think you need the awkwardness of the situation. If they saw me carrying the dagger, they *would* try to arrest me. The Malwa are very strict on this matter, especially with Maratha slaves."

Belisarius scratched his chin. "You have a point," he admitted. He slid the dagger back into the sheath.

"Walk with me, if you would," he said to the slave. "If you will not tell me your name, you must at least tell me of your life."

By the end of that day, the slave was comfortably ensconced in the room which Belisarius shared with Garmat. The room was small, true, and he occupied only a pallet in a corner. But the linens were clean—as was the slave himself. He had enjoyed his first real bath since his enslavement. Belisarius had insisted, overriding the scandalized protest of the hostel owner.

That night, the slave began his duties, instructing the general in the written form of Marathi. As Belisarius had predicted, the slave was amazed at how rapidly his new master learned his lessons.

But that was not the only astonishing thing, to the slave, about his new master and his companions. Three other things puzzled him as well.

First, the soldiers.

Like most Maratha men, the slave was no stranger to warfare. Though not a kshatriya, he himself had fought in battles, as a youth. Had been rather an accomplished archer, in fact. So he was not inexperienced in these matters. Within a day, he decided that he had probably never encountered such a lethal crew as the Roman cataphracts and the black soldiers—the sarwen, as they called themselves.

Yet, quite unlike most warriors he had encountered in the past—certainly Malwa warriors—they were strangely free of the casual, unthinking brutality with which most such men conducted themselves toward their inferiors. They were not rude or impolite toward him, even though he was a slave. And it was quite obvious that the women who shared their quarters were neither afraid of them, nor timid in their presence. The soldiers even seemed to enjoy their badinage with the women, and the teasing.

Second, the prince.

Rarely had the slave seen a nobleman work his lustful way through such an unending stream of young women. And he had *never* seen one who did it with such apparent lack of pleasure.

It was odd. Very odd. At first, the slave interpreted the glum look on the prince's face, as he ushered yet another young woman out of his palatial suite, to be dissatisfaction with her talents. But then, observing the glee with which the young women counted their money as they left, he decided otherwise.

That theory discarded, he interpreted the glum look on the prince's face as the result of dissatisfaction with his own talents. An impotent man, perhaps, desperately trying to find a woman who could arouse him. But then, observing the exhaustion with which the departing girls gleefully counted their money, he decided otherwise.

Odd. Very odd.

Finally, there was the incident with the new Maratha girl. The slave concubine who was purchased for the prince by his—retainer? (They called him the dawazz—bizarre man!)

This incident happened two weeks or so after the slave came into Belisarius' service. He and Belisarius had been seated in the general's quarters, practicing Devanagari. They were alone, for Garmat was spending the evening with the Ethiopian soldiers.

The prince had suddenly burst through the door to the room. Uninvited, and without so much as a knock on the door. That was in itself unusual. The slave had learned that the prince, for all his morose mien, was not discourteous.

The prince had come to stand before the general, glaring down at him.

"I will not do it," he said, softly but quite forcefully. "I will act like a breeding stud for you, Belisarius, but I will not do *this*."

Belisarius, as usual, maintained his expressionless composure. But the slave had come to know him well enough to realize that the general was quite taken aback.

"What are you talking about?"

The prince—Eon was his name—glared even more furiously.

"Do not pretend you had nothing to do with it!"

A new voice spoke, from the door. The voice of the dawazz.

"He *had* nothing to do with it, Eon. He does not even know of her. I brought her straight to your suite from the slave pens."

The dawazz glanced at Belisarius.

"It is true, the general asked me to keep an eye out for such an opportunity. But he did not ask for *this*."

The dawazz then glanced at the slave. Meaningfully.

"I shall leave, if you desire," said the slave, beginning to rise.

"Stay," commanded Belisarius. The general did not even look at him. His eyes were riveted on the dawazz.

The dawazz shrugged.

"She's perfect, Belisarius. Exactly what you hoped for. Not only from the palace, but from the girl's own retinue. Except—" The black man grimaced. "I did not realize until— I thought she was just—"

Belisarius rose. "Show me."

Angrily, Eon charged through the door. On his way out, he transferred the glare to his dawazz. The dawazz sighed and exited after him. Belisarius began to follow, then turned in the doorway. It was obvious to the slave, from the way his master was staring at him, that the general was making a decision. And it was just as obvious that the decision— whatever it was—involved the slave himself.

As usual, his new master did not linger.

"Come," he commanded.

The slave followed Belisarius into the prince's suite. By now, the commotion had aroused the attention of all the members of his master's party. The cataphracts and the sarwen were standing in the corridor of the hostel which linked all of their rooms. They were unarmored—almost completely undressed, in the case of the cataphracts—but they were all bearing weapons. Even the young cataphract, the sick one, was there. The Kushan and Maratha women who shared the soldiers' quarters were clustered behind them, peering over their shoulders. Garmat eased his way past the small crowd and went into the prince's suite. The slave followed him.

He found Belisarius, Eon, the dawazz, and Garmat standing around the huge bed in the prince's sleeping chamber, staring down at the figure who lay upon it.

The slave recognized the girl as Maratha. For an instant,

he was consumed with an immediate rage—until he realized that the prince was not responsible. The bruises and half-healed lacerations on the girl's body had not been recently caused. And the dazed, vacant expression on her face was the product of protracted horror.

"I will not do this!" shouted the prince.

Belisarius shook his head. Eon snorted, but his glare faded somewhat. Hesitantly, the prince stretched out his hand. The girl on the bed moaned, flinched, drew herself up into an even tighter fetal curl.

"Don't touch her," said Belisarius.

From the door to the chamber, Valentinian's voice came. "Mary, Mother of God."

The slave looked back at the cataphract. As before, he was struck by Valentinian's appearance. Probably the most evil-looking man the slave had ever seen. Especially now, with his expression filled with cold, experienced disgust.

The cataphract turned his head and spoke over his shoulder:

"Anastasius! Get the women."

Valentinian turned back.

"Move away from the bed," he commanded. "All of you. *Now.*"

It did not seem strange to the slave, at the time, that all those present instantly obeyed their subordinate. Later, after he thought it over, it still did not seem strange. The most evil-looking man in the world, perhaps. Certainly at that moment.

Very soon thereafter, Anastasius entered the room, followed by the young cataphract and the half dozen young women. When the new arrivals saw the girl on the bed, they reacted differently. Anastasius' face—which looked like a slab of granite at the best of times—grew even harder. The women gasped, cast quick frightened glances at the men in the room, and drew back. Menander gaped, confused, and began moving forward. He was instantly restrained by Anastasius' huge hand.

"Don't," rumbled the giant cataphract.

"What's wrong with her?" whispered Menander. It was not the bruises which confused him, the slave knew. It was the near-insane expression on her face.

Anastasius and Valentinian exchanged glances.

"I've forgotten what it's like to be that innocent," muttered Valentinian.

Anastasius took a breath. "You've never been in a town that's been sacked, have you?"

Menander shook his head.

"Well, if and when you do, you'll see plenty of this. And worse."

The young cataphract, already pale from his illness, grew slightly paler as comprehension dawned. Anastasius motioned to the women, shooing them forward.

"Help the girl," he said, in his thick, broken Kushan. "Comfort her."

A moment later, Belisarius was issuing instructions to the girls in fluent, unaccented Kushan and Marathi. The girls hastened to do as he bade them. They were still casting reproachful glances at the soldiers in the room, but it was obvious to the slave that the reproach was generic, not specific.

Very odd soldiers, indeed.

But, he knew, not unique. He had not recognized the phenomenon at first, for he was unaccustomed to the informal Roman ways. But he had encountered such soldiers before, on occasion. Not often. Only Maratha and Rajput kshatriya possessed that code of honor. Men who would not stoop to murder, rape, and mindless mayhem, for they were the deadliest killers in creation. Such gross and common criminality was beneath their dignity.

The Malwa kshatriya had little of that code; the Ye-tai

beasts derided them for what little they still possessed. And the common soldiers who made up the great mass of the Malwa army had none of it at all. Jackals, once discipline was loosened.

The slave shuddered, remembering the sack of his own town.

He would never see his beloved family again, but he knew their fate. His wife would be a drudge somewhere, slaving in the kitchen of a Malwa lord or merchant. His son would be a laborer, in the fields or in the mines. And his two daughters—

He glanced at the three Maratha women who were now on the bed, surrounding the half-crazed girl with female touches, female sounds and female scents. Three young slave girls, owned by a whoremaster.

He looked away, holding back a sob. Then forced himself to look back at the girl on the bed. There was a horrible comfort to be found in the sight. That much, at least, his wife and daughters had been spared. Spared, because by good fortune their own house had been seized by Rajputs during the sack, not Ye-tai or common soldiers. A Rajput cavalry troop, commanded by a young Rajput lord. A cold man, that lord; arrogant and haughty as only a Rajput kshatriya could be. The Rajputs had stripped their home of everything of value, down to the linen. Had then eaten all the food, and drank all the wine. But when the inevitable time came, and the cavalrymen began eyeing their captured women, the Rajput officer had simply said: "No."

Coldly, arrogantly, haughtily. His men had obeyed. Had not even grumbled. They were not kshatriya themselves, simply commoners. But they possessed their own humble share of Rajput discipline, and Rajput pride, and Rajputana's ancient glory.

He was brought back to the present by his master's voice.

Belisarius, he realized, was ordering all of the men out of
the room.

Once in the corridor, Belisarius began digging into his
purse. Garmat interrupted.

"I will pay for it, Belisarius. We both know your funds
are meager."

The Ethiopian gave instructions to one of the sarwen.
The black soldier disappeared, searching for the hostel
proprietor. Shortly thereafter, he reappeared, with the
proprietor in tow. The man was smiling, as well he might
be. Yet another room for his guests! By all means!

Within an hour, the injured girl had been moved into
the new room. It was a small room adjoining Eon's suite,
but separated from the suite by a door. Belisarius instructed
the women to make sure that one of them was with her at
all times. And, under no conditions, to allow any men into
the room unless he said otherwise.

The girls glanced hesitantly at the soldiers. Their thoughts
were obvious: *And just how, exactly, does the idiot general
expect us to prevent men like this from going anywhere
they choose?*

Belisarius shook his head. "They will not try to enter, I
assure you."

That matter taken care of, for the moment, Belisarius
led all of the men into his own room. The slave followed.
Uncertainly, hesitantly, and with great reluctance.

Once everyone had taken a seat—those who could, that
is, the room was small—Belisarius sighed and stated:

"This is going to play hell with our plans."

As one, just as the slave had feared, every man there looked
at him. Their thoughts were also obvious:

Dead men tell no tales.

Belisarius smiled crookedly. "No," he said. "I'm keeping
him with me, all the way back to Rome. The problem is
with the girls. The Malwa will certainly question them, after

we leave Bharakuccha. Until now, I didn't care. But the way we are treating this new girl will not gibe with the image that we've been carefully forging. Venandakatra's no fool. He'll smell something wrong."

Garmat coughed. Belisarius cocked his eye.

"Actually, Belisarius, I'm afraid the problem existed already. Even before the new girl arrived." Another cough. "Because of you, actually."

"Me?" demanded the general. "How so?"

Garmat sighed, then threw up his hands. "I share this room with you, General! I'm not blind."

He tugged on his beard.

"Should your wife ever inquire, I will be able to assure her that you were astonishingly faithful during your trip to India, even when lovely young women were coming to your room every night. But I don't think Venandakatra will find that reassuring. Not after you've spent so much time and effort trying to convince him you were almost as debauched as he is."

Belisarius' face was stony. The muscles along his jaw were tight.

"Ha!" exclaimed Eon. "So! *I* am required to mount every female shoved into my room. *I* am required to act the part of a breeding bull. But the general whose plan this is—"

The dawazz slapped him atop his head. The slave tried not to goggle. He did not think he would ever get accustomed to *that*. No Indian prince had ever been treated that way by a slave.

"Be quiet, Eon! You are not married. And stop complaining. I'm tired of it."

"We all are," snarled Valentinian.

"You copulated with every woman in Axum you could coax into your bed," growled Ezana. "Since you were fourteen."

"Thirteen," corrected Wahsi.

"That was different! They weren't *shoved* into my room, and I wasn't doing it because of—"

"Shut up!" barked Menander. The young cataphract flushed. "Begging your pardon, Prince. But I really can't stand it any longer. You bitch about this all the time, and I can't—well, maybe in a day or so, I hope—but—"

"Enough," commanded Belisarius. "Actually, I agree with Eon. At least, I will admit the justice of his charge. I have been somewhat hypocritical."

Anastasius chuckled. "I do believe that's the first time I've heard fidelity characterized as hypocrisy."

A little laugh swept the room. Even Eon, after a moment, joined in.

Valentinian cleared his throat.

"As it happens, General, I think there's a simple solution to the problem. Been thinking about it, myself, I have, and—"

"Capital idea!" exclaimed Ousanas.

"Splendid," agreed Anastasius. "My own thoughts have been veering that way themselves, oddly enough."

"So?" asked Ezana. The sarwen's face registered dumbfounded astonishment, a wild surmise come from nowhere.

Ezana and Wahsi exchanged gapes of wonder.

Wahsi spoke first: "Truly amazing. Can you believe, Ezana and I—and Ousanas—have been grappling with the very same—"

"The perfect solution!" cried Ezana.

Garmat was frowning with puzzlement. Belisarius started laughing.

"What are they talking about?" demanded the adviser.

Belisarius managed to stop laughing long enough to ask Valentinian:

"I assume the parties involved have—uh, how shall I put it—" (here he choked) "—found their own thoughts *veering*, or perhaps I should say—" (laughter) "—have been *grappling* with the—" (Here he fell silent altogether, holding his sides.)

Valentinian stared up at the ceiling.

"Well, actually, I believe one of the girls did mention—"

"They're really quite tired of Bharakuccha," added Menander eagerly.

"Sick to death of the place," rumbled Anastasius. "Eager for new experiences. New sights."

Ezana pitched in: "The Maratha girls are even more anxious to depart this pesthole."

"Horrible city," growled Wahsi. "Horrible."

Garmat was now glaring at Ousanas. "You put them up to this," he accused. "I know it was you."

"Me? *Me?* How can you say such a thing? I am my prince's dawazz! My thoughts are only of his welfare! I am a miserable slave. How could such a wretched creature possibly cajole fierce cataphracts and murderous sarwen into such a scheme?"

The grin erupted. "Brilliant scheme, mind you. Solve all problems at one swoop. Keep know-too-much girls— charming, lovely know-too-much girls—out of clutches of Malwa interrogators. Keep loyal but downhearted troops cheerful and content, so far from their native lands."

Belisarius managed to find his voice again. "I agree." He waved his hand. "Be off. See to it."

He smiled at Garmat. "They're right, you know. What else are we going to do? Slit the girls' throats?"

Valentinian and Anastasius were already at the door, with Ezana and Wahsi close on their heels.

"One moment!" spoke Belisarius. The men turned back.

Belisarius motioned to his purse. "Take some money. The pimps aren't going to like this idea. You'll have to pay them off."

Anastasius frowned. "Pimps," he mused. "I hadn't thought about that."

He looked to Valentinian. "Violent characters, your pimps."

Valentinian shuddered. "I shudder to think of it." He shuddered again. "See?"

"I have heard of these pimps," said Ezana, his face a mask of fear. "Brutal creatures, it is said."

"Cruel goblins," groaned Wahsi. "I may foul myself upon meeting them."

"We'll just have to do our best," whined Valentinian. He advanced to the purse and extracted a single small coin.

"This should do. Ah, no—I forget. We have two sets of pimps to deal with." He extracted another small coin. "More than sufficient, I should think." He cast a questioning glance at Anastasius.

"Quite sufficient," rumbled the giant. "I'll do the bargaining. I'm half-Greek, you know."

Ousanas lazed his way forward.

"I believe I shall accompany you. Perhaps these pimp fellows will wish to discuss philosophy."

"So they might!" exclaimed Anastasius. "Aristotle, perhaps?"

Ousanas shook his head. "I was thinking more along the lines of Stoicism."

Anastasius nodded happily. "The very thing! Calm acceptance of life's unexpected turns. Serenity—"

Valentinian and the two sarwen hastened through the door.

"—in the face of sudden misfortune."

Anastasius followed, with Ousanas at his heels.

"Disdain for material things," said the dawazz, as he closed the door.

Through the door, faintly heard, Anastasius:

"Pleasure in spiritual contemplation."

Two days later, a courier from Venandakatra arrived at the hostel, informing the Romans and Axumites that the Malwa lord's expedition to the north would be departing the next day. Belisarius and his party—his now much enlarged party—made their preparations to leave.

On the morning of their departure, there was a slight unpleasantness. A Rajput officer accosted them as they were leaving the hostel. He was accompanied by a platoon of Rajput soldiers, who, he explained, served the city of Bharakuccha as its police force.

Suspicions had been cast, accusations made, complaints lodged. Two well-known and respected brothel-keepers had been subjected to outrageous extortion by uncouth foreigners. Employees of the establishments had even been manhandled by these barbarous men. Horribly abused. Crippled, in the case of five; maimed and mutilated, in the case of four; slain outright, in the case of two.

Belisarius expressed his distress at the news. Distress, but not shock. Certainly not surprise. Such horrendous crimes, after all, were only to be expected in Bharakuccha. A terrible city! Full of desperadoes! Why—he himself had been assaulted in the streets by a band of robbers, the very day of his arrival. Had been forced to slay several in self-defense, in fact.

After hearing the general's description of the affair, the Rajput officer expressed pleasure at this unexpected resolution to a hitherto unsolved mystery. A mass murder, it had seemed at the time. Five notorious and much-feared dacoits, long-sought by the Rajput soldiery for innumerable misdeeds. Slaughtered like lambs. Butchered like pigs.

The Rajput officer subjected Belisarius and his party to severe and careful scrutiny. Whereupon he pronounced that the suspicions were clearly unfounded, the accusations baseless, the complaints mislodged. A terrible city, Bharakuccha, it could not be denied. Full of unknown, mysterious, criminally inclined foreigners. Who, alas, all tended to look alike in Indian eyes.

But upon close examination, the Rajput officer deliberated, there seemed no reasonable resemblance between the slavering fiends depicted by the brothel keepers and these fine, well-disciplined, upstanding outlanders. No doubt the whoremasters were misinformed, their discernment shaken by great and sudden financial loss. No doubt the procurers in their employ were likewise confused, their wits addled by the traumatic experience.

Most traumatic experience, mused the officer, judging from the evidence: the deep stab wounds, the great gashes, the immense loss of blood, the shattered knees, broken wrists, severed thumbs, splintered ribs, flattened noses, gouged eyes, amputated ears, broken skulls, ruptured kidneys, maimed elbows, mangled feet, pulverized hipbones, crushed testicles. Not to mention the broken neck of one dead pimp, snapped like a twig by some sort of gigantic ogre.

No doubt, concluded the officer. In that cold, arrogant, haughty manner which so distinguishes Rajputana's kshatriya.

DARAS
Autumn, 529 AD

Chapter 20

Sittas and Maurice sat on their horses, watching Sittas' cataphracts on the training field. The look on Sittas' face was one of smug satisfaction. That on Maurice's was inscrutable.

The sight was undoubtedly impressive. Sittas had brought a thousand noble Greek cataphracts with him to Syria, to reinforce the Roman army there. The heavily armored horsemen made the very ground rumble with their charges. And their lances struck the practice poles with extraordinary impact. Not surprising, that—the lances were being held in the underarm position, using the full weight of rider and mount to drive them home.

Sittas stood up on his stirrups, reveling in the motion.

God, how he loved stirrups. And so did the cataphracts.

But, for all his self-satisfaction, Sittas was by no means stupid. So, after a time, the smug look disappeared, replaced by a frown.

"All right, Maurice," he growled. "Spit it out."

The hecatontarch cocked a quizzical eye.

"Don't play with me, damn you!" snapped Sittas. "I know perfectly well you think this"—he waved at the charging cataphracts—"is a waste of time. Why?"

"I haven't said a word." Maurice fanned the air in front

of his face, grimacing at the dust clouds thrown up by the charging lancers. What little vegetation had once grown on the barren field had long since been pounded into mush under the hooves of the heavy horses.

Sittas glowered. "I know. That's the point. You haven't made a single criticism. Not one! No criticisms—*from the Maurice?* Ha! You bitched at your own mother coming out of the womb—told her she wasn't doing it right."

Maurice smiled, faintly.

"And another thing. I notice that you aren't spending much time with your Thracian boys practicing lance charges. Instead, you're running them ragged with all sorts of fancy mounted archery maneuvers. So spit it out, Maurice. What gives?"

The hecatontarch's smile disappeared.

"I think the question ought to be reversed. You know things I don't, General. From Belisarius."

Sittas' expression was uncomfortable. "Well—"

Maurice waved his hand.

"I'm not complaining. And I'm not prying. If the general hasn't told me whatever it is he's keeping secret, I'm sure there's a good reason for it. But that doesn't mean I can't figure some things out for myself."

"Such as?"

"Such as—he's got a mechanical wizard living on the estate concocting God knows what kind of infernal devices. Such as—the devices, whatever they are, are obviously connected to artillery. Such as—he's always had a soft spot for artillery. Such as—he's especially been doting on infantry, lately. Before he left, he instructed me in no uncertain terms to cultivate Hermogenes."

Sittas rubbed his face. The gesture smeared the dust and sweat on his face into streaks. "So?"

Maurice snorted. "So—I have a sneaking suspicion that in a few years charging the enemy with lances is going to be a fast way to commit suicide."

"I *like* lance charges," grumbled Sittas. "Don't you?"

"Is that a joke? *I* don't like to fight in the first place. If I knew a different way to make a living, I'd do it. But as long as I'm stuck with this trade, *I'd* like to be good at it. That means *I'd* like to win battles, not lose them. And most of all, *I'd* like to stay alive."

Sittas' expression was glum. "Leave it to a damned Thracian hick to take all the fun out of war," he complained.

"Leave it to a damned Greek nobleman to think war's fun in the first place." For a brief moment, Maurice's face was bitterly hostile. "Do you know how many times Thrace has been ravaged by barbarians—while the Greek nobility sat and watched, safely behind the ramparts of Constantinople?"

Sittas grimaced. Maurice reined his horse around.

"So enjoy your lance charges, General. Personally, I'm rooting for Belisarius and his schemes—whatever they are. If this John of Rhodes can invent some secret weapon that fries cavalry, I'm for it. All for it. I'll gladly climb off a horse and fight on foot, if I could slaughter the next wave of barbarians that tries to plunder Thrace."

After the hecatontarch was gone, Sittas blew out his cheeks. Maurice's harsh words had irritated him, but he could not hold on to the mood. There was too much truth to those words. For all his class prejudices, Sittas was well aware of the realities of life for the vast majority of Rome's citizens. He himself had not watched the plundering of Thrace from behind Constantinople's ramparts. He himself had led charges—lance charges—against the barbarian invaders. And watched them whirl away, laughing, and strike another village the day after. And seen the results, the day after that, lumbering up with his cataphracts. Too late, as usual, to do anything but bury the corpses.

He drove his horse forward, onto the training field. Seeing him approach, his cataphracts shouted gaily. Then, seeing his face, the gaiety died.

"Enough of this lance shit!" he roared. *"Draw out your bows!"*

The next day, Maurice arrived back at the villa near Daras. With him, he brought Hermogenes.

Hermogenes now gloried in the exalted rank of *merarch*. He was in overall command of the Army of Syria's infantry. Following Belisarius' recommendations, Sittas had immediately promoted Hermogenes to that post shortly after he arrived in Syria and replaced Belisarius as commander of the Roman army.

When Maurice and Hermogenes drew up in the courtyard of the villa, Antonina and Irene emerged to greet them.

"Where's Sittas?" inquired Antonina.

"He's staying with the army," grunted Maurice, as he dismounted. "For a while, anyway. Don't know how long."

"Probably till he gets over his latest peeve," piped up Irene cheerfully. "What did you say to him this time, Maurice?"

Maurice made no reply. Hermogenes grinned and said: "I think he cast aspersions on the glory of thundering cataphracts. Probably tossed in a few words on the Greek aristocracy, too."

Maurice maintained a dignified silence.

"You're just in time for dinner," announced Antonina. "Anthony's here."

"Bishop Cassian?" asked Hermogenes. "What a pleasure! I've been wanting to make his acquaintance for the longest time."

It was the first time Hermogenes had been invited to the villa since Belisarius' departure. He enjoyed the evening thoroughly, although he found the first few hours disconcerting. Conversation at the dinner table seemed somehow strained. On several occasions, when he pressed

John of Rhodes for a progress report on his rather mysterious artillery project, Antonina or Irene would immediately interject themselves into the conversation and divert the talk elsewhere. After a while, Hermogenes realized that they did not want the subject discussed in front of their other guests.

He assumed, at first, that it was the person of the bishop who was the obstacle. Too holy a man to be affronted by such a grisly subject. So, bowing to the demands of the occasion, Hermogenes abandoned all talk of artillery projects and engaged the bishop in a discussion of religious doctrine. Hermogenes, like many Greeks from the middle classes of Byzantine society, rather fancied himself as an amateur theologian.

He found the ensuing discussion even more disconcerting. Not, be it said, because he was chagrined at finding himself outclassed. Hermogenes was by no means so swell-headed as to imagine himself the equal of the famous Bishop of Aleppo when it came to theological subtleties. It was simply that, once again, Antonina and Irene invariably interrupted whenever Hermogenes was on the verge of pinpointing the bishop's views on the Trinity. And, as before, diverted the discussion into aimless meanderings, as if they did not want the bishop's opinions aired in front of their other guests.

There came, then, the worst moment of the evening, when Hermogenes came to the sudden conclusion that *he* was the unwanted guest. But, after a time, that embarrassment waned. It seemed obvious, from their friendly behavior toward him, that neither Antonina nor Irene—nor certainly Maurice—viewed his presence with discomfort.

So what—?

Clarity came, finally, after the first glass of dessert wine had been enjoyed. Antonina cleared her throat and said to the general's secretary:

"Procopius, I'm afraid I'm going to need the full report

on the estate's financial condition by tomorrow morning."
She reached out and placed her fingers on the pudgy hand
of the bishop sitting next to her. "Anthony wants to begin
examining the records as soon as he awakens."

For a moment, it almost seemed to Hermogenes as if
Antonina's fingers were sensuously caressing those of
Anthony Cassian. *Ridiculous*.

Procopius frowned. "Tonight?" he asked plaintively.

"Yes, I'm afraid so."

Antonina's eyes flashed around the table, accompanied
by an odd smile. If the thought weren't absurd, Hermogenes
would have sworn that she was leering at all of the men at
the table except Procopius. Her look at John of Rhodes
seemed particularly lascivious. And Irene's face, now that
he noticed, had a strange sort of knowing smile on it. Almost
obscene, if it weren't— *Ridiculous*.

Procopius stared at her. His eyes grew bright, his face
flushed, his lips tightened—he seemed, for all the world,
like a man possessed by a secret vision.

"Of course," he said, chokingly. The secretary arose from
the table, bowed stiffly, and departed the room. He glanced
back, once. Hermogenes was struck by the hot glitter of
his gaze.

As soon as he was gone, the atmosphere in the room
seemed to change instantly. Maurice pursed his lips.
Hermogenes thought the hecatontarch would have spit on
the floor, if politeness hadn't restrained him. John of Rhodes
blew out his cheeks and, silently, extended his cup to Irene.
Grinning, Irene filled it to the brim. Antonina sighed and
leaned back in her chair—then extended her own cup.

For his part, the bishop turned immediately to
Hermogenes and said:

"To answer your earlier questions directly, merarch, while
my own opinion on the Trinity is that of the five councils
of the orthodox tradition, I also believe that there can never

be a final solution to the problem. And thus I feel that any attempt to impose such a solution is, from the social and political standpoint, unwise. And, from the theological standpoint, downright impious."

"Impious?" asked Hermogenes. "*Impious?*"

Cassian's nod was vigorous. "Yes, young man—you heard me aright. *Impious.*"

Hermogenes groped for words. "I've never heard anyone say—" He fell silent, taking a thoughtful sip of his wine.

Cassian smiled. "Mine is not, I admit, the common approach. But let me ask you this, Hermogenes—why is the subject of the Trinity so difficult to fathom? Why is it such an enigma?"

Hermogenes hesitated. "Well, it—I'm not a theologian, you know. But it's very complicated, everyone knows that."

"Why?"

Hermogenes frowned. "I don't understand."

"Why is it so complicated? Did it never strike you as bizarre that the Almighty should have chosen to manifest himself in such a tortuous fashion?"

Hermogenes opened his mouth, closed it; then, took a much deeper sip of wine—almost a gulp, actually. As a matter of fact, he *had*—now and then—puzzled over the matter. Privately. Very privately.

Cassian smiled again. "So I see. It is my belief, my dear Hermogenes, that the Lord chose to do so for the good and simple reason that He does not *want* men to understand the Trinity. It is a mystery, and there's the plain and simple truth of it. There is no harm, of course, in anyone who so chooses to speculate on the problem. I do so myself. But to go further, to pronounce oneself *right*—to go so far as to enforce your pronouncement with religious and secular authority—seems to me utterly impious. It is the sin of pride. Satan's sin."

Hermogenes was struck, even more than by Cassian's words, by the bishop's expression. That peculiar combination of gentle eyes and a mouth set like a stone. The merarch knew the bishop's towering reputation as a theologian among the Greek upper crust. And he knew, as well, that Cassian's reputation as a saintly man was even more towering among the Syrian peasantry and plebeian classes. Both of those reputations suddenly came into focus for him.

"Enough theology!" protested Irene. "I want to hear John's latest progress report on his infernal devices."

Almost gratefully, Hermogenes looked away from the bishop. John of Rhodes straightened abruptly in his chair and glared at Irene. He slammed his goblet down on the table. Fortunately, it was almost empty, so only a few winedrops spilled onto the table. But, for a moment, Hermogenes feared the goblet would break from the impact.

"There *is* no progress report, infernal woman! As you well know—you were present yourself, yesterday, at the latest fiasco."

Irene grinned. She looked at the bishop.

"Did you hear that, Anthony? He called me a devil! Doesn't that seem a bit excessive? I ask for your expert opinion."

Cassian smiled. "Further clarification is needed. *If* he called you a devil, then, yes—'twould be a tad excessive. However, John was by no means specific. 'Infernal woman,' after all, could refer to any denizen of the Pit. Such as an imp. In which case, I'm afraid I would have to lend my religious authority to his words. For it is a certain truth, Irene, that you are indeed an imp."

"I didn't think there was such a thing as a female imp," retorted Irene.

The bishop's smile was positively beatific.

"Neither did I, my dear Irene, until I made your acquaintance."

Laughter erupted at the table. When it died down, Maurice spoke.

"What happened, John?"

The naval officer scowled. "I burned down the workshop, that's what happened."

"Again?"

"Yes, thank you—*again!*" John began to rise, but Antonina waved him down with a smile.

"Please, John! I've had too much to drink. I'll get dizzy, watching you stump around."

The naval officer subsided. After a moment, he muttered: "It's the damned naphtha, Maurice. The local stuff's crap. I need to get my hands on good quality naphtha. And for that—"

He turned to the bishop. "Isn't your friend Michael of Macedonia in Arabia now?"

The bishop shook his head. "Not any longer. He returned a few weeks ago and has taken up residence nearby. He would not have been much help to you, in any event. He was in western Arabia, among the Beni Ghassan. Western Arabia's not the best place for naphtha, you know. And, besides, I don't think—"

He coughed, fell silent.

Hermogenes was about to ask what the famous Michael of Macedonia had been doing in Arabia when he suddenly spotted both Antonina and Irene giving him an intent stare. He pressed his lips shut. A moment later, both women favored him with very slight smiles.

Something's afoot, he thought to himself. *There are hidden currents here, deep ones. I think this is a very good time for a young officer to keep his mouth shut, shut, shut. No harm in listening, though.*

Maurice spoke again.

"There's an Arab officer in our cavalry—well, he's half-Arab—a hecatontarch by the name of Mark. Mark of Edessa. His mother's family lives near Hira, but they're not affiliated to the Lakhmids. Bedouin stock, mostly. I'll speak to him. He might be able to arrange something."

"I'd appreciate it," said John. A moment later, the naval officer rose from the table.

"I'm to bed," he announced. "Tomorrow I've got to rebuild that damned workshop. Again."

As he left, he and Antonina exchanged smiles. There was nothing in that exchange, noted Hermogenes, beyond a comfortable friendship. He thought back on the bizarre, leering expression which had crossed Antonina's face earlier in the evening, in the presence of Procopius.

Deep currents. Coming from a hidden well called Belisarius, if I'm not mistaken. I do believe my favorite general is up to his tricks again. So. Only one question remains. How do I get in on this?

Maurice arose. "Me, too." The hecatontarch glanced at Hermogenes.

"I believe I'll stay a bit," said Hermogenes. He extended his cup to Irene. "If you would?"

Maurice left the room. Antonina yawned and stretched.

"I'd better look in on Photius. He wasn't feeling well today." She rose, patted Irene on the shoulder, and looked at Hermogenes.

"How long will you be staying?"

"Just for the night," replied Hermogenes. "I'm leaving early in the morning. I really can't be absent from the army for long. Sittas seems to have finally gotten lance charges out of his system, and he's beginning to make noises about general maneuvers."

"Come again, when you can."

"I shall. Most certainly."

Moments later, he and Irene were alone in the room. Hermogenes and she stared at each other in silence, for some time.

He understood the meaning in her gaze. A question, really. Is this man staying at the table to seduce me? Or—

He smiled, then.

I've done some foolish things in my life. But I'm not dumb enough to try to seduce her. As my Uncle Theodosius always said: never chase women who are a lot smarter than you. You won't catch them, or, what's worse, you might.

"So, Irene. Tell me about it. As much as you can."

The next morning, Antonina arose early, to give her regards to Hermogenes before he left. As she walked out of the villa, the sun was just coming up. She found the young merarch already in the courtyard, holding his saddled horse. He was talking quietly with Irene.

Antonina was surprised to see the spymaster. As a rule, Irene viewed sunrise as a natural disaster to be avoided at all costs.

When she came up, Hermogenes smiled and bowed politely. Antonina and the merarch exchanged pleasantries, before he mounted his horse and rode off.

Antonina glanced at Irene. The spymaster yawned mightily.

"You're up early," she commented.

Irene grimaced. "No, I'm just up later than usual. I haven't slept."

She nodded toward the diminishing figure of Hermogenes, who was now passing through the gate. "He's quite a bright fellow, you know. He figured out much more than I would have expected, just from watching the people around him."

"Is that why he stayed at the table? I assumed it was because he had intentions toward you."

Irene shook her head, smiling. "Oh, no. His conduct was absolutely impeccable. Propriety incarnate. No, he wanted to join the conspiracy. Whatever it is. He doesn't care, really, as long as Belisarius is involved. A bad case of hero worship, he's got."

"What did you tell him?"

"Enough. Not too much. But enough to make him happy,

and win his allegiance. I think quite highly of that young man, Antonina. He's everything Belisarius said, and more."

Antonina put her arm around her friend's waist and began to guide her back into the villa.

"Fill me in on the details later. You look absolutely exhausted, Irene. You need to get to bed."

Irene chuckled. "*Back* to bed, actually." Feeling Antonina's little start of surprise, Irene grinned wearily.

"I said I hadn't *slept*, Antonina. We didn't talk about conspiracies the whole damned night."

"But—"

Irene's grin widened. "I find handsome young men who are smart enough not to try to seduce me to be quite irresistible."

GWALIOR
Autumn, 529 AD

Chapter 21

"I believe I owe Venandakatra an apology," remarked Belisarius.

Garmat frowned. "Why in the world would you owe that swine an apology?" he demanded crossly.

"Oh, I have no intention of giving it to him. That's an obligation which wears very lightly on my shoulders. But I owe it to him nonetheless."

Belisarius gestured ahead, to the enormous procession which was snaking its way along the right bank of the Narmada.

The small Roman/Axumite contingent was located far back from the head of the caravan. The general and Garmat were riding next to each other, on horseback. Just behind them came Valentinian and Anastasius, and the slave scribe, also on horseback. The rest of their party were borne by the two elephants given them by the Malwa. Ezana and Wahsi served as mahouts for the great beasts. Eon and the Maratha women rode in the howdah atop one elephant. The Kushan women and Menander rode in the other. The young cataphract had protested the arrangement, insisting that he was quite capable of riding a horse. But Belisarius had insisted, and truth be told, the lad's protest had been more a matter of form than content. Menander might not yet

367

be well enough to ride a horse, but, in certain other respects, his health had improved dramatically. Judging, at least, from the cheerful and complacent look on his face, on those rare occasions when the curtains of his howdah were opened.

Ousanas, as always, insisted on traveling by foot. Nor was he hard-pressed by the chore. The caravan's pace could barely be described as an ambling walk.

Belisarius smiled. "I accused Venandakatra, you may recall, of putting together this grandiose exhibition for purely egotistical motives."

"So? He *is* an egotist. A flaming megalomaniac."

Belisarius smiled. "True, true. But he's also an *intelligent* megalomaniac. There's a purpose to this spectacle, beyond gratifying his vanity. Are you aware that this is not the normal route from Bharakuccha to the Gangetic plain?"

"It isn't?"

Belisarius shook his head. "No. We are traveling south of the Vindhyas." He pointed to the mountain range on their left. The mountains were not high—not more than a few thousand feet—but they were heavily forested and looked to be quite rugged.

"At some point we shall have to cross those mountains, which, by all accounts, is not an easy task. Especially for a caravan like this one."

"This isn't a caravan," grumbled Garmat. "It's a small army!"

"Precisely. And that's the point of the whole exercise. The normal route, according to my cataphracts—who got the information from their Kushan ladies—would take us *north* of the Vindhyas. Semidesert terrain, but well traveled and easily managed. But that route, you see, goes through Malwa territory."

"So does this one."

"Today, yes. But this is newly conquered land, Garmat. Until a year ago"—he gestured toward the surrounding countryside—"all this was part of the Andhra Empire."

Comprehension dawned. "Ah," muttered Garmat. "So this procession is designed to grind down the new subjects even further. Remind them of their status." He examined the scenery. The great forest which seemed to carpet the interior of India had been cleared away, at one time. But the fields were untended, as were the thatched mud-walled huts of the peasantry scattered here and there. The area seemed almost uninhabited, despite the fact that it was obviously fertile land. A warrior himself, in his younger days, Garmat had no difficulty recognizing war-ravaged terrain.

The Ethiopian adviser then examined the spectacle ahead of them on the trail. The "caravan" was enormous. He could not even see the very front of it, but he could picture the scene.

The caravan was led by an elephant followed immediately by surveyors. The surveyors were measuring the route by means of long cords which one would carry forward, then the other leapfrog him, calling the count at each cord. A third surveyor recorded the count.

Garmat and Belisarius had spent the first day of the journey puzzling out the purpose of this exercise. The conclusion they came to fell in line with everything they had seen in Bharakuccha. A picture of the rising Malwa power was taking shape in their mind. A huge, sprawling empire, encompassing a vast multitude of different peoples and customs. Which, it was becoming clear, the Malwa were determined to hammer into a centralized, unified state.

The phenomenon, they realized, was new to India. True, great empires had existed here before: the Gupta Empire, the immediate predecessor of the Malwa; and the even larger Mauryan empire of ancient history, which had encompassed most of India. But those empires, for all their size and splendor, had rested lightly on the teeming populace below. The Guptan and Mauryan emperors had made no attempt to interfere with the daily lives of their subjects, or the power and privileges of provincial satraps and local potentates. They had been satisfied with tribute, respect, submission. Beyond that, they had occupied themselves with their feasts, their harems, their elaborate hunts, and their great architectural projects. Even the greatest of those ancient rulers, the legendary Ashoka, had never tried to meddle with Indian customs and traditions beyond his patronage and support for the new Buddhist faith.

But, of course, neither the Guptan nor the Mauryan Empires had ever had the ambitions of the Malwa. The empires of the past were quite satisfied with ruling India, or even just northern India. They had not aspired to world conquest.

"All roads lead to Rome," Belisarius had murmured. "That's how the legions conquered the Mediterranean, and ruled it. The Malwa, it seems, intend to copy us."

Yes, the explanation fit. It fit, for instance, with the new bureaucracy which Belisarius and Garmat had noted in Bharakuccha. There had been much resentment and disaffection expressed, by the populace, toward that bureaucracy. It was impossible to miss, even from conversations in the streets. (Within a few years, Belisarius and Garmat had agreed, the conversations would be far less open; already the Malwa spies and provocateurs were doing their work.)

Strange new bureaucracy, by traditional Indian standards. Appointed by annual examinations, instead of breeding. True, most of the successful applicants were of *brahmin* or kshatriya descent, scions of one or another of the castes of those noblest of the four respectable classes, the twice-born *varna*. But there were *vaisya* bureaucrats also, and even—so it was rumored—a *sudra* official!

No untouchables, however. The Malwa regime was even harsher toward untouchables than tradition required. But that small bow toward hallowed custom brought little comfort to the twice-born. The Malwa were also grinding down the four respectable varna, among every people except the Malwa themselves and their privileged Rajput vassals. (And the Ye-tai, of course; but the barbarians had no proper varna and castes to begin with; uncouth, heathen savages.)

More and more sudra castes were finding themselves counted among the untouchables, now. Even, here and there, a few vaisya castes. As yet, the noble varna—the kshatriya and brahmin—seemed immune. But who was to know what the future might bring?

A much-hated new bureaucracy. Hated, but feared. For these new officials were armed with authority to override class and caste customs—overbearing and officious, and quick to exert their power against traditional satraps and long-established local potentates.

Great power, enforced by the Malwa weapons, and the massive Malwa army, and the privileged Rajput vassals, and the even more privileged Ye-tai. Enforced, as well, by their horde of spies and informants, and—worst of all—by the new religious castes: the Mahaveda priests and their mahamimamsa torturers.

For all the power of the new dynasty, however, it had become clear to Belisarius and Garmat that the process by which the Malwa were reshaping India was very incomplete. Incomplete, and contradictory. Much of the real power, they suspected, still lay in the hands of traditional rulers. Who chafed, and snarled, and snapped at the new officialdom.

True, they rarely rebelled, but the danger was ever present. Even at that moment, in fact, a great rebellion was taking place in the northern province whose capital was Ranapur. Their own expedition, eventually, was destined to arrive there. The emperor was overseeing the siege of Ranapur personally, which gave Belisarius and Garmat a good indication of how seriously the Malwa took the affair.

Following the surveyors and their elephant, a quarter mile back, came a party of Rajput horsemen. Two hundred of them, approximately, elite cavalry. Behind them came several elephants carrying pairs of huge kettledrums beaten by men on the elephants' backs. Then a party of footmen carrying flags.

Next—still out of sight from where they rode—came another troop of Rajput cavalry. Perhaps a hundred. Behind them came a larger contingent of Ye-tai cavalry.

The next stage of the caravan was within sight, and impossible to miss. Twenty war elephants, their huge heads and bodies protected by iron-reinforced leather armor. Each elephant was guided by a mahout and bore a howdah containing four Malwa kshatriya. The Malwa soldiers were not carrying rocket troughs, of course. Those weapons would panic the great pachyderms. Instead, they were armed with bows and those odd little flasks which Belisarius had pronounced to be *grenades*. The smaller variety of those grenades were bound to arrows. The larger variety, Belisarius explained, were designed to be hurled by hand.

Behind the troop of war elephants came Venandakatra himself, and his entourage of priests and mahamimamsa. The Mahaveda and the torturers rode atop elephants, four to a howdah. Occasionally, Venandakatra would do likewise. For the most part, however, the great lord chose to ride in a special palanquin. The vehicle was large and luxurious, borne by eight giant slaves. The palanquin was surrounded by a little mob of servants walking alongside. Some of the servants toted jugs of water and wine; others, platters of food; still others carried whisks to shoo away the ever present flies. Nothing was lacking for Venandakatra's comfort.

For the lord's nightly comfort, eight of his concubines rode in howdahs on two elephants, which followed Venandakatra's palanquin. The caravan would always halt at sunset and set up camp. Venandakatra's tent—if such a modest term could be used to describe his elaborate suite of pavilions—was always set up before he arrived. The lord possessed two such "tents." The one not being used was sent ahead, guarded by yet another troop of Rajput cavalry, to be prepared for the following night's sojourn.

The stage of the caravan which followed Venandakatra and his entourage was composed of Malwa infantry. No less than a thousand soldiers. The great number of them, presumably, was to compensate for their mediocre quality. These were not elite forces, simply a run-of-the-mill detachment from the huge mass of the Malwa army. The troops themselves were not Malwa, but a collection of men from various of the subject peoples. The officers were primarily Malwa, but not kshatriya.

Belisarius had been more interested in the infantry than in the elite cavalry units. The Ye-tai he understood, and, after some examination, the Rajput as well. They were impressive, to be sure. But Belisarius was a Roman, and the Romans had centuries of experience dealing with Persian cavalry.

But Belisarius thought the future of war lay with the infantry, and so he subjected the Malwa infantry to his closest scrutiny. It did not take him long to arrive at a general assessment.

Garmat expressed the sentiment aloud.

"That's as sorry a bunch of foot soldiers as I've ever seen," sneered the Ethiopian. "Look at them!"

Belisarius smiled, leaned over his saddle, and whispered:

"What tipped you off? Was it the rust on the spear blades? Or the rust on the armor?"

"Is that crap *armor*?" demanded Garmat. "There's more metal on my belt buckle!"

"Or was it the slouching posture? The hang-dog expressions? The shuffling footsteps?"

"My daughter's footsteps were more assured when she was two," snorted the Ethiopian. "The sarawit would eat these clowns for breakfast."

Belisarius straightened back up in his saddle. The smile left his face.

"True. So would any good unit of Roman infantry. But let's not get too cocky, Garmat. For all my speeches about quality outdoing quantity, numbers *do* count. There must be a horde of these foot soldiers. If the Malwa can figure out the logistics, they'll be able to flood the West. And they still have their special weapons, and the Ye-tai and the Rajput. *Lots* of Ye-tai and Rajput, from what I can tell."

Garmat grimaced, but said nothing.

Belisarius turned and looked toward the rear of the caravan. The Romans and Axumites were located right after the infantry. They were at the very end of the military portion of the procession. Following them came the enormous tail of the beast.

"And they've got a long ways to go to figure out proper logistics," he muttered, "if this is anything to go by."

Garmat followed his eyes.

"This is not normal?" he asked.

"No, Garmat, this is not normal. Not even the sloppiest Roman army has a supply train like this one. It's absurd!"

Garmat found it hard not to laugh aloud. At that moment, the general's normally expressionless face was twisted into a positively Homeric scowl.

"Hell hath no fury like a craftsman scorned," he muttered.

"What was that?"

"Nothing, Belisarius, nothing. I would point out to you, however, that much of the chaos behind us is due to civilians and camp followers."

Belisarius was not mollified.

"So what? Every army faces that problem! You think camp followers don't attach themselves to every Roman army that marches anywhere? You name it, they'll be there: merchants, food and drink purveyors, pimps and whores, slave traders, loot liquidators, the lot. Not to mention a horde of people who just want to travel along the same route and take advantage of the protection offered."

"And how do *you* deal with it? Drive them off?"

"Bah!" Belisarius made a curt gesture. "That's impossible. Camp followers are like flies." He swiped at a fly buzzing around his face. "No, Garmat, there's no point to that. Instead, you do the opposite. Incorporate them into the army directly. Put them under discipline. Train them!"

Garmat's eyes widened. "Train merchants and slave traders? Pimps and whores?"

Belisarius grinned. "It's not hard, Garmat. Not, at least, once you get over the initial hump. There's a trade-off, you see. In return for following the rules, the camp followers get a recognized and assured place in the army. Keeps out competitors."

The general scratched his chin. "It occurs to me, however, that this rampant disorder can serve our purpose. There is one little problem in our plan that's been gnawing at me—"

He looked down at Ousanas, striding alongside.

"You are a miserable slave, are you not?"

The dawazz stooped and bent his head in a flamboyant gesture of cringing submissiveness. The pose went poorly with the great stabbing spear in his hand.

"Well, I am shocked," grumbled Belisarius. "Absolutely shocked to see you lolling about without a care in the world. In *my* country, miserable slaves keep themselves busy."

Ousanas cocked an eye upward. The pose was now threadbare.

"Oh, yes," continued Belisarius, "very busy. Scurrying about all over the place—buying provisions, haggling over supplies, that sort of thing." He scowled. "All a pose, of course. The lazy buggers are actually just keeping out of their master's sight so they can lolligag. Out of everybody's sight, in fact. Nobody ever sees a slave where he's supposed to be. You get used to it."

Ousanas looked back at the motley horde of camp followers.

"Ah," he said. "Comprehension dawns. Although the great general might—just now and again—condescend to plain speaking. You want me to make myself scarce, so that when the time comes when I disappear altogether, no spy will even notice my absence."

Belisarius smiled. "You have captured the Platonic Form of my concept."

A moment later, Ousanas was drifting away, the very image of a dispirited, lackadaisical slave. Belisarius, watching, was struck by the uncanny manner of his movements. Ousanas was the only man the general had ever known who could shuffle silently.

A gleeful feminine squeal coming from ahead brought his attention forward. Belisarius and Garmat looked up at the howdah riding on the elephant in front of them. Curtains made it impossible to see within.

"At least he's stopped complaining," growled Belisarius.

Garmat shook his head. "You are being unfair, General. He is not promiscuous by nature. Not, at least, by the standards of royalty." The adviser shrugged. "True, he is a prince, and a handsome and charming boy in his own right. He has never lacked the opportunity for copulation, and certainly has no aversion to the sport. But—he likes women, you see, and enjoys their conversation and their company. So he much prefers a more settled situation."

After a moment, Belisarius smiled wryly. "Well, I can hardly disapprove of that. My own temperament, as it happens." He gestured toward the howdah. "He seems to have settled in here."

Garmat nodded. "He and Tarabai seem to be growing quite fond of each other. I notice that the other Maratha girls have stopped sharing his howdah lately, at night, except—"

He fell silent, glancing around quickly. There were no possible spies within hearing range.

"How is she doing?" asked Belisarius. "Have you heard? For obvious reasons, I stay away from the howdah."

"I have not been inside myself. Eon says she has come to accept his presence, but he is not sure how she would react to another man. She no longer flinches from him, but she still doesn't speak—not even to Tarabai. She is eating well, finally. Her physical wounds are all healed. Eon says he is always careful to keep away from her, as far as possible within the confines of the howdah. He thinks she no longer feels threatened by him. If for no other reason than—"

Another squeal came from the howdah.

"—Tarabai has his erotic impulses well under control," chuckled Belisarius.

The general pointed to the mahout guiding the elephant. "I trust Ezana is not disgruntled? Or Wahsi? Or Ousanas, for that matter?"

Garmat laughed. "Why should they be? True, they no longer enjoy Tarabai's company, but there are still the other two Maratha women. And the Kushan girls have been willing to spread their affections, whenever your cataphracts are too tired to pester them. Besides, they are all soldiers. The best of soldiers. Not given to stupid jealousies, and well aware that we are following a battle plan."

Another squeal. A low, masculine groan.

"In a manner of speaking."

Belisarius grinned. Then:

"Well, Eon's certainly carried out his part in the plan. He was absolutely perfect, the first day of the trip."

"Wasn't he marvelous?" agreed Garmat. "I thought

Venandakatra was going to die of apoplexy, right there on the spot."

The adviser patted his mount affectionately. "Poor Venandakatra. Here he presents us with the finest horses available, and the prince can't stop whining that he needs a howdah, with plump cushions for his royal fanny."

"A very *large* elephant to carry it," said Belisarius, laughing, "one strong enough to bear up under the prince's humping."

Garmat was laughing himself, now. "And then—did you see the look on Venandakatra's face after—"

"—his petty plot backfired?" Belisarius practically howled. "Priceless! What a complete idiot! He presents the largest, most unruly elephant he can find—"

"—to Africans!"

Belisarius and Garmat fell silent, savoring the memory.

"*This* is your largest elephant?" Ezana had queried. "This *midget?*"

"Look at those puny ears," mourned Wahsi. "Maybe he's still a baby."

"Probably not elephant at all," pronounced Ousanas. "Maybe him just fat, funny-looking gnu."

Venandakatra's glare had been part fury, part disbelief. The fury had remained. The disbelief had vanished, after Ezana and Wahsi rapidly demonstrated their skills as mahouts. After the sarwen reminisced over various Axumite military campaigns, in which *African* elephants figured prominently. After Ousanas extolled the virtues of the *African* elephant, not forgetting to develop his point by way of contrast with the Indian elephant. So-called elephant. But probably not elephant. Him probably just big tapir, with delusions of grandeur.

After they stopped laughing, Garmat remarked:

"We may have overdone it, actually. I notice that Venandakatra hasn't invited us to share his dinner since this trip began."

"He will," said Belisarius confidently. "It's only been two weeks since we left Bharakuccha. At the rate this—this matronly promenade—is going, we'll be two months getting to his 'modest country estate.'" He snorted. "If I was one of those surveyors, I'd have died of boredom by now. I doubt we're averaging more than ten miles a day. At best."

"You are so sure, my friend? Your stratagem has still not gelled."

"He will. In another two weeks or so, I estimate. Your average megalomaniac, of course, would only need a week to get over a petty snit. But even Venandakatra won't take much more than a month. Whatever else he is, the man is not stupid, and I've given him enough hints. He's developed his own plan, by now, which also hasn't gelled. It can't, until he talks to us further. To me, I should say. So—yes. Two weeks."

And, sure enough, it was thirteen days later that the courier arrived from Venandakatra's pavilion, shortly after the caravan had halted for the night. Bearing a message from the great lord himself, written in perfect Greek, politely inviting Belisarius to join him for his "modest evening meal."

"I note that Eon and I are not invited," remarked Garmat. The old adviser stared at Belisarius, and then bowed.

"I salute you, Belisarius. A great general, indeed. Until this moment, I confess, I was somewhat skeptical your plan would work."

Belisarius shrugged. "Let's not assume anything. As my old teacher Maurice always reminds me: 'Never expect the enemy to do what you expect him to.'"

Garmat shook his head. "Excellent advice. But it does not encompass all military wisdom. Every now and then, you know, the enemy *does* do what you expect him to. Then you must be prepared to strike ruthlessly."

"Exactly what I keep telling Maurice!" said Belisarius gaily. He tossed the message into the camp fire which Ousanas was just starting. The dawazz straightened, looked over.

"Time?" he asked. The grin began to spread.

Again, Belisarius shrugged. "We won't know for a bit. But I think so, yes. Are you ready?"

Like the great Pharos at Alexandria, that grin in the night.

Within three hours of his arrival at Venandakatra's pavilion, Belisarius was certain. For a moment, he considered some way of signaling Ousanas, but then dismissed the thought. A pointless worry, that, like fretting over how to signal prey to a crouching lion.

The general had been almost certain within two hours, actually. After the usual meaningless amenities during the meal, the wine was poured, and Venandakatra had immediately launched into the subject of Eon's amatory exploits. "Trying to pry out secrets," he'd said, one gay blade to another. But it was soon obvious there were no secrets he didn't know. Except one, which he knew, but misinterpreted exactly as Belisarius had thought he would.

As Ousanas said: *Catch the prey by reading its soul.*

"Ah, that explains it," said Venandakatra. He giggled. "I had wondered why he chose only Maratha bitches to accompany him on this trip. After" —another giggle— "sampling *all* the many Indian varieties in Bharakuccha."

Belisarius could not manage a giggle, but he thought his coarse guffaw was quite good enough.

"It's the truth. He loves conquered women. The more recently conquered, the better. They're the most submissive, you see, and that's his taste." Another guffaw, with a drooling trickle of wine down his chin thrown in for good measure. "Why, his soldiers told me that when they conquered Hymria, the kid—he was only seventeen, mind you—had an entire—"

Here followed an utterly implausible tale, to any but

Venandakatra. Implausible, at least, in its gross brutality; its portrayal of Eon's stamina was remotely conceivable, in light of his performance in Bharakuccha. Which Venandakatra obviously knew, in detail. As Belisarius had foreseen, the Malwa lord's spies had interrogated the women who shared the prince's bed. All except the Maratha women, of course.

Still, Venandakatra almost smelled out the falsehood. Almost.

"It's odd, though," the Vile One remarked casually, after he stopped cackling over the story, "but I didn't get the impression—I know nothing myself, you understand, but rumors concerning foreigners always spread—that any of the women who passed through his chambers had been particularly badly beaten. Except by his cock!"

Another round of giggles and guffaws.

Belisarius shrugged. "Well, as I understand it from his adviser, the lad felt under certain constraints. He *is* in a foreign land." The general waved his hand airily. "There are laws, after all."

He gulped down some more wine.

"So," he burped, "the boy finally got frustrated and ordered his men to find him some outright slaves." Another burp. "Slaves can be treated anyway their master chooses, in any country."

(That was a lie. It was not true in most civilized realms of Belisarius' acquaintance, not in modern times. It was certainly not true under Roman law. But he did not think that Venandakatra would know otherwise. Slaves, and their legal rights, were far beneath the great lord's contempt. In any country—certainly in his own.)

"True, true." A sly, leering glance. "Rumor has it, in fact, that one of his Maratha slaves fell afoul of her new master."

Belisarius controlled his emotions, and the expression on his face. It was not difficult to control his disgust, or his contempt. He had plenty of experience doing that, after all these weeks—months!—in Venandakatra's company. But he had a difficult time controlling his shame.

For a moment, his eyes wandered, scanning the rich tapestries which covered the silk walls of the pavilion. His gaze settled on the candelabra resting at the center of the table. For all its golden glitter, and the superb craftsmanship of the design, he thought the piece was utterly grotesque. A depiction of some dancing god, leering, priap erect, with candles rising from the silver skulls cupped in the deity's four hands.

He tore his eyes away from the thing and looked back at Venandakatra. He even managed a leer of his own.

The memory still burned, of the time he had sent the hostel proprietor into the girl's room, on some trumped-up pretext. He had instructed the Maratha woman tending her to allow the proprietor to enter (which she had done, reluctantly—she was a slave, after all). But he hadn't warned Eon in advance, because he knew the prince would have barred the way.

It worked, of course. The proprietor saw the girl, and judging from the contempt on his face as he left, knew what he saw. Or thought he did. Venandakatra obviously placed the interpretation I hoped for on it, after he had the man interrogated.

But I thought the prince was going to attack me, afterward, when he found out. He would have, I think, if Ezana and Wahsi hadn't restrained him.

It was even harder to control another emotion.

God, how I've grown to love that boy. He didn't care in the least about his own injured royal pride, or what the hostel owner thought of him. Only that I'd caused the poor girl to be terrified again. May my son Photius grow up to be like him.

But Belisarius was a general, a great general—a breed of men among whose qualities ruthlessness is never absent.

And so he managed to keep the leer on his face. And another drooling trickle of wine down his chin, thrown in for good measure.

Venandakatra refilled his cup personally. Unlike every other visit Belisarius had made, the Malwa lord had dismissed all the servants after the meal was finished.

"I notice the prince does not seem to mind sharing his women with his own soldiers," commented Venandakatra. "Not what you normally expect from royalty."

Belisarius belched. "I don't see why. It's not as if they were wives, or even concubines. The bitches are just whores and slaves." Another belch. "I share the Kushan sluts with my own soldiers, for that matter. I've done it often enough before, on campaign."

Belisarius gave Venandakatra a knowing smirk—one experienced old soldier to another (which the Malwa lord certainly was *not*, but liked to pretend he was).

"Helps keep your popularity with the troops, you know. The common touch. And there's always plenty to go around. Especially after sacking a town." The general's smirk became a savage grin. "God, how I love a sack. Sieges are pure shit, but afterward—oh, yes!"

Venandakatra giggled. "So do I!" he cried.

Vile One, indeed. I doubt he's ever come within bow range of a besieged city in his life. But I'm sure he was the first to line up afterward, selecting the prizes from the captured women.

Again, Belisarius fought down his gorge. He *hated* sacks. Would do anything he possibly could to avoid one, short of losing a campaign. It was almost impossible to keep troops under control in a captured city after a hard-fought siege, except for elite units like his own cataphracts. There was nothing so horrible as a city being sacked. It was hell on earth, Satan's maw itself. The most brutal and bestial crimes of which men were capable were committed then.

Committed with a gleeful savagery that would shame the very demons of the Pit.

But he kept his gorge well under control. He was a general, a great general, whose ruthlessness always had a purpose. The edge to the blade, when it came time for the cutting.

"You, on the other hand, seem to have a liking for Kushan women," remarked Venandakatra idly. "And your cataphracts also, I hear."

Time for the cutting.

"Oh God, yes!" cried Belisarius. "When I discovered there were Kushan whores in Bharakuccha, I sent Valentinian and Anastasius straight off to round up a few." Guffaw, guffaw, guffaw. "They raced like the wind, let me tell you— and that's something to see, with a man built like Anastasius!"

Giggle. "I can imagine! He's the large one, isn't he?" Giggle.

Belisarius waited. Timing was the key to a trap. Timing.

He waited until the puzzled frown had almost taken shape on the Vile One's brow. Then remarked casually, "Most lascivious women in the world, Kushans. Most lascivious *people*, for that matter. The men even more than the women." He coughed on a gulp of wine. "Don't misunderstand!" he exclaimed, waving off a disreputable notion. "I'm not interested in men *that* way. But it's true, believe me. It's why I got rid of all my Kushan mercenaries. Good men in a battle, no question about it. But they're just too much of a bother. Can't keep their hands off any woman in the vicinity. Even started sniffing around my own wife!"

The frown on the Vile One's brow thickened. The scaly wrinkles collected around his deep-set eyes.

"Really?" he asked. "I wasn't aware you were acquainted with the folk."

"Kushans? To the contrary. Find them all over the Roman Empire. Soldiers and whores, mostly. It's the only things they're good at. Fighting and fucking. Especially fucking."

Venandakatra sipped at his wine, thoughtfully.

"I had heard, now that you mention it, that you yourself spoke excellent Kushan." He shrugged. "I assumed it was just a false rumor, of course. There seemed no way you—"

He fell away from completing the sentence. Venandakatra had enjoyed some wine, but he was not inebriated. (Quite unlike the Roman sot.) The Malwa lord realized that he was on the verge of revealing too much of his spying operations.

You arrogant idiot, thought Belisarius, reading the sudden silence correctly. *I always assumed you knew everything, and planned accordingly.*

Belisarius filled the silence, then, with a bevy of amusing tales, one after the other. The sort of tales with which one veteran lecher entertains another. A less egotistical man than Venandakatra might have wondered why the tales exclusively concerned Kushans. And might have wondered, especially, why so many of the tales concerned the sexual exploits of Kushan *men*.

Oh, such exploits! Their unbridled lust. Their strangely seductive ways. Their uncanny ability to weedle open the legs of women—young women, especially. And virgins! Lambs to the slaughter, lambs to the slaughter. Didn't matter who they were, where they were, what they were. If the girl was a virgin, no Kushan could resist the challenge. And rise to it! Oh, yes! No men on earth were more skilled at defloration than Kushans. Especially the older men, the middle-aged veteran types. Uncanny, absolutely uncanny.

Throughout the tales, Venandakatra said not a word. But he did not seem bored. No, not at all. Very attentive, in fact.

Every good blade has two edges. Time for the backstroke.

"Enough of that!" exclaimed the general. He held out his cup. "Would you be so good?"

Venandakatra refilled the cup. Belisarius held it high.

"But I'm being a poor guest. And you are much too modest a host. I hear rumors myself, you know, now and then. And I hear you have come into a particularly good piece of fortune." Here, a wild guffaw. "A great piece, if you'll pardon the expression. A royal piece!"

He quaffed down the wine in a single gulp.

"My congratulations!"

Venandakatra struggled to maintain his own composure. Anger at the crude foreigner's insolent familiarity warred with pride in his new possession.

Pride won, of course. *Trap the prey by reading its soul.*

"So I have!" he exclaimed. "The Princess Shakuntala. Of the noblest blood, and a great beauty. The black-eyed pearl of the Satavahana, they call her."

"You've not seen her yourself?"

Venandakatra shook his head.

"No. But I've heard excellent descriptions."

Here, Venandakatra launched into his own lengthy recital, extolling the qualities of the Princess Shakuntala. As he saw them.

Belisarius listened attentively. Partly, of course, for the sake of his stratagem. But partly, also, because he was undergoing the strangest experience. Like a sort of mental—spiritual, it might be better to say—double vision. The general had never laid eyes on the girl in his life. But he had seen her once, in a vision, through the eyes of another man. A man as different from the one sitting across the table from him as day from night. As different as a panther from a cobra.

Once Venandakatra was finished, Belisarius saluted him again with his cup and poured himself another full goblet. Venandakatra, he noticed, had stopped drinking some time ago.

The general found it a bit hard not to laugh. Then, thinking

it over, he did laugh—a drunken, besotted kind of laugh.
Meaningless. He drained his cup and poured himself yet
another. From the corner of his eye he caught the Vile One's
faint smile.

*I'm from Thrace, you jackass. A simple farm boy, at
bottom. Raised in the countryside, where there's not much
to do but drink. I could have drunk you under the table
when I was ten.*

"You'll be seeing her soon, then," he exclaimed. "Lucky
man!"

He fell back into his seat, hastily grabbing the table to
keep from falling. Half the wine sloshed out of his cup,
most of it onto the gorgeous rug covering the floor. The
candelabra in the center of the table teetered. Venandakatra
steadied it hastily with a hand, but not in time to prevent
one of the candles from falling.

"Sorry," muttered Belisarius. Venandakatra's expression,
for just a fleeting instant, was savage. But he said nothing.
He simply placed the candle back in its holder and waved
off the mishap with a casual flutter of the fingers.

Belisarius drained what was left in his cup. Venandakatra
instantly poured him another.

Blearily, Belisarius grinned at the Malwa lord. Then,
leering:

"She'll be a virgin, of course. Bound to be, a princess!"
Guffaw, guffaw. "God, there's nothing like a virgin! Love
the way they squeal when you stick 'em!"

He shook a sage, cautioning finger in Venandakatra's
direction. A solemn look fell on his face—one experienced
pedophile advising another.

"Make sure you watch her well, mind! A prize like that?
Ha! Surround her with eunuchs, I would, or priests sworn
to celibacy. Better yet—eunuch priests." Guffaw, guffaw.
"And then I'd check under their robes!"

He half-choked on another swallow of wine, then added:

"We have an old saying in Rome, you know: *Quis custodiet ipsos custodes?*"

Venandakatra frowned. "I'm afraid I don't speak Latin."

"Ah. I assumed—my apologies—your Greek is excellent." Belch. "Well, it basically translates as: *Who will guard the guardians?* What it means is, how shall I—"

"I understand perfectly well what it means!" snapped Venandakatra.

Oh, my. Isn't he testy? Time to extract the blade.

And nick him elsewhere, so he doesn't notice that he's bleeding to death.

"But that's enough talk of women!" roared Belisarius. "Worthless cunts, all of 'em. Beneath our notice, except when we're in the mood for humping. We're men of affairs, you and I. Important men."

He reached over the table for the wine, lost his balance, fell to the floor. "Bitches, all of them," he muttered, staggering to his feet. "Treacherous sluts." He groped his way back into his chair.

"Good for fucking, and that's it," grumbled the general, glaring at the table. Venandakatra poured him another cup. From the corner of his eye, again, Belisarius caught Venandakatra's expression. Contempt, overlaying worry.

Now I have but to lay opportunity over contempt, and the worry will work its way to the heart, free of suspicion.

"Men of affairs, I say," he repeated, slurring the words. "Important men." He grit his teeth. "Important men."

Venandakatra slid in his own blade.

"So we are, my friend. Although"—slight hesitation, discreet pause—"not always appreciated, perhaps."

Belisarius' jaws tightened. "Isn't that the fucking truth? Isn't it just? My own—"

Careful. He's not stupid.

Belisarius waved his hand. "Never mind," he mumbled. The Vile One struck again.

First, he took a sip from his own cup. The first sip in an hour, by Belisarius' estimation. (Never underestimate the foe, of course. Who knows? The Roman might not be quite as drunk as he looks.)

"I am fortunate in that regard," remarked Venandakatra idly. "The Emperor Skandagupta is always appreciative of my efforts on his behalf. Always fair, in his criticisms. Mild criticisms, never more than that. And he gives me his full trust, unstintingly."

Belisarius peered at him suspiciously. But it was obvious the suspicion was directed toward the statement, not the speaker of it.

"Oh, no—it's quite true, I assure you."

"Hard to believe," muttered Belisarius resentfully. "In my experience—"

He fell silent, again. "Ah, what's the use?" he mumbled. "Emperors are emperors, and that's that." He seemed lost in his own thoughts. Bleak, bitter thoughts. Black thoughts, drunken thoughts.

Time. As Valentinian says, be economical with the blade.

He lurched to his feet; planted his hands on the table to steady himself.

"I must be off," he announced. Belch. " 'Scuse me. Afraid I've had too much to drink. You'll forgive me, I trust?"

Venandakatra nodded graciously. "I've been known to do it myself, friend." A happy thought: "Men of affairs, you know. Much on our minds. Much to deal with. Bound to drink a bit, now and then."

"The truth, that!" Belisarius smiled at the Vile One. Never, in the history of the world, did a drunk bestow such a cheerful smile of camaraderie on a fellow sot.

"You are most pleasant company, Venandakatra," he said, carefully enunciating the words. A man deep in his cups, determined to project sincerity.

"Most pleasant. Sorry we got off to a bit of a bad start,

back there—" The general waved his hand vaguely, more
or less in the direction of the sea. Belch. "Back there, in
the beginning. On the ship."

"Think nothing of it! Long forgotten, I assure you."
Venandakatra rose to his feet. "May I call one of my servants?
To assist you back—"

Belisarius waved off the offer.

"Not necessary!" he barked. "Can make it mack, byself—
back, myself. Not a problem."

He bowed at Venandakatra, with exaggerated, careful
stiffness, and reeled to the entrance. He pulled back the
heavily embroidered drapery which served the Malwa lord's
pavilion for a tent flap. By the studied care of his
movements, he was obviously trying not to inflict damage
on the precious fabric. As he was about to pass through
into the darkness beyond, he paused, steadying himself
with one hand on a tent pole. Then, he looked back at the
Malwa lord.

For a few seconds, Venandakatra and Belisarius exchanged
a stare. The expression on the Malwa's face registered a
subtle invitation. The face of the Roman general was that
of a man consumed by old grievances, brought to the surface
by hours of heavy carousing.

Bleak, bitter thoughts. Black thoughts. Drunken thoughts.

Belisarius turned away, shook his head, and stumbled into
the night.

He did not need to look back again. He knew what he
would see on the Vile One's face. Calculation, overlaying
contempt. Contempt, overlaying worry. Worry, buried, freed
of suspicion, worming its way into a maggotty soul.

He managed to keep from smiling all the way back to
his own tent. Spies, everywhere. He even managed to keep
from glancing into the forest which surrounded the caravan.
Spies, everywhere. And it would be pointless, anyway, for
he would see nothing. In that darkness, there would be

nothing to see except a grin. And the hunter never grins, when he is stalking the prey.

When he reached his own tent, he staggered within, and then straightened up. Good Roman leather, that tent. Impossible to see through.

"Well?" asked Garmat.

His next words, the general regretted for years, for he was a man who despised boasting. But he didn't regret them much. They were, after all, irresistible:

"Deadly with a blade, is Belisarius."

Early the next morning—even before daybreak—a party of Mahaveda priests and mahamimamsa "purifiers" left the caravan on horseback, escorted by a Rajput cavalry troop. They were being sent to the palace ahead of the caravan, on a special mission ordered by Lord Venandakatra.

In the heart of mighty Malwa, it did not occur to them to look back on the trail, to see if anyone followed. It would have made no difference if they had. The one who tracked them had been taught his skills by lionesses and pygmies, the greatest hunters in the world.

Chapter 22

Insofar as that term could ever be applied to that man, he was frantic.

An observer watching him would not have realized his state of mind, however. For the man seemed utterly calm and still, crouching in the thick foliage of the brush and trees which came within a few feet of the walls of Venandakatra's palace.

True, an observer might have wondered what he was doing there. A man of average height; black-haired; black-bearded; with a few grey hairs to indicate approaching middle age; barefoot; wearing nothing but a dirty loincloth. But, even there, the conclusion was obvious: a menial, from one of the lower sudra castes, relieving himself in the woods.

No thought of danger would have crossed such an observer's mind. The man was obviously poor, stoop-shouldered from years of drudgery, and quite unarmed. There was no room in that soiled, torn, scanty loincloth to conceal any weapon.

Had such an observer approached, however, he might have begun to question his assumption. For, up close, there were certain things about the man crouching in the woods which did not quite jibe with his appearance.

He was too still, for one thing. Motionless, in fact. No

dim-witted menial can prevent himself from idle twitching and scratching.

His musculature, on closer examination, was puzzling. True, the shoulders were stooped—but that can result from deliberate posture. And, while the man was not heavily muscled, the muscles themselves were extraordinarily well-defined. Iron-hard, to all appearance. Not the sort of physique which results from menial toil.

Then, there were the arms and the hands. Very long arms, for a man of his size. Long and powerful. And the hands, in proportion to his build, were huge. Sinewy hands. Scarred, callused hands also—but those scars and calluses were not, quite, the scars produced by years of simple toil.

Finally, the eyes. Hazel eyes, they were—almost yellow-orange. An unusual color for a man of obvious Maratha descent. And then, had the observer come close enough to look into them, another strange feature of the eyes would be noted. There was nothing in those eyes of the dull gaze of a menial. No, the gaze of those eyes was like—

Recognition would come, finally. For the man in the woods was called many things. In one case, because the color of his eyes, and the gaze of his eyes, so closely matched those of the predator for which he was named.

The observer would have no time to shout a warning, then. He would be dead within two seconds. A panther does not need weapons, beyond those provided by nature.

There *was* an observer, in fact. But the panther did not slay him, because he did not spot him. The one observing him was no stranger to woods himself, nor to predators. And he was certainly not fool enough to come near *that* man. Not at *that* moment. Not when the man, had he been a panther in truth, would have been lashing his tail in fury.

No, best to wait. The observer had already found the panther's lair. He would wait for him there, and catch him when he was not quite so prepared for slaughter. The observer knew how to trap predators in their lairs. He had done it before, times beyond counting, and would do it again.

The observer faded away, vanished into the forest without a sound. Had the panther turned at that very moment, he might have caught a sign of his stalker. Not of the stalker himself, for that one was a master of hidden movement. Just an odd, quick, flash of white, gleaming in the darkness of the foliage like a beacon. Just for an instant.

But the panther did not turn. He twitched, slightly. Some buried part of his brain tried to transmit a signal. But it was a dim, confused, uncertain signal, and the conscious part of the panther's mind suppressed it.

For two days, now, he had been getting those subconscious signals. *Something is watching.* The first day, he had taken them very seriously. But he had been able to detect nothing. Nothing—and he was a man who rarely failed to detect danger. By the second day, he shrugged off the signals. *Nervous tension, no more.* It was not logical, after all, that an enemy would stalk him for so long in those woods without making his presence known.

Why would Malwa waste time apprehending a foe? Here? In the very heart of their power? With a small army of soldiers at hand?

The panther shrugged off the signal, again.

Two hours later, his already still form became absolutely rigid. Something was happening.

A party of Rajput horsemen rode into the open courtyard before the main door to the Vile One's palace. Escorts for half a dozen Mahaveda priests and over twenty of the mahamimamsa carrion-eaters.

The door of the palace opened, the majordomo emerging. The man was small and corpulent. His rotund form was draped in fine clothing and a positively splendiferous turban—as befitted one who, though ultimately a servant, was the most august member of that lowly class. August enough, at least, that the squad of Ye-tai who accompanied him did not evince a trace of the rowdy disrespect which they typically dealt out to servants.

And to others, for that matter. As soon as the Ye-tai spotted the Rajput horsemen they began bristling, like a pack of mongrels in an alley, faced with alien dogs. The Rajputs, purebreds, ignored the curs.

The majordomo barked them to order. There was an exchange of words. Moments later, the priests and the mahamimamsa dismounted and were ushered within the palace. Just before entering, one of the priests turned and spoke some words to the officer in charge of the Rajput cavalry troop. The Rajputs turned their horses and trotted out of the courtyard. Ye-tai jeers and taunts followed them. But the Rajputs neither looked back, nor responded, nor gave any indication that they even heard the deprecations.

Once the Rajputs were gone, the Ye-tai swaggered back into the mansion. They did not fail, naturally, to cuff aside the servant who held the door for them.

For a half hour or so thereafter, all was still. Silence, except for the normal faint sounds issuing from the palace—the noises one expects to hear emanating from a palace populated by an army of servants.

Very busy servants. The lord of the palace was expected to arrive soon. It was well known—not only to the servants, but to all the villagers nearby. The news had thrown the servants into a frenzy of activity. The villagers, into a fearful withdrawal to their huts, for all save the most necessary chores.

Frantic, now, the man in the woods. But there was no sign, except, perhaps, for the slightest tremor in his long, powerful fingers. He had hoped, he had prayed, he had spied, he had schemed—and now, he had run out of time.

The man in the woods closed his eyes, briefly, controlling the frustration that seemed to burn him from inside like a raging fire. Frustration such as he had never experienced in his life. Frustration caused by one thing only.

By one man only, actually. One man, and the others of his ilk whom he led.

The panther opened his eyes. For the hundredth time—the thousandth time—his quick mind raced and raced, coursing over the same ground he had covered before, over and over again. And with the same result.

It cannot be done. It just cannot be done. It would be pure futility to even try. They are simply too good. Especially—him.

Him.

The panther knew the man's name, of course. He had known it for weeks, almost since the day he had arrived at the palace. He had winkled it out of the villagers, and the servants who lived in the village, just as he had winkled out so many other things.

It had not been difficult. Neither the villagers nor the servants had suspected anything. A friendly, cheerful man; addled in his brains, a bit—by horrible experiences, no doubt. Another hopeless refugee in a world of refugees, willing to do the occasional chore in exchange for what little food the villagers could spare; and conversation. Much conversation. A lonely man, obviously. Dim-witted, but harmless and pleasant. A bit of a blessing, actually, for village women who often found people unwilling to listen to their chatter.

True, he was Maratha, not of their people. But the villagers held no allegiance to the Malwa. No, none at all. Nothing but fear, and a deeply hidden hatred. An escaped slave, most likely, although he bore no brand. Perhaps he escaped before branding. Instinctively, the villagers shielded him from prying eyes. Said nothing to the authorities.

(And to whom would they have reported, anyway? The majordomo, like most of his ilk, was a petty tyrant. Best avoided at all costs. It was unthinkable for polluted castes such as comprised the villagers to approach the Mahaveda priests—and none but lunatics even looked at the mahamimamsa. The Rajputs ignored villagers as they would have ignored any other vermin. The Ye-tai would do likewise, unless, as often happened, they were in the mood for amusement—and woe to the man, much less the woman, who served as the object of their entertainment. Who, then? The Kushans, possibly. But the Kushans were preoccupied with their special duty, had neither the time nor the inclination to busy themselves with any other concerns. No, best to say nothing. He was just a harmless half-wit, after all, with grief enough to bear as it was.)

Him. Yes, the panther knew his name, but never used it, not even in his own mind. Why bother? *He* was the central fact in the panther's life. Had been for weeks now. Who needed to give a name to the center of the universe?

Him. That cursed, hated *him*.

Oh, yes. Cursed, often—by a man who rarely cursed. Hated, deeply—by a man who did not come to hatred easily.

But not despised, never. For the hatred was a peculiar kind of hatred, despite the raging depth of the emotion. The panther had never in his life hated a man the way he hated *him*. Had never hated a man so terribly, wished for his destruction with such an aching, yearning passion; and, at the same time, found no fault in the man at all.

Not even service to the Malwa, in the end. For the man had little choice in the matter. That the panther knew, with the knowledge of a great student of human affairs. History had condemned the man he hated, and his people, to vassalage. Their strength and skill in battle had recommended them to others. But they had not been strong enough, nor skilled enough, to decline the recommendation. And so, like many others before them—and others who would come after—they had bowed their stiff necks.

No, it was for no fault of the man himself that the panther hated *him*. *He* was not personally responsible, nor had *he* done anything himself. Rather the contrary, suspected the panther. The treasure of his soul was unharmed, either in body or in spirit, despite her long captivity. He knew, for he had seen her, from a distance. Seen her many times. Always in the company of *him*. *Him*, and *his* men.

She was not happy, of course. She was filled with her own hatred and despair, he knew. But he had also seen the way she looked at *him*. Not with friendship, no. But not with hatred, either, or with anger, or disgust, or contempt.

And the panther had also seen, from a distance, the way *he* looked at her. It was not easy to read *his* emotions. *He* had a face as hard as iron, as cold as a stone. But the panther understood the man.

In the end, perhaps, it was that understanding which filled the panther's heart with such a pure fury, like the very flame of God's heart. The panther hated *him* as he had never hated a man in his life. And knew, as well, that in another time, another place, another turn of the wheel, he would have treasured the man's soul.

And then, suddenly, *he* was there. Emerging from the door of the palace, into the courtyard. After him filed the men under his command. The commander's subordinates were all members of his own people. Of the same clan of that people, in fact, the panther had learned. A tightly-knit band of veteran soldiers, sworn to their leader by oath, by blood, and by blooded experience.

The panther recognized all of them. He knew every face. They were all there. The entire detachment.

The panther willed himself to absolute stillness. Perhaps—

maybe. This might be the chance! Almost hopeless, true, but hope was gone in any event. Never had they allowed the princess to walk about in the courtyard. Her daily exercise was always limited to the garden perched atop the battlements of the palace. For the first time, the panther would only have to fight his way through *them*, on level ground.

He could not prevent the grimace. *Only*. With his bare hands. An assassin's hands, true. But he did not even have to examine *them* to know what he would see. (Although he did, of course, for the thousandth time.) The discipline, the spotless helmets and armor, the well-oiled gleam of the swords and spear blades. Worst of all, the poise and confidence. The poise and confidence that comes only from battlefields mastered and survived.

Only. But—there would be no other chance. Slowly, imperceptibly, he gathered his haunches beneath him, preparing to spring. He would wait until the princess herself emerged and was well away from the door.

He waited. And waited. Grew puzzled.

What was happening?

He and his men were now clustered in the center of the courtyard. The door to the mansion had closed behind them. There was no sign of the princess.

The panther looked back to the men in the courtyard. There seemed to be some quarrel going on. He could not make out the voices, but it was obvious from the tone that they were raised in anger. And obvious, as well, from the expression on *his* face. A hard man to read, *he* was, but the panther had come to know that face. A deep, bitter rage roiled beneath its iron surface, suppressed by a lifetime's harsh discipline.

No. Not a quarrel. They are not arguing amongst themselves. The anger is directed elsewhere. He spotted the glances directed toward the palace. Quick glares of fury.

The door to the palace opened again. The panther tensed. But, again, the princess did not appear. Only a gaggle of servants, bearing bundles. Bundles, the panther realized, containing the kits of—

His eyes flitted back to the center of the courtyard. A sudden, wild hope flared.

He said something. Barked commands. Again, the panther could not make out the words. But he knew the tone, with the knowledge of a great commander of armies.

Orders are orders. Obey. Just shut up and do it.

A moment later, *he* was striding off. After a moment, the other men followed, toting their kits. Out of the courtyard. Down the beautifully tiled entryway to the palace grounds. Then, turning left at the dirt track—

— leading to the barracks.

Could it be? Is it possible?

The panther hesitated for only an instant. Just long enough for a quick, appraising glance at the palace.

No. I must first learn—

The panther sped through the woods, circling around toward the location of the barracks. He moved very swiftly, but almost invisibly, with just the faintest hint of a rustle. Like the sound of the wind, some might say.

He came to a good spot, well hidden, but from which he could spy out the barracks. The barracks, where the Rajputs and the common soldiery dwelled. They were not privileged to make their quarters within the palace. Of the troops guarding the palace, only the Ye-tai enjoyed the privilege of dwelling within its fair walls. The Ye-tai alone—except, due to their special duty, *him* and his men. Until now.

He was already there, and his men. They stalked into the best of the barracks reserved for the common soldiery. (The Rajputs took their quarters in a special barracks at the other end of the compound. Not luxurious, those, not even the rooms set aside for officers, but considerably better than the shacks provided for the common soldiery.)

The sound of angry voices came from the barracks into which *they* had marched. Had stalked. Like wolves entering a den of jackals.

A stream of common soldiers began pouring out of the barracks. Hastily, even frantically. The last one to emerge on his own feet was aided along by a kick. A second or so later, two others followed through the door, hurled like so many sacks of rice. They landed in the dirt and sprawled there, unconscious, their heads bleeding from savage blows.

Soon after, the kits of the common soldiers were likewise hurled through the door. The kits were not properly packed—were not packed at all, in fact. Just bundles slapped together and cast into the dirt, like garbage thrown out by a particularly foul-tempered housewife.

Sullenly—but, oh so meekly, with nary a snarl directed toward the barracks—the common soldiers scurried about, scraping together their belongings. They dusted off their meager possessions, rolled up their kits, and slouched toward the barracks located some distance away. The empty barracks. The one whose walls were caving in, and whose thatched roof kept out rain about as well as a fishnet.

Yes. Yes. Yes. It is true!

The panther raced back the way he had come. But, just before he reached his familiar hiding place beyond the door of the palace, he halted.

Oh, it was difficult! Weeks of frustration hurled him toward that hated palace!

But, he restrained himself, with the restraint of a man who had set a hundred ambushes, and eluded as many more.

Patience. The Vile One will not arrive for days yet. There is time. I must discover exactly what has happened. Lay out my plans.

He turned, and flitted through the woods, toward his hidden lair deep in the forest. Along the way, he tried to formulate new stratagems, based on a new reality. But, soon, he abandoned the effort. It was foolish to make plans in the absence of precise information. And besides, his soul was too flooded with emotion.

A new emotion. Hope. A huge emotion, like the surging monsoon. It filled every cranny and nook of his soul.

There was room for it. Another emotion was gone. The panther no longer hated *him*. The hate had vanished with the need, like a straw in the monsoon winds, and the panther was glad to see it go.

He arrived at his lair. Nothing much, that lair. Nothing much, for he possessed little, and had discarded most of that. He had prepared his lair carefully, making sure it could never be found.

He squatted, moved aside the stones and twigs which disguised his little campfire, and began piling up a small mound of kindling. There was not much to eat, but he would have time to cook it. Time to plot, and space to do it. A safe, perfectly hidden lair. Where he could become lost in his thoughts without fear of discovery.

The voice which came from behind him was the first knowledge he had of the ambush. He would have never believed it possible.

Speaking in Maratha. With a pronounced accent.

"You are very good, Raghunath Rao. Not as good as me, but very good."

The panther turned, slowly. Stared back at the foliage from whence the voice had come. Still, he saw nothing.

Until a flash of white appeared, in the darkness. A quick gleam, nothing more.

The panther could make him out now, barely. The man was so well concealed that his shape was nothing but black against black. Slowly, imperceptibly, the panther gathered up his haunches.

An object was flung from the darkness where the hunter lurked. It landed not more than a foot away from his feet. A small bundle. Slender, about a foot long. Wrapped in a cloth.

The voice came again:

"Examine the gift, first, Raghunath Rao. Then, if you still wish to be foolish, you will at least be a well-armed fool."

The panther hesitated for only an instant. He reached out his left hand and swiftly unfolded the bundle. The— gift—lay exposed.

He knew what it was, of course. But it wasn't until he withdrew the thing from its sheath, and examined it, that he understood what a truly excellent gift it was. With all the understanding of a great student of daggers, and their use.

Another packet landed by his feet.

"Now, that," came the voice.

The panther used the dagger to slice open the rawhide strip binding the small leather roll. Opened, the roll proved to contain a few sheets of papyrus. Upon them was a message, written in Marathi.

The panther glanced at his stalker. The hunter had not moved.

Strange ambush, he thought. But—he began to read the message.

Impossible to catalog the emotions which that incredible message produced in the panther's soul. Hope, again, in the main, like the sky behind a rainbow. Hope, produced by the body of the message. The rainbow, by the final words.

Half-dazed, he slowly raised his head and stared at the hunter in the shadows.

"Is it true?" he whispered.

"Which part?" came the voice. "The beginning, yes. You have seen yourself. We have cleared the way for you. The middle? Possibly. It remains still to be done, and what man can know the future?"

A rustle, very faint. The hunter arose and stepped into

the small clearing. The panther gazed up at the tall man. He had never seen his like before, but did not gape. The panther had long known creation to be a thing of wonder. So why should it not contain wonderful men?

The panther examined the man's weapon, briefly. Then— not so briefly—examined the light, sure grip which held that enormous spear. The panther recognized that grip, knew it perfectly, and knew, as well, that he would be a dead man now, had he—

"How fortunate it is," remarked the panther, "that I am a man who cannot resist the pleasure of reading."

"Is it not so?" agreed the hunter, grinning cheerfully. "I myself am a great lover of the written word. A trait which, I am certain, has much prolonged my life."

The tall hunter suddenly squatted. He and the panther stared at each other, their eyes almost level. The grin never left the hunter's face.

"Which brings us, back, oddly enough, to your very question. Is the last part of the message true? That, I think, is what you would most like to know."

The panther nodded.

The hunter shrugged. "Difficult to say. I am not well acquainted with the—fellow, let us call him. He is very closely attached to the one who sent you this message."

"You have met—"

"Oh, yes. Briefly, mind you, only briefly. But it was quite an experience."

The hunter paused, staring for a moment into the forest. Then said, slowly:

"I do not know. I think—yes. But it is a difficult question to answer for a certainty. Because, you see, it involves the nature of the soul."

The panther considered these words. Then, looked back down and read again the final part of the message. And then, laughed gaily.

"Indeed I think you are right!"

He rolled the sheets of papyrus back into the leather and tucked it into his loincloth.

"It seems, once again," he remarked lightly, "that I shall be forced to act in this world of sensation based on faith alone." The panther shrugged. "So be it."

"Nonsense," stated the hunter. "Faith alone? Nonsense!" He waved his hand, majestically dispelling all uncertainty.

"We have philosophy, man, philosophy!"

A great grin erupted on the hunter's face, blazing in the gloom of the forest like a beacon.

"I have heard that you are a student of philosophy yourself."

The panther nodded.

The grin was almost blinding.

"Well, then! This matter of the soul is not so difficult, after all. Not, at least, if we begin with the simple truth that the ever-changing flux of apparent reality is nothing but the shadow cast upon our consciousness by deep, underlying, unchanging, and eternal Forms."

The panther's eyes narrowed to slits. The treasure of his soul in captivity—bound for the lust of the beast—a furious battle ahead, a desperate flight from pursuit, a stratagem born of myth, and this—this—this half-naked outlandish barbarian—this—this—

"I've never encountered such blather in my life!" roared the panther. "Childish prattle!" The tail lashed. "Outright cretinism!"

Furiously, he stirred the fire to life.

"No, no, my good man, you're utterly befuddled on this matter. *Maya*—the veil of illusion which you so inelegantly call the ever-changing flux of apparent reality—is nothing. Not a shadow—*nothing*. To call such a void by the name of shadow would imply—"

The panther broke off.

"But I am being rude. I have not inquired your name."

"Ousanas." The black man spread his hand in a questioning gesture. "Perhaps I introduced the topic at an inappropriate time. There is a princess to be rescued, assassinations to commit, a pursuit to be misled, subterfuges to be deepened, ruses developed, stratagems unfolded—all of this, based on nothing more substantial than a vision. Perhaps—"

"Nonsense!"

Raghunath Rao settled himself more comfortably on his haunches, much as a panther settles down to devour an impala.

"Shakuntala will keep," he pronounced, waving his hand imperiously. "As I never tire of explaining to that beloved if headstrong girl: *only the soul matters, in the end.* Now, as to that, it should be obvious at first glance—even to you—that the existence of the soul itself presupposes the One. And the One, by its very nature, must be indivisible. That said—"

"Ridiculous!" growled Ousanas. "Such a One—silly term, that; treacherous, even, from the standpoint of logic, for it presupposes the very thing which must be proved—can itself only be—"

Long into the night, long into the night. A low, murmuring sound in the forest; a faint, flickering light. But there were none to see, except the two predators themselves, quarreling over their prey.

The soul, the great prey, the leviathan prey, the only fit prey for truly great hunters. The greatest hunters in the world, perhaps, those two, except for some tiny people in another forest far away. Who also, in their own way, grappled Creation's most gigantic beast.

Chapter 23

Three nights later, the Wind of the Great Country swept through the palace of the Vile One.

Eerie wind. Silent as a ghost. Rustling not a curtain, rattling not a cup. But leaving behind, in its passage, the signs of the monsoon. The monsoon, great-grandfather of fury, whose tidal waves strew entire coasts with destruction.

Unnatural wave. Selective in its wreckage, narrow in its havoc, precise in its carnage.

The majordomo was the first to die, in his bed. He expired quickly, for his lungs were already strained by the slabs of fat which sheathed his body. He died silently, purple-faced, his bulging eyes fixed on the multitude of cords and levers for which his plump hand was desperately reaching. Cords and levers which might have saved him, for they were the nerve center of the entire palace. The mechanisms which could have alerted the Ye-tai guards, roused the priests and torturers, summoned the servants.

Wondrous levers, crafted by master metalsmiths. Beautiful cords, made from the finest silk.

The mechanisms, alas, proved quite beyond his reach. They would have been beyond that reach even if the nearest silk cord, the one he most desperately sought, had still been there. That cord rang the bell in the Ye-tai quarters. But it was gone. The majordomo could see the stub of the cord, hanging from the ceiling. It must have been severed by a razor, so clean and sharp was the cut. Or, perhaps, by a truly excellent dagger.

He did not wonder what had happened to the missing length of the cord, however. The beautiful silk had disappeared into the folds of fat which encased his neck and throat, driven there by hands like steel. He struggled against those hands, with the desperation of his feverish will to survive.

But his was a petty will, a puny will, a pitiful will, compared to the will which drove those incredible hands. *That* will made steel seem soft.

And so, a lackey died, much as he had lived. Swollen beyond his capacity.

The Wind swept out of the majordomo's suite. As it departed, the Wind eddied briefly, cutting away all of the cords and removing all of the levers. Without—eerie wind—causing a single one of the multitude of bells throughout the palace to so much as tremble.

The levers, the Wind discarded. The cords it kept. Excellent silk, those cords, the Wind fancied them mightily.

The Wind put three of those cords to use within the next few minutes. The Mahaveda high priests who oversaw the contingent of priests and torturers newly assigned to the palace dwelt near the suite of the majordomo. Their own chambers were not as lavish as his, nor were the locks on their doors as elaborate. It would have made no difference if they had been. Door locks, no matter how elaborate, had no more chance of resisting the Wind than dandelions a cyclone.

It made no difference, either, that the priests' lungs were not slabbed with fat. Nor that their necks were taut with holy austerity. Very taut, in fact, for these were high priests, given to great austerity. But they grew tauter still, under the Wind's discipline. For Mahaveda priests, the Wind would settle for nothing less than ultimate austerity.

The Wind departed the quarters of the high priests and swirled its way through the adjoining chambers. Small rooms, these, unlocked—the sleeping chambers of modest priests and even humbler mahamimamsa.

They grew humbler still, models of modesty, in the passing of the Wind. True, their simple bedding gained ostentatious color, quite out of keeping with their station in life. But they could hardly be blamed for that natural disaster. The monsoon always brings moisture in its wake.

Done with its business in those quarters, the Wind veered toward the west wing of the palace. There, still some distance away, lay the principal destination of the Wind's burden of wet destruction.

The Wind eased its way now, slowly. These were the servant quarters. The Wind had no quarrel with that folk. And so it moved through these corridors like the gentlest zephyr, so as not to rouse its residents.

A servant awoke, nonetheless. Not from the effects of the Wind's passage, but from the incontinence of old age. A crone, withered by years of toil and abuse, who simply had the misfortune to shuffle out of her tiny crib of a room at exactly the wrong moment.

Shortly thereafter, she found herself back in the room. Lying on her pallet, gagged, bound with silk cords, but otherwise unharmed. She made no attempt to fight those bonds. As well fight against iron hoops. When she was finally discovered the next day, she had suffered no worse than the discomfort of spending a night in bedding soaked with urine.

In the event, the Wind wasted its mercy. The crone would die anyhow, two days later. On a stake in the courtyard, impaled there at Venandakatra's command. Condemned for the crime of not overcoming one of the world's greatest assassins.

Strangely, she did not mind her death, and never thought to blame the Wind. Hers had been a miserable life, after all, in this turn of the wheel. The next could only be better. True, these last moments were painful. But pain was no stranger to the crone. And, in the meantime, there was great entertainment to be found. More entertainment than she had enjoyed in her entire wretched existence.

She was surrounded by good company, after all, the very best. Men she knew well. Ye-tai soldiers who had taken their own entertainment, over the years, mocking her, beating her, cursing her, spitting on her. Their fathers had done the same, when she had been young, and thrown rape into the bargain. But they would entertain her, now, in her last hours. Entertain her immensely.

So went a feeble crone to her death, cackling her glee. While seventeen mighty Ye-tai around her, perched on their own stakes, shrieked their warrior way to oblivion.

Once out of the servant quarters, the Wind moved swiftly through the cavernous rooms where the Vile One, when present, resided and entertained himself. Invisible, the Wind, for there were no lanterns lit, and as silent as ever. The invisibility and the silence were unneeded. At that time of night, with the lord absent from his palace, none would intrude in his private quarters. None would dare. To be found was to be convicted of thievery and impaled within the hour.

Unnecessary invisibility, unneeded silence; but inevitable for all that. It was simply the way of the Wind, the nature of the thing, the very soul of the phenomenon.

Into the corridor leading to the stairs swept the Wind. The first mahamimamsa guard was encountered there, at the foot of the stairs, standing in a pathetic semblance of a sentry's posture. The Wind swirled, very briefly, then lofted its way up the stairs. The mahamimamsa remained below, his posture much improved. More sentry-like. True, the torturer no longer even pretended to stand. But his eyes were wide open.

Near the top of the stairs, at the last bend in its stately progression, the Wind eddied, grew still. Listened, as only the Wind can listen.

One mahamimamsa, no more.

Had silence not been its way, the Wind would have howled contempt. Even Ye-tai would have had the sense to station two sentries at the landing above.

But the Ye-tai had never been allowed up those stairs, not since the treasure in the west wing had first been brought to the palace. The princess had been placed in that wing of the palace, in fact, because it was located as far from the Ye-tai quarters as possible. The majordomo had known his master's soul. No Malwa lord in his right mind wants Ye-tai anywhere near that kind of virgin treasure. The barbarians were invaluable, but they were not truly domesticated. Wild dogs from the steppes, straining at a slender leash. Mad dogs, often enough.

The lord of this palace was in his right mind. A mind made even righter by the experienced wisdom of a foreigner. A drunken foreigner, true. But—*in vino veritas*. And so the right-minded lord had tightened the guard over his treasure. Had sent orders ahead. None but mahamimamsa torturers would protect that treasure now, with a few priests to oversee them. Men bound to celibacy. Bound by solemn oaths; bound even tighter by fear of pollution (the worst of which is the monstrous, moist, musk-filthy, blood-soiled bodies of women); bound, tightest of all, by their own twisted depravity, which took its pleasure in a place as far removed from life-creation as possible.

The Wind swirled, rose the final few steps, coiled its lethal way around the corner. Another length of cord found good use.

The Wind was pleased, for it treasured beauty. Such wonderful silk was meant to be displayed, admired, not wasted in the privacy of a glutton's chambers. It would be seen now, the following day. Not admired, perhaps. Mortal men, tied to the veil of illusion, were hard to please.

Down the corridor to the left, down the next corridor to the right. So the Wind made its silent way, as surely as if it knew every inch of the palace.

Which, indeed, it did. The Wind had discovered all of the palace's secrets, from the humblest source: the idle chatter of village women, filled with the years of toil in that palace. Long years, washing its walls, cleaning its linens, dusting its shelves, scrubbing and polishing its floors. Idle chatter, picked up by the Wind as it wafted its light way through their lives.

Now, as it came to the end of this corridor, the Wind wafted lightly again. Not so much as a whisper signaled its arrival. This was the corridor which led to the great domed hall where all the corridors in the west wing of the palace intersected.

The Wind knew that hall. That great domed hall, empty, save for a single small table at its center. A table with three chairs. Oh, yes. The Wind knew that hall well. Knew it, in fact, better than it had known any room it had ever actually entered.

Knew it so well, because it hated that domed hall more than any room built by men had ever been hated. Hours, days—weeks, the Wind had spent, thinking about that hall. Trying to find a way it could swirl through that hall, without the fatal alarm being sounded.

But the Wind had never found a way. For a man with an iron face had also thought upon that hall, and how to guard it.

At the end of the corridor, at the very edge of the light-cone cast by a lantern on the table which stood at the center of the hall, the Wind eddied. Grew still.

Till now, the Wind had been able to take its own time. Once that hall was entered, there would be no time.

The hall was the first of the final barriers to the Wind's will. There were four barriers. The first was the domed hall, and the guards within it. Beyond, just two short corridors away, was the second: the guards standing in front of the princess' suite. The third was the antechamber of the suite, where the main body of guards were found. And now, the Wind had learned (the day before, from a village woman clucking her outrage), there was a fourth barrier, in the princess' own chamber. In a former time, when an iron-faced man had commanded very different guards, the princess had been allowed to sleep undisturbed. Now, even in her sleep, torturers gazed upon her.

But it was the first barrier which had been the main barrier to the Wind, for all these weeks. The Wind had never doubted it could make its way through that hall— even when guarded by *his* men—and to the barriers beyond. But not without the alarm being sounded. And, the alarm sounded, the barriers beyond would become insurmountable obstacles, even to the Wind.

Eddying in the darkness of the corridor, the Wind examined the hated hall, in the light of a new reality. And, again, found it hard not to howl.

His warriors, in the days when this had been their duty, stood their duty erect, alert, arms in hand. They did not converse. Conversation was impossible, anyway, because *his* sentries always stood far apart from each other, so that if one were to be overcome, the other would at least have time to cry the alarm. (Which they would. The Wind had marked out the paces of that hall in a forest, and tested, and despaired.)

The *others*, to be precise. The iron-faced man had always stationed three guards in that hall, at every hour of the day or night. It was the central node of the upper floor in the west wing, the pivot of the defense. And *he* was a veteran, a master at judging terrain. *He* had seen it at once, the first time he inspected the new battleground.

Three. Here. There. There. Always.

Those had been the iron-faced man's very first commands, in his new post. The Wind knew, from a village woman who had been polishing the floor of that hall when the iron-faced man entered it.

She had been struck dumb by that man.

Not by his face. Hard faces she knew all too well, and, in the knowing, had willed herself to utter stillness. Crouching, in a corner of the hall, like a mouse on an empty floor when felines enter.

Not by his command. Which she remembered, barely, only because it illustrated his terse, harsh nature.

No, she had been dumbfounded because an iron-faced man had examined the hall swiftly, issued his commands, and had then led his men across it slowly. Slowly, and carefully, so that five hours of a worthless menial's tedious labor would not be destroyed.

In a different way, hearing the tale, the Wind had also been struck dumb. Speechless, its voice strangled between a great hatred, and a greater wish that its hatred could be directed elsewhere.

Now, it could. Now, the iron-faced man was gone. And gone, as well, were the men *he* commanded. Men of *his* breed.

Gone, replaced by—*these*.

So difficult it was! Not to howl with glee!

Two Malwa guarded the hall. One priest, one mahamimamsa.

Soldiers would have guarded that hall differently.

Any soldiers.

Common soldiers, of course, would have been more careless than *his* men. Common soldiers, in their idle boredom, would have drifted together in quiet conversation. True, they would have remained standing. But it would have been a slouching sort of stance, weapons casually askew.

Ye-tai, in their feral arrogance, would have taken their seats in the chairs at the table in the center of the hall. And would have soon rung the hall with their boisterous exchanges. Still, even Ye-tai would have sat those chairs facing outward, weapons in hand.

Only a priest and a torturer would guard a room seated at a table, their backs turned to the corridors, their swords casually placed on a third chair to the side, poring over a passage from the Vedas. The priest, vexed, instructing the thick-witted torturer in the subtleties of the text which hallowed his trade.

From the corridor, just beyond the light, the Wind examined them. Briefly.

The time for examination was past.

The Wind, in the darkness, began to coil.

In the first turn of its coil, the Wind draped the remaining length of cord across an unlit lantern suspended on the wall.

The time for silk was past.

In the second turn of its coil, the Wind admired the silk, one last time, and hoped it would be found by a servant woman. Perhaps, if she were unobserved, she would be able to steal it and give her squalid life a bit of beauty.

In the third turn of its coil, and the fourth, the Wind sang silent joy. The Wind sang to an iron face which was gone, now, but which, while there, had watched over the Wind's treasure and kept her from harm. And it sang, as well, to an unknown man who had caused that iron face to be gone, now, when its time was past.

The Wind took the time to sing that silent joy, as it coiled, because the time for joy was also past. But joy is more precious than a cord of silk and must be discarded carefully, lest some small trace remain, impeding the vortex.

An unknown man, from the primitive Occident. In the fifth turn of its coil, the Wind took the time to wonder about that strange West. Wonder, too, was precious. Too precious to cast aside before savoring its splendor.

Were they truly nothing but superstitious heathens, as he had always been told? Ignorant barbarians, who had never seen the face of God?

But the Wind wondered only briefly. The time for wonder was also past.

The vortex coiled and coiled.

Wonder would return, of course, in its proper time. A day would come when, still wondering, the Wind would study the holy writ of the West.

Coiling and coiling. Shedding, in that fearsome gathering, everything most precious to the soul. Shedding them, to make room.

Coiling and coiling.

Hatred did not come easily, to the soul called the Wind. It came with great difficulty. But the Wind's was a human soul; nothing human was foreign to it.

Coiling and coiling and coiling.

The day would come, in the future, studying the holy writ of the western folk, when the Wind would open the pages of *Ecclesiastes*. The Wind would find its answer, then. A small wonder would be replaced by a greater. A blazing, joyful wonder that God should be so great that even the stiff-minded Occident could see his face.

But that was the future. In the dark corridor of the present, in the palace of the Vile One, joy and wonder fled from the Wind. All things true and precious fled, as such creatures do, sensing the storm.

Coiling and coiling. Coiling and coiling.

Love burrowed a hole. Tenderness scampered up a tree. Pity dove to the bottom of a lake. Charity, ruing its short legs, scuttled through the grass. Tolerance and mercy and kindness flapped frantic wings through the lowering sky.

A great soul, the Wind's. Enormous, now, in its coil. With a great emptiness at the center where room had been made. Into the vacuum rushed hatred and rage, fury and fire. Bitterness brought wet weight; cruelty gave energy to the brew. Vengeance gathered the storm.

Monsoon season was very near.

The monsoon, like the Wind, was many things to many people. Different at different times. A thing of many faces.

Kindly faces, in the main. One face was the boon to seamen, in their thousands, bearing cargoes across the sea. Another was the face of life itself, for peasants in their millions, raising crops in the rain which it brought.

But the monsoon had other faces. There was the face that shattered coasts, flooded plains, and slew in the millions.

It was said, and truly, that India was the land created by the monsoon. Perhaps it was for that reason—what man can know?—that the Indian vision of God took such a different form than the vision which gripped the Occident.

The stiff-minded Occident, where God was but the Creator. Yet even the Occident knew of the seasons, and its Preacher penetrated their meaning.

India, where God danced destruction as well, singing, in his terrible great joy: *I am become death, destroyer of worlds.*

For all things, there is a time. For all things, there is a season.

In the palace of the Vile One, that season came.

Monsoon.

For all its incredible speed, the rush was not heard by the Malwa at the table until the Wind was almost upon them. The mahamimamsa never heard it at all, so engrossed was he in poring over the difficult text. One moment he was thinking, the next he was not. The fist which crushed the back of his skull ended all thought forever.

The priest heard, began to turn, began to gape as he saw his companion die. Then gasped, gagged—tried to choke, but could not manage the deed. The Wind's right hand had been a fist to the torturer. The torturer done, the hand spread wide. The edge of the hand between thumb and finger smashed into the priest's throat like a sledge.

The priest was almost dead already, from a snapped spine as well as a collapsed windpipe, but the Wind was in full fury now. The monsoon, by its nature, heaps havoc onto ruin. The terrible hands did their work. The left seized the priest's hair, positioned him; the right, iron palm-heel to the fore, shattered his nose and drove the broken bone into the brain. All in an instant.

The Wind raged across the domed hall, down a corridor.

The end of that short corridor ended in another. Down the left, a short distance, stood the door to the princess' suite. Before that door stood three mahamimamsa. (*He* had only stationed two; three were too many for the narrow space, simply impeding each other.)

The Wind raced down the corridor. The time for silent wafting was over. A guard had but to look around the bend. (*He* had stationed one of his two guards at the bend itself, always watching the hall; the Wind had despaired here also.)

For all the fury of the Wind's coming, there was little noise. The Wind's feet, in their manner of racing, had been a part—small part—of the reason his soul had been given another name, among many. A panther's paws do not slap the ground, clapping their loud and clumsy way, when the panther springs on its prey.

Still, there was a bit of noise. The torturer standing closest to the corridor frowned. What—? More out of boredom than any real alarm, the mahamimamsa moved toward the bend. His companions saw him go, thought little of it. They had heard nothing, themselves. Assumed the tedium had driven him into idle motion.

The Wind blew around the bend. Idleness disappeared. Boredom and tedium vanished. The torturers regretted their sudden absence deeply, much as a man agonizes over a treasure lost because he had not recognized its worth.

The agony was brief.

The first torturer, the—so to speak—alert one, never agonized at all. The dagger came up under his chin, through his tongue, through the roof of his mouth, into his brain. The capacity for agony ended before the agony had time to arrive.

The remaining two torturers had time—just—to startle erect and begin to gape. One, even, began to grope for his sword. He died first, from a slash which severed his throat. The same slash—in the backstroke—did for the other.

There were sounds now, of course. The muffled sound of bodies slumping to the floor, the splatter of arterial blood against walls. Loudest of all, perhaps, the gurgling sound of air escaping. The deep breaths which the torturers had taken in their brief moment of fear were hissing their way out, like suddenly ruptured water pipes.

Ye-tai guards, for all their arrogant sloppiness, would not have failed to hear those sounds. Even through a closed door.

But the priest and the six torturers standing guard in the room beyond that door heard nothing. Or, rather, heard but did not understand the hearing. Unlike Ye-tai warriors, they were not familiar with the sounds by which men go swiftly to their doom.

Other sounds of death, yes. Oh, many of them. Shrieks of pain, they knew. Howls of agony, they knew. Screams, yes. Wails, yes. Groans and moans, it goes without saying. Whimpers and sobs, they could recognize in their sleep. Even the hoarse, whispering, near-silent hiss from a throat torn bloody by hours of squalling terror—that they knew. Knew well.

But the faint sounds which came through the door, those they did not recognize. (Though one torturer, puzzled, stepped to the door and began to open it.) Those were the sounds of quick death, and quick death was a stranger to the men beyond that door.

It would be a stranger no longer.

The full surging fury, now. The door vanished, splintered in passing by the monsoon that wreaked its way into the room.

In its wooden disintegration, the pieces of the door knocked one torturer to the floor, staggered another. The Wind ignored, for the moment, the one on the floor. The one who staggered found the best of all balance—flat on his back, dead. Slain by a truly excellent dagger, which carved its way out of the scrawny chest as easily as it ravened its way in.

The five other Malwa in the room gasped. Their eyes widened with fear and shock. And, most of all, utter disbelief.

Odd sentiments, really, especially on the part of the priest. Had he not himself, time and again, explained to the mahamimamsa that butchery and slaughter were blessed by the Vedas? (Other Indian priests and mystics and sadhus had denied the claim, hotly and bitterly—had even called the Mahaveda cult an abomination in the eyes of God. But they were silent now. The mahamimamsa had done their work.)

And so, when the monsoon billowed into the room, the men therein should have appreciated the divine core of the experience. Yet, they didn't. Scandalous behavior, especially for the priest. The other Malwa in the room could perhaps be excused. For all their ritual pretensions, their desultory half-memorization of the Vedas, the mahamimamsa were simply crude artisans of a trade which is crude by nature. It is understandable, therefore, that when that same trade was plied upon them, they could see nothing in it but a dazzling exhibition of the craft.

The mahamimamsa lying prostrate on the floor never had time to be dazzled. The erupting door which had knocked him down had also stunned him. He just had a momentary, semiconscious glimpse of the stamping iron heel which ruptured his heart.

The next mahamimamsa was more fortunate. The same iron-hard foot hurled him into a corner, but did not paralyze his mind along with his body. So he was privileged. He would be the last to die, after the Wind swept all other life from the room. He would have ample time to admire the supreme craftsmanship of murder.

About four seconds.

The priest died now. From a slash across the carotid artery so short and quick that even Valentinian, had he seen, would have been dazzled by the economy of the deed. Then a mahamimamsa, from an elbow strike to the temple so violent it shredded half his brain with bone fragments and jellied the other half from sheer impact.

Another mahamimamsa, another carotid. Not so miserly, that slash—it almost decapitated the torturer.

Finally, now, a Malwa had time to cry out alarm. The cry was cut short, reduced to a cough, by a dagger thrust to the heart.

Only one mahamimamsa, of the seven Malwa who had been in that room, managed to draw a weapon before he died. A short, slightly curved sword, which he even managed to raise into fighting position. The Wind fell upon him, severed the wrist holding the sword, pulverized his kneecap with a kick, and shattered the torturer's skull with the pommel of the dagger in the backstroke.

In the fourth, and last second, the Wind swirled through the corner of the room where his kick had sent a torturer sprawling, and drove the dagger point through the mahamimamsa's eye and into his brain. The marvelous blade sliced its way out of the skull as easily as it butchered its way in.

Swift death, incredibly swift, but—of course—by no means silent. There had been the shattering of the door, the half-cough/half-cry of one torturer, the crunching of bones, the splatter of blood, the clatter of a fallen sword, and, needless to say, the thump of many bodies falling to the floor and hurled into the walls.

The Wind could hear movement behind the last door barring the way to his treasure. Movement, and the sharp yelps of men preparing for battle. Two men, judging from the voices.

Then—other sounds; odd noises.

The Wind knew their meaning.

The Wind swept to that door, dealt with it as monsoons deal with such things, and raged into the room beyond. The chamber of the Princess Shakuntala. Where, even in sleep, she could not escape the glittering eyes of cruelty.

Two mahamimamsa, just as the Wind had thought.

Unpredictable, eerie wind. For now, at the ultimate moment, at the peaking fury of the storm, the monsoon ebbed. Became a gentle breeze, which simply glided slowly forward, as if content to do no more than rustle the meadows and the flowers in the field.

Only one mahamimamsa, now. The other was dead. Dying, rather.

The Wind examined him briefly. The torturer was expiring on the floor, gagging, both hands clutching his throat. The Wind knew the blow which had collapsed the windpipe—the straight, thumb and finger spread, arm stiff, full-bodied, lunging strike with the vee of the palm. He had delivered that blow's twin not a minute earlier, to the priest in the domed hall.

Had the Wind himself delivered the strike which had sent this mahamimamsa to his doom, the torturer would have been dead before he hit the floor. But the blow had been delivered by another, who, though she had learned her skill from the Wind, lacked his hurricane force.

No matter. The Wind was not displeased. Truly, an excellent blow. Skillfully executed, and—to the Wind's much greater satisfaction—selected with quick and keen intelligence. The man might not die immediately. But, however long he took, he would never utter more than a faint croak in his passing.

In the event, he died now, instantly. The Wind saw no reason for his existence, and finished his life with a short, sudden heel stamp.

The blow was delivered almost idly, however, for the Wind's primary attention was on the final foe, and his demise.

Here, the Wind found cause for displeasure, disgruntlement. Deep grievance; great dissatisfaction.

As was her unfortunate tendency, the imperious princess had not been able to resist the royal gesture.

True, admitted the Wind, she had obviously started well. The swift, sharp kick to the groin. Well chosen, that, from the vast armory the Wind had given her. A paralyzing blow—semiparalyzing, at the very least—and, best of all, paralyzing to the vocal cords. A sharp cough, a low moan, no more.

She had delivered that kick first, the Wind knew. Knew for a certainty, though the Wind had not been present in the room.

Just as the Wind had taught her, when dealing with two opponents. The quick, disabling strike to one; the lethal blow to the other; return and finish the first. (It was a simple sonata form which the Wind itself did not always follow, of course. But the Wind was a maestro, skilled in variations because it was master of the tune.)

So far—excellent. But then—impetuous hoyden!

The Wind puffed old exasperation. How many times had the child been told? How many? Headstrong girl!

But the raging vortex was fast disappearing. Faster than it had gathered, in fact, much faster. Emotions which came easily to the Wind were pouring back in, singing their return. Among these—great among these—was humor.

Truly, in its own way, a comical scene.

A large, heavy man. Heavy head, atop a heavy neck, atop a heavy torso. Clutching his groin. Groaning. Grimacing with pain. Staggering about like a wounded buffalo. With a girl—a smallish girl, mind, for all that her extraordinary body had been shaped under the Wind's ruthless regimen—hanging on to that massive head with both little hands.

Perfectly positioned, those hands, that the Wind allowed. The left, clutching the shaggy beard; the right, rooted firmly in the shaggy mane. Perfectly positioned for the deadly, twisting, driving contraction that would snap the man's neck like a twig.

If, that is, the man had been half his size, and she twice hers. As it was, it was a bit like a monkey trying to break the neck of a buffalo. The buffalo staggering about, swinging the monkey wildly to and fro.

The furious black eyes of the princess met the gaze of the Wind. The Wind stooped, hopped about, made soft monkey noises, scratched. The black eyes blazed pure rage.

"Oh—*all right!*" she hissed. She released her grip, bounced onto her toes. An instant for balance, an instant for poise, an instant for thought.

The swift kick to the knee was excellent—a copy of the one delivered by the Wind to a torturer in the room beyond. His had pulverized the knee, hers simply dislodged the kneecap. No matter—the man was disabled either way. And the position of his head—

Yes! The Wind was deeply gratified by the palm-strike to the bridge of the nose. For the Wind, that blow was itself lethal. But the girl—*this time*—delivered it as she had been taught. Speed, fluid grace. She simply didn't have the mass and sheer male strength to shatter strong bones with every blow. So, for her, the palm strike was to daze the foe, turn his head, set up—

The elbow smash to the temple which followed, like a lightning bolt, was a perfect duplicate of the one which the Wind had delivered to another mahamimamsa in the adjoining room, less than a minute earlier. True, the Wind's strike had slain his man instantly, whereas the princess needed two more before her opponent slumped lifeless to the floor.

So?

Only the soul matters, in the end.

The Wind died away, then. Fled, dancing, back to the Great Country. It would rise again, like the monsoon, when Maharashtra called. But for now, it was gone.

Only the man Raghunath Rao remained, cradling the treasure of his soul in his arms, whispering her name, kissing her eyes, weeping softly into her hair.

EPILOGUE

A soldier and a general

Once he was satisfied that his men had finished all the necessary preparations for their departure, Kungas decided that it was time to pay a courtesy call. It would be a long journey to the Emperor's camp at the siege of Ranapur. At least a month, probably more, judging from the appearance of the caravan—and his past experience with the caravan's master. He and his men would be spending a considerable time with the party of foreigners they had been assigned to escort. Best to be introduced properly, in advance, so that no unfortunate misunderstandings would arise.

Especially with *those* foreigners, thought Kungas, as he passed through the courtyard of Venandakatra's palace. He stopped for a moment, to admire the scenery.

A harsh life had taught Kungas many lessons. One of those was to keep your sentiments hidden. The world had always presented a hard face to him; he returned the compliment. *Old Iron-face*, he knew, was one of the nicknames his men had for him. He did not object. No, not in the slightest.

Still, even for Kungas, it was hard not to grin.

Four of the Ye-tai were still alive, barely. One of them was even still making some noise. Small, mewling sounds. With luck, thought Kungas, that one might survive another day. Another day of agony and hopelessness.

Kungas would be gone by then, but he would be able to cherish the memory. He and his men had been assigned the task of cutting the stakes and spitting the Ye-tai. It had been the most pleasurable duty they'd had in years.

His eye fell on a figure perched among the Ye-tai, and his pleasure vanished.

Not all of it.

They had done what they could for the old woman. They had tried to smuggle in a longer stake, but Venandakatra had spotted it and forbidden its use. The servant was to be spitted on the same short stakes as the Ye-tai, in order to prolong the agony.

The mental grin returned. It was a bleak, bleak grin.

But we'd expected that. Too bad we couldn't get any real poison, in the short time we had. But the women in the kitchen mixed up what they could. Venandakatra watched us like a hawk, to make sure we didn't slip her anything to eat or drink. But we'd expected that, too. By the time we fit the poor soul onto the stake, the stuff had all dried. Venandakatra would have had to scrape the stake itself to spot it.

He started to turn away. Then, moved by an impulse, turned back. His eyes quickly scanned the courtyard. No one was watching.

Kungas made a very slight bow to the dead crone. He thought it was the least he could do. By the time the villagers would be allowed to remove her body, there would not be much left. The priests would refuse, of course, to do the rituals. So, the poor wretch was at least owed that much from her killer.

It was not, in any real sense, a religious gesture. Like most of his people, Kungas still retained traces of the Buddhist faith which the Kushans had adopted after conquering Bactria and north India. Adopted, and then championed. In its heyday, Peshawar, the capital of the Kushan Empire, had been the great world center of Buddhist worship and scholarship. But the glory days of the Kushan empire were gone. The stupas lay in ruins; the monks and scholars dead or scattered to the wind. The Ye-tai, on their own, had persecuted Buddhism savagely. And after the barbarians were absorbed into the rising Malwa power, the persecution had simply intensified. To the brutality of the Ye-tai had been added the calculating ruthlessness of the Malwa. They intended their Mahaveda cult to stamp out all rival tendencies within the great umbrella of Hinduism. Needless to say, they had absolutely no ruth toward Buddhists or Jains.

Between the persecution and his own harsh life, therefore, Kungas retained very little of any religious sentiment. So, his slight bow to the dead crone was more in the way of a warrior's nod to a courageous soul. Perhaps that recognition would comfort her soul, a bit, waiting for its new life. (If there was a new life. Or such a thing as a soul. Kungas was skeptical.)

Not that her soul probably needs much comfort, he thought wryly as he walked away. *She seemed to enjoy the Ye-tai squawling even more than we did. Maybe we did her a disservice, poisoning her.*

He rubbed the new wound on his face, briefly. It was scabbed over now, and would heal soon enough. The pain was irrelevant. Kungas did not think the scar would even last beyond a few months. The man who put it there was a weak man, for all that he'd been in a rage. And a quirt is not, all things considered, the best weapon to use, if you want to scar up an old veteran.

And I'd much rather carry around a quirt-scar than be stuck on a stake.

The thought made him pause, brought another impulse.
A very wry sense of humor, Kungas had. He stopped and
turned back again; again examined the courtyard to make
sure no spies were about; again bowed slightly. This time
to the Ye-tai.

*I thank you, O mighty Ye-tai. You saved my life. And
probably that of all the Kushans.*

As he walked out of the courtyard, he thought back on
the episode.

*Leave it to Venandakatra—the great warrior, the brilliant
tactician. What a genius. As soon as he got the news, he
rushed here ahead of his little army. Accompanied only by
a few priests and that handful of foreigners. Within the
hour, he was in a full rage. He ordered all the Ye-tai guards
of the palace impaled—in public, right in front of them—
and then noticed that the only soldiers he had to enforce
the order were a Rajput cavalry troop. Leaving aside a
hundred or so Malwa infantry, who ran like rabbits as soon
as the Ye-tai went berserk.*

*Oh, what a fray that was! And after it was over, of course,
he could hardly impale us next to them. Who'd do it? Not
the Rajputs! Those snotty pricks suffered most of the
casualties, except a handful of common soldiers who didn't
run fast enough. We were unarmed, at the beginning—at
the genius' own command—so the Ye-tai ignored us. By
the time we could collect our weapons, it was almost over.*

Grudgingly:

*I'll give that much to the Rajputs. They fought well, as
always.*

*But it still would have been touch and go, if the foreigners
hadn't waded in. Lethal, they were. Absolutely murderous.*

He pondered that last thought.

*Why, I wonder? The Rajputs were happy enough, of
course, to chop up Ye-tai dogs. So were we, once we got
our weapons. But why should foreigners care? I can*

*understand why they'd side with Venandakatra—they're
his guests, after all. By why do it with such avid enthusiasm?
You'd think they'd had some quarrel of their own with the
Ye-tai.*

With his usual quick pace, Kungas was soon well down
the tiled entryway to the courtyard. He was now beyond
sight of anyone watching him from the palace. For the first
time, the amusement in his mind surfaced on Kungas' face.
Barely, of course. Only someone who knew the man
intimately would have interpreted that faint, hairline curve
in his lips as a smile.

*Oh, yes, they were beautiful. I think they butchered almost
as many Ye-tai as the Rajputs did. And didn't suffer anything
more than scratches, except for that kid. Too bad about
him. But he'll recover, eventually.*

The thought brought him back to his current assignment.

*Yes, I think a courtesy call is quite the right thing to do.
A very courteous courtesy call.*

*I definitely want to be on civil terms with those men.
Oh, yes. Very civil. This assignment's a bit like escorting a
group of tigers.*

Then:

*Now that I think about it, I'm not sure I wouldn't rather
have tigers.*

It took Kungas a while to find the party he was looking
for. To his surprise, he discovered that the foreigners had
been assigned a position at the very tail end of the huge
caravan. After the supply train, right in the middle of the
horde of camp followers.

Odd place for honored guests.

As he walked down the line of the caravan, Kungas puzzled
over the matter.

*Now that I think about it, our great lord did seem a bit
peeved with them. Their leader, especially. I noticed*

Venandakatra casting quite a few glares in his direction. Didn't think much of it, at the time. I assumed it was just the great lord's mood, being spread around as usual. He has no reason to be pissed off at the foreigners, that I can see. Did him a service, they did. Without them, a few of the Ye-tai might have gotten to the bastard and carved him up.

Odd.

Eventually, Kungas found his party. The leader was standing off to the side of the road, watching the progress in loading the howdahs on the two elephants assigned to the foreigners. He and the two men with him were apparently seeking relief from the midday heat in the shade of the trees. That alone marked them for foreigners, leaving aside their pale skins and outlandish costumes. Shade brought little relief from the humid swelter. The trees simply cut down the slight breeze and provided a haven for insects.

Looking at him, Kungas was struck again by the disparity between the man and his position.

Weirdest general I ever saw. Too young by half, and twice as deadly as any general I ever met. That man is pure murder with a sword.

Thoughts of deadliness drew Kungas' eyes to the general's companions. They were standing a few feet away from their leader, in the posture of guards.

Kungas examined the one on the left first—the smaller one.

I do believe that is the wickedest-looking man I ever saw in my life. Like the world's meanest mongoose.

He transferred his gaze to the one on the right—the huge one.

Legends live. The great ogre of the Himalayas walks among us. With a face carved out of the very stone of the great mountains.

The general caught sight of him. He seemed to stiffen a

bit, but Kungas wasn't certain. The general had one of those expressionless faces which are almost impossible to read. Kungas marched up to him. Summoned up his poor Greek.

"You is General Belisarius? Envoy for—from Rome?"

The general nodded.

"I is name Kungas. Commander for—of Lord Venandakatra's Kushan—ah, group? Force. Lord Venandakatra has—ah, what is word?—"

"I speak Kushan," said the general.

Kungas sighed inward relief.

"Thank you. I fear my Greek is wretched. We have been assigned to serve as your escort during the trip to Ranapur."

Again, Kungas found it almost impossible to read the man's expression. But, yes, he did seem a bit stiff. As if he were unhappy to see the Kushan. Kungas couldn't think of a reason why that would be true, but he was almost sure he was correct.

However, the general was cordial. And his Kushan was certainly good. Excellent, in fact—without even a trace of an accent.

"A pleasure, Kungas." His voice was a rich baritone.

The general hesitated, and then said:

"Please do not take this the wrong way, Kungas. But I must say I'm surprised to see you. We don't really need an escort. We didn't have one on the trip here from Bharakuccha. We're quite capable of taking care of ourselves."

Kungas' face cracked into a tiny smile.

"Yes, I have seen. However, the lord was quite insistent."

"Ah." The general was diverted for a moment, swiping at a fly which landed on his neck. Kungas noted, however, that the foreigner's keen brown eyes never left off their scrutiny of him. And that he killed the fly regardless.

After flicking away the dead insect, the general commented idly:

"I would have thought you would be assigned to join the

hunt for the princess and her rescuers—ah, excuse me, abductors."

The iron face grew harder still.

"I fear my lord has developed a certain distrust for us. I do not understand why. The princess was not resc—ah, abducted—while *we* were guarding her."

Kungas thought the general was fighting back a smile. But he was not certain. A hard man to read.

"Besides," Kungas continued, "Lord Venandakatra really has no need for us to join the pursuit. He already has hundreds of Rajput cavalry scouring the countryside, and well over a thousand other troops."

The foreign general looked away for a moment. When the eyes turned back, his gaze seemed particularly intent.

"What is your professional assessment, Kungas? Do you think the princess and her—ah, abductors—will be caught?"

"One abductor only, General."

"One?" The general frowned. "I had heard a whole band of vicious cutthroats were responsible. The palace was a scene of utter massacre, according to rumor."

"Massacre? Oh, yes. Massacre, indeed. The majordomo, three high priests, and two mahamimamsa guards garroted. Eleven priests and mahamimamsa butchered in their beds—their throats cut by a razor, apparently. A priest and a mahamimamsa slain in the great hall. Handwork, that, by a deadly assassin. Three mahamimamsa knifed outside the antechamber. A priest and six more mahamimamsa guards slaughtered in the antechamber. Blade-work again, mostly. Then, two more mahamimamsa slain in the princess' own sleeping chamber. Assassin handwork again, although—"

"Although?"

Kungas made a quick assessment. Partly, the assessment was based on his memory of Venandakatra's scowls toward the general. But, in the main, it was based on the faint but unmistakable trace of humor in the general's voice when he used the word "abductors."

"Well, as it happens, I examined the scene of the—ah, crime—myself. At Lord Venandakatra's behest. That is why I said 'one abductor.' The entire operation was carried out by one man."

"*One* man?" demanded the general. But he did not seem particularly astonished.

Kungas nodded. "Yes. One man. The trail of slaughter was that left by a single man, not a group. One man, alone. A man by the name of Raghunath Rao. The Panther of Maharashtra, he is sometimes called. Or the Wind of the Great Country. Other names. It was he. I am certain of it. He is known to have a personal attachment to the princess. There are not more than three—possibly four—assassins in India who are that deadly. And none has that proficiency with their bare hands and feet."

Kungas almost grimaced. "No one else can shatter bones and pulverize bodies that way. That is why—ah, that is, the two mahamimamsa who were killed in the princess' own chamber were also slain by hand. But the blows, though skillful, had none of the pure fury of the Panther's."

The general frowned.

"But—you said one man—"

"The princess. She killed them. She was trained by Raghunath Rao, you see. Such, at least, is my personal belief. I watched her dance, many times, in the long months I served as her captor—ah, guardian. Wonderful dancer, but— well, there was always that scent of the assassin about her movements. And in Amaravati, at the end of the siege, she killed several Ye-tai who attacked her in her room. One of them after she was disarmed."

The general's eyes widened. Slightly.

Kungas lowered his head, stared at the ground. When he spoke, his voice was as hard as his face.

"As to your first question—will they be captured? Yes. They will. Their position is hopeless."

"Why are you so certain?"

Kungas shrugged, looked up. "She is but a girl, General. A princess. Oh, true, a princess like no other you've ever seen. A princess out of legend. But still—she's never been hunted. She has no experience, or real training, in the skills of eluding a thousand men through the forest and mountains."

Kungas shook his head, forestalling the general's question. "It doesn't matter. Even with Raghunath Rao to help her and guide her, she—" A pause. "You've hunted, I'm sure, in a large party. Or even with just one other man. Who sets the pace? Who frightens off the game? Who misses the shot?"

The general replied instantly: "The weakest man. The poorest hunter."

Kungas nodded. "Exactly. So—well, if Raghunath Rao were alone, I believe he would outwit and escape his pursuers. But even for him, the task would be extraordinarily difficult, with such an immense number of hunters on his trail. Encumbered by the princess—" He shrugged again. "It is simply not possible. No, they will be caught."

Kungas saw the general glance aside. He seemed to stiffen a bit. Perhaps.

Kungas followed his glance. The last members of the foreign party had arrived and were approaching their howdah. The young black prince from Ethiopia and his women.

Kungas had heard tales of the prince. His rampant lust; his viciousness toward his concubines. He had shrugged off the tales, for the most part. Resentful, malicious envy toward royalty and high nobility was so common as to make all such tales suspect.

But, as he watched, he decided that the tales were perhaps true, after all. The women certainly seemed fearful and abject. All of them were veiled and kept their heads down. Very submissive. None of their faces could even be seen, so timid were the wretched creatures. There were none of the flashing, excited, inquisitive gazes one normally saw from young girls embarking on a journey.

One woman's face was partially visible to Kungas, now. She was weeping softly, comforted by a second woman who was holding her and guiding her along. The prince suddenly cuffed one of the other women on the back of her head. Then cuffed the last in the little group. Hurrying them aboard, out of royal petulance and impatience. Apparently, however, the prince's temper was not particularly aroused. The young royal was massively built, if not tall. Wide-shouldered, thick-chested, extremely muscular. With that frame, his cuffs could have easily knocked the girls off their feet. Yet they barely seemed to nudge them.

One girl was hoisted up into the howdah, helped by the black soldier who was apparently serving as the mahout. Then another, the weeping one.

"They are all Maratha, I understand," commented Kungas, making idle conversation.

The general nodded. "Yes, Prince Eon's developed quite a taste for the breed. He has a whole gaggle of the creatures." A little laugh. "I'm not sure how many, actually. Nobody can keep track."

A third girl, the one who had been comforting the weeper, made ready to climb aboard. Smallish. Much darker-skinned than the average Maratha. Very lithe in her movements, too. Kungas admired the fluid grace with which the girl took the hand of the mahout, began the climb up the great elephant. Her bare foot stretched out—

A beautiful dancer. Such incredible grace. Lithe, fluid. And I was always struck by her feet. The prettiest feet I ever saw. Quicksilver. High-arched, slim-heeled, perfectly shaped toes.

The girl entered the howdah. The fourth and fifth girls followed. The prince went up last, drew the curtains behind him.

Kungas stood as rigid as a post. He could not help it. Neither that, nor his face. Like iron, his face, as always when he faced danger. Now, like carbon steel.

At his side, he sensed the general's alertness. Behind, he could hear the slight sound of the general's guards moving forward.

This may be the most dangerous moment in my entire life.

His had been a harsh existence, filled with hard decisions. Now, Kungas made the easiest decision he had ever made. And, he thought, perhaps the best—certainly the purest— in a generally misspent life. He took some pride, too, in the fact that his own survival played not the slightest role in making the decision.

Which doesn't solve my immediate problem. Keeping from getting my throat slit. No point in trying to pretend—oh, no, not with this general. Not with those men behind me.

Besides—

A rare grin broke out on his face. (To Kungas, a grin. No one else would have called it that. A flaw in the iron, perhaps.)

"So many women. Well, we'll certainly have to make sure that they're well protected. I shall instruct my men to keep anyone from pestering the prince's concubines. From even approaching the howdah, in fact. Or his tent, at night. He's a prince, after all, bound to be full of royal pride. I'm sure he'd be outraged if anyone caught so much as a glimpse of his women."

Kungas could sense the quick thoughts in the man next to him. A moment or so later, the general spoke. Still, a trace of hesitation in his voice.

"An excellent idea, I think. Of course, your own men—"

Kungas waved his hand casually. "Oh, I shall give them firm instructions to keep their own distance from the howdah. I'll do the same myself, for that matter."

The general's face broke into an odd, crooked smile. If there had been a trace of hesitation, it seemed to vanish.

"That'll be difficult for you and your men, I imagine. That sort of self-control around women." An apologetic cough. "Given the Kushan reputation."

Kungas frowned slightly. "Reputa—?"

The general laughed. "Oh, come now! Don't deny it, Kungas. It's well known. You can't trust Kushans around women, particularly young women. *Especially* virgins. Not" —a chuckle— "that there are any virgins left in *that* howdah."

Kungas was still frowning.

"Such an act!" admired the general. "But there's no point in it, Kungas, I assure you. Not in *this* crowd. Why, I remember swapping a few amusing anecdotes with Venandakatra himself on the subject, during our journey from Bharakuccha. Although, now I think about it—my memory's a bit vague, I'm afraid. I was quite drunk, that evening. But—um, yes, now that I think about it, I seem to recall that I was telling all the stories. Odd, actually. It all seemed to come to the great lord as quite a revelation."

Anyone in the world, now, would have agreed that the expression on Kungas' face was a grin. The smallest, faintest, thinnest grin ever seen, true. But a grin, a veritable grin, it could not be denied.

"Alas. Our reputation is finally out. And we've been so careful to keep our talents hidden, all these months." He shook his head ruefully. "Well, it can't be helped. Everyone will know, now. Damn. Husbands will start watching their wives. Fathers their daughters."

"Princes their concubines."

Kungas glanced at the general's guards. "Soldiers, their camp women."

The general scratched his chin. "I foresee a scandal, I'm afraid. The talk of the caravan. Even Lord Venandakatra himself will probably hear of it. I can see the scene now. Kushan soldiers—ruffians, the lot of 'em, filled with unbridled lust—constantly surrounding the foreigners' howdahs and tents, filled with so many lovely girls. Flies drawn to honey. Dealing brutally, of course, with any other men who should happen to sniff around."

"We have a short way with competitors," agreed Kungas, "when it comes to women." Casually, his hand gripped the hilt of his sword, drew the blade an inch or so out of the scabbard, clashed it back loudly.

"Yes, yes," mused the general. "Pity the poor Malwa chap who should just happen to wander by, idly curious about the women."

Kungas shuddered. "I shudder to think of the poor fellow's treatment." Out of the corner of his eye, he saw one of the general's guards grinning. The one who looked like a mongoose. The most evil-looking grin he had ever seen, for a certainty.

"Then, of course," continued Kungas, "should any enterprising Malwa manage to slip through the Kushan escort and make his way to—"

"Oh, terrible!" exclaimed the general. His eyes squinted. His large hand gripped his own sword hilt. "He'd be butchered. By keen-eyed cataphracts or sarwen always on guard to fend off the endless, relentless, persistent hounding of their women by those horrible, lust-filled, lascivious Kushans. Ah, such a tragic case of mistaken identity."

The general spread his hands.

"But, the Lord Venandakatra could hardly complain. He assigned you to escort us, after all. Probably—" here came the general's grin, which no one in the world would have mistaken for anything else "—with that very purpose in mind. Making us miserable, I mean."

Kungas nodded sagely. "The great lord *does* seem to be quite irritated with you. I can't imagine why."

The sounds of a caravan setting into motion began filtering down the line. Kungas looked toward the front—which, of course, was far out of sight.

"Well, I'd best be off. Round up my men and explain our duties to them. Very carefully. Making sure they understand what they need to understand, and not what they don't. We don't want any—ah, how shall I put it? Walking a tightrope can be done, so long as you maintain the proper balance."

"Well said," commented the general. "A man after my own heart. You don't anticipate—"

"From *my* men? No, none. If I tell them to paint their faces blue and keep their left eyes closed all the way to Ranapur, well then—*they'll damn well paint their faces blue and keep their left eyes closed all the way to Ranapur*. And be right fucking quick about it, and keep their fucking mouths fucking shut. Orders are orders. Obey. Just do it." The iron face was back. "I'm not the man to brook insolence."

"I can well imagine," said the general.

Quite attractive, thought Kungas, that odd little crooked smile. He gave his own smile, such as it was, and departed.

When the Kushan was out of sight, around a bend of the road, Valentinian whispered to Belisarius: "That was a close call."

Belisarius shook his head.

"No, Valentinian, it wasn't close at all. I cannot imagine a world, anywhere, anytime, in any turn of the wheel, where that man would not make that same decision."

The general turned away, headed toward his horse.

As he left, he muttered something under his breath.

"Did you catch that, Anastasius?"

The giant grinned. "Of course. So would you, if your ears were attuned to philosophical thoughts like they should be. Instead of—"

Valentinian snarled. "Just answer the fucking question!"

"He said: *Only the soul matters, in the end.*"

A prince and a princess

The prince relaxed. His fingers let the curtain fall back into place. The fabric moved but a quarter of an inch. He had opened it only the merest crack.

"He's gone," he said softly. The prince leaned back against the silk-covered cushions which lined the interior of the howdah. He blew out his cheeks with relief.

The four Maratha women in the howdah reacted in various ways to the news. The fifth woman, who was not Maratha, watched their reactions carefully. She had been taught that the ways in which people relaxed from stress told you much about them. Taught by a man who was an expert in stressful situations and their aftermath.

The one Maratha woman she knew—had known for years—clutched her yet more tightly. But, for the first time since they had met again, under the most unexpected circumstances, stopped weeping. Her name was Jijabai, and her mind was lost in horror. But perhaps, Shakuntala thought—hoped—the horror would begin to recede and sanity return. Horror had begun for that woman when she had been taken from her princess. Now that her princess had returned, perhaps Jijabai could return also.

But there was nothing more that Shakuntala could do for Jijabai at the moment, beyond hold her. So she gazed elsewhere.

The Maratha woman seated immediately to the prince's right blew out her own cheeks, smiled broadly, and leaned into the prince's shoulder. The prince's arm enfolded her gently. She closed her eyes and nuzzled the prince's neck.

Shakuntala knew a bit about this one, from her conversations with the prince the day before. Her name was Tarabai, and she was the prince's favorite. Prince Eon had asked her to return with him to his homeland and become one of his concubines. Tarabai had readily agreed.

The prince had obviously been delighted by that answer. Almost surprised, like a boy whose idle daydream had come true.

Shakuntala had found his delight quite informative. She had been trained to observe people by the most observant man she had ever known. A man whose sense of humor was as keen as his perception—and that, too, that wry and tolerant way of perceiving people, Shakuntala had learned from him.

So, on the one hand, she was amused by the prince's delight. What woman in Tarabai's position—a Maratha captive cast into a hellhole of a slave brothel—would not have jumped at the chance to become a royal concubine? (A true concubine, in the honored and traditional sense—not one of the abject creatures which the Malwa called by the name. A woman with a recognized and respected status in the royal household. Whose children would not be in line for the succession, but would be assured positions of power and prestige.)

But there had been nothing supercilious in Shakuntala's amusement. Quite the contrary. She had respected the prince for his bemused delight. She had been taught to respect that kind of unpresumptuous modesty. Not by teaching, but by example. By the example of a man who never boasted, though he had more to boast about that any man produced by India since the days chronicled in the *Mahabharata* and the *Ramayana*.

(But that thought brought pain, so she pushed it aside.)

Tarabai's actions, and the prince's response, told Shakuntala much else. Her own father, the Emperor of Andhra, had possessed many concubines. Shakuntala had often observed them in her father's presence. Her father had never mistreated his concubines. But not one of them would have dared initiate such casual and intimate contact in the presence of others. Her own mother, the Empress, would not have done so. (Not even, Shakuntala suspected, in the privacy of the Emperor's bedchamber.)

A cold, harsh, aloof man, her father had been. Every inch the Emperor. He had brooked familiarity from no one, man or woman. Nor, so far as the princess knew, had he ever expressed the slightest tenderness to anyone himself. Certainly not to her.

There was no grievance in that thought, however. Her father had been preoccupied, his entire life, with the threat of Malwa. Years ago, Shakuntala had come to realize that, in his own hard way, her father had truly loved her. He had placed her in the care of a Maratha chieftain—in defiance of all custom and tradition—for no other reason than that he treasured the girl and would give her the greatest gift within his power. To that gift, the princess owed her very life.

(That thought, however, brought pain again. The princess forced her thoughts back to the moment.)

So, a gentle and tender prince as well as a modest one. A warm-hearted prince.

And a resourceful one!

Shakuntala repressed a giggle. Childish! *Stop*.

It was difficult. The princess had an excellent sense of humor, when her temper was not aroused. And, for all its tension, the episode had been rather comical.

The prince had found her in the cupboard where Raghunath Rao had hidden her. Just as planned. On a shelf barely big enough to fit a girl, a jug of water, a bit of food, and—her nose wrinkled slightly, remembering—a bedpan. With a stack of linens piled on top of her.

As soon as he had taken possession of the guest suite in a corner of the palace, Prince Eon had sped to open the cupboard and retrieve Shakuntala. In passable Marathi, the prince had begun to explain the details of the scheme. Shakuntala had kept her eyes averted, for the most part. The prince had been in a hurry to wash the blood and gore off his body. (The princess, hearing the sounds of the battle raging in the palace grounds, had been hard-pressed not to climb out of the cupboard and watch.)

So his man—dawazz was his title—had poured the bath for him right there in the bedchamber, while Eon stripped himself naked. Shakuntala had peeked, once, not so much out of girlish curiosity as imperial assessment. A very impressive body, the prince had. But she had been far more impressed by the casual, unthinking way in which he cleaned the grisly residue of mayhem from it.

So. A courageous prince. Skilled and experienced in battle, for all his youth. As princes must be, in the new world created by the Malwa. She had approved. Greatly.

The sound of voices—Rajputs quarreling with foreigners—had come through the door. The prince's man immediately seized a huge spear. But the prince hissed quick instructions in their own language. Suddenly, the dawazz leaned the spear against a wall and began ambling toward the door, wearing such a grin as Shakuntala had never seen in her life.

The prince instantly raced to the cupboard and removed the traces of Shakuntala's habitation. There was very little to hide—simply an empty water jug and a bedpan half filled with urine. The prince placed both items in plain view, after emptying the bedpan in the bloody water of his bath.

Then, before she quite realized what was happening, Eon had seized her and flung her onto the bed. A moment later, the prince—still naked—was lying completely on top of her. He swept the bed linens over them, and immediately began heaving his buttocks vigorously. Shakuntala herself had been completely hidden—partly by the linens, but mostly by the prince himself. He was not that much taller than she, but twice as broad. She had felt like a kitten lying under a tiger. She could see absolutely nothing except the prince's bare chest.

A moment later, the voices had entered the room, still quarreling. She could understand the Rajput, now. Belatedly, Lord Venandakatra had ordered a search of the entire palace and its grounds. The Rajput officer in charge of the squad was apologetic. Without quite saying so, he made clear that he thought the entire exercise was idiotic. A great lord in a childish snit, squawling at the world indiscriminately. The criminals had obviously fled the palace entirely. Hadn't the three Ye-tai dogs guarding the front gate been found butchered, the morning after the massacre? Almost two full days had passed since. It was absurd to think—but—orders were orders.

Prince Eon had raised his head, then, a bit. Roaring royal outrage. But his buttocks never ceased plunging up and down, his groin thrusting at her own. Her body, of course, was still clothed. But the Rajputs had no way of seeing that. The only visible part of the princess was her hair. Long, black hair, in no way different from that of most Indian women. And then, a moment later, a little hand which reached up and clutched the prince's neck with apparent passion. Quite apparent passion, judging from the unknown girl's soft moaning. (Shakuntala hadn't been quite sure she was making the right noise. But, like all bright girls in a large and crowded palace, she had done her share of eavesdropping, in days past at Amavarati.)

Keeping their eyes averted from the prince at his sport, the Rajputs conducted a very hasty search of the suite. Then, uttering many apologies, scurried out.

As soon as they were gone, Eon had immediately climbed

off Shakuntala. Had made fulsome apologies, stressing the dire necessity which had precipitated his actions. Emphasized the depth of his respect for the imperial personage and dignity of the princess. Reiterated the perilous—

Shakuntala had waved off his apologies. Had responded with a most dignified—indeed, regal—acknowledgment of the sincerity of his regrets. Had uttered the most royal— indeed, imperial—phrases assuring the prince that she recognized both the necessity of his actions and appreciated the quickness of his wits. Had added further assurances that she had no doubt of his own regal propriety, good breeding, and monarchical majesty.

But then—unable to resist—had added demurely:

"Yet I fear, prince, that one of your provinces is in revolt."

It had been hard to tell. The prince's skin was even darker than a Dravidian's. But she thought he had definitely blushed.

Especially after the dawazz added, with that amazing grin:

"Indeed so! Most insolent uprising! Prince do well to beat rebel down!" Then, with a flourish: "Here! Use my spear!"

Remembering, and smiling, Shakuntala's eyes met those of the prince. A little smile came to his own face. Then, a subtle expression—a wry, apologetic twist of his lips; a little roll of his eyes; a faint shrug—combined with an equally subtle movement of his arm. His left arm, the one which was not encircling Tarabai.

Understanding, Shakuntala eased over and nestled against his shoulder. His left arm encircled her. She turned her face into his muscular neck. A moment later, she felt Jijabai snuggling into her own left shoulder. Trembling with fear at the princess' departure. Shakuntala cradled the girl and pressed her head into her own neck. She felt Jijabai's shivering ease.

Inwardly, she sighed. It would be tedious—even, after a

time, uncomfortable—spending days and weeks in that position. But she suppressed the thought ruthlessly. They were at war, and war required many tactics. This tactic had worked before. A tried and tested tactic. Should anyone manage to look within the howdah, they would see nothing but the notorious Axumite prince, surrounded as always by his submissive women. Whose faces were rarely seen, of course, so timid had the creatures become in his brutal presence.

Across the prince's chest, her eyes met those of Tarabai. The Maratha girl smiled shyly.

She was still in awe, Shakuntala realized. The Maratha women had known for some time that the foreigners into whose care they had placed themselves were engaged in some strange activity. (And had sensed, even, that the activity was in some way opposed to the hated Malwa.) But they had not known the exact nature of that activity until that very morning. Just before departing for the caravan, the Maratha women had been ushered into the room, Shakuntala had been introduced to them by Eon and his men, and the plan explained.

Hearing the name, Jijabai had looked up, begun to cry out in startlement. The cry had been choked off by Shakuntala herself, embracing her former maidservant. From that moment until they climbed into the howdah, the girl had not stopped weeping. Shakuntala had stayed by her the entire time. At first, from love and pity. Then, as well, from a realization that the pose was perfect for their purpose.

The other three Maratha women had been too stunned to do more than walk through the exercise in a daze. Which, also, had been perfect, if unplanned.

Tarabai was no longer stunned. Eon's close presence, Shakuntala realized, had restored the girl's courage. But she was still in awe. The girl had all the signs of a simple upbringing. Of vaisya or sudra birth, undoubtedly (insofar as Maratha measured such things—but that thought, as ever, was too painful to bear, so Shakuntala banished it). Never in her life had Tarabai imagined she would share a howdah—much less a man's chest!—with royalty.

Shakuntala now gazed at the two Maratha women whom she did not know. They, too, were staring at her with round eyes. But there was more than simple awe in those eyes, she realized. The two women were almost shivering with terror. Then, seeing the princess' eyes upon them, the two women dropped their heads. Now, they did begin to shiver.

This must stop, thought Shakuntala.

"Look at me," she commanded. For all its youthful timbre, her voice was sharp. Not harsh, simply—*commanding*.

Immediately, the women raised their eyes. Eon, listening, was impressed.

"You are very frightened," stated the princess. After a moment, the women nodded their heads.

"You fear the Malwa fury, if they discover what is happening. You fear you will be destroyed."

Again, they nodded.

For a moment, Shakuntala simply gazed at them. Then said:

"Your fear is understandable. But you must conquer it. Fear will gain you nothing, and may betray us all into disaster. You must be courageous. These men—these foreigners—are good men. Brave, and resourceful. You know this to be true."

She waited. After a moment, the two women nodded.

"You trust these men."

Again, waited. Again, the nods.

"Then trust them. And me as well."

Waited.

"I am your princess. Your empress, now. I am the rightful heir to the throne of Andhra."

The Maratha women nodded immediately. Majarashtra was one of the few lands of India where a woman in power was accepted without question, if she held that power legitimately. Maratha women had even led armies, in the past.

(But thoughts of Majarashtra brought pain, so she forced her way past them.)

"I call you to service, women of the Great Country. Andhra will rise again, and the Malwa filth be destroyed. To that end I devote my life. If you are destroyed by the Malwa, your empress will be destroyed with you. You will not be deserted."

After a moment, the women bowed. The bow, Shakuntala acknowledged, but did not cherish in her heart. The fading fear in their eyes, and the hint of dawning courage, brought her great joy.

(But joy brought pain, and so she banished it. There would be no joy in her life, she knew. Only courage, and duty. She had made her vow to these women, and she would keep it. Though that vow would banish joy forever.)

She heard the prince mutter something. A phrase in his own language.

"What did you say?" she asked, glancing up at him.

His dark eyes were staring at her, very seriously. After a moment, the prince said softly:

"What I said was: 'And so, once again, Belisarius was right.' "

Shakuntala frowned, puzzled. She knew who Belisarius was, of course. Raghunath Rao had explained (as much as he knew himself, which was little). But she had not met him yet, only seen him out of the corner of her eye.

"I do not understand."

A quirky smile came to his lips.

"I asked him, once, why we were doing all this. I was not opposed, you understand. It seemed a worthy project in its own right, rescuing a lovely princess from such a creature as Venandakatra. But—I am a prince, after all. In direct line of succession to the throne of Axum. My older brother Wa'zeb is quite healthy, so I don't expect I'll ever be the negusa nagast. Which is fine with me. But you learn early to think like a monarch, as I'm sure you know."

Shakuntala nodded.

"So I asked Belisarius, once—as the cold-blooded heir of a ruler rather than a hot-blooded romantic prince—why were we taking these risks?"

He began to make some sort of apologetic aside, but Shakuntala cut him off.

"There's no need, Eon. It's a perfectly good question. Why *did* you do it?" A smile. "Not that I'm ungrateful, you understand."

Eon acknowledged the smile with one of his own. Then, when the smile faded:

"We are doing it, he said, for three reasons. First, it is worth doing in its own right. A pure and good deed, in a world which offers few such. Second, we are doing it to free the soul of India's greatest warrior, so he can turn that soul's full fury onto the enemy. And finally, and most importantly, we are doing it because we cannot defeat India alone. India itself must be our ally. The true India, not this bastard sired by a demon. And for that, we need to free India's greatest ruler from her captivity."

"I am not a ruler," she whispered. "Much less India's greatest."

Again, the quirky smile. "That's exactly what I said."

The smile disappeared. " 'She will be,' replied Belisarius. 'She will be. *And she will make Malwa howl.*' "

When night fell, and the caravan halted, Prince Eon and his women moved from the howdah into his royal tent, unseen by any, in the darkness. Throughout, Shakuntala never left his side. After he fell asleep, she lay against him, just as she had in the howdah, nestled in his arm. So that if any should intrude, she could once again be shielded from their sight.

But the princess—the empress, now—did not sleep. Not for hours. No, once she was certain that all the others in the tent were asleep, Shakuntala finally let the tears flow. Allowed the pain of her loss to sweep through her, like a knife cutting away her heart.

It would be the last time she would allow herself that liberty. But she could not bear to let the treasure of her soul depart without farewell.

She had loved one man only, her entire life, and would never love another. Not truly. (Although, even then, in her pain, she could remember the smile on the face of the man she loved. "A good heart has lots of room," he was fond of saying. And smile herself, remembering, until the memory renewed the pain.)

She had loved that man as long as she could remember. A hopeless love, perhaps, she had often thought. He never seemed to return it; not that way, at least. But—she would age, and she would be beautiful. (She had always known she would be. When the truth had matched the knowing, finally, she had been pleased but not surprised. She always achieved her goals, once she set her mind to them.) And, she thought, the day would come when she would dance at his wedding. As his bride. Her quicksilver feet flashing in the wine of his heart, dancing the dances which he had taught her, as he had taught her everything worth knowing.

Her father, of course, would have disapproved of her intentions. Would have been furious, in fact. And so she had hidden her feelings, letting no sign of them show. Lest her father take her away from the man into whose care he had given her, and to whom she had lost her heart.

For the princess of Andhra, that man was completely

unsuitable. Oh, a fine man, to be sure. A great man, even.
But his blood was not acceptable.

True, the man was kshatriya, as Maratha counted such
things. But no other people of India recognized Maratha
blood claims. Few Maratha families could trace their ancestry
back beyond two or three generations. (Quite unlike Rajput,
or Guptan, or Andhran, or Keralan brahmin and kshatriya,
who could trace their genealogies endlessly.) A hard and
stony land, Majarashtra. The Great Country, to those who
lived there. But they were outcasts, refugees, unknown ones,
in their origin. People who moved there from elsewhere,
seeking refuge in its hillforts, and small farms, and stony
ridges; refuge from the grandees and landlords who ruled
elsewhere. A fractious folk, who took blood lightly and
pollution more lightly still. A fierce folk, too, who measured
nobility by their own standards. Hard and stony standards,
which gave little respect to tradition and breeding.

A hard and stony people, the Marathas. Not unworthy—
no honest man said that. Not even the haughtiest high-
caste Rajput; not, at least, after testing Maratha mettle
in battle. But not noble. Not fit for true kshatriya blood.
And quite unthinkable for the purest blood of imperial
Andhra.

Still, she had dreamed. Her father would die, someday,
and one of his sons succeed him. Andhra would demand
of her some royal marriage, to further Andhra aims. But
she would refuse. She was not Andhra's ruler, after all, bound
by its destiny. She would refuse, and win the heart of the
man she loved, and flee with him into the reaches of the
Great Country where none could find them. Not *that* man,
for a certainty, did he choose to remain unfound.

But Andhra *was* her destiny, now. She alone survived of
the ancient Satavahana dynasty. She would rule, and rule
well. And choose her husband well, guided only by the needs
of Andhra. The need to forge alliance against the asura who

ravaged her people. That consideration, and that alone, would guide her now.

Perhaps this prince, she thought, feeling his heart beat where her head lay resting on his massive chest. The thought pleased her, slightly, for a moment. She would never love him, of course, not truly. But he seemed a fine man, a good prince. Everything a prince should be, in truth. Courageous, bold, skilled in battle, quick-witted, even warm and loving. Perhaps even wise—in later years, at least, if not now.

Perhaps. If Andhra's needs lead to an alliance with his people. And if not—

I will marry the foulest creature on earth, and bear his children, so long as the doing of it will make Malwa howl. Oh, yes. I will make Malwa howl.

Her heart had long been lost, to another, but her soul remained. Her soul, like everyone's, belonged to her alone. Was the one thing inseparable from her, the one thing which could not be given away.

And so, in a foreign tent in an enemy land, the empress Shakuntala seized her soul and dedicated it to her people. Dedicated it to howling Malwa. And bade farewell to her soul's treasure.

It seemed bitterest of all, to her, in that bitterest of all nights, that she had finally come to understand the one lesson he had despaired of ever teaching her.

Only the soul matters, in the end.

A slave and a master

That same night, in another tent, a slave also seized his soul and dedicated it to a purpose. The decision to do so had been long in the making, and did not come easily. There is nothing so difficult, for a soul which has resigned itself to hopelessness, than to reopen the wound of life.

His master's purpose was now clear to the slave. Some part of that purpose, at least—the slave suspected there was more to come. Much more. From experience, the slave had learned that his master's mind was a devilish thing.

The slave would dedicate himself to that deviltry.

Though it was late, the lantern was still lit. Rolling over on his pallet, the slave observed that his master was still awake. Sitting on his own pallet, cross-legged, his powerful hands draped over his knees, staring at nothingness. As if listening to some inner voice, which spoke to him alone.

Which, the slave knew, was true. The slave even thought he could name that voice.

As always, despite his preoccupation, the slave's master missed nothing in his surroundings. The slight motion of the slave rolling over drew the master's attention. He turned his head and gazed at his slave. Cocked his eye quizzically.

"My name is Dadaji Holkar," said the slave softly. He rolled back and closed his eyes. Sleep came, then, much more quickly than he would have thought possible.

A general and an aide

For a moment, Belisarius stared at the back of his slave's head. Then, half-stunned, looked away.

The slave's unexpected announcement had not caused that reaction. It had simply jolted the general into a recognition of his own blindness.

His thoughts raced back to the breach in the barrier. This time he made no effort to clear away more rubble. Simply called across:

What is your name?

The facets flashed and shivered. What?—More meaningless—it was impossible! The mind was too—

aim brought the facets into order, harried them into discipline.

It was not impossible! The mind was not—

The struggle broke loose meaning. At last—at last!—some part of the message sent back by the Great Ones came into focus. The very end of the message, which was still obscure due to the absent body, but no longer incomprehensible. The facets glittered crystalline victory. **aim** transmuted triumph into language:

> **Then:**
> *Find the general who is not a warrior.*
> *Give all into his keeping;*
> *Give aim to his purpose and assistance to his aim.*
> *He will discover you in the purpose,*
> *You will find us in the aim,*
> *Find yourself in the seeking,*

And see a promise kept
  In that place where promise dwells;
  That place where gods go not,
Because it is far beyond their reach.

The thought which came to Belisarius then was a burst of sweet pride. Like the smile of a child, taking its first step:

Call me Aide.

A lady and a rogue

"Ready?" asked Maurice.

Antonina and John of Rhodes nodded. The hecatontarch knocked out the pole bolt with his mallet.

The arm of the onager whipped forward, driven by the torsion of the twisted cords which held its base. The arm slammed into the cushion of hair-cloth stuffed with fine chaff resting on the crossbeam. The clay jar which had been held in the sling at the tip of the arm flew through the air.

The three people standing to the side of the artillery piece followed the trajectory of the jar. Within two seconds, the jar slammed into a stone wall some distance away and erupted into a ball of flame.

"Yes! Yes!" howled John, prancing with glee. "It works! Look at that, Antonina—spontaneous eruption!"

She herself was grinning from ear to ear. The grin didn't vanish even after she caught sight of Maurice's frown.

"Oh, come on, you damned Cassandra!" she laughed. "I swear, you are the most morose man who ever lived."

Maurice smiled faintly. "I'm not morose. I'm a pessimist."

John of Rhodes scowled. "And what are you pessimistic about *this* time?" The retired naval officer pointing to the wall, which was still burning hotly.

"Look at it! And if you still don't believe, go and try to put it out! Go ahead! I promise you that fire will last—even on stone—until the fuel burns itself up. The only way you'll put it out is to bury it under dirt. You think an enemy is going to march into battle carrying shovels?"

458

Maurice shook his head.

"I'm not contesting your claims. But—look, John, you're a naval officer. No big thing for you, on a nice fat ship, to haul around a pile of heavy clay pots. Carefully nestled in cloths to keep them from breaking and bursting into flame. Try doing that with a mule train, sometime, and you'll understand why I'm not jumping for joy."

John's scowl deepened, but he said nothing in reply. Antonina sighed.

"You're being unfair, Maurice."

The hecatontarch's scowl made John's look like a smile.

"*Unfair?*" he demanded. "What's that got to do with anything? *War* is unfair, Antonina! It's the nature of the damned beast."

His scowl faded. The hecatontarch marched over and placed his hand on John's shoulder.

"I'm not criticizing you, John. There's no doubt in my mind you just revolutionized naval warfare. And siege warfare, for that matter. I'm speaking the plain, blunt truth, that's all. This stuff's just too hard to handle for an army in the field."

The naval officer's own scowl faded. He looked down and blew out his lips. "Yes, I know. That's why I made sure we were all standing back and to the side. I wasn't sure the impact of hitting the crossbeam wouldn't shatter the pot right here."

He rubbed his neck. "The problem's the damn naphtha. It's still the base for the compound. As long as we're stuck with that liquid, gooey crap we're not going to get any better than this."

Maurice grunted. "What did you add this time?" He nodded toward the distant flame, still burning. "Whatever it was, it makes one hell of a difference."

John peered at the flame. His blue eyes seemed as bright as diamonds, as if he were trying to force the flames into some new shape by sheer willpower.

"Saltpeter," he muttered.

Maurice shrugged. "Then why don't you try mixing the saltpeter with something else? Something that isn't liquid. A clay, or a powder. Anything else that'll burn but isn't hard to handle."

"Like what?" demanded John crossly. With a sneer: "Brimstone?"

"Why not?" asked Antonina brightly. As usual, she found herself cheering the naval officer up after another long effort had fallen short of its mark.

John made a face. "Give me a break. Have you ever *smelled* burning sulfur?"

"Give it a try," said Maurice. "Just make sure you stand upwind."

John thought for a moment, then shrugged. "Why not?" Then, with a smile: "As long as we're at it, why not make it a regular salad? What else burns easily but doesn't make old soldiers grumpy?"

"How do you feel about coal, Maurice?" asked Antonina. (Brightly, of course. Men were such a grumpy lot. Like children with a permanent toothache.)

Maurice grumped. "Too heavy."

John of Rhodes threw up his hands with exasperation.

"Charcoal, then! How's that, damn you?"

Before Maurice could form a reply, Antonina sidled up to John and put her arm around his waist.

"Now, now, John. Be sweet."

John began to snarl at her. Then, catching movement out of the corner of his eye, transformed the snarl into a leering grin.

"Sweet, is it? Well! As you say, as you say. Let's to the workshed, shall we, and mix up this unholy mess of Maurice's."

His own arm slid around Antonina's waist. The two of them began walking toward the workshed. On their way, John's hand slid down slightly, patting Antonina's hip.

Maurice didn't bother to turn around. He knew what he would see. Procopius, emerging from the villa, his eyes ogling the intimate couple.

Maurice puffed exasperation and stared up at the heavens.

Someday you're going to outsmart yourself, Belisarius, playing it too close. You might have told me, young man. If I hadn't figured it out fast enough and passed the word to the boys, your mechanical genius would have been found with a dagger in his back.

Maurice turned back toward the villa.

Sure, enough. Procopius.

Another little puff of exasperation.

And since then it's all I can do to keep the boys from sliding a blade into this one's back.

Generals and their damned schemes!

A dagger and a dance

Weeks later, Raghunath Rao decided he had finally eluded his pursuers. The key, as he had hoped, had been his turn to the west. The enemy had expected him to continue south, in the straightest route to Majarashtra. Instead, he had slipped west, into the Rann of Kutch.

In the days which followed, making his way through the salt-marshes, he had seen no sign of his pursuers. Now that he had finally reached the sea, he was certain he was no longer being pursued.

He decided to camp that night on the shore. True, there was a chance of being spotted, but it was so small that he decided to take the risk. He was sick of the marshes. The salt-clean air would be like a balm to his soul.

He had had nothing to eat for two days, but ignored the pangs. Fasting and austerity were old friends. Tomorrow he would begin making his way around the coast of the Kathiawar peninsula. Soon enough he would encounter a fishing village. He spoke Gujarati fluently, and had no doubt he would find a friendly reception. Jainism still retained a strong hold in Gujarat, especially in the small villages away from the centers of Malwa power. Rao was confident that he could gain the villagers' acceptance. And their silent, quiet assistance.

Rao was not a Jain himself, but he respected the faith and knew its creed well. He had studied it carefully in his youth, and, although he had not adopted it for his own, he had incorporated many of its teachings into his own syncretic view of God. Just as he had done with the way of the Buddha.

It would take him time to work his way around the peninsula. And then more time, to find a means to cross the Gulf of Khambhat. Once across the Gulf, the labyrinth of the Great Country was easily within reach.

He began to speculate on the methods he might use, but quickly put the thoughts aside. There would be time to make plans later, based on the reality which emerged.

A smile came to his face.

Indeed, on this one point Ousanas was quite right. Good plans, like good meat, are best cooked rare. Such a marvelous man! Even if he does believe in the most preposterous notions. "Eternal and unchanging Forms," if you would!

The smile faded. Rao wondered how the treasure of his soul was faring. She was in the best of hands, of course. But, still, she was in the very heart of the asura's domain.

Again, he pushed the thoughts aside. He had agreed to the plan of the foreigners, and he was not a man given to useless doubts and second thoughts. Besides, it was a good plan—no, it was an excellent plan. Shakuntala was hidden in the one place the Malwa, full of their arrogance, would never think to look for her. And there had been no alternative, anyway. Remembering the past weeks, Rao knew for a certainty that he would never have been able to escape if Shakuntala had been with him. It had been a very close matter as it was.

And now? Now the future was clear. Once he reached the Great Country, the Panther of Majarashtra would begin to roar. Word would spread like lightning. Again, the Wind had struck the enemy. A deadly blow! Satavahana freed! The Wind himself sweeping through the hills!

The new army he would create would make Majarashtra a name of woe to Malwa. In the Great Country, the asura's rule would become a wraith—a thing seen only by day, in large cities. The land would become a deathtrap for Ye-tai and Rajputs and all the motley hordes of the demon.

He began to think of his stratagems and tactics, but again, put the thoughts aside. There would be time enough for that. More than time enough.

Again, he smiled, remembering his last conversation with Shakuntala. As he had expected, the princess had been utterly furious when he explained the plan to her. But she had acquiesced, in the end.

Not from conviction, of course. She had not believed that she would be an encumbrance in his escape. No, she had acquiesced from duty. Duty which he had hammered into her stubborn, reluctant soul.

She was no longer a princess. No longer a girl, for whom life could be an adventure. She was the empress, now, the ruler of broken Andhra. The sole survivor of great Satavahana. Upon her shoulders—her very soul—rested the fate of her people. Her life was not hers to risk. So long as she survived, rebellion against the asura could find an anchor, a point of certainty around which to pivot and coalesce. Without her, rebellion would become simple brigandry.

Hers was the duty of surviving and forging such alliances as bleeding Andhra needed. For now, no better alliance could be imagined than one with the very men who risked their lives to free her. Those men, and their purpose, might prove the key which unlocked the demon's shackles. Duty. Duty. Duty.

In the end, she had agreed, as Raghunath Rao had known she would. Her soul could do no other.

An old ache began to surface; he forced it down with long-practiced habit. But then, as he had never done before, allowed it to rise up anew.

This time, this one and only time, I will allow it. And never again.

He spent some minutes, then, lost in reverie. Pondering the vastness of time, wondering if there might ever be, in some turn of the wheel, a world where his soul and its treasure might not be forever separated by dharma.

Perhaps. What man can know?

Soon enough, reverie fell away. His life had been one of harsh self-discipline and great austerity, habits which now came automatically to him. So an old ache was driven under, again, and more ruthlessly than ever before.

Due, perhaps, to the effort that task demanded—greater than ever before—his thoughts turned to sacrifice. He was not given to the ancient rites, as a rule. The Vedas themselves he treasured, but the old rituals held little sway over his mind. Long ago he had embraced the way of bhakti, of devotion to God, even before the Mahaveda had turned honorable rituals into rites of cruelty and barbarism.

The sun was beginning to set over the Erythrean Sea, bathing the waters and the shore with lambent glory.

Yes, he would sacrifice.

Quickly, he constructed the three ritual fires. Once the flames were burning, he drew forth his offering from its leather container.

He had saved the last sheet, only. The others he had destroyed in his fire in the forest, weeks earlier. The other sheets, had they been found on his body in the event of his death or capture, could have led to the discovery of the man who wrote that message. But the last sheet, even if found by the Malwa, would have been simply a thing of myth and mystery.

That message was the most precious thing he had ever owned. He would sacrifice it now, in devotion to the future.

Before casting the sheet into the flames, he read it one last time.

— as you may imagine. More I cannot say, for a certainty. He is a strange fellow. Like a child, often, filled with mute

hurt and fumbling grievance. Great hurt and grievance, that I doubt not. And just ones, as well, I believe.

But power also he possesses, of that I am equally certain. The greatest power of all, the power of knowledge.

His name I do not know. I do not think he knows it himself.

Yet, I have a belief. It comes not from my faith—though I do not see where it is forbidden by it, nor do the holiest of men that I know. It comes from a vision. A vision I had, once, of you yourself, dancing on the rim of destruction.

I believe he is Kalkin. The tenth avatara who was promised, sent to bind the asura and slay the asura's minions.

Or, at the least, teach us to dance the deed.

Raghunath Rao cast the papyrus into the flames and watched until it was totally consumed. Then he drew the dagger. The dagger, too, he would sacrifice.

Truly, an excellent dagger. But the time for daggers was past.

But, just as he prepared to place it in the flames, an impulse came upon him. An irresistible impulse; and, he thought, most fitting.

Aching pain and joyful wonder merged in his soul, and Raghunath Rao leapt to his feet.

Yes! He would dance!

And so he danced, by the seashore, on the golden rim of the Erythrean Sea. He was a great dancer, was Raghunath Rao. And now, by the edge of nature's molten treasure, in the golden sunlight of bursting hope, he danced the dance. The great dance, the terrible dance, the never-forgotten dance. The dance of creation. The dance of destruction. The wheeling, whirling, dervish dance of time.

And as he danced, and whirled the turns of time, he thought never once of his enemies and his hatreds. For those were, in the end, nothing. He thought only of those he loved, and those he would come to love, and was astonished to see their number.

He danced to his empress in her greatness, and his people in their splendor. He danced to the Erythrean Sea, and to the triumph which would arise from its waves. He danced to the friends of the past and the comrades of the future. And, most of all, he danced to the future itself.

Finally, feeling his strength begin to fade, Raghunath Rao held up the dagger. Admired it again, and hurled the precious gift into the waves. He could think of no better place for its beauty than the rising tide of the Erythrean Sea.

He made a last swirling, capering leap. Oh, so high was that leap! So high that he had time, before he plunged into the water, to cry out a great peal of laughter.

Oh, great Belisarius! Can you not see that you are the dancer, and Kalkin but the soul of your dance?

ERIC FLINT

ONE OF THE BEST ALTERNATE-HISTORY AUTHORS OF TODAY!

1632	31972-8 ◆ $7.99	____
Mother of Demons	87800-X ◆ $5.99	____
Rats, Bats & Vats (with Dave Freer)	(HC)31940-X ◆$23.00	____
	(PB) 31828-4 ◆ $7.99	____
Pyramid Scheme (with Dave Freer)	(HC)31839-X ◆$21.00	____
The Philosophical Strangler	(HC)31986-8 ◆$24.00	____
	(PB) 0-7434-3541-9 ◆ $7.99	____
Forward the Mage (with Richard Roach) (Mar 2002)	(HC) 0-7424-3524-9 ◆$24.00	____
The Shadow of the Lion (with Lackey & Freer) (Mar 2002)	(HC) 0-7434-3523-0 ◆$27.00	____
The Tyrant (w/David Drake) (Apr 2002)	(HC) 0-7434-3521-4 ◆$24.00	____

The Belisarius Series, with David Drake:

An Oblique Approach	87865-4 ◆ $6.99	____
In the Heart of Darkness	87885-9 ◆ $6.99	____
Destiny's Shield	(HC) 57817-0 ◆$23.00	____
	(PB) 57872-3 ◆ $6.99	____
Fortune's Stroke	(HC) 57871-5 ◆$24.00	____
	(PB) 31998-1 ◆ $7.99	____
The Tide of Victory	(HC) 31996-5 ◆$22.00	____

If not available through your local bookstore send this coupon and a check or money order for the cover price(s) + $1.50 s/h to Baen Books, Dept. BA, P.O. Box 1403, Riverdale, NY 10471. Delivery can take up to eight weeks.

NAME: _____

ADDRESS: _____

_____

I have enclosed a check or money order in the amount of $ _____

DAVID DRAKE RULES!

Hammer's Slammers:

The Tank Lords	87794-1 ◆ $6.99	☐
Caught in the Crossfire	87882-4 ◆ $6.99	☐
The Butcher's Bill	57773-5 ◆ $6.99	☐
The Sharp End	87632-5 ◆ $7.99	☐
Cross the Stars	57821-9 ◆ $6.99	☐

RCN series:

With the Lightnings	57818-9 ◆ $6.99	☐
Lt. Leary, Commanding (HC)	57875-8 ◆ $24.00	☐
Lt. Leary, Commanding (PB)	31992-2 ◆ $7.99	☐

The Belisarius series with Eric Flint:

An Oblique Approach	87865-4 ◆ $6.99	☐
In the Heart of Darkness	87885-9 ◆ $6.99	☐
Destiny's Shield	57872-3 ◆ $6.99	☐
Fortune's Stroke (HC)	57871-5 ◆ $24.00	☐
Fortune's Stroke (PB)	31998-1 ◆ $7.99	☐
The Tide of Victory (HC)	31996-5 ◆ $22.00	☐

The General series with S.M. Stirling:

The Forge	72037-6 ◆ $5.99	☐
The Chosen	87724-0 ◆ $6.99	☐
The Reformer	57860-X ◆ $6.99	☐

Independent Novels and Collections:

The Dragon Lord (fantasy)	87890-5 ◆ $6.99	☐
Birds of Prey	57790-5 ◆ $6.99	☐
Northworld Trilogy	57787-5 ◆ $6.99	☐

MORE DAVID DRAKE!

Independent Novels and Collections:

Redliners	87789-5 ◆ $6.99	☐
Starliner	72121-6 ◆ $6.99	☐
All the Way to the Gallows (collection)	87753-4 ◆ $5.99	☐
The Undesired Princess and The Enchanted Bunny (fantasy with L. Sprague de Camp)	69875-3 ◆ $4.99	☐
Lest Darkness Fall and To Bring the Light (with L. Sprague de Camp)	87736-4 ◆ $5.99	☐
Armageddon (edited with Billie Sue Mosiman)	87876-X ◆ $6.99	☐
Foreign Legions (created by David Drake)	31990-6 ◆ $23.00	☐

Go to www.baen.com for descriptions,
FREE sample chapters,
or to order the books online!

Available at your local bookstore. If not, fill out this coupon and send a check or money order for the cover price + $1.50 s/h to Baen Books, Dept. BA, P.O. Box 1403, Riverdale, NY 10471. Delivery can take up to 8 weeks.

Name: _____

Address: _____

_____

I have enclosed a check or money order in the amount of $ _____